HELEN TOWNSEND

love
and
other
infidelities

MIRA

MIRA is a registered trademark of Harlequin Enterprises Limited, used under licence.

MIRA Books, Eton House, 18-24 Paradise Road, Richmond, Surrey, TW9 1SR

F166.512
€9.00

ISBN 978 0 7783 0233 9

60-0608

Printed in Great Britain by Clays Ltd, St Ives plc

CONTENTS

CHAPTER 1
1975

Susan

I liked the early morning, lying in bed. There was the laughter of the kookaburras and then the calls of currawongs, with shafts of light coming through the venetians; thin, cool at first, then heavy with the heat of the coming day. I liked the peace, my feeling of contemplation as I lay there.

There was no family breakfast at our house. My father went to work early. My mother lay in bed after my father departed with a face pack that was supposed to keep her wrinkles at bay. She was not to be disturbed. My younger sister, Lisa, still at teachers' college, slept in and was always late for her first class. So when I got up, it was just me in the kitchen with a simple breakfast of toast and tea before I showered and dressed and set off for the station.

I liked to walk quickly. I liked that physical sense of myself, fast and precise. Every weekday morning I walked half an hour to the station to catch the train to work, not just for the exercise, but for the pleasure I took in the trees, the birds, the changes of season, the quiet of the early morning. The houses I passed, like my parents' house, were mostly hidden by their gardens—beds of azaleas and camellias, broad swathes of fine green grass shaded by old gum trees. I loved the reds of the camellias in flower in the winter, the pinks and purple of the azaleas in spring. The gum trees housed possums and mopokes at night; currawongs, kookaburras and magpies during the day. When I was small my dad had taught me to imitate all the bird calls, and I thought I could still do a good kookaburra, and probably the mopoke. As I walked to the station I always thought of how he had taught me those calls and my mum's horrified, 'What on earth are you teaching her *that* for?'

As I walked, I also thought of the day ahead at work in the university library. It wasn't a bad job. I had taken it because I had an honours degree in English and library work seemed like a good fit. As soon as I'd taken the job it was obvious it was not a good fit at all. My work at the library consisted of stacking books on trolleys and then putting them back on the shelves or searching for requests, barely a glance in the direction of English literature. I didn't mind a great deal. In my spare time I read and read and read. I had never thought a job mattered very much. It was more something to do.

Searching for library requests led me to meeting Neil Andrews and then becoming engaged to him. He was a lecturer in the history department and ten years my senior. Once I realised he wasn't just looking for books, his attention was flattering. And from being flattered I drifted into the engagement, much as I'd drifted into the library job. It was my mother who had all the enthusiasm for Neil.

'He's aiming to become a professor,' she said. 'Just imagine being married to a professor.' In truth, I wasn't doing much imagining at all about getting married. I felt slightly sick every time my mother mentioned the flowers for the church or the drinks for the reception, which should have been a signal to me that my heart wasn't in it. I'd already had an argument with my mother about the flowers. I wanted red flowers for my bridal bouquet but that interfered with her pastel colour scheme, traditional and tasteful.

That had been the way I had lived my life. I'd gone through childhood, ticking off the boxes—primary school, ballet class, netball, high school—always more my mother's agenda than my own. I wanted to make it my own, but at that time I didn't know how. My sister Lisa was more gregarious than me and had found her own life outside the house, even though she still lived at home. Friends, men, parties, drink were mentioned in passing, but not discussed. Somehow Lisa had escaped.

I had been passionate about my university studies and I still read voraciously. It annoyed me a little that my mother used this characteristic as a way of summarising me. 'Susan,' she'd say. 'Always got her head in a book. Just as well she's marrying a professor.'

'He's not a professor yet,' my dad said.

'At least he's thinking ahead,' said my mother archly, a reference to my father's failure to book the ski lodge in time for their annual ski holiday. Dad hated skiing.

My parents' marriage was like a tennis match. Serve, volley, hit, smash, but no love in the score.

My co-workers in the library were more sophisticated than I was and certainly more in touch with what was going on in the world. It was the era of enthusiastic and impassioned feminism and the university was alive with talk of feminism. En masse, women complained that the courses were sexist, demanded feminist perspectives be included, agitated against work practices which disadvantaged women and even demanded the toilets be made unisex. All this passionate debate fascinated me, but on a personal level it didn't seem very relevant to me.

I mentioned this mildly enough one morning tea-time. Someone pushed a copy of Germaine Greer's *Female Eunuch* into my hands.

'This!' she said, 'is about you.'

I started reading it on the bus to the station that evening. The ideas jumped off the page. They were powerful, big and new. As the bus grew more crowded, it became harder and harder to read but I was drawn further and further into the book. I got off the bus and sat in a café to finish the first chapter and started the next one. It suddenly felt as if the rest of my life had possibilities I had never dreamed of. I could make choices. It was no longer inevitable that I'd follow the route my mother had so carefully plotted. I'd discussed the concept of free will in a philosophy course I'd taken, but it was a heady experience to imagine it in my own life.

The engagement didn't survive the *Female Eunuch* and the bottle of wine I drank on the next date with Neil.

'How could you, Susan?' my mother asked. 'Everything is booked.'

'Do you really think I should marry him because you've booked the church?'

'He's going to be a professor.'

'Mum!'

'What on earth will you do now?'

'Live my life as a woman, I don't know.'

'Don't be ridiculous.'

My mother was deeply upset about the loss of her future professorial son-in-law but she also sensed that I was less amenable to ticking off her boxes. She and Dad took off to England to avoid the embarrassment of my cancelled wedding. And with that I felt freer still. My parents had a beach house and

I suggested to my sister Lisa that she and I go up there for the summer. I left my job, collected a swag of books and we took off.

At the beach house, Lisa and I had always felt conscripted into my mother's relentless timetable—beach in the morning, lunch at the club, board games in the afternoon, friends over for dinner. We were 'the girls', obedient, quiet and indistinguishable from each other. And somehow that relentless regime that meant we spent a lot of time together, also meant we didn't get to know each other very well. Now Lisa and I decided to do exactly what we wanted. At night we cooked extravagant meals and shared bottles of wine from Dad's cellar. We laughed and joked about that constrained and constricted childhood of ours, everything please and thank you, white socks and clean handkerchiefs.

'Bloody nightmare,' said Lisa. 'How did we turn out okay?'

'I don't feel okay,' I said. 'I feel socially retarded and full of primal terror.'

'Take my word for it, Suzie,' said Lisa. 'You're very okay.'

'But why was it a nightmare?' I asked. 'We weren't neglected. It wasn't as if every care wasn't taken of us. We were educated, looked after, had everything we needed.'

'Not everything.' As Lisa stirred the pasta sauce, she began singing 'All You Need is Love' by the Beatles.

'We were loved. They just couldn't show it.'

'Children shouldn't have to work that out. We shouldn't be wondering about it at our age,' she said. 'Did you feel loved?'

'I think Dad . . .'

'Every time he put his head up, she put her foot down.'

We started laughing. I don't know why, except that we were drunk and we felt free. We laughed and laughed and laughed. We weren't 'the girls' anymore. We were becoming sisters.

We walked on the beach the next day. We went to the pub at night and flirted with the yachties in the bar. Other nights we sat on the verandah, cooled by the sea breeze coming up and talked about our hopes, our puzzlement at life. I was the feminist with the ideology and the ideas; Lisa was the hippie who wanted to be young and free and alive. One night she stood out on the balcony without her clothes on. I watched her standing in the moonlight, enjoying the air on her skin, young and beautiful, soft and female. I still felt enough the older sister to want to tell her someone would see her, that she might get cold, that it wasn't quite proper, but I said nothing.

I changed too. I threw aside my tasteful, pastel-coloured clothes. At university I'd always felt out of place when everyone else was wearing duffel coats, black stocking with holes and big black jumpers. That didn't appeal to me at all. I started sewing my own clothes, using bold patterns, primary colours, outrageous combinations, sensual textures. I bought beads and scarves. It was not what other people were wearing but I felt bigger, stronger, that I made a mark in the world.

When my parents came back from England my mother closed down the beach house. 'It's the end of the season,' she said firmly. But now I had a taste of independence. Lisa was still at teachers' college and had money from a teaching scholarship. I got a job in the public service as a clerk, where I noted I got paid less than men with similar qualifications. I didn't like the work but I didn't expect a lot from a job, and it allowed Lisa and me to move out of home and get a flat together. I felt more myself, closer to my sister, more separate from my mother. Although it felt brave and daring, it was only a first step. Life still scared me a little. I felt ready for more risks, more passion, but I was cautious, waiting for things to come to me.

Martin

The sea. The good life. Love. They're the important things. Plus some serious boozing. I do like a beer. Or six.

I grew up in a fibro house in a scrubby suburb way out western Sydney. The local pool was the biggest body of water around so I never got into surfing until I was at uni in Sydney, before I went away on the Oxford scholarship. While I was away, surfing became the symbol of things I wanted in life—thrills, risk and sheer pleasure; waves transitory, the ocean endless. The essence of experience, a sense of the universal.

I was on scholarships all my educational life, except for the parish primary. Oxford was the biggie. 'Don't fall for them,' said my Nanna. 'Don't let those Poms turn you. Especially the girls. Mass every week remember.'

My Nanna was Irish Catholic. And proud of it, proud of herself, proud of her family.

'Best looking family at Mass, we are,' she'd say. 'Curly hair. You can tell God loves us. So long as yer dad keeps his gammy arm to hisself.'

Everyone at Mass knew my dad had had his arm crushed in an accident.

'Nanna likes to keep up appearances,' Dad used to say.

'Such smart kids too,' Nanna would say.

'Modest like you,' Mum said but Nanna didn't miss a beat.

'From County Wexford,' Nanna said, nevermind that it was two generations ago. 'Full of fight, the six of them.'

That was the brash front we presented to the world. But it hid considerable sadness, bitterness and gloom. We were loyal to a fault but we could be harsh with each other to the point of cruelty. We wanted to be better than we were but we didn't want to admit to our aspirations. We wore our Irish Catholic origins with pride, while at the same time chafing to escape from everything they represented. Underneath it all, I felt a degree of confusion that covered a love-hate attachment to my origins.

Being Irish Australian didn't go down too well at Oxford. The Poms had their noses permanently in the air so they could look down on the colonials. They hated the Irish on principle but they'd been hating them so long they had no idea what the principle was. The dons didn't like my in-your-face attitude. There were good things about the place. Ideas were thick in the air and there were people who were brilliant and inventive. But I didn't exactly feel the warm cosy glow of welcome, except in the pubs. Pubs are an environment where I slot into remarkably well, whatever the country.

When I got back after three years in Oxford, I kicked around as a taxi driver, barman and surfer for a while. I was restless and lost at the same time, I didn't seem to fit anywhere apart from surfing and drinking and drinking and surfing. But I'd got to the stage where I wanted possessions. My parents had always been a scratch above poor. They owned their fibro house and they were forever paying off the car, but if they disappeared off the face of the earth their worldly goods would be up for grabs in a garage sale. Or more likely, straight off to the tip.

I had a poor man's materialism which surfing and cab driving wasn't going to help. On the strength of my degree I got a senior clerkship in the public service. It wasn't work and it wasn't leisure, and it felt greyer and greyer every day. I didn't last long but there was the pressing problem of rent money and beer money, to say nothing of the clothes and the more illustrious possessions I hoped to acquire. I asked around a few law firms.

The Oxford degree impressed the hell out of your average

Aussie law firm. They were *so* impressed I began to see why the Oxford lot thought the colonials were brown nosers. I began to understand about Anglophile Australians my Nanna had always railed against. The law firms were full of them. Snobbery, born-to-rule mentality, God Save the Queen and no idea of how hard the average punter has to work to earn his crust. Silk ties, crisp, ironed shirts and expensive suits. The buggers weren't even trying, it wasn't an act. They bred that way, true to type. But the Oxford degree meant they made me offers which were hard to refuse.

I consulted the family. I went to see my Nanna in the nursing home. I hated that place. It smelt of death and piss. I hated it even more that she had expected to end up there. I wished I had the money to get her out. She had her teeth floating in a cup of iridescent green and her cardie on inside out. She had cancer eating away her insides, but she still had her poor Irish dignity and her sense of humour.

'Be one of those fancy lawyers,' she wheezed. 'Queen's Counsel, then put it right up the Queen.'

'All right,' my father said, 'practice for a while then go into politics. Get a house with a driveway, trees on either side.' That was his definition of success.

But a politician needs a cause and I had never been a true believer, right from first communion. The seventies were full of causes, good causes—Vietnam, Gough Whitlam and the Governor General, rights for the aborigines, the Springboks and rugby. I was partisan, on the side of the oppressed and repressed, but I wasn't a joiner, and most of those causes were full of middle class do-gooders. It was just another place I wouldn't fit in. Political action wasn't my thing, which wasn't a view that got you into bed in the seventies.

'Your dad has hated his work all his life,' said Mum. 'It's soured him. Find something you like, love. Don't worry about the money. It isn't that important.' She said it with a sort of softness. She was soft, my mum, but it didn't make any sense because she and Dad fought about money on a daily basis.

So it was buckets of money that seduced me into joining the firm of Thomas Thomas and Rodgers, up in Macquarie Street. Top firm, all pretty private school boys, golf club membership and the rest. The buggers working there just couldn't conceive what life might be like if you weren't a lawyer. Their imagination could stretch to their clientele who were company directors or rich, old codgers wanting to change the will. But they had no sympathy for the smart bugger who could fence a truckload of suits but had the misfortune to get caught, or some poor bastard stoned out of his mind while committing some fuck-witted larceny.

My imagination stretched further. My life stretched further, at least I hoped it did. Praise the Lord and pass the dope. Thank God for Bondi on a summer morning! Soggy old Oxford hadn't done me too much damage. And I liked that law firm salary.

Thomas Thomas slotted me into criminal law.

Criminal cases had an interesting sense of threat that if you lost your case you might also lose your teeth. There were the lovable rogues and the truly bad bastards. Generally the clientele in crime were a good deal more human than your average company director. But I had no illusions. I was getting them off doing whatever they were accused of, although it was pretty clear most had done something approximating what they had been accused of, with different names and places. It was fun for a while being on first name terms with hit men, standover men, madams and thieves. It pleased old Thomas because it was a good income stream, and that put the wind up those silk ties with posh voices.

I liked Thomas Thomas, who was the founder of the firm. I thought his name was a hoot and we got on well. He was fair dinkum. His dad had been a plumber. Thomas had polish and education but he liked a rough diamond like me. Thomas didn't believe the law was a sacred calling. 'There's no spirit of the law, son, just the letter, and you better get that right.' Thomas didn't bullshit with a lot of legalese. He wanted me to build up a Family Law division to deal with the no fault divorce under the brand new *Family Law Act*.

'We'll see a big rise in business there,' he said. 'Lots of people want to get out of a marriage. Now that they can do it without being publicly humiliated, they will.' I could see his point. I could see it a whole lot better when we went to his club and had a few beers. Evidently it wasn't exactly marital bliss with Mrs Thomas Thomas, although he wasn't contemplating divorce. But Thomas Thomas understood human pain and misery and had considerable sympathy for the average punter.

The new law was an important advance. You didn't have to prove adultery. You didn't have to prove cruelty. You didn't have to engage private detectives to spy in the bedroom or have your marital misery reported in lurid detail in the papers. You just had to say it was over. It seemed that the pain and nastiness of divorce would be lessened and human dignity respected—not a bad way to make a crust. And I still did a bit of criminal law.

I joined a touch-footy team, I surfed, I drank with a bunch of blokes, and surfed some more. I saw my parents, my sisters and my little brother. I bought a grotty unit in Bondi Junction, mortgaged myself to the hilt and got a car on the never-never. I nosed round the art world. I'd always been scared of high art but I got up my courage and started looking round the galleries. I fell in love with a fluid Brett Whitely drawing and had to buy it. I bought a gorgeous painting by Grace Cossington Smith and a 1930s ceramic kookaburra. I loved that kookaburra best of all. Evidently blokes used to make these pieces in the pottery after work, just for fun. That appealed to me, and my kooka had a mean blue streak down his back and a cross look in his eye. So the possessions were coming on.

I had a girlfriend, Yvette. I'd never thought marriage was quite me, having been a juvenile witness to the most painful and destructive argument in the history of the world, otherwise known as my parents' marriage. But now, here it was in my head; the idea of love, companionship, kids. I couldn't quite define it. Where I came from blokes got hooked, they didn't make choices.

Yvette was smart and sassy, hot and dirty, bright and good looking, totally wild.

I talked to my eldest sister Kathleen and explained that while I liked Yvette very much indeed, I wasn't quite sure it was love.

'You can't expect to feel infatuation at your age,' she said. I was only twenty-six and I reckoned, unlike her, I hadn't had my passion sucked dry. She'd just married a clerk in the public service. Found him in the filing cabinet under 'D' for 'dreary'.

I asked my sister Mary, my closest and dearest sibling about love. Mary was just a year older than me and we'd always done things together. We were at the pub and Mary was seriously drunk. 'You've got to be crazy in love,' she said. 'You've got to be mad for her, can't be without her. You don't want to end up like Mum and Dad. You know they're sleeping in separate rooms since Lachlan left home.'

I was crazy for Yvette and I decided I'd marry her and let the love question sort itself out.

'Yvette, you know I like you, don't you?'

She looked at me, puzzled. I reckoned that was because she still had a hangover.

'Yvette, it's been very intense between us . . .'

She now had a really puzzled look on her face. I wasn't exactly articulate. I had a hangover too.

'So why don't we get married?'

She started giggling, then rolled off the bed laughing, and rolled around the floor.

'Darling no one gets married now, it's the bloody seventies. Oh sweetheart, don't look so bloody hurt. I love you too, but it's like I love that labrador dog of mine—I like going for walks with you, I like having you around, I like to be with you, I like to scratch you behind the ears, but for Chrissakes, no one but no one gets married these days. We haven't lived together. This is your inner altar boy speaking.'

My pride was battered. The moment she started, I knew I *didn't* want to marry her.

'Thank God,' she said.

Sex is a wonderful balm but that relationship was over.

'See you 'round,' I said as I got up to get dressed. I felt more emotionally bruised than I would have thought. Her rejection had hurt my ego, especially that stuff about the bloody dog.

'Corrupting charm,' she said as she watched me getting dressed. 'That's what you've got. I almost said "yes".'

'I'm thinking it'll be a good story for you to spread round my drinking holes.'

'You bet,' she said without a trace of shame.

I leaned over and kissed her.

'You need to watch that charm of yours,' she said.

'It didn't work on you.'

'It'll corrupt someone for sure,' she said. 'Probably you.'

Melissa

In 1975 I turned twelve. I was a brat of a kid. I gave my mum a hard time while I had a good time.

My dad died at the beginning of the year. It was awful, like a great punch in the stomach, but then I repressed all the grief and pain and loss. I didn't sit around crying or missing him or thinking about him. I felt so full of life that I couldn't cope with him dying. I sealed off the part of my mind in which I *knew* he wasn't coming back. In another part of my mind I kept a little story that he was.

You hear people say it's bad to deny things or repress things, but it worked for me. It helped me get by, along with ballet and netball and swimming and running. I danced in the ballet competitions and if I didn't win, I was still happy. When I got too tall for ballet I was heartbroken.

My dad had liked me to be in things to win. He'd come to Australia from Greece when he was sixteen, with only primary school education, so winning and making money were joyful tangible things for him. Sometimes he came to my game of netball and yelled, 'Atta girl! Go get 'em!' in his thick, Greek accent. I adored him.

Not that he knew the finer points of the game or where we were on the competition ladder. Same as he didn't know what time I had to be up to get to school or what I had for lunch. That was totally Mum's business.

My mother was a warm-hearted Mum. A good person.

Dad being Greek meant I had a Greek surname and I went to a lot of christenings and weddings. I went to Saturday Greek school for a while but then Mum and Dad let me play sport instead.

When I look back, I see just how Greek Dad really was, down to the dark shadows under his eyes and the extended family which was so big I could never remember them all. But it wasn't a big deal for me, he was just was my dad who spoiled me rotten. He was in real estate, so he wasn't home a lot. When he was, he was very physical with big hugs and kisses. Like me.

The year Dad died I pulled away from Mum. She was living proof of how much things had changed.

I wanted Mum to be exactly the same as before. But there was her grief, her heavy grief, that was always in the way. Every afternoon when I got home from school, she'd been through a box of tissues in the interval between when she got home from work and when I got home from school.

She'd brighten up when she saw me.

'How was your day, honey?' It sounded fake. I knew it was fake.

'Fine, Mum.'

She always had this worried look. There were times she was totally silent and didn't even know it.

She started working full time, which suited me because there weren't boxes of tissues hidden under the kitchen table when I got home, although they were sometimes there at breakfast.

Right near the end of the year she dropped the bombshell that things had *really* changed. We couldn't afford the house and we had to sell it.

'So,' she said brightly. 'You'll be going to another school.'

I explained the facts of my life to her. 'All my friends go to Grammar, Mum.'

'We can't afford it.'

'I'll get a job after school.'

'It's eight thousand a year.'

'Why can't we borrow the money?' I'd heard plenty of heated conversations between Mum and Dad about money. I was my father's daughter. Not being able to afford things was not an option. 'Ask the family to help.'

'What family? Did they offer help after your father died? After the funeral did we ever get one phone call?'

'We didn't go to Sylvie's wedding. Vicki told me they were annoyed about that.'

'That's right! We get an invitation a week after your father died. A week. No note saying they'd understand if we didn't or they were sorry or they'd especially like us to come. Just one of those showy vulgar invites.'

She'd never liked the Greek part of our life. Now she sounded bitter.

'We can't afford to be Greek, Peter,' she used to say to Dad. 'We can't afford the present for this christening plus new dresses for Melissa and me. I can't afford the mental strain of your mother sighing whenever I come into her field of vision.'

He never said anything.

So I could see she couldn't ask my *YiaYia*, my Greek grand-mother, or the uncles for money. Ya Ya and Thia Toula, Dad's sister always compared me to my cousin Vicki who was smaller and very feminine. I liked Vicki, and I missed Thia Toula and Ya Ya, although not enough to make a fuss. Mum had drawn a line and I knew that was it.

'I'll go to the high school then,' I said to Mum. 'I'll get a job after school. Ron Matthews said I could share his paper run.' I didn't add the price of sharing the paper run was letting him feel up my budding breasts. I was a flirt, even at that age.

'Melissa,' said Mum. 'We're moving out of Manly. We're going to a place called Annandale near the city. It's different and I don't like having to do this to you, but —'

I slammed the door on my way out and ran all the way along the beach and back. I met Sandy on the Corso and even though she was one of my best friends I said, 'We're moving to the Gold Coast. I won't see you guys anymore.' The Gold Coast sounded better than Annandale.

CHAPTER 2

1976

Susan

Family dynamics changed when Lisa and I started sharing a flat. Mum rarely visited us but Dad took to visiting on his own. It was a bit awkward at first, a little stiff. Lisa and I were amazed that he came at all. We tried to think back to how often we'd seen Dad without Mum and we concluded it had been pretty rare. She'd always treated him as a second-class citizen, 'your father' as she called him. I broached the subject on his third solo visit. By this time, Dad and I were getting along much better. After years of having a rather distant relationship, we could now talk and joke. Out of my mother's orbit I could see his humour, his acceptance of people, his concern for Lisa and me.

'Is this a *secret* visit Dad?' I was teasing him.

'Secret?' he said.

'I mean, are we allowed to mention it to Mum?' We all laughed but Dad didn't answer the question so we never did mention it.

'Are you happy Suzie?' he asked me one day.

'Very,' I said. 'I'm reading *War and Peace* again.'

He looked puzzled.

'I'm glad I didn't marry Neil if that's what you mean.'

'I'd completely forgotten about Neil,' he said. 'He faded out to bland before I'd finished shaking his hand. But I meant your work. Are you happy there?'

'It's okay,' I said. 'I think it's very hard for a woman to get ahead but I don't care that much. I'm not sure the public service really suits me. I'm not sure what I'm supposed to be doing there and no one else knows.'

'Thought so,' he said. He lit his pipe. We didn't like him smoking in our tiny flat but we didn't have the heart to stop him.

'Don't you want a better job?'

I knew my father was passionate about the law. Lisa couldn't wait to start teaching, but I'd never had the expectation that work would be an involving, important part of my life.

'There's nothing I really want to *do*,' I said. 'No burning ambition.'

'Still it seems a waste—a fine brain like yours—filling in forms in some useless government department. Why don't you come and work for me—do a few law subjects, then your articles. Not immediately, of course,' he added. 'But sometime in the future.'

'Dad! Really! I'd love to!'

It wasn't the law that attracted me, it was Dad's offer. It was having a parent who thought about me, what I might like, who wanted me there. And he did. He was beaming from ear to ear.

'Well,' he said. 'You've got the brains for it and I thought with this women's lib we'd better get a few girls in the firm.'

'Dad,' I said. 'With this "women's lib business", as you call it, you can't call women "girls". You'll have to change your language if you're going to be a feminist.'

'I could hardly be a feminist,' he said. 'I'm the wrong sex for a start. But I've always thought women should work. Mind you, your mother has a totally opposite view. I wanted her to manage the practice once you girls—'

'Women,' Lisa and I said.

'All right, women, if you insist,' he said, but he remained puzzled, the unreconstructed male as Lisa dubbed him later. 'Your mother was horrified that I might expect her to work. And I didn't *expect* it, I just thought she might enjoy it. Use her mind, which is pretty sharp and is wasted on bridge afternoons, but she reacted as if I was selling her into slavery. So that's when I hired Marg. She seems to like working . . . anyway, I'm very glad you'll come onboard, Susan.' And he stood up and hugged me awkwardly. That was a first too.

Not only did I like working for my father, but I was surprised to find that I liked the orderliness of law, putting messy situations in order. And the principles and ideas were interesting. I could see that I could end up doing any number of things, specialise in certain areas, work in different roles. I felt the work could really mean something. It was the first time I'd thought that way. I had begun to see the idea of a career was as important for women as for men, a new idea at that time.

Lisa started teaching and we moved to a bigger flat where we could give dinner parties, which we both loved. We had an easy, ordered life that suited us. We had different interests—she was passionate about teaching, I loved reading. It was a good balance. We often talked about our childhood, still trying to make sense of that distance within our family.

Lisa refused to be intimidated by our mother. She was able to deflect Mum's criticisms of her. Mum dubbed Lisa as 'impossible' and left her alone. But with me, the breaking off of the engagement to Neil always came up. 'It was such a good match,' she said. 'You're so perverse, Susan.' She dropped these sorts of remarks into our conversations continuously.

'You've got to take a stand,' said Lisa.

I'd always been the dutiful daughter. That was what my relationship with my mother had been about. Then I'd become undutiful by breaking off my engagement and I wanted to make it clear, maybe to myself more than to her, that my time as the dutiful daughter was over for ever. I didn't want to be pretending to be someone I was not. I didn't want my mother pretending either. It was more complicated than that, but I thought I could start there.

I'd been molded and constructed and made to conform. I'd changed but to make that change solid and real, I had to tell my mother I was my own person. All this was churning over inside me; now was the time to explain I really had changed.

'You must be lonely without Neil,' she said next time I called her. She sighed. 'Such a pity. You should come out for dinner.'

'I will,' I said. 'Is next Tuesday okay?'

'They have a delicious chicken at the delicatessen,' she said. 'I'll get that so I don't have to cook.'

I rehearsed what I wanted to say as I drove up there. Each time I said it out loud, I felt a tightening in my stomach and was aware that my hands were clutching the steering wheel. But it had to be said.

Mum opened the front door and we moved into the entrance hall.

'That's a very bright dress, dear,' she said, looking me up and down.

'I like red,' I said. 'I think it suits me. I made it myself.'

'I thought so,' she said. 'Paler colours are generally better.'

My mother had always said you shouldn't have a conversation until you were sitting down properly, but we'd started right there so I thought I might as well continue it.

'You know, Mum, how I dress is really my business.'

'You should know what suits you.'

'I like red. And who I marry is my business too.'

'Whom,' she said. 'It is whom you marry, not who.'

I had it in my mind to walk out, walk away, but I stuck it out. It was now or never, never mind who or whom.

'I don't want you dropping remarks about what you see as my perversity about Neil. You can think what you like but I don't care what you think.' I took a deep breath and went on. 'And if I ever do marry, just remember your tastes don't enter into my calculations.'

'A mother can surely give advice,' Mum said. But she had gone white, her hands were clenched, her arms were held stiffly by her sides as if she was containing herself.

'Mum,' I said, 'please.' For the first time, I sensed my mother was vulnerable. Behind all that control, her brittle exterior, she wasn't perhaps as certain of everything as she seemed. Part of me wanted to take advantage of that vulnerability, but I also felt an unexpected sympathy for her.

'I think it's my place to advise you', she said.

'But you never think about what I want, who I am. It's as if that doesn't matter.'

'I do have the advantage of experience,' she said.

'I don't want your advice unless I ask.'

My mother looked at me coldly and then shrugged as if dismissing the whole business. 'This makes dinner a little awkward.'

'I won't stay,' I said.

'I bought the chicken,' she said.

'I don't care about the chicken.'

'Clearly.'

As I drove back onto the highway I was singing along to the

radio. I hadn't changed her, but I felt as if I had changed—my mind, my feelings, my sense of myself. And I'd done it with more grit than I'd given myself credit for. I didn't want to hurt my mother, but it had been inevitable. Every time I went against her it seemed she became a little harder, a little more fixed, a little more distant. I hated that but I didn't know what to do about it. It was painful but familiar territory. But at least I thought, I could be happier. That was my goal—to be happy. content, without too many pressures or too many self doubts.

My relationship with both parents had changed. I had a job which satisfied me, but I wanted to find an inner life. In my family, outward appearances had been all there was—what you wore, how you spoke, your education, who you knew. An inner life was seen as a self-indulgence. I knew what was inside was important, if only to me, even though I didn't have much idea of who I was. It was a little scary. I felt I knew the characters in books better than I knew myself. But I thought I could find out more about myself, gradually, by reading, by expanding the things that I did.

This was the reason that religion became a serious pursuit. I was raised Anglican and I attended an Anglican school. My parents went to church, from convention rather than conviction. I'd gone to church as a duty, but I'd hardly gone the last ten years. Now, I thought I could find that inner life in religion. I had always loved singing in chapel and I was interested in the whole question of faith and belief. But I was looking for something, not an answer but a way of exploring questions.

I started attending St James' Church in Macquarie Street, which is a beautiful little church, built in sandstone by convicts. I joined the choir and I was given some solo pieces to sing. That was fantastic to be able to express myself like that. I felt it was me, my inner self that I was giving voice to. That sense of expression seemed like a gift. This was high church Anglican so there was a lot of music as well as incense and candles. I loved the ceremony and the ritual, which gave me a sense of being lifted out of ordinary life. I met a lot of wonderful and eccentric people, the sort of people I didn't know existed. It gave me access to a life I hadn't known before.

It was here that I got to know Martin. I knew him a little before then because he was working for my father. Dad usually employed young men who had had a conventional private school background, which I guess applied to most law graduates. Martin was extremely well educated but he was from a rough-and-ready background, which made him different. He was the only person who wasn't deferential to my father. If my father made a remark about Martin's hair or his clothes—he once wore a leather jacket to court—Martin would laugh and call Dad an old fogey. Martin believed that he was my father's equal. The other young men, deferential, polite and bland, hoped to become my father's equal.

Martin flirted with me at work but he wasn't in the office much because he did a lot of court work. He was romantically good looking with wild curly hair, was tall and rugged. He was high spirited and he seemed to affect the people around him with that spirit. When he was in the office there was more laughter. I couldn't imagine he'd be interested in me. I thought when he flirted it was his way of being polite.

I certainly didn't expect to see him in St James' Church, where I bumped into him at the bottom of the steps, one evening after Evensong. I was feeling good as I'd put everything into my solo piece.

'Ah, Lady Thomas.' Martin always called me that.

'Hello Martin. This is the last place I would have expected to see you.'

'What, me being a Mick and all? The only Tyke among all the Proddies your dear old Dad keeps in silk ties? I like the choir here. I like the resonance. I thought the solo you did was just beautiful.'

'I'm glad you liked it. I really love that piece. I put a lot of work into it.'

'And passion,' he said, 'which was lovely. It really moved me.' He paused. 'But I don't know why you mightn't expect me to see me here. You think because I'm a working-class boy brought up on the wrong side of town that I mightn't need spiritual sustenance? And that because I'm an old St Joan of Arc choir boy that I mightn't like to step in and check out one of God's other houses?' He was performing and I was aware how attractive I found him. His face was very open and mobile. He didn't have that cultivated sense of distance so many men of the law have.

Suddenly it hit me like a thunderbolt that this was a physical attraction as well as whatever else was there. I hadn't experienced this before, not with this intensity. I'd joked about it with Lisa. 'Women are supposed to like sex,' she'd said. 'You've read Germaine. When you feel it, go for it.'

Martin flirting with me in the office hadn't been mere politeness. Something was happening between us and I could see he was nervous too, which made him talk more. 'I guess it would never occur to *you* to slum it with the Micks,' Martin went on. 'But all that Latin, you'd love it. Or maybe we could check out the Salvos one night if you're into brass bands.'

'I have a weakness for brass bands but I do have an aversion to fire and brimstone.' I didn't want to seem prim and proper.

'I love the choir here but I'm not exactly devout.' I went on tentatively trying to explain myself. 'But you're right, I wouldn't think of going anywhere except to an Anglican Church.'

He kept talking as the people from the service came out of the church. Then the minister, who wasn't the regular, came to the door and was about to shut it. Martin bounded up the steps. He was full of spontaneous energy. My movements were always contained, a little calculated. I'd never been any good at ballet when I was a child because of that lack of spontaneity. I had to think about things first, I loved that freedom in Martin.

'G'day Phil,' he said to the minister. 'Jesus, mate, where were you Saturday? Murphy said you'd be coming but you didn't show.'

They had a conversation at the top of the steps and I stood there watching them. I had never heard anyone address a member of the clergy in the way Martin did.

I was falling in love with Martin right there on the church steps. I was scared stiff but excited. I looked at this man who had the grit and energy that I lacked, with good humour and intelligence. He was so alive, so sexy. I couldn't wait to tell Lisa.

Martin

I debated with myself from the age of seven about whether God was true, what it meant, what the other branches of Christianity that were so colourfully demonised by the Brothers were actually about. I never stopped wondering, although I put to bed the narrow beliefs of my childhood fairly swiftly. I wanted personal transcendence, which I reckoned I sometimes got when I heard the Eucharist sung. Or out in the surf on a clear cold morning. On other occasions through dope. Sometimes with the wrist-slitting songs of Leonard Cohen. Or various combinations of the above. But I was restless and I couldn't hang onto it.

My sister Mary, who was a doctor, had rejected religion without a second thought. She joined a commune at Nimbin and became a Greenie activist and hung around with those of similar persuasion. Mary is a total bloody fanatic by nature, and my favourite sister.

My sister Kathleen got married in a church because it pleased Mum and Dad. She had her children baptised for the same reason. Whether she believed it or not was beside the point for her. I thought about religion because I wanted to feel the expanse of the world, the possibilities of the universe, not because I wanted to believe in something.

After the split with Yvette, I was at a loose end and I met up with Phil Anderson, a Pom, who I knew from Oxford, where he'd studied divinity. We'd both done Latin and philosophy at Oxford and we used to drink and play some rugby together. He was the embodiment of muscular Christianity in looks, but with a few more brains than that lot. He looked me up when he came out to Australia. It didn't surprise me that he'd been ordained as a minister in the Anglican Church and was working in the Archbishop's office down in St Andrew's Cathedral. It hadn't made him pious. He also did some work at St James. That suited him because he was from a pretty high church background. He liked Australia. He was looking for new horizons and I think his mother had been Australian.

Phil was a remarkable bloke. Very intelligent with no worldly ambition. A faith that was general rather than particular. Obviously he was a devout Christian, but he didn't think Christianity was the only religion in the world. I never got the feeling he was running away from anything, leaving England. More that he was searching. I liked that about him. Which is how I ended up going to some of his services at St James, where the music was fabulous.

Basically we were two blokes whose friendship was based on us both being, to a certain degree, at a loose end, and a certain degree of going to the footy together. And a sense of being in the same spiritual boat, both with a direction towards enquiry.

By an excellent coincidence, my search for transcendence was how I discovered woman as mystery. My sisters had been no mystery to me. In a house with eight people, no one gets to be a mystery. Generally, the girls I'd had relationships with weren't mysterious. Most of them had been outgoing, outspoken girls who could drink and carouse as well as the men. Like Yvette.

Susan was completely different. I fell for her big time, although not at first. She was my boss's daughter and she worked at the firm. It was your basic nepotism really, considering old Thomas hadn't bred any boys. Susan was efficient and devastatingly pretty. She was shy but you knew there was a lot to her. And there was a lot of warmth. But I felt she thought I wasn't her type. I suppose I felt she might prefer someone with a bit more polish or breeding. I flirted with her but I didn't get anywhere. That was that, I thought, although I always felt a stab of pleasure when I saw her at work.

But then I saw her at Evensong and that changed everything. She was their soloist and she was totally immersed in the music. It was like a lightning bolt. Her voice was high and pure. Shining, straight, golden-blonde hair to her shoulders, a sweet delicacy about her face, lovely blue eyes. She was beyond me. This wasn't just looking at a pretty girl and falling in love. This was another world with barriers to be negotiated, walls scaled, boundaries breeched. Suddenly womanhood had mystery. The same mystery of faith and belief that I had struggled with. The mystery of woman seemed more profound, and a lot sexier.

For me it was the mystery of her dark blue eyes, mystery in how contained she was, mystery in how separate she was, how unavailable she was.

I remember after the service that night, bounding up the stairs of St James and talking to Phil, full of confusion and embarrassment, then bounding down the steps again and talking loudly to her, almost hoping she'd go away because it was almost painful to be with her, because of her effect on me. She stood there, watching me, until I felt I simply had to stick to her side, like a large, stupid dog looking for somewhere to put its energy, looking for guidance on how to stop prancing and barking and jumping. We went for coffee and had a serious conversation about all sorts of things and found that we shared the same ideas about a lot of things. She saw I wasn't just a loud boozer, full of smart remarks—that I thought about things.

She liked me, really liked me. Wonder! I became the one in her life, filling some space or some need, even while she kept that mystery. It had never taken me so long to bed a woman. I could see the way she looked at me that she liked me, but I was terrified she'd reject me, scared that the ease we had together would disappear. But when we finally did make it to bed, it was glorious. We were in love, full of passion. With all the difficulties in our relationship—and there were a few—I found no fault in her. She called my mum 'Mrs Ryan', and sat ill at ease in my parents' stuffy living room and refused the specially bought cream lamingtons. It was a different world from hers.

'She's upmarket for sure,' my brother Lachie said.

My mother was circumspect. 'You know your father and I haven't actually been happy together,' she said, when I visited her alone one afternoon. Now I lived near the beach it took over an hour to get to my parents' place.

This was Mum's first ever reference to her marital unhappiness. I think she had some weird idea that if she never spoke of it, we kids would never really know how she and Dad disliked each other, nevermind the flying missiles and the verbal slings and arrows that coloured our childhood. So I felt as if I was hearing a criminal confession in the closeness of the little kitchen alcove with the worn red laminex and the white-painted chipboard cupboards with their strange old-fashioned ventilation holes. Suddenly this symbolised the confinement of everything I wanted to escape.

'It wasn't my fault,' Mum said, 'I know that.'

We were silent for a few minutes while she made her foul instant coffee.

'But it wasn't your father either,' she said as she sat down. 'It was us together. That's what you need to look at.'

'Don't get serious about this one,' my sister Mary said over a beer. She had summoned me to the Royal George Hotel to give me her opinion. Mary was never shy of giving her opinion on the most personal matters. 'You're crazy about her but, Marty, she's wrong, she's all wrong for you.'

'What do you mean?'

'Don't get me started.'

'What do you mean by that?'

'Isn't it obvious? She's not like us. And a woman like that will want to change you. She'll get her claws into yo . . .'

I stormed out, didn't speak to Mary for a month. Just because I was from working-class stock didn't mean I was stuck with that forever. My parents had educated us so we would be different from them. Christ! I'd been to Oxford. And I loved Susan, adored her and she loved me. That was the most important thing, the only thing.

I was in love, entranced by the woman who never should have even looked at me. We were different but what did it matter? It mattered to my siblings and my parents, it seemed.

And to Susan's parents which was blindingly obvious when we visited them. We drove up to one of those leafy north shore suburbs off the Pacific Highway, where you can barely see the houses for the grand gardens. Lawn, quiet streets and gravel driveways. Money and good taste oozing bloody everywhere. Cleanliness, restraint, tidiness—all those middle class virtues. Jesus! It could send you crazy. We drove down endless streets, overhung with trees, not a soul to be seen.

'This is a place to breed madness,' I said to Susan.

She laughed. 'They're all pathologically polite so it'd be hard to tell if they're crazy. Anyway the trees are lovely.'

'I suppose they are.' But there were no kids playing cricket in the street or racing billycarts down the hill. No adolescents smoking on street corners. No overturned garbage tins. No garbage at all! No graffiti. No drunks taking a kip in the bus shelters. No bus shelters in fact.

'Shit,' I said as we drove down street after street after street of those grand houses. 'I never knew there were so many rich folks.'

'Don't say that to my mother, will you?'

I laughed. 'I'm not quite that crass.' But after meeting her mother, I had the distinct impression that I was.

I talked about politics and religion and all the other no-go areas. I sort of knew they were no-go but I was bloody nervous and her mother's endless references to the golf club made me a little crazy. The golf club sounded like a crypto-fascist front to me. I drank too much sherry, ate *all* the cheese sticks specially purchased from the delicatessen and dropped the crumbs on the floor.

Susan was both impressed and horrified. 'God!' she said as we got in the car. 'No one has ever argued with Mum like that!'

'I thought she was going to breathe fire any moment,' I said. 'It added a bit of edge to the conversation.'

'I don't care what she thinks,' said Susan. She reached over and took my hand and kissed it. 'I'm crazy about you. I love you. I love it that you could just be yourself with them. It took me years.'

Old Thomas Thomas looked at me strangely the next day at work. 'You gave us a bit of a conversational workout,' he said. 'I think Aunt Helen's ghastly sherry table was just about to have kittens the way you were going on.'

I was mad about Susan, crazy about her. I really didn't give a toss what her mother and father thought, although I thought old Thomas was basically a decent bloke. Her mother was from hell. She evidently thought I was badly brought up, lacking in refinement, wild and irresponsible—an impression that was confirmed by what happened a few months down the track.

'I'm pregnant.' Susan's words sealed it. Sealed my happiness. Sealed my fate.

She was sitting on her bed, a dressing gown drawn around her, her little foot stuck out in front of her, her face miserable, her cheeks flushed.

'I don't know what to do. I could have an abortion . . . I don't know . . . I'll . . . .'

'Darling, darling, darling, don't do that. Have the baby. Hey,

I'm an ex-Catholic, you can't have an abortion on me. I'll look after you. Honestly, I love you to eternity, you love me. Let's not stuff it up, let's just get married. Honestly, I'd hate an abortion.'

She had never known this Catholic ideologue existed. 'Martin, I don't know if I want a child. Getting married isn't a solution. Well, maybe, but it doesn't change me being pregnant. I mean, I'd not thought about children. Well, in a theoretical way . . .'

'Marriage is a reasonable proposition. I love you. You love me. We'd love a baby. Come on. Suzie.'

'It's my body,' she said in her tight and proper way but I could hear the tears in her voice. 'I'd thought I would . . . have children . . . but I'm not quite ready . . . I mean, it's so huge. It's too much.' And she started crying

And the Catholic madman dropped away, although there was something from my altar boy days that really hated the abortion. The one true religion I didn't believe in anymore had left its mark. 'I'm sorry,' I said. 'You know I'm totally selfish. I'm sorry, I'm sorry. Honestly, Susan, it's not my decision. It's yours. Truly. But if you want to get married or just live together. I'll do whatever you want. It's up to you'

'I guess,' she said. 'I don't want an abortion. But I don't want a baby, not now.' She lay back against me and I put my arms round her.

'Marry me,' I said, 'not because you're pregnant but because I love you. Not to avoid an abortion but because I really want to be with you.'

'I want to think about it,' she said. 'Marriage and baby and the whole thing. And Martin, please, please, don't pressure me. I need time alone, just to think. Maybe you should think about it too.'

I knew her well enough to give her time. I was one for snap

decisions; she liked to think about things, nevermind that I didn't see there was anything to think about. I couldn't believe she wouldn't come round, she wouldn't be able to see how happy we'd be, how a baby would be a wonderful thing for us, that the marriage would work just beautifully. We still saw each other at work and went out on small outings—to the movies, to coffee and walks in the park. She was tired and sick and I could see she needed space. I was careful not to say too much, not to ask leading questions. In short, I was acting like perfect husband material.

Well, when I was with her at least. The rest of my time I did some heavy drinking and knocked round with some of my old mates. It reminded me how much she had changed me. I'd pretty much given away that lifestyle since I met her.

Cliff was a journalist, a friend of Yvette's. He'd used me in an article he'd written on the workings of the new divorce law. He'd rung up and I'd gone to the pub with him and we'd chatted. Then he'd had a photographer come round and take my photo and it was a big feature article in the Saturday paper.

Thomas Thomas was beside himself. Said it was undignified and it was almost advertising which no law firm could or would do. Didn't want his firm in the newspaper. Didn't think it was proper. Crap, crap, crap. Then had kittens when it appeared under the banner 'No More Spying in the Bedroom'. Mind you, old Thomas restrained his ire a bit when the clients started ringing up after having read the piece.

'A divorce lawyer—you should know better than to be getting married,' Cliff said when I met him down the pub in my quiet time when Susan was thinking it all over. Not that I told him the whole story.

'What's wrong with marriage?'

'Why don't you live with her? See if it works before you get tied up forever.'

'Not that sort of girl. Not that sort of family.'

'Jesus Christ, Martin. That sort of girl, that sort of family. Are you bloody thinking of moving to some posh suburb?' he said. I suppose it did sound middle class and respectable. Was I willing to become all that for Susan? Very definitely. He was probably jealous, a battered old booze-soaked journo like him on the outside track with women.

Three weeks later Susan knocked on the door of my flat on a Saturday morning.

'I hate the way you leave your football socks on the floor,' she said, shaking her head, but she was smiling 'It's disgusting.' She looked around the rest of the disarray. 'They do smell, you know.' When she was nervous she always wanted to tidy things up. It was sweet.

'Leave the socks out of it,' I said. 'Whatever you've decided is okay. Come on, sit down.' I bundled the socks under the couch.

She smiled. 'Sorry, I am nervous. I didn't have a termination. Couldn't in the end.'

I wanted to jump up and shout a few hallelujahs, but I restrained myself. She was still carrying our baby around. *Our* baby.

'We still have a choice,' she went on. 'I can have the baby and have it adopted. I'm prepared to do that.' She had tears in her eyes. 'I mean I know you said we'd get married, but I don't want to Martin, not unless you really, really . . . I mean apart from the baby . . .'

At which I did get up and shout the hallelujahs. 'Marry me, marry me, marry me,' I said. 'We love each other. We'll love the baby. If you marry me you'll make me happy, you'll make you happy, you'll make the baby happy. By Christ, by some miracle, you might even make your own mother happy.'

'I doubt we'd make my mother happy.' We both started laughing. 'This will absolutely kill her. Serve her right.'

'A marriage based on vengeance and spite can never be all bad,' I said. 'Oh my God, I'm so happy.'

'I love you, I want to marry you but I want to talk to you about some things though,' she said seriously. 'Before we go ahead.'

'Okay. Fire.'

'It's about money.'

'You know I don't give a flying fuck about money.'

'Don't swear in front of the baby,' she said. 'That's another thing. But the money thing is important. You don't have to care about money because you're a man and you'll always be able to earn plenty. But I do care about money because I'm a woman and I'm going to depend on you for while. And I don't want to feel it's only your money. I want to have some autonomy. You might think its outrageous but I want you to give me half your salary, and then we pay things together. And when I go back to work, I give you half mine, so we always have the same amount.'

'Joint cheque account,' I said. 'I agree with you. I had parents who argued about money. Who earned, who spent, what they spent it on. They're still at it. I think what you're suggesting is fantastic.'

'Martin, that's terrific, but let's have separate accounts

'But darling, we'll be married.'

'Look, I wouldn't ask this unless I thought it would work better this way. I don't want to depend on your largesse. I want to do things together, but to really feel that I need to have a sense of independence.'

'I think you have one already.' I was elated. She was mine. It seemed unbelievable.

Of course her mother was outraged by her pregnancy, by the marriage and by me. Her father was a whole lot more civilised although it made him a bit uncomfortable. And he gave me a hard time while at the same time handing me a partnership in the firm.

'You've got a bit of grand carelessness, Martin,' he said. I thought he was referring to the pregnancy which I regarded as very grand and splendid carelessness, but he meant my work. 'Not much eye for detail. It's shown up in a couple of cases.'

'So why give me the partnership?' I asked.

'Because you're marrying my daughter. I'm just pointing out that it entails some responsibilities.'

'What?' What an old bastard he was, playing the father-in-law to the hilt. 'Responsibilities to the marriage or the partnership?'

'Both,' he said. 'You're not doing quite as well as I'd expected here, Martin, in terms of the money you bring in. You don't take notice of the detail. Okay, you're marrying my daughter, which is what the partnership is for. You need to lift your game. Law isn't theory. It's practice. That's why it's called a practice.'

I think that's what they call giving it with one hand and taking it away with the other.

Phil

They'd both been coming to St James. Martin was a lapsed Catholic with a medium-sized chip on his shoulder about the Protestant establishment. He was very likeable—he was one of the first people I looked up when I came to Australia. We used to go to the rugby together where we often argued about the game or about religion. He was loud and he liked to make an impression. I guess that had something to do with his background. He made his way in the world by virtue of his intelligence and determination. He was a very good-looking man which gave him a lot of confidence, perhaps a touch of arrogance. Not in the sense of putting other people down, but he never doubted his charm or his arguments or his actions.

I'd come to Australia with romantic dreams and a few old family connections. At home, the church seemed rife with politicking and cronyism. I had this romantic notion of finding a wonderful outback parish where such things couldn't affect me, but politicking and cronyism are part of life, not peculiar to England. But I liked Sydney and the way of life. I liked the fact Australians were so open about their beliefs, particularly about their lack of them. I loved the climate and I decided to stay.

Martin and I did a fair bit of drinking together and we did a lot of talking. Some of it was drunken raving, some of the time we hit paydirt. He was an agnostic. That didn't worry me. I was an Anglican largely because my dad had been a minister. Obviously I had very deep beliefs but I liked to poke around the philosophy of religion. I loved the rituals of the high church and the music. Martin loved the music too, although he had a terrible singing voice. I told him, tactfully, but he still sang loudly.

Susan was a different story. She had a sweet voice, with an incredible range and it was hauntingly clear. She was very pretty and very gentle in her manner. A wonderful person, beautiful and a true spiritual seeker. She was composed but you could tell she wasn't very sure of herself. She thought about the big questions.

That first night on the steps I could see the sparks between

Martin and Susan. I wanted to take her aside and tell her it was wrong, that he wasn't right for her, she could do better. Actually it wasn't that it was wrong at all. It was that *I* wanted to take her aside and ask her if she'd like to go out with me, but I was far too shy. Plus, if Martin was involved, it was bound to be no contest.

As they got to know each other I thought she would help him and guide him to explore the depths, which was great, because he did have depths. He wasn't a superficial person, despite being brash. He was amazed that a girl like her would look twice at him. I must say I was amazed too. But they were great together with a sense of intimacy and ease between them.

Mary

Martin wanted me to meet her. He was crazy about her in the way he hadn't been about Yvette or the ones before her.

'I'm taking you out to dinner with her,' he said. 'At Barnaby's. Sorry, but I think they have a dress code.' What he was saying was that I was not to wear my commune overalls and gumboots. I worked up at Nimbin month on, month off. Then I came down to Sydney to do a locum or two for a general practitioner friend and earn the income to keep the commune going. That sort of thing had always been fine with Martin. He wasn't into sartorial splendour, although he had enough vanity to spend money on clothes now he had the money.

This relationship with Susan changed the ball game. Mum had already gathered that our family wasn't quite good enough for Susan. He'd come out and tidied up the front verandah the day before he brought Susan out there. Moved the collection of cardboard boxes and milk cartons and old bikes and the lawnmower parts Dad liked to keep on there. The cleaned-up front verandah wouldn't fool a girl like Susan.

Still, I borrowed a dress from Kathleen for the dinner.

'Susan's conservative,' he said. 'Not fundamentally, but she's from a posh sort of a family. They mind the Ps and Qs.' He grinned. 'Haven't quite got her out of the habit yet.'

I had been educated by Irish nuns, who understood that the British Empire and the Protestant religion were the twin arms of British imperialism. Truly, I did not mind Susan being conservative. With a different education I might have been a conservative too, although Martin says I would have always been a rabid right winger.

But Susan had picked out this good-looking, intelligent, fun, working-class man because she wanted someone to patronise. Well, that's how I saw it. She patronised me too. She smiled sweetly but falsely. She put her head to one side. 'So Martin tells me you're involved in the commune movement?' Making it sound almost respectable.

'I think it's important to believe in something, don't you?' she said.

'You work in an office?' I asked.

'My dad's firm,' she said, 'I did my degree in English literature, but there's hardly a living in that.' That from a woman who had never had to make her own living. And she smiled, as if the three of us were united by her love of English literature. I thought I was going to put my head in my hands and groan loudly, or maybe just vomit, but I caught Martin's eye. Usually we'd wink at such crap. Now he gave me an encouraging smile.

'I'm sure we'll be great friends,' she said. She seemed nervous. I don't know what the hell she thought there was to be nervous about. 'Martin's really important to me.'

'Oh,' I said, 'I'm just his sister. I'm afraid he's plain ordinary to me.' I wanted to grab Martin and take him home with me and slap him a few times and talk sense to him. Shiny blonde hair, blue eyes and white teeth aren't everything. In fact, they aren't much at all. And her clothes, tailored and high fashion. Martin told me she made her own clothes but I don't think so. She was one of those girls who had a fortune to spend.

He rang me the next day and went on at great length about her.

'She's a mystery to me,' he said, 'I can never quite reach her. It's as if she's from somewhere else.'

She was. She was prim and proper, clever and well bred. She wasn't a Catholic either, but I couldn't really hold that against her since I'd given up the one true religion years ago.

Women were not a mystery to Martin. He grew up in a household of women; shared a bathroom with four sisters. He'd seen the depilatory cream in action. He'd seen flash new bras of black lace bought to impress our boyfriends. He'd seen the tired, old saggy grey bras with stretched straps and safety pins tossed carelessly on the bathroom floor. Our oldest sister, Maureen brought home an out-of-wedlock baby at seventeen, and, even with all the drama that resulted, it was hardly a mystery. The father's name was Sam, and the only mystery was where he'd shot off to.

We were a close family. Close, and rough at times. He saw the best and worst of women. We screamed and kicked and pulled hair. There were shared intimacies of thoughts and feelings, shared tears, pain, sympathies, understandings, truces and all out wars. The was mercy and no mercy, but there was never mystery

Maybe he craved mystery. Or maybe him falling in love with

someone so alien came from the darker side of our family life—
the flashes of anger between our parents, the violence in my
father's voice or the cold, cutting dismissal of my mother's reply.
For all the family togetherness there was, at the centre of it, two
people, deeply unhappy with each other. Martin was the one in
the middle of their fights. He was the one there with Mum when
Dad got home dead-drunk and mean. Maybe marrying Susan
was about being nothing like his parents.

So what did I think of her? Honestly? You want to know?

Okay. I didn't like her. I didn't trust her. Self righteous,
perfectly mannered, totally hypocritical—need I go on?

Little Miss Bossy Boots. Little Miss Prissy.

Mock religious, judgmental, supercilious, full of repressed
rage, repressed sexuality and contempt for others. This was
disguised by a false and patronising tolerance clothed with a
facile intellectualism, dressed up in high fashion. And she'd got
herself pregnant so he'd marry her.

It had to be my darling brother, shining with such an
innocent love of life, who fell for 'Vile Susan'.

Melissa

When Mum told me our new house would be an old house,
I was disgusted. How backward could you get? The inner west
city charm of Sydney was lost on me.

I had breasts and attitude. I played touch football with the
local boys. I'd taken to wearing eye shadow and platform shoes,
although not for playing football, obviously. I was sassy. I was
boy crazy. I had a mouth and my periods. I liked to laugh and
joke a lot. I was probably a pain in the butt.

I made friends at the new school but my real friends were back in Manly. I had it somewhere in my head that I'd go back there one day. See Ya Ya and Thia Toula, except I couldn't say that to Mum.

There was a bit of a crisis when Granny died. Mum was so sad. She sat in Granny's poor kitchen, resting her head against the table. Her big hunk of a brother was standing there looking embarrassed. He said sort of helplessly, 'It's okay, Barb.' I knew it wasn't. I had just enough understanding to realise my mother needed me, selfish adolescent that I was. I made her cups of tea, got her to talk about Granny, helped her clean out her house.

Granny was real poor and had lived in a little house which was crammed with furniture, with a shed full of more furniture out the back. This furniture was the basis of my mother's new life.

I was hardly in a state to notice that my mother had decided she wanted a new life.

Mum set up a second-hand furniture business with Granny's hoard. She rented a shop on Parramatta Road and she put Granny's furniture in it. Now I think how brave she was. Gradually she traded up from Granny's knocked-about furniture to classy antiques. When I was about fifteen, we were driving along Parramatta Road and I yelled, 'Mum, your shop's got your maiden name ' "Barb Barnett's Old Wares".' She laughed and laughed because she'd had the shop almost three years and I'd never noticed.

'Why don't you use your real name?' I asked.

'I've been using my maiden name for three years,' she said. 'Haven't you noticed on the stuff I signed for school?'

'Don't you love Daddy anymore?' I asked, breaking my rule of never mentioning Dad. Suddenly I was nearly crying. 'How can you not love Dad?'

'Darling,' she said. 'I loved your Dad. I loved all sorts of things about him but his name wasn't one of them. And this business is mine.'

'You loved him? Really?'

'Sweetheart, I loved him. Remember us together. We fought but we still held hands at the beach. Remember when he was dying . . .'

I stopped listening at that point. Maybe because I had never grieved, I wasn't sure that *I* had loved him.

I was still into loads of sport. I played netball. I ran, I was a school captain, I did well academically and I was close to my mum. Privately though, I had the feeling I wasn't leading my *real* life.

I was popular but I was skating on the surface with most people.

The exception was my friend Anna. She's from a Greek family, and for her it was important I had a Greek surname. She didn't trust the Anglo kids.

She's a thinker, I'm a doer, and for both of us it's been important to have each other. I remember when I told her my father had died, she said, 'Oh my God, that must have been awful for you.' And I thought, Awful? And I had a little stab of how sad it had been. It was a reminder that life mightn't always be the way I had decided it was.

'You don't see your family?' Anna asked. She was scandalised. For Anna, families were Greek and they pretty much lived next door, if not in the same house. I missed Dad's family but we'd never heard from them since we moved. I knew something must have happened.

Anna wanted to do drama at school but she was shy. I told her that she had to try out for Juliet in *Romeo and Juliet* which was the school play. Even Mum, who loved Anna, thought that was crazy. Anna was a small, not so pretty Greek girl with glasses. But I knew in my heart Anna could do it. I knew she wanted to, but everyone was telling her not to even bother trying. I thought you could do most things if you try. I guess I got that from my Dad. So for the two weeks before the audition, I coached her every day when we were walking home from school.

'No, Anna,' I'd say. 'Juliet is really, really tragic.' And she got more tragic and poignant and more like Juliet. I went to the audition with her. She took off her glasses and undid her ponytail and she stunned them. Everyone looked at this plain little Greek girl who was suddenly Juliet, young and beautiful and truly tragic, as only Anna could be. I thought if you believe in something, you can make it real.

Life in Annandale was real to my mother. For me, the reality was limited to my mother and my friendship with Anna. And maybe jazz ballet and netball passes and powering through the water to reach the wall in swimming. Reality was my physical energy, my love of movement, of grace. In that way I felt good about myself. I loved flirting with boys, making them feel good about me too.

I was feeling I had to move fast, really fast because I didn't belong where I was. I didn't want sadness and a box of tissues on the kitchen table.

CHAPTER 3

1977

Susan

I was five months pregnant when we married.

'A scandal!' said my mother. 'How could you do this to me?'

'I didn't do it to you,' I said. 'It's got nothing to do with you. It's Martin and me that are getting married.' I looked her in the eye. 'I'm pregnant and I'm not ashamed of that.'

'Well I am,' she said. 'I can't help it but I am.' And somehow that bit of honesty made me feel just a little bit sorry for my mother.

'Mum, I wish you could see this differently. Martin and I love each other . . .'

'Love,' she sniffed. 'That won't get you far.'

'Please come to the wedding. We're making it very small, only immediate family.'

'I suppose I should be grateful for small mercies. I'll come but I'm not happy with this, Susan.'

'I'm very happy.'

She didn't reply.

I was so madly in love with Martin, that the marriage felt sacred and special, all the more because I was pregnant. I had a vision of us sharing our lives, being together, helping each other, loving each other. It was sweet and hopefully, perhaps even foolishly, idealistic. We didn't even live together before we married.

I'd never really thought about having children but with Martin it seemed totally right once I got through all that initial angst. And I was so grateful he'd given me the time and space to do that. In the end, the pregnancy was our way of coming together, of committing to one another.

The day we went to see Phil about the wedding ceremony, Martin and I walked up King Street hand in hand. This is the turning point in my life, I thought. I squeezed Martin's hand and felt, for a moment, what it would be like to be free of my doubts and fears, free to be myself. I felt I could with Martin.

Phil greeted us at the entrance to the little office at the back of the church. 'Come in,' he said. He took us through the service, suggesting music and various special readings, giving us an understanding of their meaning. Then he ran through the service and I asked him to show me the prayer book.

'It worries me,' I said.

'We'll leave out "obey",' said Phil. 'As in "love, honour and obey". It's totally archaic.'

'I know,' I said. 'It's not that. It's more that I'm not quite a Christian in the sense of believing every single word of the Bible.' I turned to Martin for support. He had a faraway look on his face. He thought weddings were women's business. 'I'm not sure I embrace all of it.'

'Who does?' said Phil lightly and then he laughed. It sounded really odd coming from a minister, but that was Phil.

'For some strange reason Susan doesn't want to get married at five o'clock in the morning on a deserted beach,' said Martin. 'So you're the next best thing.'

'I don't quite know what God is but we love each other,' I said. I felt very passionate and sure of that. 'I believe in a great benevolent force of the universe.' I looked at Martin again.

'Do you think we should be getting married in a church?'

'It's a lovely church. And we started here as a couple.' He smiled at me. 'Nearly as good as a beach, sweetheart.'

'You've thought about this,' said Phil. 'You're both closer to Christ than a lot of other people who I marry.'

As we were leaving the church Martin said a lovely thing. 'My love just feels like it was meant to be, something I've been waiting for all my life. A gift.' He kissed me and looked into my eyes. 'What I feel is beyond what I've ever felt before.'

It summed it up—the feeling between us, the sense of the love being greater than us both. I felt absolutely, incredibly happy. Of course there were hassles. My mother kept out of it but my father had quite firm views.

'The day you were born I said to your mother that I looked forward to walking you down the aisle,' he told me. 'I'm looking forward to giving you away.'

'I don't want to be given away,' I said. 'You don't own me.'

'Don't be so prickly, Suzie,' he said. 'The compensation for having daughters is that fathers and daughters don't fight. Indulge me a little.'

'I didn't know that you needed compensation for me not being a boy,' I said. Maybe I was a little affected by the pregnancy hormones, or maybe the wedding was such a big event in my head. Every little thing loomed large.

'I don't, don't be silly.'

'Times have changed.'

'Not for me.'

'Think about it. Think what it means,' I said. 'You, my father, giving me to another man. What does that say about me?'

'It says you're my daughter who I care for and I'm giving you to another man to care for.'

'You're not. I'm giving myself to him.'

'I know that,' he said. 'You already have.'

There was an embarrassing silence then, because of the pregnancy, and his statement was left hanging, but Dad must have talked to Martin.

'Look,' said Martin. 'He's a Philip Street lawyer, living on the leafy North Shore. Of course he's traditional but he doesn't think he owns you.' He looked at me and smiled. 'No one could think that about you, Suzie. I mean he'll make you a partner one day, he's paying for the whole bloody thing. Indulge the dopey old bastard, make him happy. It's a wedding for chrissake.'

Who giveth this woman to be married to this man?

I do.

Just two lines and Dad was happy. I relented and I was glad I did. Maybe it was the whole thing of leaving the firm, giving up my career before it had even started. Then Dad told me he wanted to invite his secretary Marg.

'Dad, it's family only. And only close family.'

'She's almost family to me.'

'Dad, she's just your secretary. Don't be silly.'

'She's helped organise it. She hasn't got any family of her own.'

'No Dad. Definitely not.' But I sent her a nice bunch of flowers and that seemed to calm Dad down. Funny thing for him to want though.

On the wedding day I was very nervous but excited too. It wasn't what people call a shotgun wedding. We loved each other and this was the beginning of our life together, the two of us becoming one. I had a romantic vision of full and contented happiness. Phil married us in front of our families, with no outsiders.

He did the service beautifully, it was full of meaning.

. . . and may ever remain in perfect love and peace together, and live according to Thy laws, through Jesus Christ our Lord. Amen.

Martin

At times I wished we'd done the beach wedding. For a simple wedding ours seemed unbelievably complicated at times. And it was no use me trying to help.

'I warned you,' said Cliff. 'Deciding to get married is the last simple decision you'll ever make. You've given up your freedom. You'll be following orders the rest of your life.'

'Susan told me about the unreconstructed male,' I said. 'And you may be the last of the species.' I'd decided against a bucks' night but I was doing some serious drinking with Cliff and a few other mates, which was actually remarkably close to the concept of a bucks' night. We'd been to most of the pubs round the Rocks and were all fairly drunk. I was wearing an opera cape and we'd sung the German drinking song more times than I cared to remember.

'The unmarried male,' shouted someone, 'is the last bastion of freedom.'

We drank to that and moved on to the next pub. But my heart wasn't in it. I wanted to be with Susan.

'I think we should all go and see her,' I said to my brother Lachie. I was very drunk.

'Bad idea,' he said. Lachie was doing the lion's share of holding me vertical, the art of which seemed to have abandoned me, along with the faculty of clear thinking.

Fortunately I remember very little of what happened after that. Cliff told me the next day that it had been a top night. The thing is even when I can't remember I do know I love drinking, so I must have had a good time.

But I loved Susan more. I loved her even more on the day of our wedding. Loved her and wanted her and was sure it would work. The music, the service, everything was fantastic.

Of course my family were sitting there, a good number of them convinced that by marrying an Anglican in an Anglican church, I was securing my passport to eternal damnation.

'Get over it,' I said to Dad. 'You only go to Mass because Mum dragoons you to go. And she goes for the gossip.'

'Thank God Nanna's not alive to see this,' said Mum. By the end of the service she and the rest of them were crying buckets over it. I was glad to be free of all that narrow-minded, mean sectarianism. Susan and I were starting a new life, we were finally free agents.

Lisa, Susan's sister, was the bridesmaid. She sang a wonderful hymn. Like Susan, she had a clear, uplifting voice.

I didn't even hear the words. I was just looking at Susan with such love and tenderness. She was so beautiful. Somehow it was even more wonderful that she was carrying our child. Naturally her mother didn't think so. And had let me know.

'Look at the mother. That's what you'll have in thirty years,' Cliff had told me. I didn't believe a word of it.

With this ring, I thee wed, with my body, I thee worship, and with all my worldly goods I thee endow.

Phil

It's strange performing a marriage. I know some ministers do it as routine—for me it never is. I often get a funny feeling, as if

I'm intruding on something private. And the other thing—I feel a little emasculated. They never teach you about that in training for the ministry, but it's true. Here are two people coming together in love, full of sexual passion and I'm up there in my ceremonial frock, so to speak.

You approach the ceremony with great joy and enthusiasm, although sometimes it's not quite what you expected. Maybe it's clear the groom isn't committed, or the person the bride is eyeing so lovingly is actually the best man. It's a tricky business. Fortunately that wasn't the case with Martin and Susan.

The ceremony itself was wonderful. The marriage was a dedication to God. You could see they were both full of love and hope, and they truly wanted it to work. Susan looked gorgeous. She wore a pale blue silk dress, very simple, and a veil, like a white mantilla, pinned to her hair with a twist of forget-me-knots on each side. It enchanted me, the way she looked. It embodied who she was—so sweet, so pure.

The wedding wasn't about putting on a show for anyone. It was about what they wanted their relationship to be. I had the highest hopes for the marriage.

Send thy blessings upon these thy servants, this man and this woman, whom we bless in Thy Name.

Lisa

I was sad Susan was getting married in one sense because it meant we wouldn't be living together anymore. We'd had such a great time together, cooking and talking and sometimes going out together. But really, once it started with Martin, I knew we were on borrowed time. I loved Martin, although I did wonder if he was right for Susan. He was a bit of a heartbreaker in my book. I didn't think he was the type to stick round out of duty, so it was just as well he was so crazy about her.

He was a man's man. He liked his drinking nights and his football matches and his card nights. He liked surfing and playing football. Dad went to his club and he played golf, but he was never into that macho culture. I'm not even sure Susan understood that culture and how strong it was. I suppose I wouldn't have been either, except I saw a fair bit of it being a teacher. I did wonder how that would pan out when they got married. Susan was sure it would all run on feminist principles and idealism, but I thought Martin had a fairly entrenched case of being one of the boys. And on the wild side at that.

I was the bridesmaid. I felt so emotional after all Susan had been through. We had talked and talked and talked about the pregnancy. It was obvious to me from the start that she'd end up marrying him, but it wasn't obvious to her. And she certainly wasn't going to rush it so she wouldn't be showing at the wedding. I thought she was quite strong in that way, especially considering Mum's attitude.

'It's my life,' she said after Mum called into question her sense of social propriety and her morality. 'It's not yours, Mum. And you can't change it.'

She was a stronger person now. She said it calmly so there was nothing to discuss. It doesn't sound much, but believe me, Mum was a total bloody dragon.

'You girls keep pushing me away,' she complained to me.

I didn't argue. Susan still wanted a closer relationship with Mum. I think she thought that she would change, but Mum was intransigent.

At the wedding, I sang the hymn 'O Love divine'. That's how

I felt about it. I looked at Martin while I was singing. He was expansive and generous. There was nothing small minded about him. I thought he, more than anyone, could give her the happiness she deserved.

Afterwards he came up and hugged me tight and thanked me for singing. He was moved, had tears in his eyes. I liked that. I liked the idea that someone that emotional was becoming part of our family.

'So vulgar,' said my mother. She hated the way Martin's family were all wiping away tears, I thought they were just a lot more open about things.

And Susan deserved happiness. She was such a good, kind, giving person. You couldn't fault her.

> Oh love divine, how sweet thou art!
> When shall I find my longing heart
> All taken up by Thee?
> The greatness of redeeming love,
> The love of Christ to me.

Mary

I don't know what came over me. I cried at the service, not because he was marrying her, but because I was actually moved. Well, there's a first time for everything.

She wore some prissy little dress and an oh-so-tasteful veil with tiny flowers. Vile Susan always has such good taste that it makes you want to puke. She was pregnant and quite open about it. That amazed me. I thought she be tastefully draped to hide it. And she did look terribly pretty.

That priest was dishy. Very easy on the eye indeed. Lovely English accent, gorgeous blue eyes and such a smile.

I nudged my sister Maureen. 'Doesn't the sister of the bride get to sleep with the priest at Protestant weddings?' I whispered, 'Yeah.' She winked. 'The oldest sister.'

I don't like weddings generally, I think they just legalise sex, but this wedding was something else.

Maybe, just maybe, I thought, this can work. It was beautiful. *Lord, have mercy upon us.*

Susan

After we got married, I could really feel the baby moving and kicking. It wasn't just an idea anymore, but alive and real, a little person. I started thinking I didn't want the baby to have a childhood like mine. My mother had wanted well-mannered, accomplished, pretty children with good manners. Which sounds okay but there was no room for anything else. There was no room for not liking what she liked, for not being a person whose life she controlled.

I needed to know another way of doing it so I set about finding out.

I read a lot about a baby's need to feel secure. That security comes from the mother. I wanted to be able to accept the baby the way it was, adjusting to its rhythms rather than forcing it into my rhythms. It helped me understand a lot about myself. I suppose they were the things I had never experienced. The baby was part of me but it was also its own self. To me that had a deep spiritual dimension.

I became totally focused on the baby and Martin teased me about it. I probably was a little obsessed. I had baby dreams, I worried about the baby, I was totally involved with this little growing thing. I had a special cream that I rubbed into my stomach to stop stretch marks, but really because I liked to feel the baby there. I knitted little things, which gave me enormous pleasure.

Martin was in love with my being pregnant and us having a baby, but in a different way. I guess it's different for men. It was the idea that he was in love with although he liked to pat my stomach and feel the baby kicking.

We'd lie in bed and he'd talk to the baby. 'Don't kick your mother like that,' he'd say. 'Be gentle with her. She's a goddess, remember. And I'm god, remember. And your father.' He'd do it all in an Irish accent and then he'd tell me stories about his Irish granny who had died just before we met. The way he talked, his family seemed much more colourful and lively than my family.

I didn't really miss work, although I had a vague idea I'd go back at some time. I thought of my mother playing golf and bridge, and bitching about the gardener. I didn't want that. I felt a little lonely. Decorating a nursery and buying baby clothes didn't take up that much time. Martin's flat was in Bondi Junction and it was hard to make friends, as all the neighbours seemed to be working couples.

Sometimes I felt overwhelmed by Martin. He was so sweet but he was much more physical than me.

'I'm sorry, it's just you're my wife,' he said, 'and that's our baby in there. I want to love it and touch it, and love you and touch you, Susan. I feel so close to you, I feel you're part of me.'

'I love you too but I need my own space,' I said.

He laughed and hugged me, and then got me a cup of tea.

'This *is* a tiny flat,' he said. 'One day I'll buy you a mansion and you can live in the tower and keep me in the basement.'

'Not the basement,' I said. 'I'll need that for storage. I'll keep you in the garden shed and get you a gnome for company.' There were lovely things like waking up with him, and him bringing me tea in bed before he went to work.

I wanted to make our life together. I used to lay out the breakfast things on a little table, so we could eat on placemats and a little vase of flowers. He was always in a rush in the morning and he'd say he wasn't hungry. Then he'd buy a coffee and one of those ghastly enormous iced donuts on the way to work. At some taxi depot!

He liked going to the beach. The surf was important to him. I loved the way he was so poetic about it, although I didn't want to do much more than stick my toe in the water. But it was a big thing for him, a part of his life that lifted him out of the everyday and put him in touch with the primal forces of the world.

Together we went to Centennial Park and walked around the big duck pond. I loved the trees and he loved seeing the families of ducks there.

'Look,' he'd say. 'Whole family off to six o'clock Mass. No, that little bugger has strayed. The one up the front's an altar boy, you can tell that, but that one's going off to nick some hubcaps. He'll go to hell.' Then he'd pat my tummy. 'This one won't get religion rammed down his throat. I'll teach him to surf and he can work out the rest of life from there.'

We came from different backgrounds but it didn't matter. We wanted to be ourselves in our own little world, although at times we saw that differently. I liked to give little dinner parties, whereas his family and friends dropped in unannounced. They hardly ever rang before they came. And they stayed and drank bottle after bottle. He said that was his style. Occasionally it was fun; mostly it went on for too long.

I had to put my foot down about people dropping in unannounced one night after he'd had a long drinking session with his sister Mary. I knew Mary didn't like me. I tried really hard with her, but she'd made up her mind to dislike me. This particular night they were laughing, talking, playing music, getting drunker and drunker. I went to bed, then I woke up and heard her being sick in the toilet.

It was revolting. I told him the next day that I couldn't cope, I couldn't stand it. He agreed. 'In future, if I want to hear people being sick I promise I'll go to the pub.'

But mostly we were just happy being together, and waiting for the baby.

I was excited and scared about the birth. I woke with contractions in the early morning and we went straight off to the hospital. Martin was there all the time, doing all the stuff they'd told him in birth class, but nothing could stop the pain. I had some weird idea that I wouldn't accept pain relief, but I did. Even so it was hard. Part of me wanted it to be over so much I almost forgot about the baby, but when Martin said he could see the head, I stopped caring about the pain. Martin was very funny, like a football coach, shouting at me to push, until the nurse told him to be a bit quieter. And then, when Joshie was born . . . well, it was perfect.

They put Josh in my arms and everything changed. It was miraculous. Joshie was such a beautiful little baby. Right from the start. Perfect little face and always very content. Another perfection. I held him and Martin helped bathe him. And we just sat together, holding our baby. We couldn't stop looking at him, couldn't stop admiring him. A family—so close and warm and perfect.

Martin

I was a bit immature. I didn't think married life would be a big change. I drove Susan mad with my bachelor ways. It took me a while to see that she wanted placemats and a proper breakfast because that's the way she saw marriage. For me it looked like some awful middle-class fantasy that I'd walked into. Her towel and my towel, and a proper dinner every night. I would have been happy with black bean and beef from the local Chinese most nights.

I did try because it was important to her.

We had to have whisky, sherry and gin, and buy a sideboard to keep the glasses in, just in case someone dropped in. Unfortunately when my friends came by, they usually bought a flagon or a dozen beers. But after a while I didn't really want that carousing, drinking life. Mostly we stayed home and read or watched the tele. On weekends we walked in the park, or went to a film or a play. And we talked and talked and talked.

Susan and Mary didn't get on. I knew Mary was impossible—that is if you have any sense of social decorum—but she was fun too. But Susan didn't get that side of her and Mary didn't get past the prim and proper in Susan, which always came on strong when Mary came around. But Susan would never say anything against Mary.

'We're just having trouble getting to know each other,' she said. 'I do understand she's your favourite sister. We haven't quite clicked. Maybe when we get a bigger place it'll be easier. I don't want to exclude her, but sometimes she's just over the top.'

I wouldn't let Mary say a word against Susan, but I knew what she was thinking and what she would have said with the slightest encouragement.

The birth was rough. Basic design fault in the whole process, it seemed to me. My God, I was so scared something dreadful was going to happen to Susan. It was horrible, the whole thing, at least until I saw Joshie's head, when I started yelling and nearly got myself sent to the sin bin. Then he slithered out into the world. What a miracle. I had all sorts of wonderful, protective, loving, possessive feelings about this new life, this tiny child of ours. And I felt even closer to Susan.

I went out that night to wet his head. I got disgracefully drunk with Cliff. I told him it was definitely the last of my bachelor's nights. I'd reform entirely, stay at home, by her side.

'She's got you by the short and curlies,' he said.

'I'm a family man,' I said. 'She'll need me to help with the baby.'

Cliff became bitter. 'I'm down to the Royal George to renew my vow to stay single. Get married and you kiss your freedom goodbye along with your bloody sex life.'

He was just a piss-pot, and I felt that part of my life was over. The next morning I stayed home and tidied up the flat. Sweeping the balcony, I smiled at what a reformed character I'd become. My head was full of thoughts of my darling Susan and the baby. I would have given up anything for them.

Melissa

I had my first serious boyfriend when I was fourteen. Mike. God, I loved him. I just adored him. He was eighteen.

I got on well with boys and I flirted a lot, but I was dead serious about Mike. Honestly, I thought I'd grow up and turn into Mrs Mike. I was young and silly, but it was fun.

I just loved the physical side of the relationship and it wasn't that long before we were having sex. I suppose I should have been like a good Greek girl, like Anna, but I wasn't. Girls at school talked about being a virgin or not being a virgin. I couldn't see what the big deal was. I loved Mike, I loved sex, and the two things seemed to go together.

It was good he was older because he knew about condoms and he could buy them without a fuss. I was a little worried about what my mum would think and it's true she wasn't totally overjoyed. But in the end, she was cool about it.

'It's been ages since I stopped you doing something you wanted,' she said. 'Just be careful. Make sure you're treated well and treat him well.' I thought that was pretty cool.

I probably was a little young when I started having sex, but I was very sexually charged and I would have turned into a crazed masturbator if I hadn't had Mike. And he did treat me well. And I treated him well.

I thought sex was one of the best things about growing up.

CHAPTER 4
1978

Susan

I loved him more and more each day. I could not believe how much I loved him. He was in my mind all the time. I was overflowing with feeling for him, taken out of myself, given over to him.

Josh was the most gorgeous baby, blue-eyed, with downy hair and delicate features. He had such gentleness about him, such a sweetness. I loved the littleness of him. I loved all the things involved in caring for him—the little routines, rocking his cradle, warming his bottle, playing with him.

I was very idealistic. I knew love and security are the most important things you can ever give your child. Some people thought I was a little crazy because I took it all so seriously. Maybe I was a little too serious, but it was something I couldn't control.

I was a perfectionist. I knew I was and I wrestled with it, because of course you're supposed to be relaxed if you're going to be a perfect mother. Which is a glaring contradiction. So there I was trying to be the perfect mother by being relaxed, being giving and loving while I'm tired as hell and it's all swirling around in my brain. I'm trying to make it right so I'm less and less relaxed. Sometimes I felt I was going mad. Then I'd begin to think that a mad mother wasn't going to be any good for Josh. Those thoughts went round and round my head.

Marty was very sympathetic but I could see he was wondering what my problem was. I was trying to be sensible, trying to explain and I caught myself sounding like my mother, just a bit of an edge in my voice, which was the last thing I wanted. All that feminist stuff in my head seemed like pie in the sky with a baby. I thought about that a lot. I didn't want to be 'just a mother', but at the same time being a mother felt like the most important thing in the world. I felt the responsibility, twenty-four hours a day, seven days a week. It's not the sort of thing the baby books, or feminism, prepare you for.

The flat was too small, and not where I would have chosen to live, but despite all that, we were happy. Martin was shockingly irresponsible with money, and I was very glad I'd asked him for my own money before we married. We had a joint account. He never actually set aside money for me so we could pay for things jointly, but the principle was there. I couldn't budget because he was such a spendthrift, but I did set aside money in a separate account for things I needed, and as a start for a deposit for a house.

'You're so middle class,' he teased. 'In the working class, Comrade Susan, economics is simple. You spend what you need on necessities and then get the rest on the never never. It's all about creative debt management. Hopefully by the time you die, you've managed to spend a lot more than you've ever earned.'

'Martin, it's just paying the bills that worries me.'

'It's a division of labour. I spend, you pay the bills.'

'We should have a budget. Set ourselves a target for saving. That way we'd get ourselves a house much quicker.'

'Budget,' he said. 'Odd word. Notice how the mouth purses when you say it. The anus puckers up too. Not a spirited, easy, happy word, Susan. Contracts the heart and spirit. Confines generous impulses.' He lay back on the couch.

I laughed. 'Saving plan,' I whispered in his ear.

He screamed and rolled off the couch.

'Don't wake the baby,' I said and kissed him. I didn't want him feeling left out. I wanted us to be a family, not just a mother and baby with a father tacked on. Sometimes it was tricky getting the balance right.

Things change when you have a child. Of course that's a cliché but only because it's so true. Joshua brought us together in lots of ways. We used to stand over his crib together and watch him sleep. We used to talk about him obsessively on the rare occasions we got a sitter and went out without him. We felt the thrill of being a family when we went out with him in the stroller. But I did worry about the money. I badly wanted a house. My life revolved around Josh. Martin was a little less important to me, or maybe he was important in a different way.

Martin and I had plenty of good times. We talked about books, about politics, about religion, which was fantastic for me because I wasn't getting a lot of intellectual stimulation. Martin loved to talk about those things. He has a very enquiring mind, which the law didn't satisfy, so when he talked to me about work, it was often about his frustrations there. I knew Dad wasn't entirely pleased with Martin.

'I get scared,' I said, 'that you'll throw in the towel and become a philosopher.'

'There's an idea,' he said. 'I won't, but it's the same thing, day in, day out.'

'Like life,' I said.

'No, not like life.' He sat up and took a gulp of his wine. It was always a sign he was going to start ranting. 'That decrepit old clerk. This morning, he gives me a lesson on letter writing. *Dear Sir* must always be signed *Yours faithfully* to indicate deference. *Yours sincerely* follows *Dear Mr Smith*, because even though Mr Smith is my inferior, I am still bound to sincerity. What shit!'

'Old Staples just does things a certain way. You probably terrify him.'

'I hope so. I dropped him a note. "Sweetie, thanks for the tutorial on letter etiquette. Love and kisses, Marty".' Martin slapped his forehead. 'He got his knickers in a knot over that. It's so petty, so middle class.'

'We are middle class though,' I protested.

'Not in the way we think, Suzie. We've got to resist that. Think of your dried-up prune of a mother, minding her Ps and Qs and never noticing that there's this whole other thing called life.'

'That's not about her being middle class. It's just Mum not having a life. She obviously never got what she needed in her life. When I was growing up there were plenty of families in our neighbourhood that weren't like ours, people who were really happy and had great lives.' I looked at Martin. 'Those people had happy lives *despite* the fact they lived in comfortable houses in leafy suburbs. It is possible.'

He laughed. 'The middle classes spend all their time worrying about where they'll buy a house and whether the clothes they bought last week were the *right* clothes and what school is the *right* school for their kids. It's all about perception and status. When you're poor you're grateful for a roof over your head, that your kids are still at school and you've got a jumper to wear. So you deal with reality.'

I struggled with all this much more than I really needed to. I did care about my clothes and where I lived and I wanted my kids to go to good schools. I think most people do, no matter how much money they have. But that was Martin being Martin, wanting to be different. I thought when the time came, he'd see reason. More than that, he'd see how having our own home, planning our lives together the way we wanted to live would add to our happiness.

I really wished I had a closer relationship with my mum but she thought Lisa and I had rejected her. There was a definite whiff of burning martyr. I was living my life in a way that suited me and Martin and that made me an unsatisfactory daughter in her eyes. She wasn't a person who could forgive easily. I found it so hard. I felt so close to Joshie, and I often wondered if she had felt that close to me and Lisa. As I made friends with other mothers, I often felt sad about it when those other women talked about their closeness with their mothers. Martin understood that, although it was harder for him to understand that his mother really wasn't a substitute for my own, although I did take Joshie to see his Mum and always made her welcome at our place.

Lisa helped me a lot, which was sweet of her. She was pregnant, expecting Rosie. Sometimes we laughed over what a hard time we'd given Mum. Lisa wasn't even married, because her partner Jamie, a schoolteacher, was married and had an older child. His marriage was over, but he wasn't divorced when Lisa got pregnant.

'With the two of us conceiving out of wedlock,' I said, 'Mum's status at golf must be at an all time low.'

'It is,' said Lisa. 'She told me. And I said maybe she should forget about her social status and get to know her grandchildren.'

'I asked her over,' I said, 'to spend some time with Joshie.

She told me she knew I was just doing it to be polite, which was true. She came—it was so tense. I don't think she's interested in him. I feel awful every time I try and fail. I know she's not happy.'

'Stuff her,' said Lisa. 'When has she ever worried about our happiness?'

Compared to Lisa and Jamie, Martin and I seemed to have a charmed life. We were married, we had Joshie, we had no real financial worries. We squabbled over silly things and Martin would hold forth on not succumbing to the petit bourgeois mentality. We were still living in the flat which didn't help, especially as he couldn't see that the flat was too small and difficult with a baby. But I was sure the difficulties would pass. What couple with a baby doesn't have a few troubles?

Martin

I was totally in awe of Susan. She'd gone through so much with the birth and then she was a wonderful mother. She not only read everything; she also analysed everything ever written about children. She devised her own ideas about how Joshua would be brought up. He would be demand fed, he would not be left to cry; he would understand that we would respond to his needs. When he was old enough, he would learn that other people also had needs. He would have intellectual stimulation and emotional security. And so on. It was a little bit intense, but you couldn't fault her. She didn't cut corners because she was tired or fed up.

She devoted herself to Josh. I wasn't up to speed on the theories of childrearing. In fact, I really didn't know why you needed theories or books on the subject at all, although I felt a bit cack-handed, unable to do things the way she wanted. Typical father with a new baby. And my own family was much more casual about kids. Nobody thought about how to bring up kids. It was follow your nose, educate them, send them to Mass on Sundays. Susan worried about much deeper things. To me, Josh was this little darling with a toothless smile and inclined to leak from both ends.

I wished I could help Susan get on top of things. Occasionally I gave her a backrub or she had a cry on my shoulder. But she was more the sort to solider on.

'You overwhelm me,' she said, 'always touching me. Remember I need space.' It was a joke between us, but it had a bit of an edge at times.

So my job was to bring home the bacon. I knew having financial security was important to her but I began to get sick of the law. Bloody case after case after case. I couldn't think of the future because the endless list of cases stretching to the horizon was my future. Win or lose, win or lose. You almost never got to fight anything that was substantial or meant anything.

And old Thomas was on my back, pompous old fart. The thing was I would have got a partnership with the firm at some point anyway. The fact he'd given me one when I married Susan made me beholden to him. That's what he thought. It was as if he'd given it away, as if I wasn't good at what I did, as if the partnership didn't entitle me to the respect and equality a partnership would normally involve.

I had it out with him one night. I was pretty angry. He'd been sniping at me all day, like I was the junior clerk.

'Look mate,' I said. He hated being called 'mate'. 'I have the credentials to go anywhere. I've got this Oxford degree hanging on my wall which, I remember, you asked me to frame to impress the punters. I started up your family law division which is going gangbusters. In fact, I remember when I came here we weren't actually getting any matrimonial work except when some mate of yours got found out stuffing the sausage somewhere he wasn't supposed to. Now it's a major part of our business.'

'Lower margins of profit than our commercial work,' he said.

'Well, maybe I don't believe in bleeding people when they've got enough misery on their plate already.'

'Eye for detail, Martin,' he said. 'That's what's costing us money, not the goodness of your heart. You've got my daughter and grandson to support. That must be your first concern.'

'Oh fuck you, you stupid fucking old prick! You don't like me because I've got hair and you haven't, because I surf and you can barely walk up the fucking stairs, because your daughter's in love with me, when you wanted her to marry one of these pretty boy northshore chappies or a squatter in his RM Williams boots with what passes for a pedigree in your brown nosing, half-arsed view of the world.'

Of course I didn't actually say that.

His daughter, *his* grandson. I realised the price I'd paid. My old man would have decked someone for saying that, but now I moved into a world where you didn't settle disputes with your fists. Bastard. And I couldn't say anything to Susan.

That night I went out with Cliff, who's always happy to get plastered at someone else's expense. Susan didn't like what she wryly called my 'single man behaviour', that is, getting plastered. I didn't do it often, but sometimes it felt like the *only* thing I could do.

That night I was home really late and really drunk, so I bought a whole lot of red roses from those guys who hawk them around restaurants. And then serenaded Susan when I got home. And showered her with rose petals. She was sweet about it, but didn't quite enter into the spirit of it. Joshie had a tooth coming through. But for the most part we were happy. I thought our differences were a good thing, that we had a balance, mostly we did. God, I loved her, how I loved her.

That old bastard Thomas. He was having it on the side with his secretary Marg. All the office knew it had been going on for years and years, which is why you couldn't chip her about anything, and you pretty much had to bow down and kiss her feet if you wanted a stamp to post your gas bill. I hadn't twigged because I didn't listen to gossip. One night working late, I'd seen them through the frosted glass of her office, her with her skirt up, him with trousers half mast. Thank God for frosted glass.

Surfing was my salvation from all that crap. Some mornings I got up really early and took my board and went out into the waves. The sun on the water, the waves rolling in, the expanse of it. Even on those cold grey days, I loved it. Life felt better, smoother. And I'd have a chocolate doughnut and a coffee from the taxi depot for breakfast. Made all my troubles feel like nothing at all. And I loved Susan, loved Josh. They were my life.

Phil

Susan had a very spiritual attitude to motherhood. She had brought this little being into the world, and it was her job to nurture and protect him. She did it with such tenderness, such gentleness. She looked into Joshua's soul. She had such purity of love and spirit.

There was fierceness in her too. She would have defended him with her life.

One day I went over there and she left him with me for ten minutes, just to go out and get some stuff from the chemist. He was asleep. Nevermind that, I had instructions on how to pick him up if he woke, how to soothe him, how to let him know she would be back any moment. He knew me quite well, but for Susan, leaving me to care for him, even when he was asleep, was a big deal.

Martin's sister Mary was there as well and it was obvious there was a bit of tension between her and Susan. The thing about Mary is she's very funny and she's very straightforward to the point of incredible bluntness. I liked that in her, and she was a very attractive woman, although in a very different way to Susan. Susan took her a little seriously and she was maybe a little jealous because Mary and Martin were very close. Or maybe Mary was jealous of Susan.

Martin was like a lot of fathers—inept. He was inept with Susan and inept with the baby. He couldn't see that she needed the spiritual dimension, the wonder of this baby acknowledged. He couldn't see that she didn't want fierce hugs or embraces. That was the way Martin was, open and robust in his passions. But it was clear that Susan loved him; you could see it. Just the way she looked at him.

There was one little incident that summed up the differences between the two of them. She left Joshie with Martin to go to a concert with me. It was just a little local concert and I took her because I thought she needed to get out. And I needed to get out too. I felt depressed about my path in the ministry. Sydney

Anglicans were low church and my superiors didn't approve of my high church inclinations. Susan was always good to talk to.

'You put him down on the bunny rug,' she explained to Martin. 'Then you bring this corner over here and tuck it under him, fold this corner in and then tuck this bit in around the shoulder. That way he feels secure.'

I could see Martin wasn't really listening. When we came back, he'd wrapped Joshie up in the bunny rug, but he'd secured it with gaffer tape because he couldn't remember how it tucked. Being Martin, he thought it was a great solution. Joshie had gone to sleep and was still asleep.

Susan laughed and teased him about it but I sensed she was a little offended that he hadn't listened, that he wouldn't do it her way. Maybe it annoyed her that she couldn't go out and trust him with the baby.

Of course it *was* funny. It was typical of Martin. But there was just a little bit of tension between them over that sort of thing.

Mary

I loved that baby. Could have eaten him. Vile Susan was terrified I would. He was just such a gorgeous little smiley thing. You could see his soul. And that wriggly little body. I always had to unwrap and undress him to have a look. Drove her mad.

God! She was such a fusspot. Had to be wrapped this way, had to have the temperature in his room exactly right. He was totally germ free. I warned her they're supposed to have germs so they develop their immune system.

Her rules were just a way of keeping the punters off. She

never got close to Mum so Mum gave up trying to help Susan and just concentrated on Kath's kids. Susan probably thought Joshie might get a westie drawl if he spent too much time with his paternal grandparents. I must admit Susan was wonderful with Kathleen's kids. Kath was a smack-and-yell sort of mother, a bit hard, and her kids who were older than Josh, loved the gentleness of Susan.

Mind you, Mum still adored Josh. Spoilt him rotten when she could get her hands on him. And that, according to Vile Susan, wasn't right either.

Martin had all the right instincts for fatherhood but she didn't want him jostling Joshie or making him laugh too much or letting him fall over.

Despite it, the kid came up trumps. God I loved him. Just the sweetest thing, that boy.

Lisa

Susan was very happy when Josh was born. For a few weeks, she was dead on her feet, exhausted. But she was a fantastic mother and kept herself even tempered. I must say, watching her in those early months I learned a lot from her. I think Martin realised she was pretty incredible too. He sometimes sent her up but you could see he was bursting with love and pride.

Jamie and I lived in a tiny place, but Susan had always cared a lot more about her privacy and the way things were around her than I had. Martin didn't even know what privacy was. He made me laugh because he'd come out of the toilet and he'd be doing up his fly. Things like that drove Susan mad and he teased her about being a prude. He could be pretty funny. He didn't notice where he left his things or that papers were building up on the dining room table and he'd leave his swimmers hanging over the shower screen when she had people coming, or underpants on the bedroom floor. All that mess became a pain once Joshie began to move around.

Jamie and I were totally broke. We hadn't intended for me to get pregnant for a couple of years since he was locked into a custody battle for his daughter June, from his first marriage. Jamie's ex-wife was making all sorts of ludicrous demands and poor little June was the stepdaughter from hell. Suddenly, I was pregnant. But having Rosie was a gift. And because I hadn't planned falling in love with a married man, or having a step-daughter, and having no money, I just had to go with whatever happened and make the best of it.

Mum had virtually disowned me, but Susan was fantastic. She re-trimmed all Joshie's baby things in pink and did little embroideries on them. She knitted little cardigans and made pretty things for June as well. June adored her, which was a big plus. Susan was so good and generous with other people's kids. She had a capacity to understand their troubles and respond to them. She wasn't so good at the rough and tumble stuff but kids always connected with her. I'm a teacher and I reckon that tells you a lot about a person. We spent a lot of time together with our babies, which brought us closer than ever. I noticed as a teacher, and I think its true of parents, that nothing bonds you more than coming together to care for children.

Susan was happy but she was sometimes a little tense. She never liked second best. She wanted things to be one hundred percent and that created a certain amount of tension. But she loved Marty. You could tell because she often quoted him on things like politics or philosophy. He made her feel she was different from Mum. Of course it wasn't just that. We both found it hard not having a mother who could help us with our children, but we realised we were so lucky to have each other.

CHAPTER 5
1980

Martin

I thought our life together was paradise. We were young, in love and breeding. What more could you ever want? However, like most people with young children, Susan and I did have some stupid arguments, always over things that weren't worth fighting over.

My 1930s pottery kookaburra. I had loved that kooka the moment I saw him. He was rough and ready and bloody real.

'It's ugly,' she said. 'And having it on the bathroom shelf means I can't wipe the shelf down properly.'

'That kooka was made by a bloke who worked ten hours a day in the pottery and then did something creative at the end of the day. It's a classic piece, my darling. It has history, a soul.'

'Look, I understand the sentiment but whoever made it didn't have much skill. It's crude.'

'Naïve, dear heart. It's naïve art.'

'A stubby kookaburra with pelican feet. I really don't want it in there. We're short of space as it is.'

'I'll clean the bathroom shelf. I'll lift the kooka off and wipe the shelf. Then I'll put my kooka back. It's hard, but by God, I'll do it.'

'It's just inconvenient.'

'Well, I'll put it on the sideboard.'

She laughed. 'Please, Marty, leave it in the bathroom.'

'He's not good enough for the sideboard?'

'It's a beautiful Edwardian sideboard. I know you don't like the turned pieces and the carved back, but that kookaburra would *really* look like a workman's piece there.'

'Is there something wrong with a workman's piece?'

'When it's that ugly, there is.'

'He's a very fine kookaburra. Look at the tail.'

'Look at the head stuck on like an afterthought. And the blue all down the back. It doesn't actually look like a kookaburra.'

'The glaze ran. That adds to the charm.'

'It embarrasses me.'

'What? It looks at you while you pee?' I had raised my voice just a little by this stage.

'People think it's odd having a kookaburra in the bathroom.'

'People think it's odd? You mean your mother? She'd like a bloody Lladro glass swan I suppose.'

'Actually it was *your* mother. She asked why we had *that funny bird* there. Her exact words. *Funny bird*. And I told her you were attached to it and she shook her head and sighed.'

'Hang on, you can't stand the fruit bowl she gave us for Christmas but suddenly she's an expert on 1930s naive pottery. She scrimped and saved for that Freedom fruit bowl but we can't put that on our Edwardian sideboard because it would be just a little too embarrassing to admit we have rellies who think Freedom is upmarket.'

'Stop it, Martin! The fruit bowl's fine. Your Mum knows I like it. I use it in the kitchen and I had it on the table last time they came over. Don't be such a bully!'

'I'm a bully? This kooka, my first tentative foray into the middle-class art market and you want to get rid of him!'

'I never said I wanted to get rid of it.' She flicked me with the tea towel. 'I haven't noticed that you're all that tentative about the art market. You certainly manage to spend a little bit here and there.'

Married people in love. I was stroppy about my kooka. It *was* ugly; she was right. No name, but that kooka had a story.

I was doing a case in Newcastle the next week so I went nosing round the second-hand shops and picked up kangaroo bookends of the same genre with pretty much the same result.

'Nice touch putting a platypus tail on a kangaroo,' she said.

I laughed. 'Our naïve art period is over. I promise.'

Despite our spats, I was crazy about Susan. I was proud of her. She was beautiful, intelligent and accomplished. I loved her, I never doubted that.

We had Ben by this time, Ben the baby direct from hell. I had a bit of sympathy for Ben, because like me, he didn't cotton on to the rules. I should have been willing to sort my laundry into the three baskets that contained different categories of clothes but I never got the hang of it. I continued to put them on the floor because the prospect of being instructed in the three-basket system yet again was just too much. Or maybe because I had a hangover.

'It's simple,' she said. 'Even someone educated at Oxford should be able to grasp it.' Okay, she had me there.

'What about three piles on the floor?' I asked, 'just to ease me into the system gently.'

I had a wandering spirit, Susan was a domestic soul. That caused a few problems. And kids of course. Kids are what bond you and what divide you. Kids make you tired. I knew Suzie needed me home, but I found it really hard just to hang round the house for two days on weekends. I tried and we spent time 'as a family'. She sat there, I sat there, Ben grizzled, Joshie did something with the Lego.

'He could do with a three-basket system for those blocks,' I said. 'That bloody Lego got me between the toes when I got up for a piss last night.'

'Could you not use those words,' she said, 'in front of the children?' She had this thing about using what she called the 'correct' words. Words like 'sexual intercourse', 'urination', 'penis', 'vagina', in place of the perfectly good, everyday words most people use. It made me feel as if I was in a courtroom.

'I'm just going to urinate now, Your Honour. Pull my penis out of my daks, sorry, pants, Your Honour,' I said. 'Piss *is* the word people use, you know. Which, according to linguists, makes it the correct word.'

'Oxford again,' she said lightly. 'Maybe if you said "pee". "Piss" sounds crude, especially when you hear little children say things like that.'

'I can see we'll be calling the child psychology experts to this trial as well as the linguists,' I said. 'I give in. From now on I'll pee.'

'You're an ornament to the legal profession,' she said.

We had different discontents and different remedies.

She really felt strongly about the flat—she hated it. She wanted a garden and a cat. She even started feeding the mangy thing downstairs. She'd been squirrelling away money for a deposit on a house, which was admirable, but then we had Ben and there still wasn't enough money for a deposit. She thought the flat wasn't suitable for a married couple with kids. To tell you the truth it seemed okay to me, but she'd come from a home where everyone had their own bedroom and there was a tennis court in the backyard. I'd slept on the verandah with

Lachie, a canvas blind to keep out the rain, until I left home.

Her parents got into the act about the flat too. Her mother didn't give a fig about Susan, but she chipped me with venomous politeness about when I was going to purchase suitable accommodation for her daughter.

'No one in this family has ever lived in a flat,' she said. She said the word 'flat' as if she was referring to a sewage trap.

'We're blissfully happy,' I said. 'We like the intimacy, don't we, Suzie?'

'It'd be nice to have another bedroom,' said Susan. She had always defended me in front of her mother, so I knew that this mild comment meant this was a serious issue.

'We'll be buying soon,' I said, trying to sound like a responsible husband.

'We really need to save,' said Susan in the car on the way home from her parents' place. 'All the places we've looked at in our budget are just too awful. If you could just cut down on some of your expenses . . .'

'Okay, okay, okay.'

I took refuge in surfing. Which is cheap. I loved to go out in the very early morning, when the water was still chilly, and the sky was gun-grey with yellow streaks of dawn. Things came to me out there. Not just waves but a peace inside myself, a sense that life was a great gift. Also sadness and occasionally fear which seemed to come from nowhere. They weren't feelings that I thought about. They just washed through me and over me. It gave me some peace.

I remember being out there one morning when Ben was still tiny. I got a lump in my throat when I thought about the smallness of him, or the way Joshie slept with his stripey doll under his arm. Sometimes I was aware of being on the periphery of their lives, a slightly intrusive presence when I came into their lives in the evening or on weekends.

I'd known families like that when I was growing up. Susan and I weren't as bad as that, but I thought about families where the men didn't say a word, where they were met with exasperated sighs. My grandparents for instance. As I was sitting on my board I remembered my grandad.

'Don't backchat the women, son,' he'd say, lighting his fag. 'Not worth the trouble and strife.' And then he'd explain that 'trouble and strife' was the correct term for 'wife' shortened over many centuries, but to be remembered by men who valued a peaceful life.

The surf wasn't much on that particular day, and I was out there, waiting for the big one, a little too cold for comfort, too much time for thinking.

I thought about those families where sadness and irrelevance hung round the bloke like a bad smell. My own dad was too big a presence, too strong, too volatile, too funny, too forceful to shrink into insignificance. So he and my mother fought and screamed and yelled, which was bad enough. Yet somehow they were equals.

Susan disapproved of loud voices, yelling and swearing, which was the currency of my childhood. And her view seemed good and right and civilised. But now and then her disapproval left me bleeding out on the edges of my own life. It sounds as if I was sorry for myself. It wasn't that, it was just disquiet. And I knew things would get better. The kids would be older and easier, the money might get easier too, although God help us, we weren't poor, even if Suzie thought we were.

The sun was on my back, finally throwing a little warmth through the cold of the morning. I had an enviable life. I had a beautiful wife. I had two sons; one a cute toddler and one just a baby. I loved them. But in some way we had parallel lives, not enmeshed with each other quite the way I wanted them to be. I wanted it to be different. The thought rose up, formed and then completed itself in my mind. It was there for that moment, corrosive, disturbing.

That day I was due in court, the last day of a big case. We were fighting it all day and the next day the judgement was given. To my surprise I had won an unwinnable case, so unwinnable, Thomas hadn't wanted me to pursue it. It was a compo case, a pedestrian knocked off a bush roadside, down into a gully, with the result the poor bastard became a paraplegic. No witnesses. A driver who claimed he hadn't seen the plaintiff. A plaintiff with a healthy blood alcohol level and a tendency to annoy the judge. I thought he had a case, based purely on the tyre marks on the road which some copper had had the foresight to photograph. Plus the fact that the bastard of a driver had left the scene. I never thought my bloke had a strong case. I liked him though, so I fought it every inch of the way.

I surprised myself with the win. I surprised the client. We went out for a few drinks to celebrate—him in his wheelchair sucking beer through a straw. Back at the office I told old Thomas. He congratulated me but he was a little pissed off at the same time. When I'd taken the case he told me I had to do it outside the normal partnership agreement, that I was to bear the cost personally.

'Okay,' I said. 'But if I win, I get the fee for myself too.' He'd just grunted. Now the firm was missing out on a slice of the pie.

'It's fantastic!' I said to Thomas. 'That million dollars will make the poor bastard's life bearable.'

'I suppose so,' he said. He didn't like delirious joy on behalf of clients. Or perhaps where he didn't get some of the action.

'He'll be able to set himself up properly,' I said to Thomas. 'Decent house, specially fitted out for him, special car, nursing, maybe even a trained chimpanzee.'

Thomas didn't laugh. 'It'll help you set yourself up properly too,' he said. 'The fee should be a deposit on a nice little house.'

That got me thinking. Susan and I had looked at a few houses we couldn't afford. She had very particular ideas of what she wanted, particularly in terms of safety for the children and what she called a 'nice area'. I wanted to live near the beach, which was okay by her. She loved the beach too.

Now I had this suitcase of money I could see a way out. Two weeks earlier, we'd seen a house up above Coogee. An old, rambling, shambling house. Not beautiful, not much yard. It had been built in the twenties, crammed onto the block, low and square but roomy inside and near the beach. Some of it was fantastic, like the big sandstone verandah. Some of it was shit, like the crummy louvres. A bit of grand plastering, some seriously peeling paint and the back of the house was tacked on fibro. But what a view. I'd fallen in love with it but price was the kybosh. The afternoon of the win I took my dad out to have another look at it.

'Where's the driveway with the avenue of oak trees?' he asked. 'Shit, you got a three-foot driveway and a garage under the house.' Dad had never had much success in life, never had much money, but he liked it that I did. Unlike old Thomas. Dad was getting himself worked up over this house, thrilled by the idea of me buying it. He grinned at me. 'Christ, the price they're asking. And all that damn water out there with a pile of bloody rocks out in the middle of it.'

'Wedding Cake Island,' I said.

He looked at the peeling paint, the spongy floorboards in the hall. 'Not like it's pretentious.' He winked. 'Better get this place, son. Susan will love it.'

I paid the deposit, signed the contract and got the bank loan. I thought she'd be over the moon.

That's when the trouble started.

Susan

Sometimes love is hard.

It was hard finding time for Martin and me with two little ones in a tiny flat. I never had any doubts about having married Martin. I truly loved him but I had had unrealistic expectations. I thought I'd be happy and then I wouldn't be so knotted up inside. But children change a relationship. Neither of us realised how big the change would be but we both wanted our marriage to be happy, for our own sake and for the sake of the children. We'd both been aware of our respective parents' unhappiness

I'd been attracted to Martin's sense of freedom and ease. I still saw that in him but this often excluded me. Too often freedom meant he'd go out, get drunk and come home at three. It was a major enterprise for me to take the children to the park each day. I wanted us to have more of a shared life. I really wanted to move out of the flat, and I guess I felt a little hurt that it didn't seem to matter a lot to him. It was as if he couldn't see our life.

We did share a lot of things. I wanted to be involved with his work, but that didn't have much point because, in truth, he wasn't deeply interested in it. Sometimes he'd get fired up about a case and we'd talk about it, but mainly the law was a way of earning a living. I found a lot of things about being the mother of two small children hard and it disappointed me that he didn't give much weight to my life. He could never remember names of my friends from playgroup or what day I went to the museum with the children. I loved being with the children but I felt a little trapped, a bit marginalised.

I did all the suburban things, like joining a playgroup, but I didn't feel as much a part of that life as Lisa did. Lisa had lunch with other mothers and they went shopping together on different days. I enjoyed all that but often I longed for a bit more substance and depth. And it was even harder to get that with Martin. Our lives were busy and too often separate.

Martin thought one baby or two babies were fine, the number didn't make a difference. And even though I had really wanted a second baby, I found Ben very difficult. He cried a lot and he was difficult to settle, and Josh was still little. The unit was on the second floor and we kept the pram downstairs. There was only a tiny second bedroom for the boys so Ben often woke Josh. No wonder I was so desperate for a house! I'd been talking about it and putting money aside for a long time. Martin was keen and full of plans and ideas, but I had to keep the savings account. I did get satisfaction seeing it grow, even if it was growing slowly.

I did have Phil to talk to. We talked a lot about different things. I found him intellectually challenging, but he was also able to appreciate my life in a way Martin couldn't. Martin thought I was a great mother, but Phil seemed to understand my passion about the children. Phil understood the trouble I had joining in, or being part of something that didn't feel quite me. But it was only ever just friendship.

I was in touch with my old university friends. That was fantastic because it kept me in touch with that world, although they weren't really interested in my world. Their feminism seemed very academic to me. No one was really seriously thinking about motherhood as part of feminism, at least not in a way I could ever relate to. My friends felt I'd become a real person again when I got back to work. Sometimes I longed to go back to work, sometimes I couldn't imagine it.

I was confused about where I fitted in. At some level I'd thought marrying Martin would solve that, but even though I loved him, it didn't. At times, I still had a black hole inside of me. Martin didn't have that, so maybe he just didn't understand it. But we had such a deep bond between us, I thought that it really shouldn't matter. Sometimes we just had great fun together, watching a movie on TV sitting on the couch with a bottle of wine and then finding we'd fallen asleep in each others' arms. Or going to the park with the children on the weekend, or watching them at the beach, with Josh trying to chase seagulls.

Martin buying the house took me completely by surprise. Actually, when he came home and showed me the signed papers, it was an awful shock, like a physical blow. We had been to see the house weeks earlier and I remembered Martin had loved it. I'd said it was in a great position, because it was, but I really didn't look too closely because there was no chance of us buying it. We couldn't afford it.

But when he bought it, it was awful. I couldn't believe he hadn't consulted me. Why didn't he when we'd looked at so many houses together? We'd agreed to share money and decisions, but suddenly he had this win and it was all his money. The house had no garden where the boys could play with a ball when they were older. There was nowhere to sit outside. Lisa and I had had a lovely garden when we were growing up but this house was right up against the neighbours. The street was treeless and windswept.

'The view!' he said.

'I'd rather have somewhere the boys will be able to play cricket.'

'They'll learn to surf. This is a paradise!'

'For you, not for me.'

'Look, we'll build a bedroom for us up the top and we'll wake up every morning to the sight of the ocean.'

I didn't want an ocean view. It sounds silly, but there's something disturbing about the ocean. Existential angst maybe, which seems a silly reason for not buying a house. Of course I couldn't say that to him or I would never have heard the end of it. He wanted the house because he could see the ocean, go surfing easily and run along the beach. It wasn't really the view that I minded. It was that the kitchen was old and dirty, there was damp in the hall, and there was always the wind.

'Martin, it'll be nearly impossible to get the pram down those steps. There are no parks around. It's right down the hill to a bus stop.'

It was the first big quarrel we had had. It seemed to me that he just didn't understand my life, my needs. He thought I was throwing a gift back in his face. I thought he shouldn't be regarding it as a gift. This was our house, not his.

At dinner parties Martin had held forth on the rights of women. He didn't seem to understand those rights might include me being consulted on a major purchase. You don't have to read much feminist literature to realise that's pretty basic.

'You agreed we'd make financial decisions together,' I said. I tried to explain that even if I had loved the house, there were other considerations. I didn't like the local shopping centre. I didn't know a soul. We hadn't investigated the kindergartens and schools, whether there was a playgroup, what the local parks were like.

'I wanted to surprise you,' he said. 'To make you happy. It's a great house.'

'If you like surfing,' I said. 'It's only got two bedrooms and the kitchen's decrepit. There's only one bathroom. A pink, ugly bathroom!'

'Fuck it!' he yelled. 'It's got a view over the ocean. The kids will be able to go down to the beach by themselves in a few years. We're young. We'll fix it up. Make it even more fantastic. The kids could even share a room for a few years. They might even fucking like it. God, I didn't know I wasn't allowed to buy something fantastic for you!'

It was so painful. For him and for me. 'I don't want you buying things "for me". I don't want you making financial decisions on my behalf.' I said. 'I'm your partner, not a concubine. I don't like this house but you expect me to be thrilled. Except you *knew* I wouldn't be. Which was why you didn't even make a phone call to check before you signed the contract.'

'Oh fuck you. It's just a fucking house, that's all. I thought for one millisecond it might fucking make you happy.' He began stabbing his finger at me, his standard bullying behaviour whenever he wanted to prove his point.

He tried to make it right. 'Look, I know Ben's a bit difficult. You're tired, darling. Give yourself time and you'll love it here.'

He bought me a little car. Well, that did help the transport problem, but it added to the mortgage. I admitted that the house was a good buy in purely financial terms, but I was never in love with it the way he was. Which had nothing to do with me being tired.

People said, 'Oh let it go. It's a great house.' And I did in a way. But it still upset me.

Mary

There was a lot of the spoilt little rich girl about Vile Susan. If you'd spent your childhood in a coming-apart-at-the-seams fibro house, sharing the bathroom with seven other people and never having a room of your own, which was how Marty and I had been brought up, you wouldn't complain about a two-bedroom house with a view of the ocean.

I was just getting out of the communal life and into real estate, and this was a house you couldn't lose on. Not with that wonderful, romantic view.

I did feel some solidarity with her from a feminist point of view, but not a lot. 'God, that house,' I said. 'I wouldn't bitch too much, sweetheart. Just put it down to a bloke behaving badly.'

Vile Susan didn't appreciate that remark!

Lisa

From my point of view the house didn't seem that big a problem. Jamie and I were living in a rented sunless semi in Burwood with our Rosie and June, who was a problem on a daily basis.

But from Susan's point of view, the house issue was massive. And she had made the perfectly reasonable request that they make financial decisions together. And Coogee was a long way out of town and very unfamiliar for her. And getting the pram up and down the steps was hideous. And she was right, it would have taken just a phone call.

The thing was, if you looked at it from his point of view, he bought the house out of love for her. You could see that and you could see her reaction had cut him. But the thing was, Martin is just one of those selfish people. If he thinks something's a good idea, he's convinced everyone else is going to think it's an absolutely great idea. It was near the beach. He loved that, so why wouldn't she?

It was awful of him but he'd never been any different. He was too confident to change or start thinking about things from other people's point of view. In some ways he's quite exciting and charming because of that, although it would drive you crazy. So I think that buying the house was an act of love, a misguided act of love. But Susan was so cross, she missed seeing that. And he should have made the phone call.

Phil

I think I understood. He was buying his view of their happiness, which was big and expansive and a bit wild.

Her view of happiness was based on closeness, consultation and caution.

I helped them move in. 'Fantastic,' he said, as we carried their bed into the front bedroom. 'You'll hear the wind whistling round the house all night.'

'It'll be hard for the children to sleep,' she said.

They'd made up after the argument, but it was still there. It had shaken them both to the core and even though the argument had been patched up, they were both still bruised by it. Even though everything seemed okay on the surface, both of them were a little disillusioned with the other. The magic of their love wasn't broken, but it didn't embrace their relationship the way it had before.

They both believed in their own side in the quarrel about the house. Even 'believe' is the wrong word. Each of them saw it how they saw it.

It was an odd house. Not beautiful, but it had a lazy, sprawling charm. It was a 1920s Californian bungalow, low lying with a wonderful verandah looking out across the sea. He loved the view. She worried the children would climb over the wall and fall down onto the path. She worried about the rough, beach culture. He saw it as an escape from the place he had lived in as a child, and away from the possibility of the leafy green suburb where her parents lived. She saw it as a step down. He saw it as a step up. He saw all the positives. She saw all the negatives.

I tended to Martin's view, although I felt very sympathetic towards Susan. I understood how important joint decision making was to her. I understood his viewpoint because I was relieving at a parish in the south of Sydney, in the heart of respectable suburbia. To this day the whole experience traumatised me so much I can't remember the name of the suburb or the church. I just remember I went across a bridge called Tom Ugly's which seemed symbolic. The place was physically beautiful, but there was so much ugliness in the minds of the people at the church—closed minded, suburban ugliness.

The most outspoken people in the congregation were a group of middle-aged, hard-faced matrons, who saw Christianity as a set of rules. If you obeyed the rules God would love you. If not, eternal damnation. And they'd extended the rules to exclude the people they called 'youth', and other people they called 'foreigners'. The foreigners were supposed to go to their own churches, the youth to be disgusting in the street.

'Tut tut.' They were like a flock of gossiping galahs. 'Terrible, terrible. We're very superior.'

Suggestions of tolerance and kindness from me came up

against Old Testament injunctions of repression and punishment. I was dying inside.

And I wasn't well regarded because I added some high church touches to my services, whereas this was very low church. For me the worship lacked a sense of ceremony, of respect, of any acknowledgement of the wonder of the deity.

There were those in my flock who were tolerant and loving, but also less outspoken. I had hopes for them until I prodded the underpinning of their attitude and found them to be mawkish and sentimental. It was like wrestling with warm toffee.

'It's driving me to the brink,' I said one night when I was having dinner with Martin and Susan and Mary. They'd been in the house about six months by then, and Susan had transformed it. She had made it light and airy, colourful and casual. She was fantastic with colour. I don't think Martin really appreciated how creative she was. I wondered if she'd begun to enjoy the house a little. 'I'm a minister of religion,' I went on, after our third bottle of wine, 'and I'm beginning to hate my parishioners.'

'It pays the bills, doesn't it?' said Martin. 'And it's hardly onerous, is it?' There was a lot of financial pressure on him. The renovations to the house had cost a lot more than he had budgeted for. Susan and Martin had always argued but the sting of the disagreement about the house was often just below the surface.

'Hate's part of religion,' said Mary. 'Stand up there on a Sunday and tell them about the blackness of the world, the stains on their soul, the evil of man. Go for the Old Testament, Phil. Christ, it's not as if you have to convert them or spend the rest of your life with them. Have some fun.'

I liked Mary. She made me laugh and she was very pretty. She said she was an atheist, but with her Catholic background she could often provide a spiritual perspective which was, admittedly, a little devilish, but sometimes quite original.

She loved absurdity. 'Try pride,' she said. She stood up. 'From Isaiah. *How art thou fallen from heaven, O Lucifer, son of the morning! How art thou cut down to the ground!* Listen, you ladies with your earnest faces, your Sunday hairdos and your damning and narrow morality. He said, *I will ascend above the heights of the clouds. I will be like the Most High.* And Lucifer, that most gorgeous of angels, fell to the depths, sank his Babylon beneath the shoals. Was Lucifer Satan on Earth? We do not know. Are you Satan on Earth? Can you know? Let you who is without sin cast the first stone.' We were all hysterical with laughter as she sat down. 'See, high biblical drama.'

Susan had a different approach. As I went to go home, she pressed Fromm's *The Art of Loving* into my hand. 'Love might be more effective than hate,' she said. I had always loved Susan, and maybe that made me a little shy with her.

This book proved to be the start of a much deeper friendship, where we discussed books and prayer and meditation and a lot of other things. Unlike Mary, who ferreted out contradictions, inconsistencies and hypocrisies, I thought Susan looked for good in life.

I was growing away from Martin partly because I was getting closer to Susan. She started telling me, unconsciously I think, the sort of things that were going on with Martin, like the difficulties about the house. His enthusiasm and excitement became less contagious because I could see the other side of it.

Martin had always been less of a believer and a seeker than Susan was, at least where religion was concerned. His search had come from curiosity rather than a spiritual hunger. Increasingly, he seemed impatient when we talked about spiritual things.

The afternoon after Ben's christening, he and I went off to the rugby, then to the pub afterwards.

'I don't believe in it anymore, Phil,' he said.

'What?' I said, thinking it would be something about the rugby.

'I don't believe Ben's conceived and born in sin. I don't believe in Christian baptism.'

'I would think being born in sin was one of the most obvious truths of Christianity. It's pretty hard to argue with,' I said, waving my hand round. 'Look around.' The pub was smoky and full of bad language. There was a brawl going on in the doorway and some illegal betting somewhere else. 'Sin!'

'Hardly *original* sin,' he said.

'Originality isn't everything.'

'Especially when it comes to sin,' said Martin. 'I always go with the tried and true myself.'

'I guess the promise of the baptism is that although we're fallen, we can be redeemed, saved by a belief in Jesus Christ.'

Martin got us another couple of beers and came back to the table. 'These days I'm a million miles off being a Christian,' he said. 'I can't reconcile an all good, all knowing and all powerful entity with the things that happen every day. Eastern religions get closer. At least they embrace good and evil. I'm the classic agnostic. Some mornings, out in the surf, I feel the goodness of the world. I feel as if life's special and purposeful. Other times life feels like a random event in a random universe.'

'But don't you think . . .'

'I don't want to think anymore, Phil. I'm out of this particular debating society.'

I didn't say anything. I'd always felt he was a kindred spirit now he was saying he wasn't. More than that, he'd become dismissive as if he was joining the ranks of practical, masculine men, who earn a living, do what a man needs to do and leave God to other people. Seeking in the realm of the spiritual is put aside as a childish thing. Serious secular and material concerns are cited. Martin was married with children and I wasn't. I felt as if I'd lost credibility in his eyes, as if he was resigning from his friendship with me.

I knew Martin spent a fair bit of time at the pub because people were always coming up to him, chatting to him about the surf or the football. I'd always envied him that easy male companionship. That afternoon, just as we were about to go, we were joined by a journalist friend of his called Cliff. They chatted a bit about a few legal cases and about politics.

'We've got to go,' said Martin. 'Susan's having a few people over. She'll need a hand.'

'She's still got you by the short and curlies,' said Cliff. 'Marriage. Christ, you'd have to be desperate, wouldn't you?'

Cliff looked pretty desperate himself. It was one time I didn't envy Martin his easy friendships.

Melissa

I had almost two years with Mike. I liked older men. It meant I never went through the stage of groping in the back of cars or going down the park and having the blues shine a torch on you. I'd always done it properly, and Mike and I had tried a dozen different ways.

I started going out with men who I met at clubs. I did some wild stuff; game playing, bit of this, bit of that. I'm not ashamed of it but it's private. The thing was I wasn't one of those girls who were coy about sex and I wasn't a tease. I enjoyed myself.

It wasn't the only thing in my life. I was serious about school. I worked hard. I did well. I loved my sport. Life was pretty sweet.

CHAPTER 6
1984

Mary

I love airports. I love the feeling of going somewhere, starting on something or returning from a job well done, usually, in my case, lying in front of bulldozers to try and protect an old growth forest. Trees are a lot less complicated than people.

The commune at Nimbin that I'd been part of had broken up. It was sad, but the main thing I got out of it was that I realised most people are crazy. You can't live with them, can't work with them. It's just too hard. That's why marriage is a legal contract. Otherwise there would be a lot more of, 'So long, been good to know ya'. After my flirtation with living communally, I thought that the important thing was to save nature, especially the forests. And have a little for myself. I bought the best slice of the land from the commune and built myself a little house on it. I had a talent for house and garden, otherwise known as real estate, so I bought other bits and pieces in the area and started doing sympathetic developments. I'm anti-capitalist in principle, although there are bits of the system I like. For instance, flying back and forth from the north coast to Sydney and living two different lives.

You hardly ever meet anyone you know at an airport, unless it's pre-arranged. So when I saw my brother Martin, way up ahead on the walkway, I gave a big yell. He didn't turn around.

Martin should have known better than to hide from me. It was easy to outrun the moving walkway and I saw straightaway why he was avoiding me. He had a woman with him, and it wasn't Vile Susan. It was a lovely looking girl, young and spunky looking. She wasn't classically beautiful; in fact, her face was a little chunky, but she was very appealing. She was wearing a low-cut top and had a beautiful figure.

'Martin.'

'Hi Mary.' He leaned over the walkway side, it was still moving, and kissed me on the cheek. He was in a good mood. 'You've come out of the forest for a while?'

'I've got to earn some money,' I said. 'There's a practice in Bondi that needs a locum for three weeks.'

He was obviously with this girl but pretending he wasn't. So I busted him. 'Aren't you going to introduce me?'

They got to the end of the walkway. 'This is Melissa,' he says. 'Melissa, this is my sister Mary.' Then he did something dumb. 'Melissa is Susan's cousin.'

'You're kidding?' Tact is not my strong point. I turned to Melissa. 'Really, which side of the family? I don't believe it!'

'Melissa needs to go to the loo,' he said. 'There's one over there, sweetie.'

I don't think he even realised he'd called her sweetie, but she did and was off like a shot. I wasn't far behind, and once I was in the ladies I waited for her to come out of the cubicle.

'Hey,' I said when she emerged. 'I'm friendly fire. You don't have to worry about me.'

'I know,' she said, washing her hands. 'You're his favourite sister.'

'Can I ask you how long it's been going on?'

'Nine months.'

'Is it serious?' I said.

She looked straight at me. 'I love him. I don't think he'll leave the marriage. He loves me, but he can't.' She smiled at me tentatively. 'It's not exactly your business,' she said. 'I'm only telling you this because . . . well, you're pushing your luck really.'

'Yes I am. And he's my brother, so there's a certain merit in my curiosity,' I said. 'Is Melissa your real name?'

'Melissa Sardelis,' she said, and held out her hand. 'It's weird, but it *is* nice meeting you. One of the costs of this is that you're totally removed from normal life.' It sounded corny but she had a smile that lit up her whole face.

I didn't pry any further and I didn't gossip about what I'd found out. Martin knew he could trust me. I felt sad because I sensed a great intimacy between them that wasn't there with Susan. What might have been, what could have been. Poor baby. I was just glad he was having some relief from Vile Susan.

Susan

I loved the job. I was successful and that made me happy. It was a matter of grasping the broad picture and working out the details. For instance, we'd always put a classified advertisement in the *Herald*, near the legal notices. I withdrew that and put an advertisement relating to wills, divorce and personal injury in one of the TV magazines instead. I also commissioned radio advertisements. The response was excellent, so good we had to recruit more graduates. It was exciting to be creating something.

I also liked having my own money. It meant that I could organise the bank loan for the second mortgage and somehow

I felt that gave me more rights to do what I wanted with the house. I liked to buy little things for myself and the boys. Small changes pleased me. I'd always bought white socks for myself for five dollars. Now I went to the ten dollar brand with better ribbing. Small, silly but satisfying. And I was able to ignore Martin saying we must have this and we must have that. He wasn't good at actually having a conversation about those things. He liked what he liked and was very adamant about it. So I did the kitchen exactly as *I* wanted it. He grumbled and complained, but typically he was pleased when everyone admired it. He even put his ghastly kookaburra on one of the spice shelves.

He liked doing the public relations on TV. I lined it all up for him. He had an awful friend, Cliff, who he went drinking with, who was a producer. I didn't like him and he didn't like me, but I didn't care. I had a job to do which was to get Martin on television. I never watched. I couldn't bear it as it was so superficial, but Martin was really good at it. The performer in him got a run. It always made me wonder if he should have gone to the bar, which requires a sense of the theatrical, but he didn't have that ambition. He had always said the wigs were silly and he didn't want to be a Queen's Counsel which was what they were called back then. I liked that in Martin. Working in the firm I saw so many other solicitors and barristers who thought the law was the most important thing in life. Martin looked beyond that.

Generally Martin was happier, and we were both so busy that we had less to do with each other, which in a way was a relief because there was less bickering. I also think me working and having my own money was important to me feeling good about myself. When I'd been full time with the children, I'd always rebelled against the feminist notions of women needing to achieve full status in the workplace. I mean, raising children is a terribly important job. But the reality is that it has no status and no pay, so it is easy to feel defeated and to lose a sense of worth. Being back at work helped me enjoy life and it did give me a sense of worth, even though it was so hectic.

I was glad I had the children. I made sure I could have time off with them if they needed me. We had little projects, like getting a pup from the pound and training her. Martin thought that complicated life, but we bought Buffy anyway. To me, having pets and looking after them was a great joy, something my mother had never allowed Lisa and me to do. Martin didn't see this so he didn't help with that and all the other things I dreamed up for the children. It cut into his surfing time or his drinking time as far as he was concerned. For me it was vital the children have a happy home with lots of love and fun. The law was far less important than the children.

I wanted to share my inner life with Martin, but somehow we'd fallen into a pattern of not doing that. Somehow there just wasn't the intimacy. Maybe it was a question of time but he was a bit impatient discussing things close to the heart. It's as if all that was decided and wrapped up in a big parcel called marriage. I guess we were just different, but I felt he didn't want to know me on a really deep level. At the beginning of our relationship we'd talked about those things—little shifts of feeling, insecurities, fears, the meaning of our lives, the meaning of what we were doing with the children, but that had dried up. He was impatient with this sort of talk, I couldn't reach him. When I said something he'd cut me off, or make fun of it.

That's why Phil was such a friend. He was totally unworldly. We discussed the meaning of life, the ideas of Christianity, notions of love, of right and wrong. To have that was *so* important.

Martin

I'd forgotten what it was like to be happy. I felt young and free and sexy. I'd forgotten what it was like to love someone freely. I'd forgotten what it was like to have goodwill in a relationship. I'd forgotten what it was like to be loved, to be wanted.

I'd forgotten the physical intimacy of loving someone who wants you, so you can touch, kiss and do whatever turns you on. I'd forgotten the sweetness of waking up next to someone who doesn't have to run off to the kids or the new pup or any other damn thing. I'd forgotten what it was like to have a woman laugh at your jokes, to play games, to lose yourself in each other.

I hadn't forgotten how good sex could be. Now, I had it. Sex and love. No restrictions. I could kiss her anywhere, I could squeeze, I could feel her body. There weren't any no-fly zones; the things Susan had made me feel bad for even thinking about. It was bliss.

It was sweetly stolen time. It wasn't reality. I wasn't kidding myself. Well, I was. When I was with her, I felt as if it was forever, that this was my life. It wasn't, it couldn't be. But it wasn't just fun. It went deep. A lot more than a flirtation or a casual affair. I loved her. I looked into her eyes and I felt comfort, warmth, ease, intimacy. I was understood and loved in return.

I told myself I was a better husband because of it. I didn't care as much. I didn't want to be mean to Susan. I loved Melissa and I loved the world. Of course there was a lot of guilt. I didn't feel good about what I was doing, but I didn't dwell on it. I was aware of the deception, feeling uncomfortable, not in line with what I wanted to think about myself. But it seemed justifiable. After all, it wasn't harming Susan.

Melissa was on my mind all the time. I'd have sex with Susan and it would be Melissa. I was unfaithful in every possible way to Susan's mind, body and soul. I'd be going home, thinking of the heavy, brown breasts of Melissa, the exquisite white of the underside where the sun didn't reach, the golden fuzz of hair on her lower back, the long, brown gold hair falling across her face, her shivers of pleasure when I sucked her nipple. More, more, more.

The relationship grew in depth and intensity. If you looked at Susan and me, you'd have to say that we were suited in terms of intellect, in terms of our education, thinking and the sort of circles we moved in. Melissa was outside that. She was intelligent but she didn't give a stuff whether she read a newspaper or not. She had given up her law degree without a thought. She never read anything except crime fiction and romance. She loved the cut and thrust of business. She loved hanging round with the footballers at the club where she worked as promotions manager. She liked big physical humour and would often miss quiet irony or a pun.

'I'm a Greek geek,' she told me and laughed.

She was intelligent, not intellectual, but she wasn't anti-intellectual. She was just who she was. She took people for who they were. She lived in the present and didn't hold grudges. She was re-establishing contact with her Greek family. It didn't matter that they'd cut her off. She lived passionately and fearlessly.

'I can't leave the boys.' I'd told her a hundred times.

'Wait,' she always said. 'Wait and see.'

In the end it was she who wouldn't wait. Towards the end of the year we were constantly bickering.

'You'd probably see as much of them if you were separated,' she said one morning. We'd just made love, still intertwined.

'It'd be different, artificial.'

'It's not the boys. It's her.'

'It's the damage it would do to the boys, knowing their parents don't love each other.'

'They know it already. Kids always do.'

'We're always polite.'

'Dead giveaway.'

'Don't be silly.'

'You can't leave *her*.'

'Don't be silly, Lissy.'

'Don't patronise me. It's her. It's her father's firm. It her, the lawyer wife. It's her, Mrs Perfect. It's the house at Coogee. I drove out yesterday and had a—'

'Melissa!'

'She was there on the verandah with the boys, talking to a minister. She had on a beautiful dark blue and green dress and red beads. I looked through the fence. She looked fabulous and sophisticated, every single thing that I am not. Don't worry, they didn't see me. But it's not the kids. It's her. I know.'

'It's not.'

There were a lot of tears from her and from me, a lot of days when I thought I'd just walk out of the house and move in with her. There was a lot of pain, a lot of anger, but in the end she was right. Not about it being Susan but about the fact I could not leave. Not then. Maybe later. But Melissa wouldn't give me a later.

And the tragedy was that I loved her. And she loved me. I wanted her, I needed her. She wanted me, needed me.

It couldn't last.

The relationship with Melissa ended just before Christmas.

That Christmas I got very, very drunk.

Melissa

I told my friend Anna about Martin as soon as I met him. I was pissed off at him for asking me out, after buying me the coffee and being sympathetic. Truth was I was pissed off with him for being married.

'I can tell,' said Anna. 'It's a love-hate thing. He'll be back.'

'No way!' But he was, two weeks later. He sprang me at David Jones. Mind you, I hadn't stopped thinking about him. I'd been thinking of waiting outside his office at lunchtime and casually bumping into him. Or going back to the coffee shop. The attraction between us was that powerful.

I worried about him being married. Anna and I were into being young and free. We weren't too wild, but we wanted experiences. We weren't too worried about traditional morality.

'Everyone's got to have at least one married man in their portfolio,' she said.

That wouldn't have cut any ice except I was so madly attracted to him. I didn't want complication for the sake of it. And I always seemed to have someone to go out with. But this was different.

It went on for a year, which is a long time when you're twenty. I felt so in love. I felt like he was my soul mate. I'd never felt anything like it before. It worried me that it was so intense and so impractical. There was the constant of Susan and his children in our life, the guilt that went along with that.

At the end of the year Anna went to England for a tiny part in a film. I drove her out to the airport and we sat in the lounge drinking expensive airport brandy, lime and soda.

'Seduce the producer and make sure you get a great part,' I said.

'Oh sure. I'm there with some real big stars and he'll choose me.'

'He's a bloke, isn't he? Just do this.' I fluttered my eyelids and giggled, but really I was dying inside about Marty. I knew it couldn't go on.

'What should I do about Marty?' I asked, suddenly serious.

'Dump him,' she said. 'You've got the married man in your portfolio. Now's the time to have an affair with a dashingly attractive, repressed homosexual.'

'It's not like that,' I said.

'He's using you,' she said. 'Look, it's fine for him. He's got the wife, he's got the kids, he's got the job in his father-in-law's firm. And he's got you. Puleese. All this breast beating he's going on with about whose life he's going to ruin. Let me tell you, it's yours.'

'I think he's going to dump me,' I said. 'Not because he doesn't love me.' Anna's boarding call came over the PA. I hugged her and we wished each other luck.

I thought about what she said. She was cynical about him. But I knew Martin took his marriage seriously. He wasn't the sort to just walk out which was part of why I loved him. I decided to make it easy for him. I told him it was over unless he left Susan. Her or me, that was the choice. He vacillated, argued the toss, tried to convince me. But I'd made up my mind. It was over.

I wrote to Anna. 'I finished it but not because he doesn't love me. He just can't leave his wife.'

It was the most horrible Christmas I ever had. But the relationship was too messy, too hard.

Thomas Thomas

I knew Susan knew about me and Marg. I suppose it was unrealistic to expect she wouldn't find out working in the office.

I have two subscriptions to the opera. Just my bloody luck to have two women who adore opera. Have to see the whole season twice and I'm not exactly a buff. Anyway, I had the tickets there on my desk.

'You're going with Marg?' Susan said.

'Tonight, yes,' I said, as if it was an unusual occurrence.

She looked at me knowingly. 'Well, enjoy yourself,' she said. That was that.

I must say it was a relief to me. I'd been thinking if she found out that I'd have to leave Irene. And it wasn't practical to leave Irene. Our marriage was over in most ways but we had the girls, the house, golf club membership and all that together.

Giving up Marg was unthinkable. I couldn't live with Irene without the relief of Marg. It had kept me awake a few nights, I can tell you.

I think Susan was quite pragmatic about it. Probably understood, given what a dragon Irene is. Even though women are supposed to be the keepers of civilisation as we know it and the guardians of morality, in some ways they're more practical than men.

Susan never said another word about it.

CHAPTER 7

1985

Martin

'I think you've really come good,' old Thomas said to me. 'Your billings are excellent. Susan organising your cases is all for the good. Allows you to concentrate on the important stuff, eh?'

Christ! My father-in-law really knew how to piss me right off. The whole thing was really pissing me off. I was just going through the motions as far as marriage and work and the rest of my life went. It wasn't Susan's fault, it really wasn't, but it was if she thought she could ignite the fires of the marriage by discussing philosophy or by us having psychological insights about each other. It was just crap, crap, crap.

'By the way, old boy,' Thomas went on.

What's with the fucking old boy stuff? I know they're supposed to have a network that's running the world, but excuse me, I thought this was the end of the twentieth century, not a boy's own annual from the old fart's childhood.

'Old boy . . . I thought you might like these tickets to a charity bash . . . you and Susan. My old university college. Fancy dress. Victoriana. All those great music hall songs.'

So I went through the motions of the big night out, courtesy of old Thomas. Rented myself an opera cape and a top hat, which I lost sometime during the evening. Susan fixed herself a spectacular costume, but when the time came Josh was sick and she bowed out. I thought the babysitter could have coped with a child with a sniffle, evidently not. I went alone.

Who should I see but my old flame Yvette? I hadn't seen her since I had proposed to her, but I knew that predictably, she'd dined out on the story of my proposal, which pissed me off a little. The way she saw it was that marriage was totally unsuited for sophisticated people who were into the good times. I knew she was in with the trendy set who sniffed coke and cheated on tax, which was what life was about in the eighties for the sophisticated. It was way too heavy to appeal to me, I had seen enough of those people come undone. The people in the smart set who got heavily into drugs and hit serious trouble—bankruptcy, being struck off, jail sentences, marriage break-ups, suicides and one case of murder—were often the people who paid my bills.

I waved to Yvette across a couple of tables and that was it. Or should have been. Except, as Thomas had promised, it was a damn good night. The music was fantastic and being in fancy dress added a feeling of abandon. And I had a little too much to drink. Which was how I found myself on a table leading a chorus.

Two lovely black eyes,
Oh what a surprise,
Simply for telling a man he was wrong,
Two lovely black eyes.

I was as drunk as a skunk in a crinoline and I slid off the table on which I'd been dancing, right into the arms of Yvette. Which was when I remembered not so much that she had refused to marry me, but the time before that when we were hot and she was sassy and the sex was unbelievable.

'Dear one,' she said. 'Dear, dear, darling man. Where have you been?' She had on long knickers and one of those corsets pulled tight round the bust with her tits in their full glory pushing out the top of it. She looked smashing. And smashed.

I kissed her. Not just a hullo kiss, or a by-your-leave type of peck on the cheek, but a serious kiss on the mouth, tongue moving down the throat, explore-the-inside-of-your-head type of kiss.

'Is Susan here?' she asked when I surfaced.

'Home with the kids,' I murmured, holding myself up on the edge of the table.

It was one o'clock and the songs were sounding more and more like drunken rants.

'If *she's* at home with the baby, *you* should be home with me,' she said. 'That's only fair.'

She started giggling and groping me, so supporting each other, we weaved our way out of the hall and towards Parramatta Road, stopping on the college oval for a quick fuck on my velvet cape. Who says fancy dress isn't fun? We got into a taxi and up the stairs to her second floor unit at Glebe Point. I had a rush of memory. It was a down-at-heel little flat, with a very romantic view over Blackwattle Bay. I could feel the nostalgia factor at work as we made love on the floor. I still had in my head how she'd compared me to her labrador. It gave me some satisfaction that the dog was almost certainly dead now, and she was more than happy to have me there.

We had it together sexually. Yvette was always experimental. She talked dirty, explored everything. She pulled and bit and shrieked and moaned. She'd never been interested in polite sex and, boy, she was fun. We did it on the lounge, in the shower, on the kitchen floor. Finally after about two hours, we were well and truly and literally shagged. She rolled a joint and in silence we passed it between us.

Halfway through the joint, I sat up. One of those terrible moments where you pass from being drunk and stoned to crystal clear, sober reality. Which is not what you want in that situation.

'Christ,' I said. 'What have I done?'

'Fucked your brains out, sweetie. Mine too.'

God, I'd sworn off Melissa. That was over although I felt the pain of it every single day. I had taken the marriage vow in my head again. I wasn't all that happy but it had been the right thing to do. And now I'd given it up for this. It had been a moment of madness. 'How could I do it to Susan? How could I? Jesus Christ.'

'You did it to me,' Yvette pointed out.

'I don't do this,' I said. 'I had one affair but it's over now. Sorry, it's not about you. Believe me, please believe me.'

'Believe *me*,' she said. 'This sort of thing happens. In marriage, out of marriage. It isn't a crime or a tragedy.'

'I shouldn't have let it happen,' I said.

'Listen babe, I had a good time. Save the bleeding heart for Susan. I don't want your recriminations. She stood up, still naked, joint in hand. 'The same you that let it happen is the same you who put your tongue down my throat back in the college. The same you that's feeling the moral weight of the world happens to be the same you who wrapped my hand round your prick in the cab and wanted to fuck me on the stairs. I didn't drag you up here and there wasn't part of you that didn't want to come in. Now you're feeling sorry for yourself, you've summoned up your moral policeman who makes you feel worse than the you that made love to me on the bathroom floor. Who, I remember, was feeling pretty damn excellent. There aren't two people here, Martin. You did exactly what you wanted and now you're trying to get out of it, pretending you forgot something or that I lured you here or some such shit!'

'I'm not blaming you,' I said. 'It's me.'

'Yeah, well, you could stop blaming yourself. It's not a cataclysmic event. If you don't tell her about it, she'll never never know. Don't be such a bloody drama queen. You used to be no bullshit. That's what I liked about you.'

'I'm a married man,' I said. 'That changes everything.' A married man. In a marriage that isn't working—not quite. In a marriage where I'm an extra, in a marriage where I'm kind of not wanted.

Yvette was pissed off with me now. 'No, not everything. We had great sex, same as we always did. You loved it, same as you always did.'

'You wouldn't understand.'

'*Oh fuck off!*'

Susan

I'd had a feeling it would be a bad year. Christmas had been ghastly. It was at his sister Kathleen's. His family has no sense of restraint with food or drink or conversation. It was hot, and the food was all the traditional Christmas stuff. They sat there, eating and drinking, eating and drinking, stuffing themselves. It was a nightmare. The grandparents stuffed the kids with junk. When they started singing old Irish songs there was no stopping them. The whole clan was caterwauling on.

When I said I wanted to go home Martin said that at least his family knew how to have fun, and it was better than my mother and her low-fat turkey and her triumphant re-telling of her meeting with the sainted Sir Robert Menzies.

'At least their Christmas is restful and predictable,' I said.

'Oh, it's a hoot all round,' he said. 'So fucking joyous.'

I laughed, it was fair comment. But we had stayed too long and I wanted to go. The kids love Christmas there. They love their grandparents and cousins, especially Ben who thrives wherever there are a lot of people, but Josh and I were exhausted. Josh has a limited tolerance of noise and uproar, like me, I suppose. And I seemed to be the only sober adult.

Not one of them can sing in tune, except Mary, and the songs went on and on and on, sentimental and maudlin, full of Irish failure. Martin was smashed and when we did get home, he started playing his Dubliners records loudly, singing along to them.

'Marty, please . . .'

'Oh all right.'

And then he feel asleep on the couch. I don't know, but I felt like something had snapped. Some sort of connection, some hope that we would reconnect. It wasn't dramatic, it wasn't liberating. It was strange. I just felt as if I now had to navigate this marriage on my own. That there was him and there was me, rather than us. It didn't really make a difference on a day to day level. I still loved him. But the feeling of separateness was there, permanent, embedded.

The next morning, sitting on the edge of the bed, the kids still asleep, Martin downstairs, I felt the full weight of it again—the tiredness, the daily grind, the emptiness of this life we couldn't even talk about. I felt very disillusioned. Even though going back to work had been so fulfilling for me, I had come to see that I was unhappy with the marriage. I guess part of it was my pre-feminist upbringing. Somewhere deep inside myself, I had thought a man could fulfil me in a way that I now know is impossible.

Early in the marriage I had sensed we didn't want the same things and that he didn't know how to compromise. But I was pregnant and I desperately wanted the relationship to work. Now I'd come to the point where I knew the relationship had serious limitations.

When we married I was naïve and idealistic. You can have principles but it's the day to day stuff, the same old issues to deal with, the same areas where we repeatedly clashed. We couldn't find an easy place with each other.

I felt an emptiness, a fear of life, a loneliness.

I'd hoped exploring the spiritual dimensions of life would help but it didn't, at least not in terms of my marriage. Martin simply didn't care about those questions anymore especially because I moved to a more conventional view of Christianity. For me, faith was looking beyond the contradictions towards believing a Christian faith would give meaning, purpose and structure to my life.

As opposed to surfing.

Martin wasn't going to change. Maybe he'd never really understood who I was. All his talk of romance and mystery was a way of not facing the issues in our marriage, of not seeing me. He thought we were married and it should work. He didn't think about why it didn't or what I might need from him. Yet I gave him so much support at work and took the burden of creating our family life. I worried about his moods and his ups and downs but I felt he was oblivious to mine.

The compensation was the kids. Thank God! If I'd missed out on having children, my life would have been so empty. Of course children need loads of attention but the love is easier and flows naturally. I just adored them. There were times when it felt too much, but then I'd settle into the homework with Josh or see Ben's pride at swimming a length of the Olympic pool, and things would seem okay. Seeing how happy they were, my tension would dissolve.

They had their little anxieties and worries but they were happy children. They were having a childhood that was full of love and fun and security. I suppose I was experiencing it vicariously. And they were so different. Ben soaked it all up but Josh thought about things, worried about everything. I know he worried about me when I got stressed or tired. He worried about Martin getting angry. I think his artistic talent came from that same ability to notice small things.

After Christmas Martin and I had an enormous fight about painting the house. I'd picked the colours and I'd run them past him. He always said he was too busy or he'd look at them later. Finally I painted up a board and he agreed to the colours.

'I didn't agree to that,' he said the afternoon he came home and the front of the house had been painted. 'It's incredibly ugly.'

'Martin, you agreed to it!'

'Never!'

'Martin, I've still got the board. See, over there. I stood here. I asked you. You said yes.'

'Oh fuck. Do you have to treat our life together as if it's a court case? Have all the bloody evidence gathered up. You've probably got sworn statements from witnesses.'

'Don't be stupid. We agreed on this colour.'

'I have no memory whatsoever of agreeing to poop green. As I remember you were forever flashing bits of coloured this and that in front of my eyes.'

'You negotiate with the painter and pay for the new paint, because I refuse to do it anymore.'

He sulked but when people admired it he decided he liked it. 'You were right, puss. I was wrong. As usual. And the colours go with my kooka.' I'd moved it upstairs but now the awful thing was back on the hall table.

It wasn't as if he had any serious opinion about the colour. That's why it was so easy for him to apologise.

It sounds petty but I longed for unity, warmth and together-ness, which was there in flashes, but more often absent. It was hard to see what was missing but I felt it getting worse, not better.

Sometime around March, things picked up. He came home one night with flowers. The night before, he'd gone to some charity do at the university, he'd been incredibly drunk and hadn't come home till about four. Something must have shaken him.

He gave me the flowers and said, 'Darling Susan. You're my wife and such a good one. I'm sorry I've been so awful. Really sorry.'

That was nice. I thought I really should just take him how he is, instead of wanting something different. Things were better for a while.

Lisa

Susan is good at everything she does. I've admired her and looked up to her all my life. She's better than I am at most things. The way she stood up to Mum. She drew the line in the sand. When I did it, it just annoyed Mum. Susan has a lot of control, a lot of cool. She's a class act. And everything she does expresses who she is. She dresses beautifully, but not like other people. She always original, the last person you'd expect to use colour boldly, but she does it so exquisitely. Same with the house.

Martin is different. Every woman in the world falls for Martin because he is so good-looking and charming. Charming isn't the right word. You say charm and you think smarm. He's alive, warm, or at least he seems that way. But the funny thing is that Susan is actually oblivious to that. She isn't totally oblivious, but that wasn't why she fell for him.

My theory is that she thought she could make something of him. Jamie, my bloke, agrees with that. She got Jamie out of teaching, which didn't suit him, and into computer programming, which does. She got me to apply for deputy head and then headmistress. Jamie says Susan is a born reformer, she wants to improve everyone. There's some truth to that. She rebelled against our mother but in some ways she's quite like her. Well, not like Mum in a bad way. She's got a sweetness that somehow passed Mum by. I mean you see her with kids, not just her own, and she knows how to reach them. But she's determined. She wants to get people right. Not in a pushy way but because that's the way the world should be.

She likes people to fit into the way she sees things. I guess that's because she's very focused in her beliefs. This whole thing she does for Martin at work is incredible. The point is that he's totally unsuited to law. Dad told me about it ages ago. Martin pursues virtues like fairness and trust. Do you want a person like that running a case? No, you want someone who can seize on the best argument and pursue it, who can change horses in midstream if they have to without a qualm of conscience. That's not Martin. He should have been a professional surfer, or a philosopher. Or both.

Family law is all very well, but Martin likes it if he can talk people out of a divorce or work out some compromise so they don't fight in court. Which is not, as Dad says, the way to bring in fees. The way Dad tells it, Susan helps Martin stick to his principles and make money at the same time. Which is pretty amazing.

I love Susan. When we were kids we weren't that close, but since that beach holiday when I was still at uni, we always have been. Through all my troubles with June, my stepdaughter, she's been fantastic. She's had a good effect on June, made her feel like one of the family, which I could never do, no matter how hard I tried.

Susan and Martin have always had bad patches in their marriage. It's because they are so different. Susan always wants to pin down the reasons. She likes to analyse it and work out the rights and wrongs. It makes her unhappy and she wants to fix it whereas Martin would just cruise along, adoring her, some days less, some days more. She does tend to make things into 'issues'. I think it's better to just let things go.

One day when we took the kids for a picnic in Centennial Park and they'd all gone down to fish in the lake, Susan started talking about sex. Though she has friends, they are very intellectual and they talk about literature, recent reviews, the latest feminist books, the position of women, and whether marriage is a viable institution, nevermind what we're actually stuck with.

So that day it was a big jump for Susan to get from the theory to what she actually felt, down to the nitty gritty.

'Sometimes,' Susan said to me, 'I wouldn't care if I never had sex again.' She took a deep breath, trying to be cool. I tried to keep the same tone.

'Don't we all?' I said. 'At times?'

'Well, not men, evidently,' she said. 'Martin told me the other night that it's the most important thing in a marriage. We had a big argument about it.' I could hear the tears in her voice and I tucked my arm into hers.

'Poor you,' I said, still trying to keep it light. 'You must like it sometimes.'

'I resent it,' she said. 'Because Martin *expects* it.' She bit at her fingernail. I gave her an encouraging smile. 'How do you handle it?' she asked.

'Look,' I said. '*I* like sex, but Jamie and I have different appetites. Different times, different ways—all that. Some women don't want it as much as men. Or maybe we're not as easily turned on. Or maybe it's all the emotional energy women invest in kids. That's all. You have to find a balance, don't you think?'

'I think it's a much bigger problem than that. I feel emotionally disengaged from Martin. He still wants me. He doesn't seem to understand how I feel. I don't think he even wants to know.'

'I think you've got to find what turns you on and use that,' I said. 'Emotionally and physically. And tell him. I was so embarrassed telling Jamie I liked using a vibrator. And that I don't like porn. Things that work for me, things that turn him on. I'm very clear about no go zones. It's hard to do.'

She was looking to me for help and I could tell by her expression, this wasn't what she wanted to hear. I didn't know what else to say and I could see her closing down.

'It's about the oppression of women,' she said, 'the way men think about sex.' Then she went down to the water to go paddling with the kids. It is hard to talk about those things, especially with your own sister. I guess there are people like Susan who get right over sex. Which would be hard if you had a husband like Martin.

She didn't mention it again. I thought how hard it would be in a marriage like that. I always knew with Jamie that however much we fought, we adored each other. It wasn't like that with Martin and Susan. Not anymore. They played their parts at being husband and wife. And it was sad because they had been so much in love.

Next time we were at lunch, Martin hugged her and I could see her recoil, just slightly, but it was there.

I saw the hurt in his face, the resentment in hers.

Phil

Career crisis! It was about whether I could do God's work, whether I could be an effective minister and be a good person at the same time. I wasn't sure I had the tolerance or the patience. God gave me love and sustenance. I wanted to share it with others, but it was really hard going.

My relationship with Mary raised that question. We had always been friends. I'd seen her a lot in the early days of Martin's and Susan's marriage. She'd always flirted with me. Then, a few months ago, when Martin couldn't come to the footy, she took his ticket and came with me. And after that it moved to another plane. Well, that's what modern psychologists say. In the Bible, it tends to be a bit balder. There is a lot about who one lieth with, and who one does not lieth with (mother-in-laws, beasts, sisters etc). And I lieth with Mary with both pleasure and guilt.

'Guilt *is* pleasure!' said Mary. 'You Anglicans just don't get it, do you?'

Here I was in another suburban parish relieving for a poor

sick old fellow. I was told if I played my cards right, the parish council might choose me as his successor 'when the time came'. Couldn't bear it, the everyday stuff, the dry, distant low church services. Here I was well into my thirties, no career at all. All the ideas of making a spiritual splash (not very compatible with spirituality when you think about it) had receded. I wasn't even married and people like their ministers to be married.

There was no prospect of following in the old dear's foot-steps because the Parish Council, headed by the local busybody, had found out about my little fling with Mary and the fact that she had stayed a night or two at the rectory during the week the old bloke was in hospital. This didn't go down well at all. And while I had doubts and guilt, as well as lust and longing over the Mary affair ('You would,' Mary said. 'See, that's what religion does to people.'), I knew the relationship had to end, although I wasn't sorry it had happened. I was lonely and sex starved again. People don't think of ministers as sex starved. They think we're sexless.

I would have liked these parishioners if I hadn't been their minister. I saw them at the shops and down the river fishing. Trouble was when they saw me their faces assumed a look some-where between guilt and embarrassment. So I spent a lot of time with people, not enjoying their company, them not enjoying mine, not having a real conversation, engaging in low-grade Jesus talk. And as their minister I had to nod and smile approv-ingly at pretty much whatever was said. Jesus didn't suffer fools gladly but ministers are supposed to. As a result, the social life of a minister can be tediously pious. No wonder so many take to drink.

It was a lonely life. During the seventies, the clergyman became a sort of social pariah as people became openly antagonistic to God. By the eighties, all traditional respect had disappeared, replaced by a derisory hostility that demanded you proved the existence of God. You were also required to do something about Northern Ireland and poverty in India, which were taken to be the church's fault.

I craved connections with people who didn't automatically see me in dog collar mode. It was hard to find people to whom I was just Phil, rather than Reverend.

Susan and Martin were my very dearest friends. They respected what I did. They treated me as an ordinary person. I had performed their marriage but I'd also helped unload the truck when they moved into their new house. I christened both kids, I went there for lunch. There had been a little cooling of the relationship with Martin, but I was very comfortable with them both. And Mary, surprisingly for such a loudmouth, was absolutely trustworthy. She'd embarrass me privately (with considerable flair), but never publicly.

The house at Coogee was Martin's pride and joy, and now that the children were a little older Susan and Martin gave lunches there every Sunday. In winter, they were held in the enormous dining room with an open fire, in summer, out on the verandah. Susan had made the house gorgeous, although it must have cost a fortune with a second storey and the entire back section had been re-built.

I loved going there because I loved to see them and the children. Josh was a very thoughtful, very unusual boy. He was into art in a big way and also loved all the animals Susan had for them. Ben was more your rough-and-tumble kid with an eye for trouble. You could talk to Josh about all sorts of things like God, eternity, infinity and panthers. With Ben, you could kick a ball round endlessly and be pretty sure it might go through a window by the end of the game. They were very different, but very close.

Susan's lunches were convivial and uproarious. They went on and on and on with lots of booze and good talk. There were people they worked with, plus a few football mates, plus some of Martin's ragged and outspoken family, people from the Surf Club and some of Susan's old university friends. Martin loved the surf and adored the beach and was inclined to hold forth on the virtues of surfing. He was such a bloke.

Being in the church focuses your mind on God a lot, which of course is precisely where it should be. This gave me my special connection with Susan. We often had talks out in the kitchen as I helped her whip up the mayonnaise or grate the Parmesan. She wasn't much of a churchgoer. However she thought and read an awful lot. The Anglican Church was becoming narrower and almost fundamentalist in its outlook. I had no time for such nonsense so it was wonderful to talk to someone who was theologically curious.

Susan was thoughtful, sweet and so intelligent but there was this blackness in her too. It was the price she paid for the rest of her being so wonderful and special. I suppose I was a little in love with her. Maybe a lot in love.

She loved music with a passion. Martin did too, but he could hardly tell the difference between Bach and Beethoven, whereas she had a fine ear. Sometimes we'd sing bits and pieces to each other, to demonstrate a sequence or a transition. We had such a wonderful time, often sitting together at the piano, playing to each other or together. It was intimate and innocent.

Before she went back to work, I often used to have lunch with her and the boys during the week. When she was working, I'd pop into town and we'd have sandwiches in Hyde Park.

She knew everything there was to know about me (apart from the fling with Mary), and she let me into her life. I knew her insecurities, her fears. She craved love and also mistrusted it. I'm not one for demonising mothers, but let's just say that Susan's mother had an awful lot to answer for. All her harshness, her lack of sentiment had cut Susan to the core when she was a child.

'Do you ever wonder what you're doing with your life?' she asked me one day.

'I'm supposed to,' I said. 'Part of the job description. You can't spend too much time worrying about the meaning of life—you're so busy.'

'I do wonder,' she said. 'I despair. I want to tell you something.'

'Go ahead.'

'It has to do with Martin. But I don't want to jeopardise your relationship with him.'

That was thoughtful, but I was dying to hear out of plain old human curiosity.

'I'm in the church, Susan,' I said. 'I'm very used to dealing with information in discreet parcels. He's not overspending, is he?' She had already told me that Martin had a tendency to spend on things that weren't necessary. He'd spent an enormous amount on a custom-made surfboard, a lot on clothes and he always had a racy car. It worried her. She saw it as a character flaw, as if he was cursed with a grasping materialism. I've seen grosser materialism in pastors fighting for funds for the rectory garden. She always knew how much she had and what she spent it on. The house was lovely, she dressed well and the boys had everything they needed. She hated his carelessness. They had fought about it a few times, I'd heard barbs going back and forth, but they weren't exactly short of money.

'It's not money,' she said, looking down. She had such a sweet curve to her cheek. 'It's how we live. I don't feel as if we've really made a marriage. I try all the time but, you know, left to himself he'd be running around with old footballers and university mates and strange academics and . . .'

'. . . reprobate ministers.'

She smiled, but briefly. It wasn't like her. She liked to laugh. 'And he's off on this big ego trip about what a fantastic lawyer he is. And how easy it is. Almost as if it's beneath him. I do case reviews and almost all the ones he's lost are because I've taken my eye off the ball.'

'So it affects you? Your sense of worth? What you do for him?' I asked.

'If I was kissing him and making up to him, that would be the perfect marriage in his eyes. He doesn't want any more. It's as if he resents me wanting more. And it makes me feel . . .'

'It makes you feel?'

'I feel like nothing, like nobody in relation to him. He doesn't notice who I am.'

'People think you are the perfect couple,' I said.

She looked me straight in the eye. 'I don't think we would have got married if I hadn't been pregnant,' she said. 'We were in love, but that's not enough. We feel—unconnected. Too different.' There were tears in her eyes. 'You're right, people do think we're perfect. And we were connected back then. But it feels like a different life now. It's not his work, it's not his surfing. It doesn't work as a marriage for me. And I can't just let it go and say "Okay, I have my life." I struggle with it. It feels as if I've got this great big black hole in me. And he goes on as if life is fine. And if I talk about it he gets all loud and robust and jokey . . . Oh, I don't know.'

'People can be different and complementary,' I suggested.

'We're not,' she said fiercely. 'We irritate each other. We don't understand each other. You see I think understanding is important. He doesn't.'

'Maybe that's just the difference between men and women.'

'Partly,' she said, 'but it's more than that. I'm struggling, Phil. We have children and I know he loves me. At times I feel it could just blow away. If he saw what I'm doing at the office, how I support him, it would shatter him. His great big, fragile ego. And I'd be left. Alone in the corner. *I* feel I'm there already. This *empty* marriage. I resent it. I can't leave because of the kids, yet I hate the deception of it.'

What was I supposed to say? I wondered to myself.

'You can't give me an answer, Phil. I know that. It's too hard.'

'God will give you an answer in time,' I said. 'You underestimate how much he loves you.'

'God or Martin?'

'Maybe both.'

When we parted, I always kissed her on the cheek. That afternoon, she put her arms around me and clung to me. 'Oh Phil,' she said. 'Thank God I have you in my life.'

Phil

The job of my dreams. Well, not exactly, but a great relief. I was appointed assistant chaplain at a boys' school. I taught a little English, one history class and religion. Susan helped me get the job in the school, after years of going from parish to parish, bemoaning the state of the church and wondering about my place in it. Josh and Ben went to school there and I think Susan had had a word in the ear of the chaplain.

I taught in the high school and helped with the sports teams in the junior school. The boys were a bunch of little heathens, which was a wondrous challenge. Apart from the usual cynicism of adolescents, they were open-minded and curious when they discovered I wasn't there to ask them if they went to church or had impure thoughts. There was a reasonable number who became interested in religion, who sought life's deeper meaning, who could relate to the rituals and appreciate their meaning and resonance.

The chaplain turned a blind eye to my unconventional teaching and was pleased when I got a few extras to come along to weekend chapel.

In class we discussed everything. Sex, drugs, music, blasphemy, hope, faith, God, the devil, power, good and evil, a potent and arousing mixture of ideas, which occasionally had me reprimanded by a conventional Christian parent with fixed ideas on sin.

What is sin? Well, there are the big-ticket sins—murder, rape, child abuse, drug dealing, grand larceny. From these, we look to lesser but related categories of sin—brawling, petty dishonesty, self-indulgence, small deceptions, petty manipulations, tiny cheats, self-deception.

Even further down the sin scale, barely worth mention are the tiny sins in which our lives are steeped—white lies, failure to love, resentment, refusal to forgive, jealousy, small infidelities, gossip, cheating, greediness, over-indulgence, pinching parking places, not giving back excess change from groceries, meanness, the mean exploitation of tiny powers, bleak views, joy in others' misery, petty lust, bitterness, acrimony.

I lived in sin with Susan. I revered her, admired her and loved her, yet she was the source of my sin.

Was it my pastoral duty to hear her worries about Martin? In the beginning I thought so. In the beginning it was about her unhappiness. Then I became privy to her kind and compassionate complaints, bemoaning his unhappiness, regretting his failure to grapple with the law, his inability to understand the sensitivity of his sons, and finally, the imposition of his unhappiness, his moods, his dark moments towards her.

She was long suffering and loving but it was measured against her own unhappiness. She had hopes and dreams for Martin. She did things to improve his life most of which he didn't know about or care to notice.

I knew, deep down, that she didn't really want him to be happy. Or to be a success. That was her sin. I'm sure it wasn't a conscious thing but it was a sort of underhand triumph that she was after. She wanted the triumph of superior unhappiness a sort of martyrdom to his deficiencies. She wanted to be the better person, and except for wanting that, she was. Maybe I colluded in that superiority, forgave it, bypassed it.

So my sin was collusion, to tutt tutt and make helpful suggestions that would not work and give her love and support in her despair about him. It felt cosy but it also made me uncomfortable.

I wondered if she needed someone with a broader perspective and more experience. Mary was doing a counselling course. The subject of counselling came up at a Sunday lunch and I listened attentively to Susan's reactions, hoping maybe I could suggest she see someone.

'I did a youth counsellors' course,' I said to Mary. 'Only a weekend seminar but it's been very useful.'

Mary was never slow to take an opportunity to tease me about religion. 'That's rich, Phil,' she said. 'Your lot are responsible for human misery. Your congregations don't come crowding through the door because they're so happy. They come because they're so bloody miserable. Unhappiness is the lifeblood of the churches. You peddle sin. Every harmless pleasure known to mankind— sex, drugs, recreational thievery—the churches jump on, turn them into sins. Then, you offer redemption everlasting, but only in the afterlife. And now counselling. I thought the godly weren't supposed to need it.'

The wisteria was out and Mary looked very pretty sitting under it, denouncing religion. 'Actually it's not hard, this counselling business. Go and have a wank, I say to my patients,' continued Mary. 'Or stop sleeping with your alcoholic husband. Go out and enjoy yourself.'

The guests round the table winced at Mary's frankness. Her presence at lunch always seemed to encourage the drinking of more wine.

'That seems a strange idea of counselling, Mary,' said Susan, putting down a dish of fennel and fetta in olive oil.

'No,' said Mary. 'It's just commonsense.' She picked up a piece of fennel and let the oil drip onto the table before she put it in her mouth. I saw Susan frown slightly as the oil stain spread across the linen tablecloth.

'Commonsense often isn't sense at all,' said Susan. She was right. 'Surely counselling is something quite different.'

Out in the kitchen Susan and I chatted more about counselling. I said I thought it was useful, although I found some of the language rather clinical as a way of describing the human condition.

'What about you?' I asked. 'Have you considered it? For your difficulties with Martin?'

'Yes, I have,' she said. 'He comes home late. He avoids me. He sits drinking, staring at the TV. He gets angry over small things. He wakes early every morning. I read that those are the symptoms of depression.'

'I preferred the time when we called it grand desolation of the soul.'

'I think he'd benefit from professional help,' she said. 'Someone who could help him change his thinking, help him see things in a different light.'

'I was thinking more of counselling for you.'

'I'd go with Martin if necessary,' she said. 'But the hard part is to convince him to go. I was wondering if you could talk to him.'

This took the focus off her unhappiness.

'What could I say that you couldn't?' I asked.

'It's not what you say,' she said. 'He's more likely to listen to you.'

'Maybe you should talk to someone too,' I persisted. 'You often seem very upset, agitated.'

'I am upset,' she said. 'Which is why I need *you* to talk to Martin.' I couldn't resist Susan.

I talked to him a few weeks later, when we were drying ourselves off after showering after a game of touch. He still had the most fantastic body. He was big and strong and had an impressive grace about him.

'Susan thinks you're depressed.'

'Low level misery—flashes of—curse of the Irish.'

'She thinks it's more. I think you need to take this seriously. Talk about it. Think about it. Get Susan to help you.'

'Susan? Help me? You're kidding!' He turned to me. 'Phil, you're my oldest and dearest friend but Susan's put you up to this. Ask her why she doesn't talk to me about my depression or whatever she chooses to call my psychic state. Ask her why we need you as a go between.'

'Well, that might be the problem.'

'Shit Phil. Fucking grow up.' He was angry, slight menacing. 'You're her friend, not mine. You don't give a shit about me or what you call my depression, so don't pretend you do.' He flicked me with his towel, hard enough to hurt. 'Have some fucking integrity. If you want to play spiritual counsellor do it with us both there.' He walked out, but the next time we met it was as if it had never happened. Martin wasn't one to hold grudges.

I wanted to revive my friendship with him but he was right that we had ceased being close friends quite a long time ago. There wasn't the intimacy we had once had.

'I do care about you, Martin,' I said.

'Sure thing,' he said. 'Next you'll be hugging me.'

'He won't listen,' I told Susan. '*I* don't think he understands what is happening to him. Or wants to.'

I remained her confidante, guilty as sin.

Martin

I tried to be happy with Susan. After breaking off the relationship with Melissa and then the incident with Yvette, I tried. My unhappiness seemed shameful, to exhibit it even more so. I gritted my teeth, tried to grin and bear it.

The worst was the loneliness, going home at night. It stopped feeling like home.

'Oh hello, Martin.' It felt as genuine as the welcome in a four-star hotel. 'Ben crashed into bed at six. He had swimming this afternoon. Then Joshie and I ate dinner. We got hungry, didn't we Joshie?'

It hurt. The kids were lined up against me. I was the bruiser who was late to dinner. I was the one who was too rough in games. I wasn't such a good parent, but I wasn't as bad as they thought. I could see it in Joshie's eyes. Here he comes. All the peace and calm with Mummy will go down the tube. He'd do anything to resist me—grizzle, cry, hurt his arm, be polite or ineffectually cooperative. I could see him caught between us, the ideological battle between good and evil. Sometimes I hated him for how easily he capitulated to her, but I could remember being the child who had stood between his parents. I tried to keep the door open to the kids. Occasionally the Irish in me slammed it shut.

'There's some bread and cheese in the kitchen,' she'd say, 'and the cold lamb kebabs from Sunday. I'm putting Joshie to bed and then I'm going myself.'

Later I'd go in, and she'd be asleep, her small body resolutely defining her side of the bed. I'd reach out to her, out of desperation, and very occasionally she would allow me to make love to her. It was an allowance, a small one at that. It seemed to fuel my resentment against her, rather than pacify it. I wanted to love her. I did love her and it felt as if she was going out of her way to deny my love.

I got into the habit of putting off the loneliness, stopping at the Coogee Bay Hotel for a drink on the way home from work. Lots of faces I knew from my days doing criminal trials, lots of hard faces, lots of talk, lots of violence some nights. It was human emotion, human activity, human warmth and laughter. I'd sit there and watch, sipping my beer, gathering some sort of grim comfort, then steel myself to go home.

It was outside the hotel that the accident happened. I still can't put together quite what happened. Melissa was in my head. Warm, brown, loving Melissa. Melissa, Melissa. It was a year since I'd seen her. She was in my head most of the time.

But having a woman in your head when you're driving doesn't cause an accident. It was drizzling rain in the summer heat, the water steaming off the road as soon as it hit. Round eight. Daylight saving, the sun just about to go down, light bouncing off the wet.

He ran out on the road. I hit the brakes too late and he was on the windscreen, his face distorted against the glass. Red T-shirt. A thud as he hit the road and bounced hard against it. Two youths banging on my windscreen calling me 'cunt'.

I was out of the car. One of them tried to punch me. The kid in the red T-shirt, late teens, looked bad lying there on the road, blood coming out of his mouth and ear. I was shaking like a leaf. There was the sound of sirens coming closer, then the ambos and the cops were there. Another bloke was standing there, wearing a white apron, from the hot dog stand. 'It wasn't your fault. He ran out.' Then he disappeared. Down at the cop shop I answered questions. Polite and respectful but the cops had an edge of triumph having a solicitor in custody with two witnesses swearing I was going too fast, hadn't stopped in time, guilty as sin.

Me thinking, the kid's probably dead. Someone's son. The image in my head, his face smashed against my windscreen.

I rang Susan. No, she couldn't come down and collect me. The children were asleep. Five minutes away. She couldn't come. Her voice was cold. Bitch.

They found the hot dog man. The other blokes had chased the red T-shirt kid out onto the road. Part of a punch up. Someone else saw it too. I wasn't guilty but I'd hurt the kid. Or killed him. The cops couldn't say. He was still in intensive care.

I walked home in the rain, the boy's broken face in my head.

'I'm sorry I couldn't come,' she said. 'The children.'

'I ran into someone,' I said. 'I needed you there.'

'But it wasn't your fault.'

'Don't you understand? What it might feel like? That I might have liked you there?'

'I'm sorry,' she said, with a trace of guilt. 'The children . . . Martin . . . it wasn't your fault.'

'Oh good,' I said. 'Every time I get a picture of him in my head, his face smashed against the windscreen, I'll just remind myself it wasn't my fault. Bloody hell! That helps. Sorry, I hadn't thought of it. I just thought about some kid smashed against my car. But shit, look on the bright side. Insurance might even pay for the windscreen.'

'Martin, please . . .'

'Fuck you,' I yelled. 'This is a fucking sham, this life of ours. This is nothing. It's nowhere. This is over, it's finished.'

I had never spoken to her like that before. I'd always said I never would. More than that, I'd respected her. I'd felt her fear and abhorrence of being spoken roughly to. Now I could see her crumbling but I didn't care. I wanted to get her, punish her, make it so she couldn't despise me.

'Fuck you, you bitch!'

I went into my study, slammed the door, poured a whisky and hardly slept at all.

Josh

When I was little I had this dream all the time. It started with just an orange, moving around, suspended in air. Then, there got to be something a bit creepy about it, as if the orange skin was like the pale skin of a person. As it started moving round, I realised there was an ogre face on the other side coming towards me, but I never quite got to see the face. It was always about to come round but it never quite did.

When I was a kid, I couldn't put it all together. I remember that with the face, I felt this worry about my Mum and Dad at the same time. They didn't like each other. One of them would leave. I had to choose between them. Maybe one of them might even die. I was so frightened my heart would go fast. Then I'd wake up with a start. I was feeling I shouldn't speak because I'd say something that might make one of them leave.

Ben and me slept upstairs. Ben slept, you couldn't wake him. He never heard what was going on downstairs but I had to listen. I wanted to know what was going on. I wanted to know when the divorce would happen. Ben didn't think about divorce. Ben hardly thought about Mum and Dad. He called them 'the parents', as if they were separate from him and me.

I knew about divorce. Tom, my friend, had divorced parents. His father had a gun. His mother had hit his father with a broom. They didn't have a house anymore. His father had gone away and now he had a new baby sister.

You could sit in the cupboard at the top of the stairs and hear most things. The hearing cupboard I called it. Mum didn't like Dad's tone of voice. She thought he should take steps. She felt that something had to be done. Dad said 'fuck' a lot. They were both angry, very angry. Why it was so scary, I'm not sure, except there was the divorce there.

And then one night it was really there. Dad had come home late. I'd been to swimming and I was really tired but I wanted to know he was home. It was better when he was home and they went to bed and so they were asleep till the morning. I heard him come in the front door and I crept along to the hearing cupboard in my pyjamas. I knew it was wrong but I had to know because they are our parents—mine and Ben's. Something about a car. The police. She wouldn't do something. He'd killed a man. He was yelling loud. Killed a man. Killed a man. He said it twice. He was talking a lot more than her, a lot more angry. He shouted so loud. He hated her, you could tell. She went to bed. He went into the study.

Next morning. Ben and me were supposed to get up at seven. Half past six, Dad is there, downstairs, shouting again. I could feel the divorce. I moved along to the hearing cupboard.

'I cannot live with you. This is wrong. It's crap.' And then the door slammed. I rushed back into bed so Mum wouldn't know I'd been snooping when she came up to wake us.

At breakfast I could see Mum had been crying. 'Why are you getting a divorce?' I asked.

'I'm not getting a divorce.' She started stacking the dishwasher.

'Is Dad?'

'Of course not, darling.' But she didn't explain. Mum always explained things to us so when she didn't, I knew something was wrong.

'I think you are.'

'Whatever gave you that idea?'

The hearing cupboard, top of the stairs. 'Nothing.'

Melissa

It was summer. A year since Martin and I broke up. No, I wasn't over him. I thought about him, said his name, masturbated imagining the sex we'd had. I was attracted to other men who looked like him. I was sure he would be back.

What had he said to me?

'There's a place in my heart only you can fill.' That said everything.

'There's a place in *my* heart only *you* can fill.' Which was true. I knew he was coming back, he must be.

As Anna reminded me, it was like the thing with my father. I had learned from experience that when you thought people were coming back, it didn't always happen. But Dad was dead and Martin wasn't. And I *had* moved back to Manly. So it was possible to get what you wish for. I was part of the extended Greek family again. My Thia Toula had become the family matriarch when Ya Ya died. She had been so close with Ya Ya, but now, the differences had become apparent. She no longer dressed in black and she had her hair done every week. She wore an amazing amount of gold jewellery. The lover whom she had had for years came out of the closet. She must have decided she had treated me badly because she took me under her wing and let me stay in her flat for free while she lived with the lover. The deal was that I would cover for her if someone rang. The truth was they all knew she lived with her lover in his apartment and he went home up the coast to his wife every few nights.

I liked her. She was kind and funny and good to me. Everything seemed right on the surface, but the Greek part of me that was accepted by her was also the Greek part of me that never quite forgave her for excluding my mother and me after my father died. She didn't know that, which was fortunate for me as it turned out later.

I went and saw an astrologer. Anna had told me he was fabulous. He advised all the TV stars in Sydney. He told me that Martin and I were partners in a former life, and that's why the connection was so strong. We weren't destined to be together in this life. Then, with this revelation, he hit on me. So I refused to pay. Afterwards I thought that maybe there was some truth. Maybe Martin and I weren't destined. So I began getting on with my life.

The first six months without Martin had been so painful that I worked fourteen hours a day with a sports good manufacturer, running their endorsements. Then I had a fling with one of the swimmers to try and get over Martin, but truly, the swimmer was so in love with himself there wasn't room for me. And since it wasn't truly professional to sleep with people you're promoting, I started looking round for a summer romance. I found him down at the surf club.

It was unfortunate, but maybe also fate, that the first night with the Summer Romance was also the day Martin came back. Martin kissed me and told me that he had come to spend his life with me, while the Summer Romance was showering in the ensuite. Martin didn't know he was there. I took Martin down to the beach to talk, hoping the Summer Romance would depart. When we got back, after walking and talking and making out on the sand, the Summer Romance was sitting there on the lounge watching cricket in his boxers.

'How could you?' Martin asked.

'He's just a summer romance.'

Summer Romance made it worse by declaring deep love for me at this point. Martin made it better by propelling him out the back door. I made it worse still by putting his clothes in a bag and passing them out to him, and telling him I was sorry it hadn't worked out. Thia Toula made it even worse by turning up for the first time in six months and finding one man getting dressed outside the back door and another in the lounge room.

It sounds comic but it wasn't. Because I believe at that very point, Martin was actually prepared to leave Susan and the kids and be mine totally. The whole farce destroyed his moment of pure impulse, so it became a little less sure of itself, a little muted. When he came back later that week, it was different.

Maybe that was fate too.

Phil

Martin rang and told me he was thinking of leaving Susan. For one glorious moment I indulged in the fantasy of the comforter priest, counselling her through divorce with its pain and heartache, giving spiritual solace, reciting sombre prayers for acceptance and forgiveness, which would then slip seamlessly into a physical release, with me crying out to the heavens for our forgiveness. Tacky, but even ministers have sexual fantasies. (Especially single, middle-aged ministers) I'd been having one about the prep teacher, which I dismissed with this slimmest of chances with Susan.

'Come and talk it over,' I said. By the time he arrived I was in a less heated frame of mind. My role was not to be the hand-maiden of divorce but the sustainer of wounded marriages. As an Anglican minister I can't marry divorced people. But realistically there are plenty of good people who need to divorce and plenty of fine people who are divorced. In the Old Testament, God seems to approve of many unions which would now give a bishop apoplexy. Still, leaving a marriage is a serious matter.

I had an apartment in Potts Point, looking out across Wool-loomooloo Bay and up to the Domain. I loved the area with its thick layer of sinful humanity and I loved the view. We sat out on the balcony. Martin had never been there and I think he was surprised to find I lived in a slightly bohemian style.

'This is pretty cool, Phil,' he said, settling himself down. I got him a coffee. He was staring out over towards the Art Gallery. 'I do love her,' he said.

'She's a wonderful woman,' I said.

'Not Susan,' he said. 'Melissa.'

And he poured out the story of how he had met Melissa, the affair, breaking it off, starting it again, then about his marriage, the exclusion and alienation he felt, the sheer misery, the misery he believed Susan was suffering, the love he felt for Melissa, the depth, the passion, the wanting. He told me about the guilt he felt, the Catholic guilt and the deeper primal guilt, the betrayal of his wedding vows, his love and concern for his children.

Against that was wanting and desiring Melissa and the over-whelming love he felt for her.

There was no doubt this came from the depths of his soul. There was no doubt in my mind that his marriage was torture for him. Worst of all, there was no real problem for me in recognising what he said of Susan could be true. I didn't change my feelings and my admiration for Susan, not one bit, but I could see how these two people, both wonderful, might interact like this. It came from what I had seen the first night they were on the steps of the church. These were two people who were totally and utterly incompatible.

The Christian churches have a lot to say about faithlessness in marriage. They have not had quite enough to say about violence in marriage. They have strong views about children and marriage. They have very little to say about incompatibility.

'Melissa,' I said, 'is not the cause of this. She may be the trigger which is causing you to consider leaving Susan at this point. There is nothing magical, mystical or pre-ordained about your union with Melissa.'

'You don't understand,' he protested. 'Melissa and I . . .'

'Think about it,' I said, 'and you'll see I'm right. It applies to any relationship. It's just they appear magical and mystical for a while. There isn't one long-term relationship on the face of the Earth that is. Basically any relationship, given time, is two people rubbing along, bound by love and a whole lot of other stuff, doing the best they can.'

'In the sight of God,' he said sarcastically.

'Well everything's in the sight of God, isn't it? All seeing that He is.'

'Yes.' Martin was impatient.

'Susan may, on the other hand, be part of the cause.'

He was surprised by me saying this.

'There's a lot of factors you have to consider. She has two young children. She runs a house. She has a full-time job.'

'Same goes for an awful lot of marriages,' he said, 'that aren't going down the tube.'

'Most people find those factors stressful though.'

'Yes.'

'And on top of that you have two people who loved each other, but were, in a sense, thrown together into marriage, only to discover how very different they are.'

'So?'

'I haven't finished. You're thrown together, you're different, you have children. You have a life together. Okay, you have differences, mainly of temperament, yet I'd say you share a lot of the same values and interests.'

'What are you driving at?'

'I'm saying a lot of years are invested in this marriage, nearly ten years. Plus two young children. I don't think either of you has grappled with the area of difficulty. You've simply reacted to it. Maybe if you stepped back a little, accepted Susan as she is, asked her to accept you as you are, even had some marriage counselling, then maybe you could accept that this is a marriage made in heaven.' I couldn't see these two sorting out this mess with spiritual remedy alone.

'Hardly.'

'The blows by which God perfects us—C.S. Lewis? Maybe this marriage falls into that category.'

'I've given up God bothering, remember? And I have tried to make the marriage work.'

'Maybe not tried the right things.'

'So what will I do?'

'One. Don't leave Susan. Part with Melissa. Don't reject her, keep her as a warm memory in your heart, not a possibility. Two. Go home. Do what you can to improve the marriage. Don't judge Susan. Don't try to change her. Don't even wish she were different. Read the story of Abraham. Abraham goes back to where he was first with God, which, in your case, is when you first loved her. Find that place in your heart.'

'What if it doesn't work?'

'Give it five years. The boys will be older. If it hasn't worked by then, maybe give it away.'

He stood up. He looked a lot less burdened. 'Thanks Phil. That's actually good advice.'

A few days later I went and had lunch in town with Susan. It was clear to me she hadn't heard about the Melissa factor and I wasn't going to bring it up. But Martin had threatened to leave and that had shaken her to the core.

Martin was overwrought but Susan wasn't. If anything, she had become a little bitter, and that made her seem a little hard, which wasn't like her. But then she told me some of the things he had said and I saw the trauma she had felt. They were things Martin would say off the top of his head in the heat of the moment. They were things that Susan would take into the depths of her soul, which would scar her. That hardness was her way of protecting herself, it wasn't real. And as she talked, I sensed her terrible sadness and her sense of failure.

'If he does leave,' she began, 'I'll get Les Reese to do my side of the divorce. He represented the wife in a case where Martin represented the husband. Martin and the husband got done like a dinner.'

I felt uncomfortable. I told her what I'd said to Martin about tolerance, acceptance and giving the marriage five years.

'You seem to forget I have already put up with him all this time,' she said. 'I haven't tried to change him. I've tried to accommodate him.' She had tears in her eyes as she said this.

I took her hand. 'No one knows better than me how hard you've tried,' I said. 'But accommodating someone is a little different from accepting someone.'

'I don't try to stop him putting his clothes on the floor anymore,' she said. 'I just pick them up and take them to the laundry.' The whiff of burning martyr was there.

'And I don't expect the children's sport to interfere with his surfing. It's me who takes Joshie to soccer and Ben to swimming.'

I didn't say anything. She was churning underneath. Poor Susan. She struggled. She so wanted life to be right. She so wanted what was best for the boys.

'Divorce does terrible things to children, Phil,' she said, and all her softness, all her love was there again, but it was for her children, not for Martin. 'I've read all the literature. It's actually seen as more catastrophic by some children than the death of a parent.' I wanted to talk more, but she looked at her watch. 'I have to go.' We stood up and as she took my arm; her hands were trembling. 'He'll do exactly what he wants,' she said. 'Thank you for giving the kids another five years. That means a lot.' She had tears in her eyes.

I felt like crying myself. I thought God owed me.

Melissa

After the Thia Toula/Summer Romance fiasco Martin said he needed time. I didn't hold out much hope. At the end of the week he called and we met in a coffee shop. I was sure it would be goodbye. He sat there, a whole lot calmer and told me he'd talked to some priest, and he'd been living in a hotel to give himself time to think. He'd come up with a solution along the lines the priest had suggested.

'I will leave Susan in three years,' he said. He must have seen the look of despair on my face. 'Darling, you'll still only be in your twenties. My kids will be established in school. You know, Ben's just starting school. He's just a baby. And we'll have a whole lifetime together. And for now we'll still see each other like we did before, knowing there's an end in sight. So it's not as if we'd be waiting three years with no contact.'

'Three whole years?' I said. 'Have you any idea how lonely I've been since you left?'

At that moment Summer Romance sort of flew in, in spirit form, Summer Romance in his boxers watching cricket on TV.

There was an embarrassed silence.

'Well you sleep with *her*, don't you?' I said.

'As little as possible,' he said. Which I knew was a lie. Which he knew I knew. 'Look, it was just bad timing, Lissy. I know you had to have other lovers. I know you had to start your life again. It *was* bad timing though.'

And then he spluttered on his coffee and started laughing. And I started laughing, and we were sitting there like a couple of idiots in the coffee shop, just laughing. And then, after a mad mercy dash, three minutes later we were in bed, inside each other's heads and bodies, so inside, in so deep that it felt as if the world would be like that forever.

And it was in those circumstances that I agreed to wait three years for him.

Susan

Phil thought I sounded hard. I had to harden myself but I wasn't hard inside. I hated that the idealism, the hope of the marriage had gone. But it had. When he yelled at me like that, called me a bitch after the car crash, the whole thing felt hollow and empty. And even if he didn't leave, it was out there on the table. He'd said it when he was angry but it was also how he thought and felt. It wasn't an idle threat.

I had to be realistic. Martin threatening to leave was the turning point for me. When he bought the house he'd broken the agreement about money in the marriage. But I'd got over that. And as far as that was concerned, he'd simply gone on his merry way making other financial decisions. Now he'd yelled and ranted at me. Jabbed his finger at me.

I was devastated. I think that broke the thread between us, cut what had kept me hanging onto the marriage emotionally. I was shattered. I went straight to bed but I couldn't sleep all night.

I understood he was upset about the accident but he hadn't told me he just wanted me to pick him up. I thought I'd be at the police station for ages. And I couldn't leave the children. And I can understand he was upset but it wasn't even his fault. He's intelligent but he's got no emotional perspective. How could I leave two sleeping children alone in the house? He could have got a taxi home that night or asked the police to drive him, but he preferred to make it into a drama. It was awful but the young man recovered. I suspect Martin's dramatisation was about himself, not about the man he'd hit.

In the morning poor little Joshie started badgering me about what he'd obviously heard the night before. That night Martin didn't come home and the kids were full of questions again.

'Daddy was upset,' I explained. 'He'd had a car accident and a man was badly hurt. But it wasn't Daddy's fault. He was upset. You can imagine that, can't you?'

'Did the man die?' asked Ben.

'No,' I said. 'But he was hurt so Daddy was upset.'

'Will Daddy go to jail?' Ben asked. 'Can we visit him in jail?'

'No Ben. Don't be silly. It wasn't his fault.'

'Why was Daddy shouting at you?' Josh asked. 'It wasn't your fault.'

'Sometimes they hang people,' said Ben. 'Criminals and bad people.'

'We don't hang people in this country Ben,' I said. 'And it wasn't Daddy's fault. There's no problem. Daddy got upset and he was in a bit of a temper.'

'You say if we have a temper we're not allowed to get mad at other people.'

'Well maybe Daddy forgot that, Joshie. It would be an awful feeling to be in a car accident.'

'So will you get a divorce?'

'Of course not. It was just an argument. He knows it has nothing to do with me.'

'But he shouted at you.'

'Just for a moment.'

'Last night and this morning.'

So it went on until I finally got the boys off to bed, making as light of it as much as I could. Then, the next morning, instead of going straight to work, I stopped at Centennial Park and walked around the lake. I remembered how Martin and I used to come for walks here when I was pregnant. How he poked fun at 'walkies'. How he had never taken my needs and wishes into account. How he'd bought the house. I try not to dwell on the past but it's there.

I thought of the children, of their upset, of their need for stability and order, their desire for Martin and me to be happy. Especially Joshie.

But I wasn't going to put more work into the marriage. I couldn't. It wouldn't work. As far as I was concerned, I'd worked as hard as I could. So my concern was to protect the children. And I was determined to do that.

Martin went away for a week. I had to explain to the kids about the accident again and again, and then why Martin wasn't there, which was hard. Martin evidently didn't give that a thought. For me it was the same old thing, me holding the empty shell of the marriage while he did what he wanted. Nevermind that poor Josh was beside himself. Then Martin came back and announced to me he had decided to stay with me.

'Oh thank you,' I said. 'I'm sure we'll be deliriously happy.'

I was grateful to Phil for buying that extra time, although in the long run it was other things that would keep Martin in the marriage.

Apart from Phil, I talked to Lisa, who was always supportive.

'I think you need to talk to Dad,' she said. 'Just in case he does leave you. Be practical, Suzie.'

Dad understood, but typically for a man, he was shocked that I was thinking of my future in terms of financial security.

'It can't be that bad,' he said. 'Can't you sweet talk him a bit?'

'Dad, we're past that. We're just not suited. It might hang together but he wants to leave. He told me. He's really only staying for the kids, I think.'

'What a bastard. I always knew he wasn't right for you. What a mess this is.'

'He hasn't done anything terrible, Dad. It's just not what I thought it would be.'

'I know all about that,' he said.

'I know you do, but Martin isn't going down that route.'

'What route?'

'With Marg,' I said. 'That route.'

'Life's complicated.'

'Dad, I'm not judging you. Really.'

'What do you want me to do?'

'Look, think about it. But I'd like you to give me a seat on the board.'

'Why on earth? You're not even a partner, Suzie. You told me you didn't want to do your articles.'

'Yes but I am as important as any of the solicitors.'

'Yes . . .'

'But I don't have a stake. Except through you and Martin.'

'So if anything happened to you, and I hope it won't, but even if you retire, I'd like to feel secure here. I'd like to think that if this thing between Martin and me gets to divorce that I still have a place here.'

'Of course you would, darling.'

'There's no "of course" Dad.'

'I'll think about it. But wouldn't you be better off trying to sort out this mess with him? I mean, on a personal level?'

'Dad, I told you . . .'

He came back to me a couple of weeks later. 'I've fixed it. You get a seat on the board. Martin voted for it. I don't see what you're complaining about.'

I felt a bit defeated by that. Maybe I didn't need to be on the board. Maybe the marriage would just go on as it had. Maybe I should try to fix it, again. I felt horribly confused.

CHAPTER 9

1987

Susan

After all the drama with the car accident and Martin threatening to leave, our life seemed to settle down. But something had gone out of the marriage. That was undeniable, but it was also true that things hadn't been right for a long time. I was more clear-headed, less emotional. I saw that the marriage was important. It was important to me that it stayed intact. We had committed to it. We had two children. At times, I felt strangely impersonal about it as if it was almost separate from me, something I had to do, not be part of.

I had wanted it to work. I'd struggled and fought to make it work, yet it didn't. Was it my fault? It felt like it was his, but maybe I'd been pedantic or unyielding. But I'd tried. Maybe I shouldn't have tried. I didn't know. What more could I do?

Martin seemed more relaxed maybe because he was more distant and less engaged, although he couldn't resist having a shot at me now and then. Dad had appointed me to the board of the firm and that gave me a sense of security. It didn't really give me any power to change what Martin might decide to do but it gave me some bargaining chips.

We still had an awful lot of arguments and disagreements. We rubbed each other up the wrong way. I hated it. I knew Josh heard a lot. Ben seemed oblivious but maybe he wasn't. You can never tell with children. I knew it wasn't good for the children. Josh asked me lots of questions, about divorce in particular, but I couldn't really talk to him. I suppose I was protecting myself as well as him. I could see he needed his father and he needed me, but he thought he had to take sides.

'I think it's important to stop arguing in front of the children,' I said to Martin late one night after the children were in bed.

'Be my guest,' he said. 'I think it's important too. You were the one who started in on me about the sunscreen.'

'You being the one who let them get burnt.'

'Tanned,' he said. 'Ben just got a little brown. He wasn't burnt.'

'Let's not go over it again,' I said. 'You ended up yelling at me and storming out.'

'I said there wasn't any point talking to you because you're completely irrational.'

'Josh was crying when I put him to bed.'

'Oh yeah, and how did you bring that on? Tell him the sad story of your life.'

'He was praying when I went into his room. He said, "God, don't let them fight anymore. Please God." Then when he finished he saw me there and he started crying, saying he was sorry but he thought God might help.'

'Oh shit,' said Martin. 'Oh shit.' He didn't say anything more but when we were going to bed, he said he was sorry, I was right, and he'd make sure it didn't happen in front of the kids. He told me his parents had yelled and screamed at each other and he remembered praying about it when he was a child. That's the thing with Martin. It always comes back to him. He can't relate to it any other way.

I needed some degree of goodwill from him to make the

marriage work for the children. I thought about it a lot over Christmas when he was away surfing. I didn't make a fuss about his weekend trips and he did come for a short time on our holiday to the Snowy Mountains, although he went home three days early. He hated the mountains, I loved them, which was like so many things in our marriage.

Alone with the children in the mountains, I realised how insecure I felt. You can't live by rationality alone. It's hard to live with someone in a marriage, without the emotional sense of a marriage. It was hard to know who I was, what I was really trying to do in my life. I knew that I could do everyday things, I could look after my children, do my job, live with Martin, but I wanted more.

I decided I'd make one final attempt to resurrect the marriage as the sort of partnership we had envisaged. We couldn't go back to young love, but I hoped there could be more ease and understanding in the relationship, that we could behave in a more civil and civilised way. We hardly went out together anymore. We sometimes had sex, which he always initiated.

I tried to imagine what it could be like. Civilised, considerate. That felt a bit hollow but it was the best I could summon up.

During the last week of the holidays I was back at work and busy getting the boys' uniforms ready and new shoes and school bags. But I found time to write down all the things we needed to consider. I wrote it as a letter.

Dear Martin,

I think we would both agree that we have arrived at a point in our marriage where neither of us wishes to be. I don't believe we can go back to the beginning, which is what Phil always says we should do. I feel you have broken some fundamental conditions we agreed on for this marriage—that financial decisions should be made jointly and that you would not shout at me and bully me. However, maybe they weren't important to you and you never realised how important they were to me. Maybe we haven't talked about it enough. I feel encouraged that you did respond to my request that we don't argue in front of the children.

It would take a great burden off me if we were to make financial decisions jointly. I would like you to do more with the children, not just for my sake, but for theirs and yours. I would also like to take decisions about the house jointly, rather than me taking them and you complaining in retrospect.

I'd hope that if we could address things like this, we might regain a sense of ease, of the love that brought us together. I'd hope so.

There was more and perhaps it sounded a little impersonal, but the alternative was sounding angry, although as I wrote it, I really felt very angry at times and had to keep toning it down. The letter was long, detailed and carefully worded. I tried to lay out the facts rather than making accusations. I handed it to him and told him what it was about. He looked at me, sadly, I thought, and said he would read it.

A few weeks later, getting ready for bed, I was sitting at the dressing table putting cold cream on my face. He came in and opened the curtains and the windows, which I hate. I need the room dark and still to sleep. He liked light and the sound of the sea.

'Your letter is what's wrong with us, not what's going to fix us,' he said. 'There's nothing about sex or love or affection there. That's what's missing.' He lay down on the bed, facing me.

His body language seemed to imply that if I had sex with him he might consider the rest of the letter.

'I don't like the curtains open,' I said. 'I find it hard to sleep.'

'It's healthy to have fresh air.'

'It's cold. I think we agreed in winter we would have the curtains shut.'

'Bloody rules, rules, rules. Rule 27 for lawnmowing. Rule 45 for clothes washing. Rule 101 for not having the bloody window open. Rule 102 for having it closed. You want more rules and regulations. But I don't want any more! I'm a grown-up, a free agent. Why don't we have some freely given love here? Some commitment? Some passion? Instead of these bloody rules?'

'I'm not having sex as a bribe to get you to talk about our marriage, if that's what you mean,' I said. I lay down on the bed. The curtains were wide open and the wind was coming off the sea. I could hear the surf. I turned around to him. 'I can't even begin to think about sex while you don't respect the fundamentals of how I want our life to be. What about these other things in the letter? Why can't we work on them?'

'Work on a marriage? Work on love. It's a contradiction in terms, isn't it?' He got up and banged about the room for a while. 'Bloody wetsuit. I swear that bloody cleaner moves it. I need it for tomorrow morning.' The implication being I should know where it was. Which I did, but childishly I didn't tell him.

'Forget sex,' he said. 'Why should I care?' Well, *that* was a joke. He cared. It's the way he was made.

'Maybe the passion and commitment are missing because all these other things are out of order,' I said. 'I know the letter sounded angry. I am angry but I was honest too.'

I got up and put the cold cream away. He put his hand out to me. I took it but then he dropped it. I lay down again, facing away from him. I felt the whole thing was hopeless. I was angry—angry and hurt. I couldn't think straight. But if I said anything he'd accuse me of being angry or manipulative.

'I'll do more with the kids,' he said. There was something broken and hurt in his voice. I almost said something but we were already miles apart. He got up and stood at the window, pulling the curtain further open. I could feel the chill of the breeze.

'Your wetsuit's down in the laundry,' I said.

Martin

I had an idyllic summer. There wasn't much on at work and I'd take an afternoon off, have a surf and then see Melissa after she finished work. We'd go out to dinner and then go back to her house and make love. Or sometimes we'd watch TV together and then I'd go home. Her Aunt Toula knew about me. She'd tutt-tutt at me, although she wasn't in any position to. She'd just married George, but she'd been his mistress for twenty-five years until his wife died. The tutt-tutting was all show. I liked Toula and she liked me.

Melissa made me feel incredibly alive. She liked to dance. She loved to surf and she was pretty damn good. She went to parties. She loved movies and comedy shows at pubs. I did things with her that I hadn't done for years. She wore thong underwear and sexy bras. She took her top off in the surf, when we were right out the back of the waves. She had such brown breasts with sweet, firm pink nipples. Oh God, the look of her, the feel of her, the wildness of her.

But it was more than that. It was the closeness, the intimacy. It was being able to look into her eyes, run my finger along her lips, hold her hand while we watched TV, talk about things, laugh together. It was the sense of having someone in my life who loved and cared for me, whom I loved and cared for. We wanted the best for each other.

When Susan and the boys were still in the mountains, Melissa and I took an ecstasy tablet together. I hadn't done any drugs for years. I felt wild, abandoned, energetic. It was a crazy night. We went to a club and danced. We ran along the beach.

'Let's sleep at your house,' she said.

'Oh no, no, no.'

'I want to be your wife,' she said. 'I want to sleep in your bed.'

'It'd be wrong.' Wrong to betray Susan. That was the thought that came to me, except how was I betraying her? Hadn't I already done that? I felt a stab of guilt.

'It's just pretend. I'll never be in that house, I know that. But I just want to pretend. Please.'

'I'll show you it,' I said. 'Then we'll come back here.'

We drove over and I took her through the house and showed her everything. The boys' rooms up in the attic, our bedroom, the conservatory, the family room, everything we'd built and created. It was a very strange feeling, apart from the effect of the ecstasy tablet which made everything more vivid. But there with Melissa I felt like an outsider in my own home.

Melissa looked at the table in the hall, where Susan kept a collection of favourite family photos. Melissa stared as if for the first time realising these people were real. She got down on her knees and looked at the photos one by one. She was seeing my life. She picked up one of Ben, taken when he was three, upside down on some monkey bars. Susan had been furious that I let him, but it was the most fantastic photo, his face all lit up, his curls hanging down. Melissa looked at it for ages.

'Like you,' she said. 'Wild and free.'

I felt the weight of the house, the weight of the marriage. The phone rang. I picked it up. Melissa came and sat at my feet, running her hands up my legs, under my shorts, turning me on.

'Hi Martin. It's Lisa. Jamie and I were wondering if you'd like to come over and have dinner with us tomorrow, seeing as you're batching it.'

I liked Lisa and Jamie. Lisa was like Susan, except she had a pragmatic, everyday streak. Lisa liked me, although she was totally loyal to Susan.

'That's sweet of you, Leese, but I've got to prepare this big case going to trial any minute.'

'Oh, Susan told me there's nothing on at the moment.'

'Came in while she was away,' I said. 'A drug case. Oh God!' Melissa had her face pressed against me, rubbing up and down, moaning. I leant down and pinched her nipple.

'Ouch!'

'What?' said Lisa.

'A spider,' I said. I tried to hold Melissa prisoner between my legs but she was doing things with her tongue. 'I've got rid of it now.' Melissa escaped and was standing behind me, kissing my neck. 'North coast case,' I went on. 'Guilty as hell but it's a matter of getting the sentence down from the maximum.'

There was no case at all and it was stupid to give her that detail. I didn't know what she and Susan talked about, but they did talk two or three times a week. It was the 'e' making me blab. And Melissa biting on my ear.

'Why don't you and Jamie and the kids come out on Sunday? Susan's back Saturday and she'd love to catch up, I'm sure.' And she'd be sure to ask me about the case on Sunday. I was digging my own grave.

'Okay, lovely,' said Lisa. 'We'll bring the meat for a barbecue.'

I got off the phone and fell down on Melissa laughing. 'Spider,' I hissed. 'My spider.' We made love on the floor. It was wonderful at first. But afterwards, lying there, I knew it wasn't right, the two lives, together in the same room. It was wrong to bring her there. My two lives had to be separate. It was the only way it could work. My guilt was ameliorated by the fact that the whole thing was only for three years. But the truth was, I couldn't bear to think about it too much.

God was smiling on me. The very next day a big drug case came in and I said I'd take it, which surprised everyone in the office because I had said I didn't want to take any more junkie cases. It got me through the Sunday barbecue, which was just as well, because Lisa asked me a lot of questions about it, all in front of Susan. Maybe she had her suspicions. The details weren't the same as what I'd told her before but I fudged over that. I caught her looking at me quizzically.

Not long after that Susan handed me the letter outlining all my faults. At first I thought that maybe, even if there were two lives, I owed it to her to make the one with her as good as possible for the three years. So I looked at it. A lot of what she said about the house and the boys was true but she never acknowledged her part in that. She'd given me such a time about buying the house, that I'd let her make all the decisions after that. Now she was complaining about it.

And then there was a whole lot about my work—that really got to me.

As you know, over the years, I have put a tremendous amount of effort into supporting and promoting your career. I have made sure you get the cases most suited to your talents. I developed a scheduling system that almost automatically keeps every case up to date. I have provided you with copies of relevant judgements, and I have promoted you in the media as an expert in the area of family law. In addition, I have increased your billings by meticulous accounting for hours and costs. But you've never even acknowledged this, let alone thanked me.

Bullshit! I'd earned the money to keep her and the kids for the first six years in the marriage. It was entirely her decision to go back to work. And to be brutally frank, it was what she was paid for.

There was no bloody heart in it. No wanting it to be right for us. She felt nothing, whereas I still felt something for her, that was the hard bit. God, I still wanted her. I knew her better than any other person on the face of the Earth, but she didn't seem to have a clue who I was. I'd pursued her, cared for her, looked after her. I desired her, wanted her. She didn't want me, which was exactly why we were in this mess. Occasionally we had sex, but not with great enthusiasm or passion. I wished I could stop wanting her. I don't know why I did want her. I didn't want her like I wanted Melissa, but I did want her. And she threw it in my face.

She got to me about the kids. I felt guilty as hell about that. I'd always sworn I'd never put my kids through what I went through as a kid. I'd withdrawn from them. I needed to change that. That was it.

When she came back to work there was a big media frenzy going on about divorce. It blew up regularly, fanned by the media in low news times. The government was in a rage about divorce because the deserted mothers and kids were costing a lot in social services, although they didn't like to say so and lose the single mothers' vote. The divorced fathers were in such a rage that it seemed that the next step in Family Court security would be guards with machine guns. According to the papers the divorce rate showed no sign of abating. The moral fabric of society was disintegrating. Certainly the idealism of the no-fuss divorce was long gone.

So my old mate Cliff convened an hour-long TV special. You know, one of those things with the experts out the front—the articulate and opinionated—with a deeply divided, opinionated and generally uninformed audience. The great unwashed. If you can't make good TV out of a social crisis you should be working in a box factory

Susan got wind of it and got me on. I gave my usual spiel about enforcing judgments on maintenance. And made the quote that got me on the front pages. 'I'm not ashamed to call myself a feminist, if that is what it means.'

Susan gave me grief about that. 'A TV feminist,' she said. 'Pity it doesn't extend to how you live your life.'

A low barb. But it hit the bullseye. Somewhere I wasn't too happy about how I was living my life.

Josh

Mum said there was no divorce. I couldn't ask Dad. I asked Auntie Mary when we were on one of those long bushwalks she loves. Ben came too. We stopped to make a campfire and boil a billy, which was the best part.

'Are Mum and Dad going to divorce?' I asked.

She came over and hugged me. 'Oh Joshie, you worry, don't you love?'

'Are they?'

'Why do you think that?'

'No reason.' I put some sticks in the fire.

'You think there might be some reason?' she asked, 'for them to get a divorce?'

'Maybe.'

'No,' said Ben. 'There isn't.'

'Would them getting a divorce be a good idea?' asked Auntie Mary. 'Or a bad idea?'

'Bad.'

'You're worried because things are bad now. Even without a divorce.'

'No. Just divorce.'

She sat there building the fire up. Later she talked to me when Ben was off playing down the creek. She told me about Grandma and Grandpa fighting when she was little. She used to get sick in the stomach. I got sick in the stomach when she talked about it and I didn't know what to do. Auntie Mary didn't know. Later, she rang me up and said she was sorry she didn't have an answer. There wasn't one. She wanted to tell me she wouldn't tell anyone what I said.

I was going to ask Auntie Lisa, but I didn't because she might tell Mum. But their house was different. Uncle Jamie kissed her a lot and she sat on his knee. They had pizza out of a box too.

Phil

I had been totally ineffectual in helping Susan and Martin with their relationship. Martin had decided not to leave and had given up Melissa, but neither of them showed the slightest sign of accepting the other person, or at looking what the marriage had going for it. It was as if they had simply arrived at a point where they had decided to tolerate one another. When I went there for Sunday lunches, I felt a distance between them. At best it was play-acting.

'Did you buy the basil?'

'I thought you were going to buy the basil.'

'When you took the children down to the beach I asked you to buy the basil.'

'When I was getting their swimmers, you said you were going to the shops.'

'Not to get the basil.'

'Well, I thought someone going to the shops would get basil, rather than someone going to the beach.'

'You had already said that you would buy the basil.'

'Maybe I get confused with what I'm supposed to do and the things I'm not supposed to do. I was just thinking common-sense. I'm so sorry.'

I came home feeling very depressed.

I was over forty. I'd say ministers of religion generally suffer as many, if not more, human ills as any other group in society—alcoholism, promiscuity, gambling, broken marriages, abusive relationships, sexual perversions, criminality (of the *very* white-collar kind), and mid-life crises, which was what I was suffering.

In the early days of my career I had a very rich spiritual life and I felt that God would reveal my path. But He didn't. Or maybe He did and I didn't have the humility to see it. I liked being at the school but I was restless again. I wanted to get married but I didn't take any steps to find someone to share my life with. Mary made an occasional sinful appearance in my life. In fact I don't know why I felt it was so sinful because it didn't harm anyone and it quietened my sexual longings. Although I liked Mary tremendously, the sex *was* odd. She was fulfilling her desire to bed and corrupt a priest, albeit of the wrong denomination, and I was too lustful and too guilty to look beyond that.

Religious fundamentalism was beginning to overtake the school, although it was valiantly resisted by the chaplain. Conservative parents complained when I taught myths and legends as part of religion. I could sense a vice tightening around my life and my spirit. I felt a sense of desperation to find a place in the world.

Susan and Martin were more of a lynchpin for my emotional life than I could acknowledge, even to myself. And they were in such a mess.

I began feeling quite crazy, which isn't a good way for a man of the cloth to feel. People don't want a loon in a dog collar.

I worried a lot about John 1:1. *In the beginning was the Word, and the word was with God, and the Word was God.* Well, that's one translation, but I stayed up nights, poring over it in the original Greek. People have argued about this verse forever. You can imagine it at three in the morning.

My dear father died and I returned to England for a brief visit to my family. Back in Australia, immersed in bible study with a group of Year 12 boys, I began to feel that it was the Bad News Bible, that God was vengeful and unfair.

Drumming up some vestiges of zeal, I organised a holiday excursion to New Guinea with a group of boys from the midschool to visit an orphanage which our school had been supporting for years. The trip would help bring me and them back to the fundamentals of Christ's message. I organised flights, inoculations, permissions, on-ground transport, all with frantic energy. On the plane I collapsed with a whisky.

The orphanage was the most horrible place, absolutely steeped in poverty, situated on the edges of Port Moresby. It was poverty our money wouldn't fix. It was an under-resourced, overcrowded, ugly place, run by people with no sense of the love of Christ, or giving or mission. The headmaster was cruel and beat the children. The children cowered and knew God only in His punitive role. It was hot, dusty, unforgiving. There was no redemption in any of it. I got malaria and dysentery and came back home in a shocking state. I'd looked after the boys but I had forgotten to take the medication myself. I took a term off.

Susan came to see me while I was in a malarial fever. The moment I saw her the fever turned into a rave.

'Or lives are pointless. We have to find something, seek something higher and better. You and Martin, there's an ugliness about it. It's not right. The world should be better. Scrape the surface and there's ugliness. You must forgive Martin. He must forgive you. You must go back to where God is, when you looked at each other with adoration, when you saw what was right, not what was wrong.'

'Phil, you're not well at all.' She went to the bathroom and got a cold cloth and laid it on my forehead. 'We're all right. You mustn't worry about Martin and me.'

'Love! The love! The love! You have to have love.' I was delirious but I can remember everything I said. Through the haze of that afternoon it was as if a little voice was prompting me from off-stage. To say it! Finally. To tell her! Maybe, I thought, it was God. God, by his very nature, you'd expect to be on-stage, but that's a mistake. God mostly works off-stage as a prompter.

I took her hand. 'Do you love him?'

'Not the way I did.' Her voice was flat and hard.

'So how do you live with him?'

'In holy matrimony, Phil,' she said with a touch of irony. 'God ordains holy matrimony, doesn't he? For the children really,' she added.

'I love you Susan!' I said fervently. I could feel what was missing in my life. My temperature was nearly forty-one, and I was dripping with sweat, shaking. I was forty-one years old. The same number as my temperature! My youth had gone! But finally I knew what I needed in my life. 'I really, really, really love you Susan! Oh God, help me! Help me!'

'I love you too. Very much.' She took her hand out of mine and stood up. 'This is a very high fever. I'm a little worried. I'll call Doctor Burgman.'

She knew it wasn't the fever. It was the fever that made me speak but the feeling was there. But we never spoke of it again. The friendship didn't cool but its balance changed. She was very kind to me, very considerate, as if I was recovering from something else beside malaria. It was almost a year before she told me anything more about her and Martin.

Melissa

When I first met Martin, I was twenty. I was a student, I had no real plans beyond my next exam. I had dreams of my own business, of owning a house, but my life was free floating.

So when he came back, it was different. I was only twenty-three, but I was working. I knew where I was going in terms of business. Pretty soon after things started with Martin again, Thia Toula had married George, leaving a decent interval of two months after his wife died. Then I paid rent for her house and I bought things for it and decorated it in my own style. It was nominal rent but it made it my place. Thia Toula didn't have a key anymore.

Mum used to come and visit and helped me with the decorating. She'd been annoyed about me getting together with the Greek rellies, but she became reconciled to it. 'Get what you can,' she said, but with a laugh. Mum sometimes stayed a night, and we would have fun barbecuing out on the balcony or getting fish and chips. God! I loved it. I love my mother and she's a great inspiration to me.

Anna had been overseas acting in a British film. As soon as she was back we had regular gatherings at my place with her new boyfriend Nick and her other friends who were in the acting business. Plus there were people from the Surf Club where I was doing lifesaver training, which I totally loved. I was starting up my own business, managing sports stars, so I was pretty busy working out the finances of that and doing the business plan. Mum helped me. She was right behind me.

So Martin came into the life of a busy and successful young woman on the way up. The last time, he'd walked into a vacuum which he had filled up.

'I have three questions for you. Why? Why? And number three question—why?' said Anna when I told her and Nick what was happening with Martin and me. 'You're nuts.'

'I told a sheila I was going to leave my wife just last week,' said Nick. 'It's a good trick. She dropped her knickers in no time. And hey, I don't even have a wife.' He moved out of Anna's kicking range. 'Seriously, it's the oldest bloody trick in the book. And I love the three years. That gives it *real* credibility.'

'Did he tell you his wife doesn't understand him?' asked Anna.

'Well, she doesn't.'

Nick hooted. 'That he's never felt like this before?'

Anna started giggling. 'That it's just the kids keeping him there?'

Nick put his arms round Anna. 'That he's never had sex like this before?'

'Those things might be clichés because they're true!' I said, but not with great conviction.

'Oh yeah,' said Nick. 'Clichés are true. Let me see—it's young love. Or *true* love maybe? He swept you off your feet. And of course, love conquers all, especially when you're head over heels. You're his love goddess, he's your first love. That makes it *so* special. Love hurts, but you love him to death. He's the apple of your eye and for him, the love of a good woman—'

'Shut up, Nick,' I said.

'Very darn clever, Nick,' said Anna. She looked at me. 'Can't you see though? The clichés are true, right to the one where he doesn't leave his wife. Melissa darling, married men *don't* leave their wives—in three months, three years or three decades.'

'Take our mate John,' said Nick. 'Madly in love with a married man. Married man finally understands he's gay, finally understands he's been living a lie. Sizzling sex. But does this married man leave his wife? No! It's John that slits his wrists and spends two weeks in St Vincents.'

They went on and on. I denied it, nursed the specialness of Martin and me, remembered everything Martin had said, the sex, being at his house. I could see there was a problem. I could see that they had a reason for their concern. So I made a deal with Anna. I would try something else.

I hunted down the Summer Romance. His name was Jimmy. He was an Irish backpacker with a good line of patter, a lovely Irish brogue and blue eyes. He was still living in the same back-packers' house down the road.

'I'm sorry about what happened, chucking you out of my place,' I said. 'It was very bad manners.'

'Christ, you Australians,' he said. 'You can see you're descended from the Irish. Except you've gone feral.'

'I'm half Greek,' I said. 'I don't want to bullshit you.'

'You're half Greek, sweetheart. So I don't want to bullshit *you*. You've probably got a village full of swarthy fellows waiting to defend your honour.'

'Look,' I said. 'I'm madly in love with him. But everyone tells me I'm crazy because he's married and he says he's going to leave his wife in three years.

'Excuse me if I join in the general hilarity,' said Jimmy.

'So maybe I thought I should just try a little harder with someone else. Maybe I am young and naive.'

'Pleased to be of service,' he said. 'I presume you're asking me to sleep with you?'

'Yes. On a trial basis.'

'Last time it wasn't a trial at all.'

'Good.'

'Is he going to come busting in again?'

'No, I promise.'

'Promises promises.'

So I slept with Jimmy. I liked him, I really liked him but it had got off on the wrong foot. I mean he wasn't going to woo me and fall in love with me. He knew he was just an experiment. And so did I. I was doing it to prove I loved Martin. And I did love Martin. But I did have doubts. Three years seemed so long.

I slept with Jimmy twice and I began to like him more. He was smart. He was funny, he was unattached. He loved surfing, and for an Irishman, he was good.

'I hope you've got over your friend,' he said in the morning.

'Because I'm going over the Nullarbor tomorrow. And then somewhere called Broome. And then Uluru. And some other hot and crazy places. And much as I like you, Miss Meliss, I can't see our future writ up in lights. Can you?'

'No,' I said. 'But thanks. You're a lovely guy.'

Martin was away and that week I thought about Jimmy quite a lot. Not as much as I thought about Martin, but enough to unsettle me. A week later I saw Jimmy down the Esplanade with a girl. He didn't see me, but I felt rejected. And then Martin called me, and his voice sent shivers through me. It's fate, I thought, a sign. I'm meant to be with Martin, despite what everyone else said.

Mary

Martin told me he was back with Melissa. He was back in love, happy, getting loads of sex, more himself.

'Then you have to make the decision,' I said. 'How serious is it?'

'Very,' he said. 'I'm leaving.'

'Well, it's sad, but it's probably the best decision. When are you leaving?'

'Three years.'

'Three years?'

'Yes.'

'Isn't that a little unfair?'

'I don't think so.'

'It puts everything on hold.'

'Not really.'

'You'll never sustain it. Two lives, three years.'

'It'll be fine.'

'I think it's unfair to her.'

'It's not. The boys will be that much older. The house payments will be down to nothing. It gives her time to see that it can't work. I tell you, Susan will see a separation in a very positive light in three years. All the heat will be out of it.'

'I meant Melissa. It's not fair to Melissa.'

'Oh,' he said. Then he collected himself. 'She's prepared to wait. We've talked it over.'

'It's a very bad arrangement, Marty.'

'I hardly think you're in a position . . .'

'Don't lawyer me.'

'All right, tell me why you think it's so bad for Melissa.'

'Susan too,' I said. I think that was the first time I had ever considered Susan's welfare. But on balance, over the years, I had reluctantly come to admire her, perhaps even like her a little.

I bought him another drink and explained in words of one syllable. Marty is a wonderful person but he does tend to see things from his point of view.

He phoned me a week later. 'That was good what you told me. I can see it is hard for Melissa. But I adore her and I'm really trying to make it work for her.'

He can be sweet too, as well as stupid. I told him it was a disaster waiting to happen.

Lisa

I had a stepdaughter running wild. Jamie was being retrenched from his job and Rosie was having her umpteenth ear operation. The PE teacher at school was marrying an ex-pupil and I was out of my mind worrying what the papers might say if they got hold of it. Then Susan came over and told me she was having problems communicating with Martin. I was so scattered and mad I wasn't sure I actually communicated with anyone, certainly not enough to have problems in communicating. I just wasn't doing it. Jamie and I seemed to kiss in the morning, kiss is the evening, but there was hardly time for deep and meaningfuls.

Susan had told me about the letter earlier in the year. I think she should have let the work thing go. Dad had complained about Martin on and off and he probably was disorganised, but no one can tell me that Martin was a total dud. Well, Dad even admitted their family law division was the biggest in the city and that it made a bigger profit than anything else apart from their commercial work.

I loved Susan, and I admired her so much. I thought she could have done a lot for Martin. In a way, she had. It hurt her that he didn't notice.

And I thought he'd do a lot for her, but what works for Martin with a lot of people, his charm, just did not make an impact with Susan.

But maybe, as much as anything, it was about sexual appetite and passion. I began to wonder whether he had affairs, because the two of them just weren't compatible. Even on holidays he always came back early. That was a bit suspect if you ask me.

But there is something about being sisters. She saw I was stressed and took me out to dinner. We went Italian which was nice, because it was warm and intimate, although Susan, as usual, wanted the sauce without cream and no added salt and nothing with bacon. But that's just Susan. And she gave me some totally off the mark advice about the wayward stepchild. She thought Ben was hard to handle. Ben was a middle-of-the-road kid in a family of over achievers. He was gorgeous and sociable and impulsive, but there was no way he was going to get a girl pregnant or get picked up for selling drugs outside the school where I was headmistress. Which was pretty much where June was heading. I guess that sounds harsh, and it was a little, but sometimes I thought Susan didn't appreciate how easy her life was.

Anyway, she was sympathetic. She had talked to Jamie about some contract work. For which I was truly grateful, except when I was on my lasagne, after an entrée of garlic prawns, and she was still fiddling with a green salad, I felt a pang of 'why aren't I more like Susan?' Why can't I lose weight? But it was a momentary thought. I'm not like her, and anyway that control and self-discipline does have a cost.

She thought about relationships in a totally different way, almost analytically, but maybe that was also to do with where her marriage had taken her.

'We're committed to this,' she told me. 'So it's a matter of being able to communicate to Martin my needs and the needs of the children.'

'Maybe writing a letter wasn't the way to go,' I suggested. Over dessert (me gelati, Susan, black decaf) she agreed with me.

'I know. It was wrong. I don't know what I was thinking. I should know Martin better. He reacted very emotionally.'

'Which is what you expect in marriage,' I said. 'An emotional reaction.'

'I guess I'm scared of the emotions,' she said. 'The emotions bring us to hostility and aggression and flare ups and arguments. I wanted agreement on the basics.'

'The basics are the emotions. It's Martin wanting you and you not wanting him. It's companionability and living together.

Maybe it doesn't matter what the words are. It's letting things go that aren't important. I can't think when Jamie and I last sat down and had a rational discussion. We have a PMT row every month or so, but basically, it's just two people looking out for each other.' I was pleading with her to see things differently.

'We're not like that.' She looked pained. 'Maybe I'm not like that.' She had tears in her eyes. 'I can't be someone else.'

'Oh Suzie. You can only be yourself. But you've got such a good heart, maybe that's what you need to be offering, however difficult it is. Maybe that's the direction you should be heading. Instead of trying to put everything in order. You're so good at order, but in a marriage, order isn't everything.'

We talked around this a bit more. Martin wasn't bad, she agreed, only the wrong person for her. He was self absorbed, insensitive. And he was demanding. I read this as he wanted sex more than she did. This was as painful as ever for Susan and I changed the subject. I remembered that holiday at the beach when I stood naked on the balcony. I had the feeling back then that she'd wanted to do it too. She'd laughed about it, responded to it, but it wasn't her.

'It's admirable what you're doing, trying to save the marriage for the children. But if it can't work, you've got to let it go. I know the kids will survive. They're good, robust children. I see lots of kids who survive divorce. They go through a lot. They suffer a lot. They learn a lot. A couple of years on, they're no different from any other child.'

'I guess not,' she said. 'I have actually thought about that. I know it's possible. But it scares me to death, just putting them through that.'

'Do you think we're better off because our parents stayed together?' I asked her.

'Well, at least we didn't go through the trauma of divorce. At least we grew up in an intact family.'

'Do you include Dad's secretary in that "intact family"?' I asked.

She laughed. 'I actually get on with her all right. I mean, it's never acknowledged but she knows I know. It works for them I suppose. Not for Mum, but I'm not sure anything much works for Mum.' She paused. 'I sometimes worry I'm like her. You don't think I am, do you?'

'I can't imagine sitting with Mum, and her having tears about her marriage and feeling all this heartache and pain. Can you?'

'No.'

'So put that out of your head. This marriage mightn't work. You've tried, and Martin has too, in his way. And perhaps maybe the more you understand divorce is possible,' I said, 'the more creatively you can deal with it.'

'It's not just the children,' she said. 'It's also the sense that I've failed.

That's the problem with Susan. She does succeed in most things. Success or failure. Right or wrong. Black or white. Most people expect failure or compromise, so success is an occasional unexpected pleasure. Susan has higher standards. She does not like to fail.

CHAPTER 10
1988

Martin

The world I shared with Melissa was totally different from anything I'd ever known. There was a closeness, a meeting of minds, a natural intimacy, which simply flowed between us. It existed on a physical level, then flowed through to an emotional level. We both craved physical closeness, and we were passionate in our sex life. I did things I never did with Susan. We played games and invented fantasies. We tried a hundred different positions. She loved the smell and the feel of me. She wanted me. It was rain after a drought.

I loved Melissa. It was different from the love I had felt when I met Susan. With Susan, I had been trying to win her, to arrive at the heart of her, to be allowed to share her, mind, body and soul. With Melissa, it just happened. There was no striving, no effort. It was an immediate and deep understanding.

It made me resentful of Susan. But I still wanted Susan. We still made love, although not very often. I wanted not to want her, but my head isn't made that way. I was there in bed with her. We were married. It seemed natural to have sex, although she didn't think so. And when we did, I thought of Melissa.

Melissa and I loved the sea. We liked sleeping nude, long hot days and nights. We were both volatile. We'd shout and argue, then it was gone. And she was much more emotionally practical than I was. Or Susan, for that matter.

'I had a bastard of a day,' I'd say.

'Poor baby,' she'd say, massaging my neck.

Whereas Susan tried to analyse things. 'What exactly happened?' Susan would have asked.

'I had this conference. Jones versus Jones. We lost control of it. The husband and wife were yelling at each other.'

'It's better not to conference those cases,' Susan would have said. 'You should think about it beforehand. Make it part of a checklist. You know that list I've already given you. We could add "Potential for conflict".'

'Oh yes,' I said. 'Potential for verbal violence, potential for physical violence, potential for abuse of me, either verbal or physical, potential for me decking someone, potential for you walking in on a brawl, potential for arson later on. Come on.'

'And we should have procedures for terminating at the point where conflict does arise,' said Susan without missing a beat. 'There'd be all sorts of liability if there was a physical dispute.'

'Yeah, would they pay for my teeth or would I pay for theirs?'

'Martin, this is a serious matter.'

'Susan, this is the end of a very long and stressful day.'

'I was only trying to help.'

Maybe it's unfair, but what Melissa said always left me feeling I could handle it, whereas what Susan said always made me feel I'd handled it badly. Melissa gave me energy. Susan's responses put me on notice.

Perhaps the worst thing was that the comparison was always there for me. I wanted to let go of Susan, stay in the marriage for the boys and break cleanly after three years. I still thought

I could do it but the dogged presence of Susan in my head, with me point scoring against her, counting her wrongs, nursing my rights, also made me feel I was letting Melissa down.

Susan

Any sense of faith I had had now seemed to fail me—in life, in God, in whatever. Life wasn't so much the mystery that Phil and I had talked about. Instead it felt more like a catastrophe. I'd lost my way in everyday life. I needed guidance, parameters, a sense of direction. I sang in the choir at the local church but I felt the need for more strength, more passion, more commitment. The tensions of everyday life overwhelmed me—the squabbles, the burden of it.

I confided in Phil, and while he was sympathetic he was starting to get a little nutty. He always delighted me because he was so idealistic, so mystical, so imaginative. But he lived a very protected life in some ways. He was a single man supported by the church. What *could* he know about relationships?

And I talked to Lisa. Lisa is a wonderful person, but she's very concrete with her solutions. I felt lost.

'Tell Mrs White I'm running late,' I said to Josh one morning as I dropped the boys off. 'I can't keep the appointment with her. Say I'll phone her and talk to her.' That morning I just couldn't go into the school, I don't know why. I despised people who told white lies. I despised myself even more for making Joshie deliver the message.

'You told her that last week, Mummy,' he said.

Life started to unravel. I was doing all the usual things but I found myself less and less able to do them. I'd wrestle and struggle with myself but it didn't work. I had a fear eating away at me, and I didn't know what it was about.

At work, I'd be sitting at my desk, making a list of things to do and my eyes would fill with tears. I'd have to shut my office door and pull myself together. I'd always pushed things forward. Now it seemed as if things were simply running and I wasn't needed. Even Martin's cases ran like clockwork now. I'd sit at my desk and think how I'd devoted myself to this legal practice and its success. What did it matter? It was just a law firm office, not a great and noble cause. I'd spent years helping Martin with his career but he didn't even notice.

What had happened to the woman who had been doing her masters in English literature, the woman who sang solo at St James? Now I sang at the local church, my voice wasn't what it had been. I felt as if my life had been put aside for other people, other things. I'd lost myself.

I wanted a way to keep me from feeling the sadness and fear that welled up within me. I hated feeling so bitter towards Martin. I felt as if not only the world had forgotten me, but God had too.

I couldn't help how I felt about Martin. He'd been the instrument of so much of my unhappiness, but he was unwilling to acknowledge that. And it certainly wasn't possible to share much with him.

He was happy. I resented that. He hated work, in an abstract way. He had his surfing and his touch football. He read a lot and started going to films. I don't like the cinema but he began to go regularly. He was true to his promise and took more responsibility for the boys. I was jealous of that too. As their mother I looked after them, taught them things, read to them, checked their homework, prepared their meals, organised their schedules. They loved me but they complained to me and about me.

Martin just had to turn up to a soccer match and he became their hero. He lapped it up. He took them to soccer all that winter, while I sat at home paralysed, unable to do anything, anxious, jealous, scared of losing them to him.

I stopped giving our regular Sunday lunches. I simply couldn't do it.

I made a decision to cut my working week down to three days to see if I could regain my sense of balance. It meant a substantial cut to my income and things were tight. We had school fees and I'd insisted on a new bathroom for the boys and a proper laundry, which cost almost double what we'd budgeted. Somehow I took that as my fault, although it didn't come anywhere near all the things that Martin had spent recklessly over the years. He'd spent thousands on a pair of antique gates for the house, which was silly because it wasn't the sort of house for gates. He'd bought them on an excursion with his father, who loved buying junk with a touch of grandiosity. We'd had a fight about it, and he'd got sulky and still hadn't organised for anyone to install them.

I didn't need to feel guilty but I did.

'It's your decision,' he said, when I told him I was cutting my workload. 'But we won't be able to afford Betty.' Betty was our nanny, who had been with us since the children were tiny. She still came in the afternoons to look after the boys when they came home from school, to pick them up if they were late, to take them to sport, to mother them when I wasn't there.

'I'm keeping Betty,' I said. 'I need her on the days I do work.'

'Well, I'm sick of bloody Betty.' Betty annoyed Martin because she refused to do housework. She was a nanny, not a char. I thought that was reasonable.

'She's the boys' nanny, not yours. And they adore her.'

'Well then, the cleaner.'

'I'm not getting rid of the cleaners. I need two days off, not two days cleaning.'

'So what's the solution? Things are tight, you've said so.'

'We could sell off those gates, couldn't we? Maybe the custom-made board? Or your naïve kookaburra you're always telling me is worth such an enormous amount. Or send back those awful American shirts you insisted on ordering out of that catalogue and you've never worn.'

He wouldn't hold my eye. He shuffled through the day's mail.

'We lead a very good life,' I said. 'And this isn't forever, although I don't want to be bound to working.'

'But it's okay for me to be bound to work?' he snapped.

'I thought we agreed my primary responsibility was for the children.'

'Except they're at school during the two days you have off. And you still have bloody Betty. Sorry, I don't get this primary responsibility.'

'I'm feeling very rundown,' I said. 'I simply can't work at the moment.' I wanted to say I organised the house, kept the family running, took responsibility for the kids, liaised with the school, as well as working. I wanted to say this was my life, that it counted, but it all seemed too trivial, too small, when set against his work.

'Okay!' he said and threw up his hands. 'You're stressed. But *you* work out how we'll manage. You're the financial genius.'

'You could cut out some of those weekend conferences,' I said. 'I don't think they're necessary.'

'The firm pays for them.'

'Admin expenses are paid for by the firm, but expenses like these come off your fees. I explained that to you a hundred times.'

'Oh yeah, the company version of the three-basket laundry system.'

'Nobody else seems to be baffled by it. Even the ones who aren't Oxford graduates.'

'Anyway I thought I was supposed to network.'

'Well yes, but there have been an awful lot recently. And flying to places for cases when most of it could be done by phone.'

'Isn't that my decision? Professionally?'

'Maybe think about whether it's needed. And cut your personal expenditure.'

'Oh great! I'll start taking a cut lunch. And maybe I should get the bus home. And give up my membership at the surf club.'

'Look, Martin. We're not poor people.'

'Certainly not. We've got a new bathroom and laundry and a nanny and a cleaner. We're so rich you don't even have to work anymore!'

'I'm still working three days a week. Which is a lot more than a lot of people with kids aged eleven and eight do. I just can't cope anymore. I need some respite.'

'Okay. Fine. Do it.' But he said it coldly, and walked out of the kitchen. A moment later he reversed down the drive, way too fast. I didn't know where he was going and he didn't come back till late that night.

I took the boys to the museum to get information for Josh's science project and went to bed straight after dinner.

Phil

I was in trouble. I'd recommended that our school stop funding the orphanage in New Guinea. I'd not only recommended it but

I made a great song and dance about it, about the immorality of sending money to that place. Of course the place turned out to be the baby of some church luminary. I should have let it go at that point. But I wouldn't, sitting up there on my moral high horse. Instead, I asked the boys in my religion classes to contribute to a village in Nigeria run by another church organisation.

The school chaplain asked me to keep supporting the school in New Guinea. He was a good man. He promised he would work to restructure our contribution so that it went to teaching materials only, and he'd see if there was a way we could transfer the headmaster who worked there.

'What about sacking him?' I asked.

'Phil,' he said. 'It's you they're talking of sacking. Help me out here. Let this New Guinea thing go. Forget about the Nigerian village or at least make your contribution privately.'

'I'm reluctant,' I said.

'I'm reluctant too,' he said. 'I'm reluctant to help you when you won't help yourself. You're being pig-headed.'

'So don't help me,' I said.

'Think!' he said. 'I love what you do with the boys. You've got a gift. But there are plenty of people who'd actually like to see you out of here. You're high maintenance.'

'I'm sorry,' I said. 'Just this place in New Guinea . . .'

He looked annoyed. 'You're not going to change anything there. Firstly, there's a brochure that's already been printed showing a picture of the place. So it is somebody's baby. If you persist you'll probably lose your job and have a hell of a time getting another one. And for some unknown reason I'm trying to set it up so you can take over my job when I leave.'

'It's just that place was so—'

'Phil, stop! If you feel strongly enough about it, resign over the issue, try to change things from outside. But be prepared to go to another city because it'll be hard for you to work here in Sydney. That's how near the edge this thing is. Make your choice.'

Another city? Susan, I thought. I couldn't leave Susan. So although I didn't quite drop the Nigerian village, I kept a lower profile.

Susan was not well. She'd stopped her Sunday lunches and lost weight. She was working less and delegated more of what she did with the boys to the nanny and Martin.

One afternoon we were sitting out in her tiny courtyard, drinking tea.

'The Vicar and his lady friend,' I said lightly, pouring her another cup. 'So here we are.'

'Yes,' she said listlessly. 'I should be watching the boys swimming.'

'In my experience boys swim quite well without watching,' I said.

'Ben asked me to come and time him,' she said. 'The squad coach won't do it. And it's his carnival next week.'

'Are you going to the carnival?' I asked.

'I'll have to,' she said.

'Susan,' I said. 'You seem so sad.'

'Swimming carnivals lose their gloss after a while.'

'Has anything in your life got any gloss at the moment?'

'Not at the moment.'

I could see tears in her eyes. 'Oh Susan, I hate to see you unhappy.'

Susan began to cry, silently, tears running down her cheeks. 'I'm so useless, Phil, so useless. You know, the boys don't need me, work doesn't need me. Rodgers said last week he heard of an office manager on $20,000. I earn much more than that. And Martin doesn't need me.'

I sat closer to her and put my arm around her, and stroked her hair. 'Susan, you're . . .'

At that moment Martin drove up the driveway with the boys. I thought he'd be horrified to see me with my arm round his wife, but he got the boys out of the car and shooed them into the house.

'Have a shower, hang your togs out and put on your PJs,' he yelled. 'Then we'll have the biggest fry-up in the history of the world.' Ben ran inside without a glance at us but Joshie looked at me holding his mother, then ran in.

Martin walked over. I guess it became clear to him that I was comforting Susan, not embracing her. Maybe it had been clear to him from the start, and I was the one who didn't know what I was doing.

'Hey, sweetheart,' he said to her. 'What's the matter?' He put his hands on her shoulder, but she got up to fiddle with the tea things.

'I'm okay,' she said. 'I was just telling Phil about that business with Rodgers saying I was only worth $20,000, and no one stuck up for me.' She looked at him.

'I sent a memo round the office,' he said. 'Demolishing that particular argument very soundly. I didn't suggest a rise outright because it would have looked like self-interest but the facts certainly suggested it."

'I'll fix the boys up,' Susan said.

'I'll fix the boys,' Martin said. 'You sit down and chat with Phil. He picked her up and twirled her round. But not with love. It was somehow an ironic gesture. It showed on his face, and on hers.

'Not that I expect any thanks.' That meanness wasn't like Martin at all.

Josh

I thought Mummy had cancer. Not sunburn cancer but an inside one. She cried a lot when she thought we weren't watching, but sometimes I could hear her when she said she was having a sleep in the afternoon. She had more sleeps because cancer makes you tired.

Ben hated school. He told his teacher she was a bitch. He got into bad trouble but he didn't take the note home. I signed it for him, the way Dad signs. When he had detention, I asked Betty to pick us up late because we were swimming and then I hid down near the tennis courts until Ben got out from detention. He didn't want to tell Mum and I didn't want to tell her.

Ben did a lot of things but I never told on him. I never told him about the cancer either because he was too little.

I was going to ask Auntie Lisa but she would have told Mum. I just wanted Mum to get better. Then I had an idea that Auntie Mary could give her pills, or something because Auntie Mary is a doctor. She always keeps secrets.

'So you don't want me to tell your Mum that you think she has cancer,' she said sounding like she didn't believe me about the cancer.

'I know she has cancer.'

'You don't know, Josh. It's really wrong to say a person has cancer just because they're tired. You have to do blood tests and look inside their body. That's the only way to find out.'

'You find out. But don't tell her I know.'

'I won't tell her that you *think* she has cancer. I don't think she has cancer, but *if* she does, we can probably cure it.'

'You can die. Even sunburn cancer can kill you.'

'It's not called sunburn cancer. It's skin cancer or melanoma. And cancer doesn't always kill people.'

'Someone told me you get cancer and die.'

'Well, someone was wrong. A lot of people with cancer live. Your grandma had cancer. She's alive, isn't she?'

'I guess.'

'I have lots of patients who have cancer and most of them are still alive.'

'How will you tell if Mummy has cancer?'

'I'll tell her I'm worried about her and ask her if I can do some tests.'

'Are you worried about her?'

'Yes, I am. Something is wrong but maybe not cancer. Probably not cancer.'

'Do you like Mummy?'

'Yes, I do. And if she has cancer we'll do something. And I'll tell you.'

'The truth?'

'The truth.'

Mary

Martin had said he would leave Susan in three years' time. The three-year clause always worried me. But when I thought about it I wondered if it was just me. I'm a very decisive person. Wham, bam, thank you mam, and it's done. Relationships, work, religion, sex, politics, that's how it is for me.

I'd got married about five years after Martin did. Stayed with Tim for a year. Woke up one morning, looked at him sleeping. I still thought he had a nice face but I realised it wasn't working. So before he woke I packed my bag, wrote a firm but compassionate note saying it was over and I was off up the north coast for a year. I like spending time up there. I do well in real estate. I don't care about the money but it is fun. I suppose I do care about the money a bit. I got Mum and Dad into a better place, and I'm financially secure. But I'm not into possessions the same way Marty is. Not that Marty thinks he is. Just likes his toys.

Up north I got involved in setting up a women's health practice. The philosophy was great—to provide excellent service, to change the parameters of medicine so they favoured women. Then the nurses got shitty and decided it was a co-op and they should get the same pay as the doctors. Well, I'm not working to support nurses. So again, I packed my bags and buggered off back to Sydney where I bought my own little piece of heaven in Lavender Bay.

That's what you realise as you get older—the ideals you hold dearest, like communality and radicalism, may not actually be the ones that suit you personally. And the things you thought hardly mattered, like family, matter a great deal.

Like Joshie.

I can't tell you what that kid was like. It was just a quality. He was a heartbreaker, full of longing. He wanted life to be good. He worried at it, like the proverbial dog with a bone. He was always looking for the hole in the dyke so he could stick his finger in. He was always looking out for his Mum, for his Dad, for Ben.

Ben was different. A bundle of joy. Giggles, smiles, wild,

rash and daring but the world didn't touch him the same way it touched Joshie.

Joshie was a lovely-looking kid. He looked more like Susan but he had a dreaminess about him that she didn't have. And I have to say she did a great job with him. She never pushed him, always encouraged him, gave him a lot of love and, as a result, he had this quiet confidence. He was a wonderful artist. He just loved to draw and his talent was amazing. But with all that came this sensitivity and an antenna for trouble.

He thought Susan had cancer. He knew he could trust me but he didn't know if I liked Susan enough to do anything about it. That's all pretty remarkable for an eleven-year-old child of the male sex.

Susan wasn't my favourite person, but I liked her more than I used to. She had real strengths I admired. She worked hard. She thought about how to bring up her kids. She loved her kids, maybe in a way Marty and I had never been loved as kids. She had a wonderful voice. She gave all those lunches for years, even though in a way, they weren't quite her.

I didn't call her Vile Susan anymore.

I realised she had weaknesses. She cried. She hurt. She loved Phil being so in love with her but she was careful not to hurt him or exploit him. All that counted with me.

So when Joshie talked to me, I thought I should talk to her. Which was actually tough to arrange because even though we saw each other often, we had never had a comfortable tête à tête. I didn't drop in on Susan or go out with her. It wasn't that sort of relationship. I annoyed her; she annoyed me, although I'd stopped wanting to provoke her. And when I thought about it, I realised I was quite fond of her without actually liking her very much. Maybe that's what family is.

But now she'd reduced her workdays so she was at home some days. I rang her one morning, said I was in the neighbourhood and told her I needed to talk to her.

'Okay,' she said, sounding surprised. 'I'll put coffee on.'

Joshie was right. There were signs that things weren't right. The house, which was usually beautiful, with fresh flowers, and very neat and tidy, was actually a bit of a mess, with the newspaper on the floor and some dead hydrangeas in a vase. Nothing like my brothel of a flat but unusual for her. And Susan was thin, dressed in an old Laura Ashley print dress, her hair drawn back, no make-up, her eyes tired. Or maybe she had been crying.

We sat down in the conservatory. She got up and shut the window and pulled an old jumper round her shoulders.

'Boys at school?'

She nodded.

'Marty at work?'

She nodded.

I'm not much good at chitchat.

'I'm worried about you,' I said. 'You don't look well. I noticed last week. I'm not your doctor but maybe you should get a check-up.'

'I have a check-up twice a year,' she said. 'I had one with the boys before they went back to school. Then I have another when I have my flu shot.'

'And your doctor gave you the okay?'

'Yes.'

'Did he do a blood test?'

'No.'

'I would have done a blood test. Iron, cholesterol, cell count, other things.'

'Maybe I should go back.' She bit her lip. 'Get more tests.'

'Look,' I said. 'I don't want to alarm you but you have lost weight. You look drawn. Maybe your GP doesn't see you often enough to notice the difference but I can see it. How do you feel?'

There was a long silence. A little bulbul came and sat on the pergola outside. Susan looked at me.

'I feel okay. A little tired, which is why I'm working less. It's hard running a house and looking after the kids and doing a full-time job. Maybe it's just accumulated tiredness.'

I got up. 'Well, go and see your GP and set your mind at rest. And mine too. I've got to be off now.' I surprised myself by leaning over and kissing her.

I let myself out. She was just sitting there, staring at the bulbul hopping about on the wisteria. I hoped she was all right.

A few weeks later she rang me. 'I had the blood tests and some other tests and I'm fine,' she said. 'Physically.'

Her tone was still a bit stiff but I sensed something had shifted between us.

'That's good,' I said. 'I'm relieved to hear it. You were probably right—you were just tired.'

'And depressed,' she said. 'My doctor said I'm depressed.'

'That's no good.' I felt very nervous. I wanted to ask her why she was depressed but I wasn't sure that I could. I hate being rejected and Susan had the power of cool rejection down to a fine art. I wanted to build a bridge. 'Do you want to come out to lunch?'

'Well, yes,' she said. 'That would be nice, Mary.' We made the arrangements and then she went on. 'I was touched you noticed, Mary. It was nice.'

Then I felt guilty because it was Joshie who had noticed, but I couldn't tell her that. But in a way, I was pleased she thought it was me. Except I knew about Melissa. I had an inkling, even though I didn't think she knew, that perhaps it was related to her depression.

Susan

I soldiered on. I took the kids to school. I saw my Dad at work. I saw Lisa, Rosie, June and Jamie. Lisa's was a very dysfunctional family but in a way it was a family that had more cohesion than ours. June was a troubled kid, but maybe that kept something alive at the heart of the family. Martin and I seemed so lucky on the surface but the heart of it was dead. I worried it affected the kids. I knew it affected me.

Summer came and Martin decided to teach the boys to surf. He took them to Nippers at the surf club and then taught them body surfing himself. I hated the whole thing. I'd always been scared of the waves. I was sure he wouldn't use sunscreen. I was convinced they'd be stung by blue bottles and get their necks broken by dumpers. They did get sunburnt a few times and we had terrible arguments, but they loved it.

Martin came and went as he pleased. The kids went to school and came home from school. I paid the bills and organised the house. They went to swimming and music and soccer practice. Betty came and went. There was an occasional frosty call from my mother. The kids went to stay with Martin's parents.

Phil, like Mary, noticed I wasn't well although he was attuned to my spirit and feelings rather than my physical state. I had always confided in Phil. I had always loved Phil. I knew he was hopelessly in love with me, but it could never have been that sort of relationship. Nevertheless, we were good friends.

In the depths of my despair I sometimes wondered why Phil was the only close friend I really had. Yes, I had old friends whose company I enjoyed, and there was Lisa, but she was frantically busy as a headmistress. I worried that maybe I had cut myself off from the world. I'd never been one to display my emotions or tell people about my personal life. I felt as if I was living in a dream, where all the people I knew were at a distance, that they didn't know me at all.

So when Mary, of all people, said she was worried about me, I felt such a surge of emotion that I could barely speak. On one hand, I felt quite threatened because I had always thought Mary didn't like me at all, although we seemed easier with each other over the last few years, and she has certainly been a wonderful aunt to the children. Both of them, Joshie in particular, love her. I felt enormous gratitude to her for noticing and then for offering her help.

When she asked me to lunch I was a little worried. She and Martin are extremely close so I had to be careful not to say anything about him, but also not to let anything get back to him about me that I didn't want him to know. The thing was I didn't want Martin to be aware of my vulnerability, my fragility. He'd already had a go at me about reducing my work hours. More than that, I didn't want him to know too much, to intrude on me when I was feeling so down. I couldn't trust him to support me which was part of why I was feeling as I did. He was, as far as I was concerned, a hostile force. I didn't want to tell Mary that.

It all sounds very convoluted and paranoid. But that's what my life had come to.

We went to a small café in Bondi. It was a good place with

exquisite Italian food. I think she had chosen it knowing how fussy I was. I warmed to her even more.

'Did your GP prescribe antidepressants?' Mary asked me almost as soon as I sat down. 'They're relatively new and you may have to see a psychiatrist to get a prescription. But they can be amazingly effective.'

'The GP prescribed them and I think they are beginning to work,' I said. 'I was very worried about taking them though. I don't like my mood to be dependent on a chemical.'

'Well, it won't be forever. It's just an imbalance in the brain they're fixing. It's no reflection on you as a person.'

'Maybe I'm too independent,' I said. 'I like to rely on myself.'

'Me too,' said Mary. 'But even people like us need outside help.'

Then we ordered and we talked about the children and her work and my work. Being depressed made it hard to feel enthusiasm about those areas of my life, even though I was still committed to them, especially the children. Mary was kind and sympathetic and she understood. To some extent at least.

'If you want to knock this depression on the head,' she said, 'you could think of going to a counsellor.'

'Maybe,' I said.

'You don't like the idea?' she asked.

'I don't like the idea of giving myself over to someone else I don't know, because when I analyse it my unhappiness doesn't amount to much. I'm a very private person.'

'Confidentiality is the absolute keynote of a good counsellor,' she said. 'I don't think you need to worry about that.'

'I guess not. It's just you hear about people re-living childhood traumas. All that drama. The idea appalls me.'

'You have to think carefully about what you want,' she said. 'What you want, what works, what suits you. I can give you stuff on different types of counselling, tell you who I think is good, who's a bit of a ratbag.'

'Didn't you used to do counselling?' I asked. Even though I felt better about Mary I wouldn't have wanted someone like her as a counsellor.

She laughed. 'Used to is the operative phrase. It was a bad case of medical arrogance. Then I saw some real counsellors at work with drug addicts and alcoholics up the coast, which gave me a sense of proportion about my own skills.'

Later, I thought back to what she had said. I also thought back to what Phil had said about the language of counselling. He'd called Martin's depression a 'grand desolation of the soul'. My depression felt like that. It went deep, right to the very heart of me. I needed spiritual remedy. I had always talked to Phil about such things but I sensed, much as I loved him, we were on different wavelengths for the present.

It was odd, but I remembered how I had got to know Martin at St James, where he told me he'd been 'hanging around churches'. He'd been interested but in a different way than me. He didn't seem to have a personal need anymore. He claimed he found what he needed in surfing. Ludicrous though it seemed, I could understand it. The ocean has a vast, spiritual feel to it. I had talked and thought about spirituality a lot. I attended our own local church and I enjoyed it. I liked the structure, but it all seemed very black and white. More about the rules for good living, rather than the meaning of life. Following the rules offered me no remedy for my malaise. I decided to start hanging around churches, to find a way of living my life.

Melissa

A married lover has some serious disadvantages, the main one is that you don't get to see him all that often. But I had the promise of a future and I lived on that.

Sometimes I felt really jealous of Susan. She was legit, I was illegit. She had his children. They shared the house, a life. I was his love but I was on the fringes of his life. Not forever, I told myself.

I didn't feel guilty about Susan and I certainly didn't bear her any animosity. Well, not much. But it wasn't as if I was breaking up a happy home. Even in the short time I'd known her, I could see why she and Marty would not get on. She was nice, but a different sort of person to him.

I spent a lot of time with Anna who had just done an amazingly successful miniseries. Her boyfriend Nick was big on the comedy scene. He was on TV, she was on TV, both flying high. I was doing okay workwise. I knew in a few years I'd be running my own company managing sports stars. But unlike Anna, I wasn't there yet. Somehow she and Nick felt that gave them the right to hassle me about my relationship with Marty.

Their romance (was it on? was it off?) was kicked along big time by the media. There's no doubt it made the whole thing more highly charged. They believed their own publicity. This was it. Love!

'So you know how I feel,' I said. 'You know why I've stuck with Martin.'

'Darling,' Anna said. 'The difference is Nick isn't married and we're not having a secret affair with a three-year contract.'

'Having you and him flashed all over the cover of *TVWeek* and you saying, "It feels so right" is somehow superior to what I have with Martin?'

'You know what happened to you and Marty last time.'

'And we're back together again,' I said. 'We've had a relationship for four years. You're looking at eighteen months and you think it's the same.'

'Except we can be together all the time. Besides, Melissa, four years is bullshit. You've been apart far more time than you've been together.'

'We've been together in my mind.'

'Which is different from reality.'

'I've been his all that time.'

'Except those other guys you slept with.'

'Don't be such a bitch!' It'd been a little spat, but now I was yelling at Anna. 'You've always said it won't last. But it has lasted. It's there. I don't like everything about it. But fuck it, Anna, this is my life! Don't you understand, Martin is my life! Okay, he comes with Susan and two kids. If I have to wait three years or four years or five, it's worth it. But for me, this is as good as it gets. Fuck you!'

I burst into tears and threw myself on my bed. Anna sat down beside me and said she was sorry. It was so hard, all of this, so hard. But I loved him. I really loved him. More than anything on the face of the Earth.

Martin

When I'd gone back to Melissa, I'd had a picture of how it would be with Susan. It would be calm and easy. It would be detached and polite. It would fall into place. Then, one morning, I would pack a small suitcase, shake hands, thank her politely and walk out the door.

It didn't work that way. The relationship was full of guilt, full of anger.

The boys pulled me every which way. Joshie asking me about his mother's birthday present. Ben telling me that Susan was too tired to take him and his friends to a film. Josh suggesting I buy flowers for Susan. As if he knew!

And Susan! She wanted family things like holidays. Individual things, such as me not having breakfast in bed because it left crumbs, me not using her shampoo and not leaving the porch light on. And sometimes nice things—cooking me a roast or buying me a shirt. Things which brought this abstract thing called my marriage to mind—to the understanding I was living with this woman, that I was going to leave this woman.

I knew, she didn't.

Sometimes I felt fury at her for being present in my life with my folded socks and my ironed shirts, and my children. 'Your father', 'Daddy', 'Dad'. It brought to mind who and what I was constantly. Except I was inconstant, living this other life.

I fantasised about Susan dying in a car crash. Or a sudden, freaky closing of a heart valve. Yeah, I'm ashamed I thought about it enough to know I needed her demise to be quick. It was the easiest solution, even if it was only a shameful fantasy. I'd be the grieving widower, comforting my sons, giving due reverence to the memory of my dear wife, a year or two later gently introducing the boys to Melissa, to be a much loved step-mother, to step into Susan's shoes, to be the wife. But it began to get fuzzy and uncomfortable here, guilt-ridden with the wrong-ness of those fantasies, making me feel I should leave immediately—leave her, leave the car crash fantasy, the lying, the fake weekend conferences, the fake surfing and the fake nights out at football.

The details were so sordid. Who had been at the conferences? What had been discussed? Who won the footy? It all needed research. Or action, like rinsing out my wetsuit, bringing home a suitcase of crumpled clothes when I'd spent the weekend naked in bed with Melissa.

Surely, I thought, she must know. Surely she should have the decency to end it? Surely she shouldn't have to put up with it? Surely it was up to her to end it?

My life was complicated, sometimes almost ruinously. I couldn't afford it, emotionally or financially. I gave an extravagant bottle of perfume to Melissa and I'd find myself bringing home flowers for Susan. Keeping the girls happy. God help me!

The guilt corrupted and corroded me. Susan wasn't well and I responded with anger. I needed her well and strong. I needed her nasty and vicious but she wasn't, never had been. I needed proof of her badness to justify my own.

I called on the God I hadn't had since childhood. The God who judged and punished, the God with the rulebook and the set of regulations, the God who brought you into line and made you toe it.

Amazingly I found myself at confession one evening at St Mary's Cathedral. 'Forgive me father for I have sinned.'

'How long since your last confession?'

Where do they get off? Thirteen years. Thirteen years. Since then I'd married in the Queen's church and then had my children christened there. Since then I'd sworn and blasphemed and forsaken God. Since then I'd loved mammon more than God. But I wasn't there for those old sins, but my marriage. I'd fallen in love. My wife didn't love me. I wanted to leave my wife. I refused to give up my mistress. I wanted to divorce my wife. Big, big sins.

But this priest wasn't in touch with the God of my child-hood. The God of my childhood would have threatened pain and punishment and eternal damnation. He would have summoned up fire and brimstone and called a moral halt to what I was doing. But this priest didn't have the heart for judgement and punishment. 'Think of how unhappy you are,' he said. 'Think of why. God will guide you. God is with you. God hasn't cast you out. Remember that.'

I went out into the early evening and walked along Art Gallery Road. I looked over to the park where young men played football. I envied their innocence and despised my lack of it. I went and sat behind the art gallery and looked over to where Phil lived on the cliff going up to Potts Point. Phil loved cleanly, nevermind that it was my wife. He loved steadfastly. He had loved me too, but I'd rejected him.

I sat there feeling completely alone. But still angry at her. And at God.

CHAPTER 11

1989

Melissa

Martin liked our self-contained world. He liked playing house and being cocooned from the outside world. He felt free to be himself. I wanted him to feel my place was his home, his real home. But I was always aware of his other world—Susan, Joshua and Ben—the house at Coogee. It felt as if they owned him and I had him on borrowed time. That's where he had his clothes, his possessions. That's where his kids were, it's where Susan was. And Susan was his wife. That's where his friends went, where his family visited. That was his phone number, his address, his house, his junk, everything. He didn't know how hard it was for me sometimes.

I made the best of it. Thia Toula's house was a dark little semi, with windows on the south, so I'd put a skylight in, and I painted it the most outrageous colours. I wanted him to have the house imprinted on him, to remember it, to love it, to have flashes of it through his head.

He didn't talk about Susan much. I knew some things—she had plain cotton sheets, so I had wild ones with red poppies. She wore pyjamas. We slept naked. She liked the windows closed. We both liked them open. She liked teacups so I had mugs. She was restrained and tasteful. I was not so tasteful. I liked an extravagant, over-the-top look. I'd seen their house and it was beautiful. I'd never know where to start with a house like that, let alone have the money, so I did my thing and tried to feel good about it but I was always aware I was competing with her. Sometimes I got hurt, like the time I bought him a fluffy bathrobe.

'Not really my style,' he said. 'A bit kitsch.' That was before he saw his name embroidered on the pocket, which evidently made it even more kitsch. It also meant I couldn't return it. We had an awful blow-up about that. Did he love her more than he loved me? Did he love her at all? Did he fuck her? Answer: obviously 'yes'. My head went crazy for a week. Some things I just couldn't think about, didn't want to ask him. He loved me, not her. He told me that.

We went to the movies and sometimes to clubs, but mainly we went to the beach or stayed at home. I didn't mind. We cooked and ate, we talked and laughed a lot and fooled around. He loved me. He knew this was hard for me, but he didn't really know how hard. He had two worlds. I had one, where he was an occasional visitor.

'It's going to end,' he said. 'Remember that. If it's good now, think of how fantastic it'll be when we're living together. Fantastico, bellisima!'

'I'm Greek not Italian,' I said.

'All wogs to me,' he said, and kissed me.

But he was uncomfortable with other people around. 'I can trust you,' he said. 'I don't know about other people.' He was scared of someone seeing him and telling Susan. Sometimes, I wished that would happen. Sometimes I thought about how easy life might have been with the Summer Romance.

For us to go to Anna's wedding together was important for me. 'Come. You have to. Please, please.' I begged him. 'I'm a bridesmaid. You'll be letting me down seriously if you don't come. It's safe. It's really safe.' It wasn't as if he and Anna had friends in common.

He agreed to go, nervously. We felt like school kids sneaking out for a secret date.

I spent the day of the wedding with Anna at her parents' house in Leichhardt. We had a beautician there, a masseur, her mother, her aunts, her bridesmaids and a lot of nervous, rowdy Greek blokes downstairs. I was chief bridesmaid, one of five. It took all day to get our hair, nails and make-up done. I love that stuff! We all looked so gorgeous it was amazing.

Suddenly I felt teary, not about Anna, but because I wasn't a bride and wouldn't be in the foreseeable future.

'I'll end up like Thia Toula,' I said. 'I'll never ever ever get married till Susan dies.'

'God knows when that will be,' said Anna.

'How could you wish someone dead?' said one horrified bridesmaid who had had no experience of life. Anna and I had been casually wishing people dead for years. Now I had the thought that my happiness was only possible at Susan's expense. Not her death of course, but other things. Those things would cost her, I knew that. I didn't like to think about it. I only had Martin's word for the emptiness of his marriage. She was as unhappy as him. Their eventual separation would be a good thing for her. I bought that, but in all that bridal finery, all the wedding emotions, I began to realise I didn't know. Did she love Martin? Did she think Martin loved her? I knew Martin well enough to know he had the capacity to see the world the way it suited him.

I got teary, the mascara began to run and the beautician was swabbing my face in panic. 'Have an "e,"' suggested Anna. 'It'll cheer you up.'

'Yeah and she'll be bouncing down the aisle in front of you,' said another bridesmaid.

'It's shocking,' the beautician said to Anna. 'A wedding is a sacred event. How could you?' We felt slightly ashamed, but it washed away in the wedding hysteria. We went downstairs after the men had left and waited for the cars.

Anna kissed me.

'Don't touch her,' said the beautician and touched up Anna's lips, then swabbed my cheek. 'No kissing!'

'You and Martin will be doing this one day,' Anna whispered. 'Have faith.' She could sense I was on precarious ground, that I had touched the flimsiness of my connection with Martin.

The wedding was noisy and opulent and showy and beautiful the way a Greek Orthodox wedding always is. As we walked into the church, I thought, this is my very best friend getting married. I'm her bridesmaid. When I looked around for Martin, I couldn't see him. I searched the faces anxiously. I wanted him to smile at me, to be proud of me. I started feeling panicky, wondering whether he'd come. It was only at the end of the ceremony as we walked down the aisle that I saw him, up the back in the darkest corner of the church. I felt hurt. He should have been sitting where he could see me, where I could see him, so we had eye contact, so we were there *together*. I felt betrayed.

Back at the reception, he was even more edgy, almost beside himself. 'There are bloody photographers here,' he said. 'And a film crew. My mate Cliff, his show is filming this.'

'Anna's the celeb,' I said. 'They've come to photograph her, not you.'

'I can't take the risk,' he said.

'It's only *Woman's Day* and a tiny TV spot,' I said. 'Susan's too upmarket to read that. And you told me she doesn't watch commercial TV. It's not like we're talking *Vogue Interiors* or anything.' He didn't like that. I wasn't supposed to make jokes about Susan.

'This is risky.' He was frowning, staring off into the distance.

Suddenly I felt angry. 'Go then,' I said. 'Go back to her and your real home. Don't be with me. Go back to Susan forever and she'll never ever know. But if you do, it's over with me. This day is important to me.'

'Don't be stupid,' he said. 'I'm here, aren't I?'

He stayed skulking up the back, which didn't do him any good at all. The photographers went right up to where he was to take shots of the ice sculpture, which was of a swan and a princess. I knew *he'd* think it was tacky. *I* thought it was fantastic.

When we sat down to the wedding feast, I tried to make him jealous, flirting with every man at the table. I wanted to break his mood, but I couldn't. He talked politely to a few people but he certainly wasn't advertising that he was with me. No gestures of affection, no kisses blown, no couple jokes between us.

I watched as Anna and Nick danced the bridal waltz. They looked so beautiful, a symbol of what love should be. This wasn't just anyone. This was Anna, the person closest to me, besides Martin and my mother. Like sisters, we'd grown up together and here she was in her fairytale dress, while Martin was making sure *Woman's Day* didn't capture his soul. I was the one he loved but it was Susan that he was tiptoeing around. I danced with the best man, who was Nick's best friend. I danced close and flirta-tiously, Martin pretended he didn't see me.

We got a taxi back to my place in silence.

My house has steep front steps and I went up ahead of him, holding my gold satin dress up off the steps.

'We're supposed to be living together some time this year,' I said, staring down at him.

He didn't say anything.

I went into the house and along to the bedroom and started undressing. Not for sex. My shoes were killing me, the dress was scratchy and I was angry.

He came into the bedroom and watched me.

'Will we be?' I asked. 'Living together?' I chucked the gold shoes into the wardrobe.

He sat down on the bed, looking sad. 'I promise we will be.'

Why did he have to promise? That seemed to make it less certain. I heard the doubt in his voice.

'If you're not sure, tell me now.' I lay back on the bed, still in my golden bridesmaid underwear. He sat on the edge of the bed, looking at me.

'I am sure.' He rolled over on top of me and kissed me. 'Sure and certain, all rolled up and signed off. I love you, Meliss.' He drew back, my head cradled in his hands. He looked into my eyes. 'You know that.'

'Enough to leave her?'

'Yes. Enough to leave her.'

'Enough to leave the kids?'

'Enough to leave them. I need to be sure I don't lose them though.'

'This year?'

'Yes.'

I kissed him. 'Enough for us to get married and have a kid?'

He was moving up against me. 'The whole thing, Melissa. The whole thing.'

'Because I want your baby. At the wedding, I thought, I wanted to get married. It's not just that. It's the baby. Your baby.

Inside of me. And being a family.' I felt the loss of my own family as a child. It had been cosy, my mother and me, but not quite a family.

'I want that too. Our baby. Growing inside of you. You and me together.'

Susan

I had always been very influenced by Phil and had loved to hear him talk about the rituals of high church, the mystery. We'd talked about going beyond the idea of God as a regulatory being. We were both more interested in mystery and the infinite nature of creation, and our own finite nature.

'It's the universe of God we're talking about,' he used to say, 'the vast complicated unknown mass that is God. That's what we need to contemplate. Not worry about stray bits of behaviour.' Unfortunately contemplating the vast complicated unknown universe of God had not helped the desolation of my soul. I suppose I was getting a little cynical about Phil's theological perspective as he seemed to lurch from crisis to crisis himself. I was looking for a spiritual perspective that would help me live with greater ease.

I had seen a little about St Anne's on a religious program. I can't even remember what appealed to me. Maybe it was the guiding hand of God that took me in there one Sunday morning. It was a small suburban church, near a main road, with wire grills over the stained glass. Not very inviting. However inside there was a warmth, in both the people and the building. People smiled and said hello, but there was no prying. The old woodwork was clean, and the church was decorated with vases of white daisies. It was sparse and scrubbed. Something rather Protestant about it appealed to me.

But it was the sermon that really attracted me. 'God loves you,' said the minister, 'exactly as you are. He doesn't need you to be good or to be spiritual or to be holy. None of that is required. Trying too hard to be all those things might make it a little hard for you to get close to God. Come just as you are. He accepts you. He loves you.'

The sun was shining through the window, making a square of sunlight on the floor. I was sitting at the end of a pew. I remember it so clearly. My eyes filled with tears. I felt a great surge of gratitude, of acceptance, that sent shivers down my spine. All my years of trying to be good, trying to please everyone, trying to do the right thing. But with God, I could and should be myself. No trying, no striving, I was loved as I was. It was an enormous revelation, a different slant on what Phil had been telling me.

'So often we think God is counting up our good works and our bad works, checking out sinners and saints,' the minister went on. 'The message of Jesus is that God loves sinners as much as saints. He loves us for ourselves because of what we are.'

The need to be good, the fixed idea of who I was, the burden of who I was, felt as if it was falling away.

I kept going Sunday after Sunday. The boys were old enough to be home for a few hours by themselves and this was my time. Gradually, I could feel I was developing a different idea about myself, freeing myself from judgment, my own and Martin's. I thought about my marriage a lot. I wanted it to work. I wanted it to be better, but I didn't have to become a different person. I had thought I had to be right about things, be able to defend any decision I made, but that wasn't it at all. I felt freer. My relationship with Martin didn't change but I felt less a victim of the marriage. I felt more like a person in a bad marriage. And in the end, if the marriage didn't work, so be it. Well, I felt like that on good days, not all the time. I wanted to be able to do something constructive to help the relationship, but I didn't know what.

Of course the changes that were happening to me were gradual. Not being sure of what was going to happen was a little disturbing. For the first time in my life I wasn't using rules and regulations as a guide of how to behave and referring to codes of conduct to judge myself.

I had no alternative but to believe I was loved as I was. By God, if not by Martin.

I began to take pleasure in small things again, like my knitting and buying the perfect sock. And doing an occasional Sunday lunch.

Lisa

Susan doesn't read gossip mags. She despises them, calls them my secret vice. So when I saw someone in *Woman's Day* who looked very like her husband in a crowd shot behind the ice sculpture at Anna Gialouris's wedding, I didn't know whether to say anything to her because I couldn't be absolutely sure it was him. I'd been suspicious something was going on. He'd become very removed, very distant. Jamie thought I was just drumming up gossip but the thing is, Susan is my sister. So while it may have been interesting gossip if it had been anyone else, this was different.

I knew there was a possibility that even if Marty was having an affair, Susan would turn a blind eye. Still, I thought it was my sisterly duty.

I asked him. In front of her. That way they both knew what I knew. Or didn't, as the case may be.

Sunday lunches had become rare, but this one was a big lunch for Dad's birthday, plus a few other people who had been regulars at those lunches. Susan had done it beautifully, with a big madras checked tablecloth, baskets of bread, gorgeous dips and lovely Mexican platters. It was so beautiful without being overdone. She has such a talent for making people feel good.

We came to dessert and everyone was very relaxed, even Mum which was a miracle.

'You know that actress Anna Gialouris?' I asked Martin casually across the table.

I swear he sort of started, but Jamie said he just turned to look at me.

'Can't say I do,' he said.

'She's in that series "Rumours". She's hot.'

He didn't ask why I thought he might know Anna, which I thought was very suspicious, although Jamie thought it was completely natural. Susan *did* ask, which I thought was significant.

'Why would Martin know her?'

'There were pics of her wedding in one of the weeklies. And there was someone who was a dead-ringer for Marty in the crowd.'

'Impersonator,' said Martin. He laughed. 'I get it all the time.'

Later in the kitchen, I asked Susan if she'd like me to bring over the magazine.

'Why?' she said. 'No, I don't think so.'

I went home and had another look at the picture. Even Jamie said it had to be him.

Phil

Sunday lunch, bliss! It lifted my spirits, made them soar. It had been so long since Susan felt up to putting on a Sunday lunch. I'd done a christening at the school chapel that morning with twins who had the good fortune to have wonderful parents, who reminded me a little of Martin and Susan when they first married—seriously good people, full of faith and hope for the future.

Which wasn't my position exactly. In fact my future was looking particularly grim. The school board had taken a very dim view of my New Guinea adventure and my subsequent support of the Nigerian project. I'd gone to great lengths to prove how bad the New Guinea project really was, but I missed the point. What counted was that the school had supported it, people had put their hearts into it. It had made *them* feel good, nevermind the outcome. Maybe that's what charity is about

The growing shift in the school towards fundamentalism meant I was under attack from all quarters, having to justify my lessons where I talked about interpretation rather than the literal meaning of the scriptures. I got the boys to debate whether Jesus was man or God, whether He could be both at once. These are the things children long to discuss. God as a mystery wasn't acceptable either. But God was truly a mystery to me. My faith was to keep faith even when I didn't have faith.

I wanted a sign from God. Maybe it was the re-appearance of Susan's Sunday lunches.

Lisa and Jamie were there, lovely Mary trying to tempt me, and a few people from the law firm.

I had been to Susan's new church and I liked the preacher's approach very much indeed, but it was a little too plain to engage me emotionally. No trimmings! But Susan was more relaxed, easier on herself, less inclined to judgement, more inclined to heart over head. She took her old pleasure in small things, like the colour of her table linen, the pattern in her rug and the scent of her lavender. Her attention to these details had always charmed me.

I saw quite a lot of Joshie at school and I coached Ben in the school's worst soccer team. The tension in the house had taken a toll on the children, especially Josh. He was a little too serious for his age, a little too dark. He often showed me his drawings, which were always black and white, and I thought there was a poignancy and a loneliness in the figures he drew, quite remarkable for a boy his age. He couldn't talk about them, but I thought at least he had some outlet. Even though I cared deeply for both him and Ben, I cared most about Susan. I could admit that to myself now. She was the love of my life.

Martin was telling a wonderful story about a con man selling cane toad farms on a party plan, but I joined Susan in the kitchen to help roll the hot brandy snaps, then fill them with Italian custard. Lisa and Mary helped for a while and there was general hilarity at Mary's ineptitude, until she was sent out of the kitchen. Such a scene would not have happened a year ago.

'Lisa,' said Susan. 'I need a word with Phil for a moment. Could you check the drinks?' Lisa was a bit put out. Like me, Lisa likes to know the gossip and I suppose the prospect of Susan confiding in me must have been galling. Which somehow made the whole thing even more pleasing. A minister of religion shouldn't have such feelings, but I did.

'How do you think Martin treats me?' Susan asked.

'Do you really want me to answer?'

'Yes, and truthfully.'

'Well, he's offhand,' I said. 'And irritable.'

'And what about me to him?'

The hard one. I winced. 'Same sort of thing,' I mumbled.

'Do you remember how it was when we first got married?' she asked.

'Oh it was wonderful,' I said. 'That wedding, how you were then, is my benchmark. It was so full of feeling and reverence for each other and the institution of marriage.'

'I don't feel we could ever get that back,' she said. 'However, I want your advice on getting the marriage back on track. I feel so much better, so much more myself, I think I can do it. I think what has happened has been damaging for the children. They don't see any love or any spontaneity. I thought that as long as the marriage was intact and we were halfway civil, it didn't matter. But then I realised that's exactly what I saw in my parents' marriage, maybe that's why I've repeated it. Both my parents wanted to be better than the other. They wanted Lisa and I to be good. Everybody was good, better or best. That's what counted.'

I nodded encouragingly.

She popped a broken brandy snap into her mouth with almost a wanton look. 'So what would you suggest?'

She looked so pretty and relaxed and funny with the brandy snap in her mouth. She looked sexy, she looked beautiful.

'I thought it would be obvious. Seduce him!'

I might as well have hit her. She looked stunned, then pulled herself together.

'I wouldn't have expected that from you,' she said coolly. 'It's such a male answer.' She picked up the tray of brandy snaps. 'I'd better serve these.'

She avoided me the rest of the afternoon. When I was saying goodbye, she was upstairs.

I was shockingly upset. I've never ever said anything like that to Susan before, but the thing was she looked and seemed different. It felt like the right thing to say, yet it obviously wasn't. Maybe it *was* a male answer. Parts of her had relaxed but evidently not that part.

The incident ate away at me all afternoon and that night I did an outrageous thing. Mary and I were a little drunk. She gave me a lift and one thing led to another and I slept with Mary again (and agreed to wear my dog collar to bed, for her Protestant minister seduction fantasy). That didn't feel good because I'd promised myself I'd never become involved with Mary again. It didn't seem *seriously* wicked, not the sort of thing that God at His most benign would condemn me for, although I couldn't imagine He would actually like it very much. If I'm truthful, I'd have to say that the whole relationship was based on irreverence really. It *was* fun of course, but it made me uncomfortable. And while I haven't taken a vow of celibacy, I suppose I would like to be generally chaste.

The worst thing was that I betrayed Susan's confidence, telling Mary what I had said to Susan about getting the marriage back on track, and Susan's reaction. My only excuse is that I was drunk and upset by Susan's rejection of me.

Predicably, Mary found it very funny. 'You told her *what*?' she said.

'It'd work, wouldn't it?'

'Yes but she wouldn't do it.'

'How can you be so sure?'

'Look,' said Mary. 'I'm fond of her. I think she has a lot of integrity and she's certainly a lot more relaxed than she used to be. But Susan and sex? You've got to be kidding.'

'I can't see the contradiction.'

'Of course *you* can't. You're in love with her. But she's buttoned right up. To within an inch of her life.'

'She's a very attractive woman. That's what's bothering you.'

'I'm not jealous. Men always think that when women comment on other women. And I'm not saying she has no sex appeal. She simply doesn't have any interest in sex, you can see that. God, why do you think Martin is with Melissa?'

I looked at her perplexed and Mary went quiet. Realised she'd given it away. So he hadn't given up Melissa. That explained a lot.

Mary got up quickly and started getting dressed. 'You're probably right,' she said. 'I've got to go.' She leaned over and kissed me. I could smell Mary. Earthy but lovely Mary. I wondered what Melissa was like.

Later, I thought about telling Susan about Melissa. But the thing is that Susan wanted the marriage to work and this would mean the end of it. Also, I couldn't be sure how serious this relationship with Melissa was. Maybe it was just a little fling. I was drunk when I was with Mary, and she was drunk too. I couldn't remember exactly what was said. Martin would brush me off if I tried to talk to him. Or deny it. Or punch me. I thought I'd keep my mouth shut. I was a little afraid of Martin.

Susan

I was amazed at Phil at lunch. How could he? When I was asking him seriously for advice? Surely he couldn't believe I should use sex as some sort of manipulation?

I felt close to Phil. I'd told him a lot about my feelings and we had a similar approach to life. Now I realised he was just a man. Maybe a man who had never really grown up. I suppose that was part of his charm. But Phil had fallen off the pedestal I had placed him on for so many years. I suppose he was just expressing what a lot of people think. But it wasn't the way I thought. It wasn't the way I operated.

I hadn't enjoyed the sexual side of our marriage for a long time, but it didn't seem that sex itself was a problem, more a symptom of the problem. How could I enjoy sex with Martin when I felt he didn't care about me, didn't notice what I did for him and the family? I decided to talk to Lisa about it. Lisa is more practical about marriage than me. I was knitting her a jumper, and she came over so I could measure it up against her. After that we sat on the verandah and had a cup of tea.

'Lots of women do use sex to manipulate men,' she said, looking out to the island. I wondered if she was paying attention.

'Don't you think it's wrong?' I asked.

'Theoretically, I suppose so. But it happens. It's part of it.' She was paying attention, but she was calm and detached, which made me realise that I wasn't.

'It goes against my principles,' I said. 'My feminist principles.'

'What about your Christian principles?' she said. 'Maybe that's what Phil was saying. Seduce him to strengthen the marriage?'

'What *are* you suggesting.'

'I'm not suggesting anything. But you're getting very indignant and hot under the collar.'

'I'm not indignant.' I looked at her and thought about it. 'I guess I might be.'

'This is hard for you. It'd be hard for anyone.'

'I suppose. I think sex should be an expression of something.

It certainly was when I first met Martin. I seemed to be a willing partner then . . .'

'You seemed to be? You sound tentative.'

'Well, I was a bit prudish, I suppose. But remember me telling you how sexy he was, how physically attracted I felt. I did want sex with him. Now I've been having sex for years when I haven't wanted to.'

'Do you ever say "no" because you don't want to?' asked Lisa, looking pained.

'Sometimes. But mostly I just make sure I'm not available. I'm asleep when he comes in, I get up very early in the morning.'

'Can you imagine *wanting* sex with Martin?'

'Not at the moment.'

'Oh dear.' She looked out to the island again. 'So what would happen if you said "no" every time?'

'Unfortunately I think sex is so important to him that the marriage would fall apart.'

'You put up with it for that reason?'

'Yes.' I felt tearful at her questioning. 'And I'm surprised you seem to think Phil's idea is a good one.'

She leaned forward and put her hand gently on my knee for a moment. 'Not at all,' she said. 'But just talking about it, it seems to me you're drawing all these different lines in the sand. You're outraged when silly Phil suggests you seduce Martin to get the marriage back on track. However, you *do* have enough sex to keep Martin in the marriage, even though you don't want to have sex.'

'Well, I suppose it is contradictory.' What Lisa had said was true, and painful. I knew she didn't want to upset me, that she was trying to get me to look at things. 'But why does it matter so much?' I asked. 'Is it that important?'

'Sex is hardly trivial,' said Lisa. 'If you have sex without wanting to, you're putting the very core of your personality at risk, the very core of your being. Not everyone believes that, but I do.'

'But I've been doing it for years.'

'And you've had a very severe depression and a lot of unhappiness. At the very least you're cut off from your physical and sexual self. You are strong, Susan, but you're vulnerable too.'

'Lots of women don't like sex,' I protested.

'Look, sometimes I have sex just because Jamie wants it and I can see he needs something from me. And I might enjoy it or not, but it's a gift to him.' She smiled. 'Without telling him. Look, it happens, and it happens more often with women. At least I'd think so. I mean don't take me as an expert. And in a loving, giving relationship, maybe that gift can work as an occasional thing. But sex is the deepest, most intimate thing we do.'

'I'm not really sure about that,' I said. 'But what can I do?'

Lisa was tentative. 'I know we have different ideas about this but I don't think you can keep on having sex when you don't want to, and come up smiling every time. It doesn't work like that. Sex isn't like taking your turn putting out the garbage.'

'I want the marriage to work.'

'I don't know what to say. Some marriages don't work. This sex thing is a big problem. In my book anyway.'

'What would you do?'

'I'd leave. But I know you don't want to do that.'

'I have thought of it, and it's a possibility in my head. But I worry so much about the kids. Jamie left and look at what's happened to June.'

'June's that way because her mother is a bloody neurotic

manipulator not because of the divorce. Don't get me started on that.'

'The divorce couldn't have helped.'

'No,' said Lisa. 'It hasn't. That's life. And it could have been worse for June if Jamie had stayed. I don't know. You and Martin are a lot better off, a lot more rational. Maybe you should agree to simply having a marriage of convenience.'

I felt tears in my eyes. 'That seems grim,' I said. I sat there, almost unable to restrain my tears. 'It's so far from . . .'

Lisa hugged me. I was crying on her shoulder now.

'It is a long way from where you want to be,' she said. 'But you know, you'll get to where you're going, even if you don't know where that is.'

'What do I do in the meantime?' I blew my nose and sat down again.

'Talk to him,' she said. 'If he agrees that he wants the marriage to work, you could think about marriage counselling.'

'You think that would work?' I asked.

'Don't know.' Lisa laughed. 'I've got a halfway good marriage, a mad stepdaughter and plenty of other problems of my own. God, I put on two stone last year. Do what you need to do, Suzie. If it works, you're damn lucky. Otherwise you can at least say you tried.'

Mary

Susan phoned me and told me she was thinking that she and Martin might go to marriage counselling together. She hadn't said anything to Martin yet and she wanted to have lunch with me and just run a few things past me about Martin and her.

Of course, I said, that would be fine. It would be fine if it wasn't for Melissa, but I could hardly say that, could I?

Never, ever before had we talked about Martin but she did all the right things, as Susan always does. Was I comfortable? Did I understand it was confidential? I was not to feel pressured. We agreed to meet in a small restaurant in Woollahra.

It was small, elegant and full of ladies lunching lightly and wearing expensive, understated clothes. Thin women in beige linen, except for me and Susan.

'Look at us,' I said. 'Who would have ever thought we'd be Woollahra lunchers?' She laughed. 'I mean me,' I added.

Susan looked different. She was thinner and her hair was cut short and boyish which made her look younger and softer. And her clothes were softer too—cotton trousers and an Indian shirt, the usual fabulous colours, but less starched looking than usual. We each ordered a glass of wine. This was going to be a tough talk. Had she found out about Melissa? Had Phil told her what I'd said about her?

'I'm glad we've become better friends,' she said. 'It means a lot to me.'

'Me too.' I decided I would not lie about Melissa.

'Family's very important to me,' she said.

'Me too,' I said. 'Well, parts of it. When you have five siblings you can afford to be a bit choosy.'

'I need your help,' she said, 'as family.'

Maybe I should lie about Melissa, I thought.

The waiter brought our wine and took our orders.

'You know about Martin and me, don't you? The general state of the marriage?'

'Look, he doesn't talk about it, you know.'

Which was true. He talked about Melissa until I was tired of hearing about Melissa. I liked Melissa. She was young and she was smart and she was good looking and sexy. Which were all the reasons Martin was with her. The trouble was, they were the only reasons. I thought back to how I'd scoffed at Martin's talk of the mystery of Susan. Now I had to admit there had been something to it.

'There's a lot of tension, a lot of disharmony,' she said staring straight at me, her eyes astonishingly like Josh's.

'I'm aware of that,' I said. 'I imagine that's part of why you've been so stressed.' If I was going to lie, which I wasn't sure I would, I could at least be sympathetic. I had a good swig from my glass of wine. I needed something to see me through.

'Not really,' she said. 'I think I've been stressed because I had a lot of very rigid ideas, especially about myself. That makes anyone stressed. But I do feel I've become more forgiving, less hard on myself. I'm different. It's this church I've been going to. I know you're not a believer, but it's made a difference to me.'

'I can see it in your face,' I said.

The waiters brought our lunch, breaking her hold on me for a moment. Susan could be very intense.

'Martin doesn't see it,' she said. 'He's angry about me not working full time. He pays lip service to me not being able to, but he doesn't mean it. Which is a pity.'

'You mean he can't see you have changed?'

'No, he can't. Which would be okay if I didn't care about this marriage. I want it to last, and it can't last as it is.' This was the moment to tell her about Melissa. 'The thing is,' she went on, 'he doesn't see the consequences if it breaks up. He doesn't understand how it damages the children, especially Josh. Don't you agree?'

'Sometimes,' I said, 'but children can be better off with separated parents who are not fighting.'

'Maybe,' she said, 'but not in this case.' Her mouth was back in its old firm line. 'Especially Josh.' She was tense. 'It may happen, I know that. I want to be sure that it doesn't if I can help it.'

'Very commendable,' I said. 'What's your plan?'

'I want him to come to counselling, so we can work on the problems together. That's what I want to know from you—whether you think he'd have any interest in working on the marriage.' She looked very vulnerable.

I sipped on my wine. I could tell her about Melissa. But that would blow the whole thing apart forever. Which wasn't what she wanted. And even though Martin was enmeshed with Melissa, there was still a chance for Susan, maybe. And maybe she was right about the children. I remembered my conversations with Josh, his distress about any possibility of divorce, his sensitivity, his black drawings. And even Ben, cheerful and robust, was at a vulnerable age.

'Maybe it would work.' I said.

'Good,' she said. 'I'm glad you think so. I actually feel scared to ask him. He's likely to make some biting reply. He overreacts to me.' She toyed with her salad. 'If you felt comfortable about it, I wouldn't mind if you mentioned it to him—if you think it really is a good idea,' she added hurriedly.

'I'm sure I could. But not in a devious way. I'd have to tell him the idea comes from you and I've been talking to you.'

'That's okay.' She pushed the salad round her plate again. 'There's something else.'

'What's that?'

'Well, I've been thinking that Martin needs a reason to

change. I mean, he's never mentioned divorce and I never have either. I don't want it and neither does he, as far as I know.'

'That's good then, isn't it?' I felt awful about my duplicity about Melissa. But there was nothing I could say. Or should really. But this wasn't the sort of conversation to make someone in my position feel virtuous.

'Not really, because Martin doesn't seem to really care about the state of the marriage. He doesn't care about my unhappiness. There's no incentive for him to change.

'So what's the incentive?'

'If he thought divorce was a possibility. Not that I want it for one minute,' she added quickly. 'But if he thought it was a possibility and he realised what he could lose . . .'

'Money? Kids?'

'Well everybody loses out in divorce in that way. But he could lose his partnership. I don't think we could both stay at the firm. I'm on the board of the firm. So I have to consider my best interests and the firm's best interests.'

'What do you mean?'

'Look,' she said. 'It sounds awful but I'm the sort of person who looks ahead. Martin and I couldn't work at the same place. If there was a divorce, I guess I'd be looking at protecting me. I'm not vindictive but that's just the way it is. Martin is innocent like that. It's one of the things I liked about him. But he's also much more materialistic than me, although he'd never ever admit it. But he does place store by his possessions—his house, his car, his boys' toys. If he thinks about all that and about losing his partnership, he might look at the marriage differently.'

Whew! Something different from the gentle and civilised Susan. I'd always despised the middle class, thought they had soft centres, but there was true grit here.

I admired her.

A few weeks later, Martin and I were drinking in the Royal George, which had become a trendy watering hole, rather than a hangout for the intellectually disaffected. Even though he professed great happiness with his life, darling Marty was beginning to look like a middle-aged man having an affair and telling lies.

I ordered two rums with beer chasers. I thought we needed fortification for the night ahead. I had just come back from Byron where I was supervising the building of my first block of townhouses.

'Susan's got a share in one of them,' I said. 'It'll be a very good investment for her.'

'You didn't ask me.'

'You told me you didn't have any money,' I said. 'So how are things?'

'Flat out.'

He tossed the rum down.

'What do you think Susan will want when your three years are up?'

'Three years?'

'When you go and live with Melissa.' I could see he'd done a thing that is very characteristic of our family; a dreamed up grand scheme, not much attention to unpleasant details or even to the execution of the plan. 'You know, Susan might be one of those clients you're always telling me about—who really want blood.'

'Susan's fair-minded,' he said. 'Melissa and I can live pretty cheaply and I make a lot. When the kids are grown up, I might buy Susan's share of the house. I love that damn house.'

I explained it to him in a way that was brutally clear. 'Susan will protect her interests, which might mean your interests suffer a bit of a blow. You could lose the partnership if you divorce. In fact, you probably would.'

'Have you been talking to her?' He looked alarmed. 'I mean you aren't exactly friends, are you?'

'We are, much more than we used to be. We went out to lunch.'

'Does she know about Melissa?'

'No.'

'Why did she tell you?'

'Don't shoot me. I'm the messenger, that's all.' I finished my rum. 'She thought you'd rant and rave at her but that you might listen to me.

'Fuck! I had no idea she was thinking of divorce.'

'She's not. She wants to avoid divorce. But she does want things to improve.'

'And how is that going to happen?'

'You've been living in la la land. What made you think your divorce might be amicable when you've dealt with divorce cases for almost fifteen years? You've got two women here. You've got obligations to them both. You've got two kids. And you haven't give a thought to anyone or anything. With the grand exception of your dick.' I was angry with him.

'It's love,' he said. 'Not sex.'

'Whatever. Do you love Susan?'

He sat there. He sighed, angry. 'Too much has happened.'

'She'd like to fix the marriage up,' I said. 'She's not happy, it isn't good for the kids. She'd like to see you happy.'

'Christ! *I* am happy,' he said. 'With Melissa.'

'Susan has changed,' I said. 'She's softer. But she's also a realist unlike you, my dear little brother. So she's thought about divorce and what it might entail. But she thinks if you went to counselling together that the marriage might work. She wants it to work. She hopes it'll work.'

'Why is life so fucking hard?' he said bitterly.

'Yeah, it is tough,' I said. 'You've got a house on the cliff at Coogee. You've got two gorgeous kids, two gorgeous women. A high-paying job. Get over it, Marty. You've just got to make some choices.'

He shook his head, and sighed. 'It's too complicated. And whatever choice I make, I'm going to be as guilty as hell.'

'So *are* you going to make a choice?'

'I have to. For Melissa's sake. But the choice is killing me. Duty versus love. Because whatever happens, I don't think what I have with Susan will ever be anything like what I have with Melissa.'

'Maybe it's not just a simple choice between Melissa and Susan. Maybe there are other issues, for instance, status versus disgrace?'

'What do you mean?'

'You leave Susan and you go and live in a semi in Manly belonging to the woman you've left your wife for. The woman is impressive in her way but a bit down the social scale from Susan. You become a suburban solicitor rather than a top divorce lawyer. You don't have a house on the cliff at Coogee. People talk about you and your troubles with undisguised pleasure. You're not on TV anymore. You're a part-time father, diminished in the eyes of your children. Not a pretty picture.'

'Shit Mary, I don't give a toss about that. Except the kids.'

'Marty, we've been rich, we've been poor. Rich is better. You pay people to do your shit work, you do what you like. Believe me, I have done serious self-examination of the revolutionary conscience. And I look at you—status and money do count.'

I could tell he was pissed off because bought himself a whisky and didn't buy me a rum.

'I never had a revolutionary conscience,' he said. 'I like money but I don't give a shit about status. In fact, I positively dislike it. And I wouldn't mind a bit being poor.'

'You're not on TV now,' I said.

He got that tight-lipped look he got as a kid when he was angry and he was about to punch me. I moved back a bit, and gave him my childhood look that said I wouldn't stop taking the piss out of him whatever he did. Okay, he was still a working-class larrikin in some ways, but money and possessions mattered. And he had a stunning ability in the area of self deceit.

'Fuck you,' he said, and walked out.

Josh

Dad drove us to school every Monday. It was better than when Mum drove because he took these crazy short cuts and he swore at the traffic and sometimes he went fast or in the bus lane and got booked. He told us good stories about drug cases or a robberies.

'Why don't you tell us about the divorce cases, Dad?' I asked.

'Josh is crazy about divorce,' said Ben. 'Josh talks about divorce all the time.'

'Shut up,' I said and gave Ben a bad look. 'I want to know why people get divorced.'

'I can't tell you about divorce cases,' Dad said. 'They're private.'

'But why do people get divorced?'

'Irretrievable breakdown of marriage,' he said.

'Which means?' said Ben sarcastically.

'Irretrievable means you can't get it back. Breakdown means it's fallen apart. Like if you fight all the time.'

'I hear you fighting. Quite a lot.'

He looked at me. 'I'm not getting divorced however much you want me to,' he said. I thought he was serious.

'I don't want you to get divorced, Dad.'

'Josh, we're not getting divorced.'

Nobody said anything the rest of the way to school. I felt upset.

'Don't worry about things that might never happen,' he said as I was getting out of the car. But he said 'might'. And they did fight. I could hear them.

Martin

I was between a rock and a hard place. Mary was right, even though she read me totally wrong as caring about status. But it was true I hadn't given a lot of thought to the practicalities. Typically, Susan had, and had it all worked out to suit herself. Oh fuck, maybe that's not fair. Susan wanted me to go to counselling so we could live more amicably together. If I left the marriage now, I was out of the partnership. Susan would have the numbers and it would mean a big loss for me.

And the whole thing was precarious. Phil knew something had gone on, although he probably thought it was in the past, Mary knew, Lisa suspected, bloody Cliff had twigged and harassed me so I'd told him about it and sworn him to secrecy. But that was hardly reliable, Cliff lived and died by gossip. Susan could find out and then all hell would break loose. Well, I didn't know what would happen but there was a sense of my life unravelling.

And there was Josh, with his talk of divorce, the pain in his eyes. We tried not to fight in front of the kids, but I'd been one of those kids with an antenna for parental brawls, and I knew he was the same. Weighing up every word. Trying to forestall it. He was going to high school, but he was small for his age and not tough like Ben. I couldn't do it to them.

I devised a plan. I would go to counselling. Susan would come to see that the marriage couldn't work. The children would be a little older. If the decision to separate came from Susan, we'd come to a better financial arrangement. Maybe I could even stay in the firm and she could start up a branch office in the west. She was good at that sort of thing.

Telling Melissa that we had to put off moving in together for another year was the hardest thing because I knew she wouldn't understand. I felt sick but I knew Mary was right. I had to make the hard decisions. I loved and adored Melissa. I wanted to be with her, but it wasn't the right time now.

'Look,' I said to Melissa. 'It's a financial decision, and if we rush it will have long-term ramifications on what we can do and the sort of life we can enjoy together.'

'Tell me,' she said. She was quite unlike herself, hard, almost cold.

'Susan wants me to go to counselling, for the marriage.'

'Yeah, well, of course, you'd want to get the marriage right before you move in with me.'

'Melissa, listen, if she feels right about ending it, she's not going to be after my blood and neither is the court. We might even settle it out of court, and save ourselves $20,000.'

'Or not,' she said.

'She's in a very fragile state,' I went on. 'She can't even seem to work full time. It's quite stressful the way we live.'

'Sure,' she said. 'You fuck her, you fuck me, she doesn't know, I do. She has a house and kids. I live on a promise. Poor *Susan*.'

'I *love* you,' I said.

'But not quite enough.'

'More than enough. I just hadn't thought this through. I love you, Melissa, but I don't want some shitty divorce where I'm fighting forever about money and access to the kids.'

'Whereas I'm available any time it suits you. Do you have any idea how hard this is on me? That I can't introduce you to my family, that I only know one of your sisters, that we can't go out in public, that most nights I don't even get to see you, you have to go home, that I don't take holidays because we can't go away together, that you're with another woman in every sense of the word.'

'She'd know otherwise.'

'Oh I see. Oh yes! Of course! That's it! You fuck her just to trick her. It's like wiping the lipstick off your collar and not having my name in your diary and admiring her cooking. You just have sex now and then, so she won't make a fuss about the divorce and so she won't suspect I exist, even though she knows you don't love her. And according to you, she doesn't even like sex so I can't help wondering why you don't keep your hands off her. This arrangement stinks. This arrangement is the stupidest thing we ever thought of. If you had any guts you'd get on the phone now and say, 'Susan, I'm leaving you. I'm leaving that fucking job, which *you* tell *me* you hate. You'd say, do your worst, Susan, but I'm never going to sleep with you again!'

'It's hard for you. It's hard for me. I don't want to make it harder by rushing it at this point.'

Melissa just stood there.

'I'm going to think about this,' she said eventually. 'Because I really don't think there's much here for me.'

'Melissa.' I went to touch her but she leapt backwards. 'Don't argue with me. I'll think about it and then tell you what I think. This is my decision.'

I moved towards her.

'Don't!' she said. 'Go.'

I left. I felt torn apart. Torn by her, by Joshie, by the whole damn mess of it. I sent her flowers. I wrote to her, asking for just another six months.

'It's finished,' she wrote back. 'Six months, three months, three weeks, tomorrow. If you loved me and you didn't love Susan, none of this would be a problem. But it is. So I'm out of the equation.'

Melissa

I was in a fury, in a jealous rage. All this stuff about Susan. All this pacifying Susan. Susan, Susan, Susan. That was all our relationship seemed to be about.

Martin sent flowers.

I sent them back.

He sent letters.

I sent them back unopened.

He made phone calls. I hung up. If I heard his voice, cajoling, begging, pleading, I'd fall for him all over again and we'd back in the same situation.

At first I was angry. But then I began to feel sad and pitiful.

I'd known, in some part of my head, that the three years

wasn't for real. He was right that it needed to be planned and organised. And he wasn't anywhere near doing that. As long as I was there, wanting and loving him, then he didn't have to make a decision.

I wasn't trying to force a decision. I was beyond that.

I'd been listening, understanding, sympathising, wanting him. I'd loved him, more than I could imagine. But it was all so secret, so not part of life. I knew all about Susan and Josh and Ben, but they didn't know about me. Sure, I saw Mary occasionally but none of the rest of his family. I was nothing, no one. If he died I would have been the mysterious mourner at the back of the church, the mysterious woman in a headscarf by the grave, like the lover in an old Hollywood movie.

When I'd looked in the mirror I didn't feel so good about how I looked anymore. Susan is beautiful. I am not but it was as if I always had youth on my side, but now I was nearly twenty-seven, which isn't so youthful. And Susan had actually got more beautiful. And for the first time in all this with Martin, I thought my life is going. I'm getting older, I'm getting nowhere. God, in three years, I'll be thirty.

It wasn't that I didn't love him but part of me was getting lost and smothered. It was too painful living like that.

I didn't stop loving him. I simply could not be with him anymore.

CHAPTER 12

1990

Martin

I had lost Melissa. I tried everything, but she made it clear it was over. I sent her flowers and she sent them straight back to the office. Thank God Susan didn't see them. I called her and she hung up. I knew what she was saying—that either I tell Susan or the relationship was finished.

I did think of telling Susan, of leaving her, of finishing the whole bloody mess, but I couldn't. Maybe it was cowardice, maybe it was playing with the kids in the surf, driving them to school, putting them to bed at night. Maybe it was the vows of matrimony and the Catholic choirboy still lurking in me. I don't know. Maybe it was feeling frozen in the headlights as my life went on around me. Maybe it was the sense of unreality, that Melissa could not have gone out of my life. Maybe it was guilt that Melissa deserved better than me. Maybe it was the feeling I should give the marriage one last shot.

'I've found a marriage counsellor who might suit us,' Susan said. 'And I'd like to make an appointment for us both. We can't have children growing up in this environment.'

'What environment?' I didn't feel like a permanent resident in my own house.

'Sniping and snapping and fighting. It makes me tense. I'm sure it makes the kids tense.'

'So it's me that's doing the sniping and snapping.'

'I didn't say that. You always misinterpret what I say.'

'Always?'

'You do it on purpose.'

'So what's the purpose?'

'Lawyer stuff, Martin. Prove a point rather than listen to what the other person is saying.'

'Oh really. And you used to tell me I was such a crook lawyer.' I felt the bitter taste of loneliness.

'I never said that,' said Susan.

'Along those lines.'

'Stop harassing me.'

So it went on, until we found ourselves in the therapist's office. Wendy, tall, big-boned, raw-faced Wendy. I took an immediate and unfair dislike to her. Wendy who had the Desiderata taped to the back of the door. I wanted to tell her it was just a modern concoction, not ancient monkish prose, but that would have got things off on the wrong foot. Witch Wendy.

'So what are you here for?' she asked me.

'Susan asked me to come.'

'I guess I'm asking you why you did come. If it's more than pleasing Susan?'

'Not much more. No.'

'What about the children?' Susan flared.

'Let's just concentrate on Martin,' said Wendy calmly. 'I'd like to think I can offer you more than just pacifying your wife. In fact I don't think that falls within my range of skills.' She had, perhaps, a slight sense of humour.

'I don't hold out a lot of hope for this process,' I said, looking at her pebbled ceilings. I hate those pebbled ceilings. They suck the life out of a room.

'Contempt prior to investigation,' said Susan, on edge.

'No,' I said. 'We've both tried to work out our difficulties—without success.' I looked at Susan for the first time since we'd arrived.

'How was the experience of trying that?'

'Frustrating,' said Susan. 'The marriage was something we thought would work but didn't.'

'It felt empty,' I said. 'Trying to breathe life into something that's gone. Like nothing.'

'Nothing at all?'

'Yes.'

'How long have you been married?'

'Thirteen years.'

'Has it been nothing all that time?'

Melissa came flooding into my mind, the children, the sadness of my marriage, the time we had wasted, the way we had started, the way things had gone wrong, the entrenched misery and bitterness. Susan with Josh as a baby. Susan sitting on the bed in my flat, her little foot stuck out in front of her. Susan singing at St James. That moment of purity which had turned to a pebbled ceiling and a tattered Desiderata poster and a therapist looking at me kindly.

'My minister mate once said if we were ever in trouble to go back to the beginning,' I said. 'Abraham did in his search for God. In the beginning, the very beginning, we had something. But it would be hard to get back there.'

Susan started crying. Her nose went red and her eyes were watery. To my shame, her tears aroused my contempt rather than my compassion.

Susan's tears. Often I had believed they were manipulative. But maybe they weren't now. I couldn't reach out to her, take her in my arms and comfort her. And did I really want to? I didn't know.

What did I feel? I had become a heartless bastard with her, maybe more so since I lost Melissa. And I'd been selfish and stupid about Melissa, thinking she would wait forever. What sort of hopeless idiot was I?

'What about getting to some other place?' said Wendy, handing Susan a tissue, but looking at me. 'Some place not as passionate as where you started but where you would both be comfortable?'

'Comfort!' I said to Wendy. 'Is comfort the aim of life? Sounds like clean hand towels in the bathroom, wipe your feet on the mat, nice manners at the table, pressed collars, the dog in front of the fire, sex with your eyes shut and probably your legs crossed too, conversations that mean nothing, a general agreement to not really live so you won't notice when you really die. I don't want to be comfortable!'

'Hmm,' said Wendy. 'Comfortable seems to be a loaded term.'

There was a long silence

'We're exploring your life,' she said. 'That could provide a bit of discomfort.'

There was another silence.

'If you're prepared to do it.'

I didn't say anything. I wanted to be happier but Susan didn't feel like part of the happiness equation. What would it be like to be happy with Susan? I felt as if Susan no longer loved me, but we had a marriage, a home, children.

The grief and blackness in my soul. The fuckedness of life.

Susan

At the start of the counselling with Wendy, Martin argued the toss on every single thing. Therapy wasn't going to work. He could change, I could change but you couldn't change a relationship. Or he couldn't change, I couldn't change and the relationship was as good as it got.

'It's unnatural,' he said. 'Telling your most intimate secrets to a stranger.'

'There's a long tradition of human beings doing it, from the wise women to the confessional,' said Wendy mildly. 'Psychotherapy and counselling are maybe the modern equivalent.'

'With the add-ons about your toilet training and whether you ever saw your parents having sex,' said Martin. 'Before we get to penis envy and the Oedipus conflict.'

'They're tabloid journalism terms you're talking in,' said Wendy. 'We're looking at the real issues of your marriage here.'

Martin raised his eyebrows. She wasn't intimidated by him like I was. Or sick of him. Maybe, I thought, he really does want to do something about the marriage. I wanted him to do something about the marriage. I wanted it better, although I couldn't quite envisage what I wanted. I was in this process now, and it had been my idea, but I could see that I was very critical of Martin. And I felt ashamed because in an awful way that's what I was here for—to reform him, change him, show him he was wrong. And I wondered if he thought the same about me. And that made me wonder if it could work. I wondered if I could change, if he could, most importantly, if we could.

Wendy ploughed ahead. 'One way of working is to deal with specific issues. We'd need to decide on a hierarchy of areas you could negotiate,' she said, 'starting with the least controversial.

From that process we come up with a list of issues and areas of conflict in the marriage. It's a concrete way of working that takes in the basic conflicts, but it's not rigid.'

The idea of the list was that we would put all of the issues that bothered us down on paper. Once this was done we would start to negotiate the least contentious areas and gradually move down the list. During this process we'd explore issues and how we thought about them. We'd look at approaching issues in new ways, letting go of the past. It sounded good to me.

I suppose in this way, Wendy thought like me. A list was my sort of process, much less natural to Martin. So I suppose it was to be expected that Martin would poke fun at the concept, complain and bicker about the details. He called it 'The Ryan Marriage Grievance File'.

'It's fantastic,' he said. 'We can minute it. We can add bylaws. We can make rulings. My God, it opens up a whole new way of having a relationship that people have never thought of before.'

Over the next couple of weeks we worked on drawing up a list. Martin participated in the process but I could see the only things he cared about were my sexual compliance, and getting to a point where we didn't bicker, which was on my list too. And he insisted on putting his awful, ugly pottery kookaburra on the list. To me that was a sign he wasn't taking it seriously.

The list emerged as follows:

housework
the garden
house maintenance
shopping and meals
family rituals, such as breakfasts, bedtime procedure, etc
family outings

money issues
children—each parents' obligations
behaviour in front of the children
doing things for one another
place of the pottery kookaburra
resolving conflicts
expressing anger
consideration for each other
behaviour in private
displays of affection
sex

'Each issue you deal with is a learning process in negotiating with each other,' said Wendy. 'Understanding your differences and your areas of congruence.'

'I'm looking forward to congruence,' said Martin sarcastically, 'Meanwhile, I am starved of affection.'

'Meanwhile, I am starved of consideration,' I said.

'It might work,' I said to Martin as I walked out.

He looked at me without hostility. 'It might,' he said and for a moment I thought he was going to hug me. But he didn't.

Martin

Starting with my mate Cliff, I'd been the media darling for the two-line grab whenever the *Family Law Act* was in the news. I'd been in newspapers, magazines, radio, current affairs TV and supposedly serious panel shows.

Family law and divorce was becoming a bit old hat for TV. The new sexy stuff was stalking and paedophilia, which both had a legal angle, but the media generally went with the psychologists. And those psychologists were versatile. Stalking, paedophilia, anorexia, repressed memories and the rest. God, you gotta love television, don't you? It's a funny business, picking the stuff that's going to tickle the fancy and arouse the indignation of the nation. Princess Di was magic for bulimia, but Fergie couldn't do it for the fatties.

Anyway, Family Law had pretty much had its run, but when one of the morning shows was organising a segment, Cliff's researcher called me. I was a little reluctant.

'The mums will love you,' Cliff said. 'throw in a bit of sympathetic marriage advice too. Not from your own marriage, of course' he added sarcastically.

I ignored that. 'Morning TV, refuge of the desperate,' I said, 'How come you're producing that shit?' A bit more of that went back and forth but I said I'd do it.

The front guy was one of those good-looking bland blokes, sporting fake tan and oozing fake sincerity. 'Do all divorce lawyers work this hard to avoid a divorce?' he asked after I had given some cautionary tales on divorce and its costs.

'Look,' I said, 'I'm not a psychologist but when you've seen as many marriages go wrong as I have . . .' Somehow I made the perfect segue from lawyer to kindly marital adviser. Which was more than a little ironic considering my own marriage was a complete mess. But I had wicked witch Wendy feeding me lines on a weekly basis about my own marriage. It was a shock to find myself regurgitating it on national television as if I believed it. Well, I did believe it, but it didn't really seem to be quite working for me. At a head level perhaps, but not at a heart level.

Susan told me there was another offer as a result of the TV

segment. 'One of those magazines wanted us to talk about our marriage,' she said. 'I said we'd rather not. Then they said they'd like you to do a weekly column. Q&A stuff.'

'I'll do it,' I said. 'At least it'll pay for Witch Wendy.'

'I wish you wouldn't call her that,' Susan said.

So I did the column. They liked my style. Martin Ryan, the human face of personal misery.

The other ironic thing was that however bad my relationship with Susan was, my relationship with old Thomas Thomas just got better and better. Part of that was due to chance. One night when I was working late, I came across his secretary Marg, who was in an awful bloody state. She lived in an investment property which was owned by the firm and she paid pretty nominal rent. But it wasn't a permanent arrangement. She'd had a bit of an inheritance, which Thomas had told her to put in property. She'd put it into one of those damn trusts that went down in 1989. Evidently she'd said something to Thomas and he'd brushed it aside and when I came across her she was thinking of letting the cat out of the bag with Susan's mother, which was not a good idea from anyone's point of view. I counselled her against it and had a little chat to Thomas the next day.

'Very good,' he said, 'Wouldn't have done anyone any good at all.'

'Especially you,' I said.

He ignored that.

'Look,' I said to him. 'You can't just leave Marg hanging. Just fix it. Life tenancy of the flat. Pension from the firm when the time comes. Plus restructuring her investments so she'll always have something to fall back on. And put it in writing. That's all you need.'

He was very relieved and Marg was relieved and a couple of

weeks later he asked me to lunch at his club. Being invited there for lunch was something.

'Look,' he said. 'You got me thinking about retirement a bit more concretely. Your family law stuff's a steady business. And all those corruption enquiries and white-collar crime, they're quite good for us too. All in all I'd say you have a fair breadth of vision.'

'Well thank you,' I said. No 'I told you so' from me. I thought maybe he was finally going to nominate me to join his wanky club.

'Your, um, difficulties with Susan seem, well, it's back on an even keel, isn't it?'

I hadn't even known she'd confided in him. It took me by surprise so I just nodded and mumbled.

But the drink had got to him and he was opening up. I wasn't too keen on knowing his thoughts on life and love but there was no bloody stopping it all falling out his stuffed shirt once he'd undone a few buttons, so to speak. 'That's marriage, isn't it? You're lucky if it's halfway bearable. It's more of a partnership really, for the children and the social reasons. Wouldn't marry if I had my time again. Probably most men wouldn't.'

Fuck! What could I say?

'See, I think you have it in you to run the place. I mean, when I retire. All I want out of it is a chairman's salary and a car. But it'd be your show.'

Fuck, what could I say?

'So that's settled, is it?'

'Fine by me,' I said. 'Thank you.' And I was smart enough to give a little speech on the goodness of his heart and the wisdom of his counsel.

I'd started to like Witch Wendy. I thought she was a pleasant and sensible woman. Trouble was, our marriage was far from either pleasant or sensible. 'Addressing the concerns of both parties' gave it a shape and substance that it didn't quite have in real life, however much I might want that. I struggled for the ideal but I struggled against the reality.

And I so missed Melissa. Warm, sensual Melissa.

Witch Wendy tried. 'How do you feel about the garden, Martin?'

'Oh I love that garden!'

'What about you, Susan?'

'I love it but it takes time and commitment. I'd like some help from Martin, but not just as an act of largesse.'

'Do you feel a sense of largesse, Martin? When you mow the lawn for instance?'

Witch Wendy probed and probed. What was happening for us? Where did our resistance lie? Did we have similar issues in other areas of our lives?

These were more constructive questions than the ones Susan and I wanted answers to, like——Why is he so selfish? Why is she cold and aloof?

We started to work our way down the list. We got past housework which included the three-basket laundry system and although Susan complained that I often slipped, she also had to admit there was an improvement. And as Wendy said, we were after progress, not perfection. We got stuck on the garden because I stubbornly refused to concede that lawnmowing was a man's ordained duty. The argument was also about the concept of 'lawn'. To me, it was green plants you could walk on, preferably without bindies. To Susan, it was a sown expanse of bent and rye grass and nothing else. To her, the flaming wand that Ben and I had bought from the hardware shop and used to eradicate non-bent and non-rye plants was a horribly hostile tool. To me, bending over and picking out weeds with a fork was the height of idiocy.

We were only on the second item on the list and already we were striking what Witch Wendy termed 'variations in value systems'.

House maintenance disputes revolved around whether my father should be called in to give, what was, according to me, wisdom. According to Susan, his advice fell a long way short of wisdom.

'A class issue!' I proclaimed.

'A competence issue,' she said. 'And it's a matter of considering my feelings.'

'Well, I don't think it's considerate moving my board wax off the dining room table when it hasn't been requested,' I said.

'We agreed we'd have a family meal every evening on the dining room table.'

'The fucking dining room table rules,' I said, hitting my forehead. 'God, I haven't brought myself up to date on those this week!' Pathetic, I know.

Anyway, I finally agreed that consideration included noticing what other people liked and what other people were doing. Or, if I wanted a change, I made—'an application for change'.

So it was a surprise to me when Wendy's sessions began to work, when my homecoming ceased to be treated like that of the pesky beggar returning to the castle. Meals ceased to be battlegrounds of venomous politeness, childcare became something to be shared between two parents rather than a battle for moral superiority.

Recounting my sins in a jocular tone doesn't mean that the list wasn't actually having a profound effect on me. Hail fellow well met, may be okay in the pub but it's no good around the house. But I didn't feel it was quite me doing this. Or quite Susan. There was an element of pretence but Witch Wendy told us that 'a sense of self-consciousness was normal in the initial stages'. And it did feel, dare I say, more comfortable.

And then there was the matter of old Thomas, offering me succession. True, the money would be nice, which would take pressure off the marriage. Would that mean the marriage would become better or did it mean I would leave?

Christ! What the hell was I doing?

It all felt like a betrayal to Melissa, my true love. Melissa who tugged urgently and insistently at my heart, who I wanted, in contrast to Susan, who I merely owed. Melissa, who I had lost.

I think Wendy would have referred to my state as 'conflicted'.

Melissa

For six months I was in a complete funk, depressed and sad. While my mum and my friends were kind, it was clear they felt a great relief that Martin was out of my life.

I couldn't imagine I'd ever love anyone else like I loved Marty. I knew he loved me. It was a case of wrong time, wrong circumstances.

One day, walking round the Callum Park, I asked my mother's advice about the heartache I felt. There's a little beach there where you can sit on the sand under the ti-trees. We sat there for ages until the tide came in and we had to scramble up the hill. The more I talked about him, the more I missed him, the more I wanted him back. I was trying to think it through, not just react to my feelings.

'Maybe love is all that matters,' I said. 'I know he loves me and I love him.'

'I loved your father,' Mum said, 'and I loved someone else before then. He was called Julian, and I loved him more than I ever thought I could love your father. But now they've both been dead so long, and I know I loved your father more.'

'Was Julian married?'

'He was a drummer,' she said, 'which is worse.'

'Why didn't you marry him?'

'He asked me and said it would make him happy, and he'd give up drugs and settle down. And he'd be famous. And we'd make a baby.'

'Didn't you believe him?'

'No. Maybe because I could see something in him he couldn't see himself. He was sincere but I wasn't sure. And he didn't give up his drug habit and he didn't settle down and he didn't become famous. And sometimes, maybe because I loved him, I wondered if that was my fault for not marrying him.'

'And what about Daddy?' I asked. 'Was that just a calculated decision to get married?' This was the closest we had ever come to talking about my father.

'I was twenty-nine, an old maid back then, so it was partly a calculated decision. It was also a decision to make him happy and make me happy and have lots of little children and a good life. And even though he got heart disease and we only had one child and he was shocking with money, it worked. At first I wasn't sure if I loved him. I never loved him like Julian. But he slept beside me for fifteen years. We had a child together. We argued. We made love. We ate together. We made a home and a life and we grew together even if we didn't grow old together. And I still miss him. I often think about Julian because he was the dream of my youth, but I don't miss him.'

It was getting dark as we walked past the old sandstone buildings of the asylum up towards the main road.

'So what do you think I should do?'

'It's far too important for me to give you an opinion,' she said. 'You have to decide.'

My mother's story reverberated in my head for months. She wanted me to understand Martin was not a good choice. And she was right, if a union with marriage and children was going to be the story of my life. But what if my life story was to be about something else? What if it was going to be about love? About an ideal rather than an institution? I thought about it a lot. I knew I still loved Martin.

My bedroom overlooked the courtyard, a mass of over-grown greenery. At night there was the smell of night jasmine and gardenias and potent spurts of smell from my withering tobacco plant. It was quiet and I felt my mind was stripped naked, free of preconceptions, free of the past. I often lay on my bed, the window open, drinking in the smells, thinking of Martin.

Up until I left Martin, I had dreamed, lazily and uncon-sciously, that my life would follow certain lines. I'd grow up—inevitable—I would work—necessary—I would fall in love—hopefully—I would marry—eventually—and have children. I thought I was on the way, just waiting for Martin to join me.

Maybe I started thinking differently because this separation from Martin was so incredibly painful. It had been just over six months and it still felt unbearable. My mother's story resonated in a way she hadn't expected. I wanted true love.

The natural, simplistic life story of marriage and children fell away. It might happen, it might not. But I wanted to pursue the more elusive, more abstract, more difficult concept of true love. Because that is what I felt. That was the height of my experience. That was my achievement to date. Loving Martin had brought me to both the highest and lowest points in my life.

I was twenty-seven years old, and I'd never thought about my life before, not in this way. Love was a risky venture. I was a risk-taker. I always had been. It felt right, almost ordained.

In this spirit I made an appointment with Thomas Thomas and Hargraves, specifically asking to see Martin. I made the appointment in the name of Melissa Barnett, using my mother's maiden name.

I remembered the office dress code. I wore a low-cut yellow silk and lace sleeveless shift printed with red flowers, a denim jacket and running shoes.

Susan was there, a little softer, less stitched up than I remembered her. She was my enemy but she didn't look the part at all.

'Mr Ryan will be with you in a moment,' she said. It took me a moment to realise she was talking about Martin. 'If you don't mind filling in your details.' She handed me a clipboard without a flicker of recognition.

Ten minutes later she ushered me into Martin's office. It was just as well she was chatting to me because he went as white as a sheet. He turned away for a moment and then he must have gathered himself, gave me a nod.

'Please sit down,' he mumbled when Susan finished the introductions.

'Oh God!' he said when she closed the door behind her. 'Oh God!'

I sat there and he came and knelt at my feet and put his arms around me and held me. I put my arms round him, feeling him, smelling him, my face in his neck. He was shaking.

'I thought you'd never come back,' he said. 'I felt so lost without you, Melissa.'

'I want to be back with you,' I said.

'I want that too,' he said. 'I want that so much.'

Then he looked up at me, and shook his head as if in disbelief. 'Talk about brash.'

'Style,' I said and kissed him.

'What if she recognised you?'

'Even old office girls are entitled to a divorce. Anyway, she didn't.'

We looked at each other. We were both thinking sex. 'I'm not that brash,' I said.

'Me neither,' he said.

'I've come to tell you two things,' I said.

'Fine,' he said. 'I know I've had my head in the clouds.' I loved him. He was trying to sound resolute and grown up.

'No,' I said. 'I did. I thought this relationship would go a certain way. I thought you'd leave Susan. But maybe you can't. And that's your decision, not mine. I love you and it's your decision to do with that what you will.'

'I'll try . . .' he began. I put my hand over his mouth.

'Don't tell me,' I said. 'Let's just have what we have. Let's just do what we do, which is love each other. It'll be how it should be. You know, these past three years I've spent more time worrying about Susan and how she's reacting than I have thinking about you and me. And we only have one thing going for us, which is that we love each other. There's a whole lot of other stuff but this is what we've got. It's enough. It's enormous.'

'Meliss, I will, I mean it, I will leave.'

'Don't talk about that stuff. Don't even think about it now. Tell me you love me.'

'I love you so much,' he said.

Josh

They started being nice to each other. Dad sometimes made jokes and Mum sometimes laughed. And sometimes he kissed her when he came home.

I grew three inches by June. I stopped listening in the hearing cupboard, not just because I was too big, but it seemed like a little kid thing to do.

Dad was happy I was in the rowing team, happy I did okay at school. Mum thought I should drop rowing and do more school work. I wanted to spend more time drawing. I loved to draw. But they weren't fighting.

'We agree to disagree, don't we, dear?' he said to her at dinner one night. We had dinner together every night Dad was home. She liked water on the table and he always got it. He put ice in it which annoyed her, but he put the ice in every time.

'Can you help me buy Mum a birthday present?' I asked Auntie Mary.

'How much have you got and do I get a commission?' she asked.

'And can I come?' said Ben. 'And could you lend me the money to buy her a present too?' I always lend Ben money and he never pays it back.

I bought a really nice pot of lavender and Ben got some pencils on special, which just happen to be the exact same pencils he needed for school. He's too old to give Mum a drawing but Auntie Mary didn't say anything.

Auntie Mary bought her a silk scarf with a pattern of waratahs.

I had to remind Dad it was Mum's birthday. He bought her a jacket. She said it was nice and everything but she never wore it.

Martin

I was so much in love. I felt complete again, our connection reignited. Melissa had come back with a generous, uncomplicated love. Nothing but love she told me. At the time it was irresistible.

It was so generous, so like her, but for me there *was* more than love. There was a complicated piece of immorality, which left me living a perpetual lie. It was a lie that I might justify to myself on the grounds of love and necessity but it was a lie all the same, which sat there in my gut night and day. It was a lie around which I practised numerous deceptions about where I was going, what I was doing, who I was with. It was a lie about what I spent, whom I gave my time to, about what I did.

It could not go on but I couldn't stop, not right then.

What *was* the relationship with Susan about? The therapy was working and we were getting on better, but it wasn't like what I had with Melissa. Why didn't I just up and leave? Ben was coming up to the end of primary school. Josh was in high school and more settled than he'd been for years. So why not just go?

The therapy was working, but it was also an exercise in deceit. Deceit and truth. As we got further down the list, it became more personal, more heartfelt, more difficult. *Doing things for each other* took months, Wendy valiantly trying to stop us re-hashing all the old arguments about the house, the kooka-burra, all those resentments I held.

It wasn't just the resentment but the pain of the rejection. And I remembered the love I'd felt—the extraordinary passion, the wanting, the needing, the love of her. I remembered it and the dreams we had.

'Can't you remember?' I yelled at Susan during the session. 'Don't you remember what it was like, how much I loved you, that you rejected me, every single day, in lots of different ways, all the time. Can't you remember that?'

'You never knew who I was,' said Susan. 'The things I wanted were just whims or middle-class fancies that you chose to diminish.'

The night after that therapy session I could not go to Melissa. I simply could not go. But I couldn't go home either. The Susan at home was too removed from the pain and hope of that memory. I rang them both and told them I'd been late working with a client and I was bunking down in a sofa bed in my office. For once I wasn't lying.

Phil

I was out on my ear. I had got carried away with the church campaign against homosexuals and gave my opinion that Jesus would have accepted homosexuals, that maybe God created homosexuals, and that the church needed to re-think. Which is obvious. But not politic to say to a group of Year 12 kids. Although I was glad because the group included at least two homosexual boys, one of whom was in agonised contortions over his sexuality, and the other who wore blue eyeshadow to class.

There was also my relationship with the gay divorcee, Mrs Andrews, teacher of French. In fact, I merely wiped her tears and gave her a few little encouraging pats, but this was sufficient encouragement to my enemies. The whole thing snowballed. Suddenly I was out of the school, out of a job.

They were very civilised about it, as such institutions generally are. All the bloodletting is done in private. They gave me a farewell afternoon tea and a kindly, if not a glowing, reference. The afternoon tea almost broke me. The kids who I'd taught over the years came. They gave me such sustenance and loyalty, I was overwhelmed. I saw their qualities, and contrasted them with mine, the chief of which was stupidity. I could say it was a matter of principle but it was more a failure to compromise.

There I was stripped down to the bare bones. Was I even a minister in anything but name? My life had been interwoven with the church from my earliest years. Only now did I feel how powerful that connection had been, how much more it meant than just the brand of Christianity I had been born in to.

I had very few prospects in the church. But I was a man of God. I wanted to do good. I wanted to grow in my spiritual life.

And there was Susan. I was not the centre of her emotional life but she was the centre of mine. I fussed about the hopelessness of it, worried about its effect on me, what it said about me, prayed about it, wanted to let it go. But couldn't or wouldn't. I was a mess.

Jenny Andrews, gay divorcee and teacher of French, had fancied me more than I thought. She courted me with the proceeds of her divorce settlement with consoling excursions to the opera, visits to her holiday house, visits to the theatre, which were all a balm to my bruised state.

She was a great one for gala events and cocktail parties and opening nights, which was how we ended up at the opening night of *Uncle Vanya*. Wonderful, wonderful, wonderful and Jenny insisted we go to the cast party afterwards. Which was where I saw Martin and met Melissa.

'Oh dear,' I said to Jenny. 'There's my friend Martin. With another woman. Not Susan. You know, I told you.' I'd told Jenny of my relationship with Susan and she had classified me, simplistically I thought, someone with a 'love addiction'.

'Always socially difficult,' said Jenny.

I bowled up to Martin, Jenny on my arm for courage. It was obvious the woman on Martin's arm wasn't just a casual acquaintanceship. He had his arm around her and as I made my way to him through the crowd, he kissed her on the neck. When I got to them, they were talking to the wonderful Anna Giapoulos who played Sonya. Martin went white and the woman looked abashed but I simply added my congratulations to the general chorus of praise until Anna was spirited off.

Then I turned to Martin. 'And your friend is . . .?'

'Melissa.'

He still had his arm round her but they looked stiff and uncomfortable.

'I'm Phil,' I said to her. 'I'm a long-time friend of Martin and Susan.'

'He's talked about you,' she said nervously. She wasn't a beautiful girl, but there was something lively and attractive about her even in her shocked state. And she had a beautiful figure.

'Well, he did talk to me about you,' I said. 'A few years ago.' She blushed.

'I hoped it was over,' I said, 'although I had my suspicions.'

'Phil's a minister,' said Jenny. 'He's very honest and plain speaking. And he's having a life crisis.' Jenny drank too much.

'Has been ever since I met him,' said Martin.

'You can hardly talk,' I said to Martin. 'How could you do this to Susan?'

'Go away, Phil.' Martin was openly hostile. 'Fuck off.'

I didn't want a scene. I'd said my piece and I felt my old fear of Martin. We went over to the bar.

'He's a bloody bully,' said Jenny. 'Just like my husband. Got very snaky when I got found out, I can tell you.' She'd already told me but she told me again.

Martin rang me early next morning in a frenzy. 'Phil, before you do anything with the information, can we just have a drink?'

'Jenny said you're a bully. I think I agree with her. I've been bullied by parents, by the bloody headmaster. I'm not in the mood to be bullied by you. Stuff you, Martin.'

'Are you going to tell Susan?'

'Are you?'

'Of course not. Come on, Phil.'

'Piss off, Martin.'

After I'd spoken to Martin, Melissa rang me. At first I was sure Martin must have put her up to it, but it became obvious he hadn't.

'I got your number from Martin's diary,' she said.

I was a bit sniffy but I agreed to meet her for a cup of coffee. We met in one of those dingy Kings Cross coffee shops, all black tiles, chrome benches and no soul.

'Martin dreads Susan knowing,' she said, 'but in a way it would be a good thing for me because it would probably be the end of his marriage. But he worries about his kids. And the way it would end. He has this romantic notion it must end well.' She looked all misty and I thought I was not the only crazy person in the world.

Then she told me all about her theory of love but how it didn't quite work for Martin. She worried how tortured he was by the whole thing. I could see *she* was a romantic and I warmed to her. After all, so was I with my love for Susan.

'The situation is of his making,' I said. 'It seems a bit hypocritical to be tortured about it.'

'*Will* you tell Susan?'

'Will you give up Martin? For the greater good? For the marriage? For the sake of the children?'

'I did,' she said, 'for over six months. It didn't help the marriage and I nearly went crazy.'

'Six months isn't very long.'

'*Will* you tell Susan?'

I didn't say anything to her but I decided not tell Susan for the moment. I took her point that it would end the marriage. I think she really wanted that. But that wasn't my reason. I thought maybe Martin would see sense or maybe the counselling would help. I realised I didn't know much about human relationships, I couldn't cope with this. I wanted to get away from it all. It was Lisa who gave me the solution.

I was hoping she could give me a job at her school. But she didn't have any vacancies for English or religion and, anyway, I wasn't quite the right brand.

I felt downcast.

'Oh Phil,' she said. 'Maybe you should go back into the ministry.'

'Can't,' I said. 'It's all "thou shalt nots" at the moment. I can't take them on. I have no family left. I've never married. I've never had a job of substance. I'm totally uninterested in money or possessions. I like high church, thinking about God and going to the theatre and football. Otherwise, I'm nothing.'

'Adolescents say that sort of thing to me every day,' said Lisa. 'At least you're not suicidal with parents who need to be notified. You haven't taken drugs or done obscene graffiti at the railway station. You could hitchhike round Australia. Go and work in Thailand. Spend a year in Turkey.'

'I couldn't leave, I worry about her.'

'It's none of your business,' said Lisa. She was so practical. 'I worry about her too but it's none of my business either. Susan's made that clear, even when I tell her things I think should concern her.' I took that to mean that she had found out about Melissa too and Susan hadn't wanted to know. It was sad, but it eased my mind.

Lisa was right. I needed to get away. I got a job as a boarding master in a boys' school in North Queensland. I just wanted a place to be. I didn't want to get involved. It was an easy job—no politics and you just had to supervise the boys' study periods and chat to the ones who cried at night.

Susan

I worked on the list and its outcomes in good faith. I tried to make things easier for him. I realised that I am a perfectionist and not everyone else is.

But there was a fear there. What if this didn't work? What would happen to our lives?

And a fear if it did work. At times I felt inexpressible rage. I liked water on the table for the evening meal. I liked it without ice in the jug. He doesn't drink water with meals but he always put ice in the jug. Just that one little habit made me feel almost murderous.

The same rage at my birthday. A black soft kid jacket. I couldn't wear it to work. I don't like black outside of work. I've never worn it. I never will.

I felt churlish, angry, childish.

I gave the jacket to Lisa. Why didn't I just tell him? Because it would blow everything wide open and the children would be unhappy.

Some days I felt really crazy, that I couldn't live this way.

I tried to be nice to him. I longed to feel the way I was acting. Wendy talked about congruence coming slowly, but sometimes I saw myself acting out this charade forever.

It had become clear in therapy how big an issue my judgement of Martin's work had been, and how important it was for him to feel he was the breadwinner. Which he was. But I had made it possible.

'Whatever you feel, Susan,' said Wendy, 'perhaps it would be constructive to let go of that particular issue.'

'I don't believe that Susan ever lets go of these things,' said Martin smugly.

'You're accusing Susan of saying she'll do one thing but secretly or privately do another?'

'I suppose I am.'

'If she says she's prepared to let go of it and you say she's not, you could also be accused of the same fault, couldn't you? You have to have a certain degree of trust for this process to work.'

'If I say I have trust that she has let go of it and I don't really have trust that she has, isn't that a lack of honesty too?' Martin was forever getting into these legalistic arguments.

'Not if you're aware you don't trust and you are prepared to work on that and let it go.'

'Basic hypocrisy. That's what you're suggesting?'

'I'm suggesting good faith rather than cynicism,' said Wendy. 'Have you read Sartre on bad faith. He was a French existentialist.'

'I know who Sartre is.' Martin bristled.

'That's good,' said Wendy with a slight touch of irony.

I could have added a bit about Sartre and bad faith but it's hardly the point when you're trying to fix up your marriage, is it?

'I look at our list,' said Martin. 'We've done the garden and that's going swimmingly. We've done house maintenance. We've done money and we're working up to the nitty gritty of the list. The fate of my kookaburra and my need for affection and sex. But all the stuff we've done is the mechanical stuff. If the lawn is mowed and the repairman cleans the leaves out of the gutter and I call the plumber, it's done. And if I have the feeling that Susan is merely tolerating my lawnmower man and my flamethrower style of weeding, it mightn't much matter. What I'm saying is that further up the lists, standards go up.'

'Standards should have been high right from the start,' I said. 'But I've accepted the way you do what you call the "mechanical stuff", even though I think it's about how we live. I've been prepared to let it go. But attitude matters, wherever we are on the list.' Of course, that had to apply to my attitude too, which remained a question mark in my mind. Wendy kept trying to bring us back to those important questions but it seemed to me that both Martin and I were going through the motions, skating on the surface, maybe because we were both afraid of what lay beneath. I often thought of what Phil said about going back to the beginning. I was a long way from that.

'When we get onto sex,' said Martin, 'or even to affection,

you've got to admit it's more complex emotionally. It requires we look at attitudes, not just actions.'

He was so pompous, so lawyerish, even though he thinks of himself as a boyish free spirit because he surfs.

'You don't seem to care what *my* attitude to sex is,' I said. 'When you want it, you want it.'

'What we're talking about is a congruence of behaviour, thought and feeling,' said Wendy. 'I think we need to accept that congruence takes time. Change takes time. We have to work at all levels.'

So we moved to Martin's pottery kookaburra. I wanted someone to break it, knock it over, demolish it in some grand gesture. But it scared me dreadfully when Ben once knocked it. It didn't break or chip, but I had found myself trembling

'It's the one thing in the house which is mine,' Martin said.

'Apart from your Whiteley drawings,' I said, 'and the antique gates in the garage and the Cossington Smith painting. And those 1930s cut-glass leadlights and the ebony elephants.'

'You've made those yours,' he said. 'The kookaburra is mine and mine alone.'

'I don't find a need to designate things as "yours" or "mine",' I said. 'Surely they're just ours?'

'They're all yours. That's why you don't care. I'm just clawing the kookaburra back.'

'Don't worry. He's yours.'

'And you hate him. Maybe that's why you hate him.'

'On one level,' said Wendy, 'you're talking about a matter of taste. Martin loves the naïve pottery kookaburra. Susan, you're averse to it. Is that right? But on another level you see your individual stake in the relationship is related to the possessions of the marriage.'

'That's the problem with this whole process,' said Martin. 'It's *her* therapy to fix *me* up. That's how she sees it.' He started jabbing his finger at Wendy.

'Don't jab at me like that, please,' she said.

She could say things like that to him. Stop him in his tracks. If I did it, it would turn into a series of endless recriminations.

We went on, weekly session after session, clawing away at each issue, trying to make the relationship work. I still bridled at the inept lawnmower man he had engaged. I had agreed to say no more about the money issue and my part in Martin's career because I saw he could not admit that I had made him a success. I wasn't letting these things go even though I stopped saying anything. Maybe that was bad faith but it seemed that made life easier and the marriage tolerable, which was all I wanted.

The children were happy. I told myself that again and again and again. That was what I wanted. That was my aim. The counselling was working. I never expected to be happy and in love. And I wasn't. But it distressed me.

I couldn't shake the feeling I had given up something. Maybe integrity or maybe I was a little stubborn. The changes we had made seemed to satisfy Martin and the children, but not me. Some days I felt very emotional, as if my life was a sham. The congruence wasn't really happening. I don't know why.

I turned to my faith at those times. I came back to what I knew best—that even though I had faults and frailties, I was loved and accepted by God. In a sense, that was Phil's gift to me. All the years we had talked, he had always talked about God as a loving presence in life, not a judging or angry deity. So prayer and church always gave me a sense of acceptance, a sense of the continuity, whatever mistakes I might make. I truly missed Phil. I'd only received one letter and it sounded as if he was a little off-beam.

Martin wasn't dismissive of my faith. He said it was a gift, a gift he didn't have. I think he was sincere. When he talked about the past, I thought it wasn't just me who had turned from him but that he had turned from me too. All those discussions we used to have, all the ideas we discussed—they didn't interest him any more.

I was scared of the list. Scared of getting to those items so important to Martin. Because I didn't believe in my heart that I was connected with him on a physical level. I'd never thought it as important as he had. I tried to think how it had been at the beginning. We had been passionate. But then we had had the children and we'd never really factored in that it changed things. Martin had been the same and I'd changed, but we'd never lovingly discussed that. Was that why things went wrong?

I accepted sex as the price of the marriage. When had I started to feel that? Why was I like that? Was it something to do with me or had it happened because the relationship didn't work. But that's what happened, occasional, quick sex which I didn't want but I consented to. I didn't feel anything much but I didn't mind that much. Lisa hadn't understood that, but it was the truth.

Martin said he wanted me to engage with him. God knows what he wanted. I'd hoped for a shift in my feelings towards him. But it hadn't happened. He still felt alien, hostile. I didn't want him, not sexually. Even the way he wanted me felt wrong.

Melissa

I was on about love. It was still my ideal but like all ideals it was constantly challenged by real life, by events, by the things people said. It felt as if life was closing in on me.

Martin's friend Phil knew about us. To be honest, I hoped he would tell Susan but he didn't. He took off to somewhere in Queensland and Martin breathed a sigh of relief.

And I was left with love.

'You do have a choice,' said Mary to me. Mary came and saw me sometimes. She owned a little house up the road and she was putting in for re-development. This day we went to lunch at a new place down on the Corso. I liked Mary. All her nonsense about the revolution when she was such a capitalist. And good at it because she thought outside the square. She was like that with relationships too. She'd been married once, very briefly, never had kids. Like me she wasn't following the 'normal' path.

'I don't see this as about having a choice or not,' I said. 'I've decided to pursue love. And Martin is the one I love.' We had a view over the beach. It was a perfect day, the waves rolling in, a cold, sharp blue.

'You're making a choice not to look for love elsewhere. You're making a choice that allows him not to make a choice. You're making a choice not to have children. You're making a choice not to get married.'

'I could have a child.'

Mary raised her eyebrows. 'I like you, Melissa,' she said. 'But I see Martin in a lot of pain, and you with your bloody head in the clouds. And you're headed for more pain, no doubt about that.'

'That's my decision.'

'Martin has a life. He's had it for thirteen years. He doesn't seem to be able to understand why he's committed to it, although it's blindingly obvious to everyone else.'

'He says it's the kids.'

'Maybe there are other things.'

'Like what?'

'Marriage vows, possessions, even Susan. He's not immune to Susan.'

'Neither am I.'

'Have another drink,' she said, pouring me one. 'I hated Susan. Now I like her. I've always liked you. I love Marty, but maybe if you weren't around, there might be a chance for him and Susan. For the kids not to have to suffer through a divorce.'

'I love him,' I retorted. 'And we already tried being apart.'

A month later, Thia Toula died suddenly of a heart attack. It was horrible, the suddenness of it, and for me it resurrected the death of my father in an unexpected way, so I made fewer demands on Martin, wanting to spend more time with my mother to talk about my father. It was a raw, childish grief, which my mother ministered to. I wondered what my father would have thought about me and Martin. Would he have been the outraged Greek father or would he have understood, like Toula?

'He knew about Toula and George,' said my mother. 'He helped her, bought the house so she wouldn't have to live with Ya Ya.'

A month later, I was surprised to find that I was the sole beneficiary of her estate. My cousins all protested that I was the nominal beneficiary and that I was supposed to share it with them.

'No,' said my mother. 'No, no, no, no. The money Toula had was from your father. This is her way of paying back your father.'

She told me the whole story. When Toula wanted to move away from Ya Ya, my father had bought a house for her. He had financed it by providing her with a guarantee. After my father had died, Toula had handled her money badly and the bank had called in the guarantee. Which was why my mother had had to sell our house and move to Annandale and why I had nothing to do with the Greek relatives.

'Why didn't you tell me?' I asked my mother.

'Two reasons,' said my mother. 'Your father loved Toula and it was true she had never had any experience with money. Second, I thought if you were not on bad terms with her or even on good terms, which is what is happened, she would at least leave you the house. And I was right.'

I wanted to give the money to my mother. It was rightfully hers but she said she didn't need it.

'At least let me take you on a holiday,' I said. 'Five star.'

'I hate five star,' she said. 'I'm two-star maximum person. Let's get a little fibro shack on the beach and cook for ourselves at some place with no nightclubs and no activities.'

'You shouldn't have married a Greek real estate agent, should you?'

'We were happy.' Did I believe her? 'Love is very complex,' she went on. 'It gets down to habit sometimes, even where it starts with passion.'

'Are you talking about Martin and me?' I asked.

'No,' she said. 'Martin and his wife.'

Anna was pregnant, her baby due next year. I congratulated her but I felt hollow and empty. Her pregnancy brought back all my longing for a child. For so long it had seemed impossible. But now I decided I had to talk to Martin about it, however difficult that was. Susan had taken the boys camping the whole weekend, so we were spending the entire weekend in bed. I loved it— eating together, reading together, watching videos together, making love three or four times a day.

I was talking to him about Anna's pregnancy. 'It's what I want too,' I said. 'For us. To have a baby.'

'But you told me this was only about love. Not leaving Susan or marriage or any of the rest.' He sounded indignant, as if I was trying to trick him.

'But you said before that you wanted a child.'

'I know,' he said. 'But things are a lot more complicated now.'

'It's you that made them complicated. It's you that changed the ground rules.'

'And then you came back. "It's all about love." That's what you said.' He moved a little away from me, so we weren't quite touching.

'Having a baby is about love,' I said. 'And I really want your baby.'

'We don't need kids. We've got each other.' He leaned over and kissed me but it didn't feel like love to me. There was something cold, even calculated. He lay there, looking at the ceiling. 'Truly, I don't want more kids. I'm sorry, but the older they get the harder it is. The more I feel the responsibility.'

'When did you decide this?' I felt sick with disappointment and anger.

He turned towards me and started stroking my hair. 'Look, I'm not ruling it out completely. I don't mean I won't have a child with you, at some point. But if you said to me you didn't want a child, that would be fine with me.'

'How do you think that makes me feel? You have two with Susan and none with me?'

'Having children isn't a competition. We're in a relationship not a bloody race, Melissa.'

'I don't want a child because I'm competing with Susan!'

I said. 'I want a child because I'm with you. I want our baby with you. I thought you wanted the same thing!'

'Christ! It's different from the nappy ads. Kids are hard work, time, money, devotion, pain.'

'Love is all those things,' I said.

'Meliss, you've got your head in the clouds. You don't know what it's like, you don't know what a responsibility it is, how hard it is.'

I'd got out of bed by this stage and had my bathrobe wrapped around me. 'Maybe nobody who has never had children should ever actually have children because they won't ever understand what it is to have children. Is that what you're saying?'

'I'm saying we're in a relationship where we aren't in a position to be central to each other in a lot of ways. And until we are, we shouldn't even be thinking about having a child.'

'Fuck, fuck, fuck you,' I said. I threw a cushion at him. I was so angry. 'I've given up thinking about us being together. I've given you that, I've given you love. And you tell me now that I'm not even allowed to think about something that is important to me. Fuck you!' I hit him hard with the pillow. 'I was brought up by a single mother. I know how hard it was for her. But she did it. She never fucking complained about the time or the money or the commitment or the pain. I don't think she ever even thought about it.'

He looked at me. 'I bet she did.'

'Anyway I don't need you to have a baby. I've got this nest egg from Toula. I can just do it. I don't need help from you. If you're going to have love without obligations, so can I.'

At that, he got up and walked out.

I was shaken to the core. Scared of losing him. Scared of our fight. Scared of never having a child. But when he came back the next day, we made up, made love. Then, although it was winter, we went out into the surf, in wetsuits, but it was still too cold. For the first time ever I felt a little fearful being out there, the beach deserted, a great rip running. But then I looked at Martin and I felt exhilarated by the risk, by our sense of bravery. I felt okay. It was the right setting for love to re-appear, and the wrong setting to ask questions or make plans and babies and houses. I had to forget that stuff. Susan, and all those other things, there was no answer. There was just me and Martin together.

CHAPTER 13

1991

Susan

Wendy went on a long overseas holiday during summer and Martin and I were left to our own devices. I must say, he tried. He did try.

He was a lot more considerate around the house and he came on half the summer holiday with the kids, whereas for the last few years it had only been a few days at the most. That was the thing about Martin. He wanted us there, as his family, but he didn't want to be there.

We were staying down the Snowy Mountains, a place I loved and the kids loved. It was so quiet, I enjoyed the walking and the cold nights and the sense of isolation. The boys went fishing and on little excursions by themselves and swimming in the cold river. It made me feel me alive.

Martin didn't like it, because it wasn't the beach, but that year he threw himself into it, and he took the boys off riding and fishing which was fine by me. We were staying in a little chalet, very simple, and we cooked each night outside on the barbecue and I even made our own bread. We sat around in the evening and played Scrabble or Monopoly. It felt like family life should.

Martin and I slept in the top bedroom and we could see the stars and hear the wind in the trees, or sometimes, a sudden storm.

We'd lie in bed reading. One night I was sure he was going to ask for sex because he started touching me. But he didn't. He just held me after we turned the lights out.

'Susan, I just want you to know I love you.' He kissed me on the forehead and then rolled over and went to sleep.

The next day, the call came from Sydney and he had to leave. He bustled around as if his departure was unexpected and there was some great drama. The kids and I were used to it.

That day the boys took a packed lunch. They went out along the river, boiled the billy and caught fish. I walked along the riverbank to an old hut where I sat and thought.

The hut was stone, with no roof, the old summerhouse of a family, who had come from Sydney in Victorian times. There were apple trees and berries planted around it, and it seemed to hold a reverberation from those simpler times.

Martin had seemed sincere when he said he loved me. I thought he did love me. Or he had the feeling that for him counted as love. I shouldn't complicate this but people mean different things by love. But anyway, I no longer had any of that feeling for him. It felt painful, a vacuum. I didn't know what I thought or felt, but it wasn't love. It wasn't hate. It was more a sort of fatigue in his presence. I couldn't love him the way he wanted. Maybe I had never been able to.

I felt bad when he said he loved me and I wished I felt differently. I know sex for him is an important element of that love. I felt painfully far from a real intimacy with him.

I thought about faith, love, right and wrong. I wanted to know what to do, how to live my life. I had been a good wife, a good mother. I had said I wanted the marriage to continue. Now we'd come to the point of dealing with love and affection in our counselling sessions I began to see what it all meant.

There's a sort of cold in the mountains, even when the sun is blazing. You find it suddenly, in a shadow, in a breath of wind, when a cloud suddenly passes over the sky. But that day it was blazing hot, the insects humming around me, the heat coming off the ground. I took off my shoes and walked through the thick grass down to the river. I stood on a smooth stone, letting the water run across my feet.

I went back to the hut. I had waves of feeling coursing through me but I can't put in words what the feeling actually was, except it was deep and powerful. There was a wide doorstop to the hut. I sat on it. I was praying without words. I saw I could not give to Martin what I did not have. I could offer him what I had, what I could. That was all. I felt the cold and saw a bank of black cloud coming over the mountaintops. It began to rain, suddenly and fiercely, and I walked back to the chalet, the icy rain beating against my face and body.

Josh

Mum was worried. Dad acted happy but he wasn't.

Ben started high school with me, and he was always in trouble. He'd always been in trouble before but it didn't matter so much in primary school. I tried to look out for him. He was in my house at school, but the thing was Ben didn't care. There wasn't one thing about school he liked.

I got him to come to debating for the house competition on Tuesdays because Ben is a really good speaker. He's not shy like me. And he can have an argument and make people laugh. So I thought he'd like debating. But that's when things got bad.

Dad said he'd come and collect us on his way home because

we finished at 5.30 and on Tuesday he always went to the meeting at the Surf Club. Which was good because Mum didn't like us coming home late.

We did debating practice in the music rooms on the top floor. From there, you could see right out onto the road, not close, but you could see it. Dad's car was there, parked up the hill from the gate where we always met him.

'There's Dad's car,' I said to Ben. 'He's early.'

'Let's finish this,' he said. Debating was the first thing he'd ever liked at school. And I could see he was just itching to demolish this guy's arguments.

Ben was the last speaker and he got up and he was going for it, but halfway through he said, 'I hate this fucking school,' straight to the debating master, who started to say something. But Ben was just out of there not even taking his bag, and I took off after him. He was gone and I couldn't find him. I went back and got his bag. The debating master was really angry.

'Tell your brother he's out of the team and he reports to me first thing.'

'Yes, Sir.' I was so angry I wanted to tell on Ben and get him into trouble but he was sitting in Dad's car. I guess Dad saw him coming out of the gate and drove down the hill like he always did. Ben was angry and I thought Dad had already bawled him out about something.

Later I told him what the debating master said, but he didn't say anything. He didn't do any homework either, just played on his Gameboy.

Next day, he went off really early and by the time I got there, it was all over the school that Ben flooded the washrooms and wrote stuff in texta all over the headmaster's door and the staff corridor.

He said if they suspended him he'd do the same again, and he was going to run away and no one could stop him and he hated everyone. He was yelling at teachers. Mum came and got him. Everyone said he'd be expelled for sure.

Which he was. Except because Mum had worked so hard for the school and is secretary for the fete and stuff, they agreed to take him back.

Ben wouldn't go. He said he wanted to go to reform school and meet cool guys. He seriously thought that's what would happen because he watched too many movies. Mum wanted him to go back to school but Dad said he should go to the high school and take the consequences. Ben finally left our school and went to the high school, but I don't think he went too often.

About a month after, he told me that afternoon in debating he'd seen a lady get out of Dad's car, while he was making the speech, and Dad got out, and they were kissing, real kissing.

The divorce was back.

I told Ben maybe he should talk to Dad in case it was a mistake. He said he talked to Dad and Dad told him it was a mistake, but Ben knew it wasn't a mistake. And Ben was scared if he told Mum she might kill herself or something. I told him that wouldn't ever happen but I knew why he'd done all that stuff at school. That's what Ben does when he's upset. I draw pictures of people all hunched up or dying or something.

I thought we should tell Mum. What happened wasn't Ben's fault but he was in trouble. I said I'd tell Mum and Ben said he'd kill me if I did. We fought and he punched me really hard and made me promise I wouldn't tell Mum about the lady. I didn't even tell Mum why I got a big bruise on my arm. She was really angry because I wouldn't tell her anything about Ben.

I had the dream every night.

Melissa

Martin told me what had happened with Ben.

'So somehow, even though you told me it could never happen, Ben actually saw us,' I said.

'He never saw us,' said Martin. 'He hates that school. Always has. He's like me. Hates the establishment.'

'Oh,' I said, 'Like you, Mr Lawyer? Hates the establishment?'

Then he gave me a big rave about how he hated the establishment, which was why he was doing work on some police corruption investigation. He was stinging and nasty and I felt put down. He couldn't admit that we had been sprung and how awful it was for the kid.

'I love you,' I said. 'But sometimes, you know, you use that to pour shit on me. I don't care whether you're establishment or not. It's crazy saying Ben is like you and that's why he flooded the bathroom. It doesn't make sense whereas it makes a whole lot of sense that he saw us.'

Anyway we made up, like we always did. I had to let it go. Can't fight with him about that sort of stuff because its like a raw wound. Trouble is there seemed to be more and more raw wounds in our relationship.

Anna's baby. That was another one. It was so hard for me. I went to the birth and they asked me to be godmother and I was a mess of tears for a week after, visiting Anna every day. But Marty and I couldn't talk about it because we'd end up in a bad space.

But I loved him. He was my love and my life. And he loved me. He could be so tender and beautiful. That's what made it so difficult.

Sometimes, almost too difficult.

Mary

I asked Joshie what had happened and he told me.

I thought I should tell Susan. It was no use talking to Marty. He'd do his bullshit act like he did on Ben.

Joshie begged me not to tell, at least till he talked to Ben some more.

Ben wouldn't talk.

I decided to think about it, not act in the heat of the moment. Telling Susan was the right thing to do. I decided I'd do it in a week or two. I'd see if I could talk to Ben first.

Lisa

June got pregnant. She'd always been up and down with her weight so I didn't pick up she was pregnant until she was seven months. I saw her in the shower one morning and I knew.

I told her it was okay, it would be fine. Which is true of almost everything if you look at the big picture. But I was amazed how calm I was. The worst had happened and it wasn't as terrible as it might have been.

She decided to keep the baby and then try to get an education. I went to the birth. It was a turning point for June and me.

She laboured right through the night and most of the next day, and when she was finished, and tucked up with the little fellow, I was completely stuffed. So stuffed that when I walked into the hospital coffee shop and sat down, I barely noticed the man sitting at a table next to mine, until he got up to go. Then I realised it was Martin, with a woman who looked washed out and teary.

I've suspected for years that Martin might be having a series of affairs but Susan had made it pretty clear she didn't want to know about it. Now here he was with this woman.

'Hi Martin,' I said, getting up.

He was cool as a cucumber. 'Hi Lisa.'

'June's just had the baby,' I said. 'A little boy.'

'Great,' he said. He was always lovely to June and Rosie. 'She's come through okay?'

'She's great,' I said. 'This might even be the making of her. But I wouldn't have expected to see you here.'

'No,' he said. 'I was just getting a deposition signed by a new mother who's a client of mine. Wants an AVO against her husband and we had to act fast. This is her sister, Melissa.'

'Hi,' I said, and the woman nodded and stood up. She seemed upset, which I thought was understandable.

Well, that was all okay.

'Give June my love,' he said.

'Sure,' I said. 'We'll probably come over with the baby in a few weeks.'

'Great.' He smiled and gave me a nice hug, the sort that always makes you feel good about Martin. The woman smiled stiffly at me and got up to follow him, obviously ill at ease. He started walking and she trailed after him.

I sat down again, to have my cuppa, but I was still watching them out of the corner of my eye. At the coffee shop door there was a rack of jump suits for babies. She stopped and touched a little suit, the way women do.

'Come on, sweetie,' he said impatiently. He must have forgotten I was there.

She glanced back. I was staring at her and she turned away quickly.

'Susan doesn't want to know,' said Jamie when I told him the story. 'That's the truth and you know it. And when it comes down to it, I suppose you could call a client's sister "sweetie".'

'You could not,' I said. 'How can I not tell her?'

He put his arms round me and hugged me. '*Fermez la bouche*, sweetheart. Button it up. This is a mess and you're best out of it. For all we know she knows and doesn't want to know. There are plenty of marriages like that. Which is why I'm so glad ours isn't.'

I thought Susan needed to know. I'd pick my moment.

Susan

I was aware, every day, of how much the atmosphere at home affected the boys. It was better than it had been, but it wasn't right. For years Josh had seemed like the vulnerable one. But Josh had matured. It seemed as if he'd got beyond his childhood worries and become his own person. Now Ben was troubled. And although Ben was tougher he didn't have Josh's inner resources.

I never realised how strong his feelings were about school. He didn't like the school we had chosen for the boys and had romantic notions of how 'free' he might be at the local high school. But I never thought it would come to anything beyond some adolescent grumbling. When they rang and told me what he'd done, I almost couldn't believe it. It seemed the sort of thing someone else's child would do. Even though he wasn't happy at school, he didn't seem quite that unhappy, or quite that disturbed.

Martin and I went straight to the school. Even then we could have contained it. I wanted Ben to be responsible for his actions but also to realise that Martin and I were the parents and we made the decisions.

'You're only worried about the shame this brings on you,' said Martin. 'And you can't bear the thought of your kid at a public school.'

'It's not that,' I said. 'We can't discuss this now. Ben's upstairs.'

'He should go to the high school. He can wear the consequences. It might be better for him anyway.'

'Martin. Not now.'

'This isn't acting out, as you call it. It's bloody close to criminal behaviour. And you want to kept him wrapped in cotton wool.'

Ben knew we disagreed and it gave him power. We couldn't send him back. It would be me sending him back. Here he was, going into puberty, with Martin telling him he was old enough to make his own decisions. I was powerless, so he went to the high school. I was very angry with Martin and Martin was in a fury with me even though he got what he wanted.

It was in this context that we went back to our first therapy session for the year with Wendy. It was in this context that we moved into our discussion of our behaviour in private, displays of affection and sex. It was in this context I told Martin what I was prepared to offer. I simply offered him what I could. I suppose you could call it a 'no frills' deal. I told him the truth, that I couldn't find a way into sexual intimacy with him, that I didn't know what I felt, but I was prepared to return to a regular sexual relationship because it was so important to him.

'Just wait,' said Wendy. She looked very concerned. 'This doesn't seem a very constructive way to go—for either of you. We really need to discuss this.'

But Martin didn't wait. He sprayed around some vicious remarks, a few snide comments and then he left the therapy session in a rage, went home, packed his bag and left the house.

The marriage was over.

Martin

It started off as a shit year.

Well, right at the beginning, when we were in the mountains, I thought for a moment that we could get the marriage to work. I was thinking that if it could, I'd give up Melissa even though it would break my heart. I knew that the life we were leading wasn't fair to Melissa. So one way or another I should bite the bullet. I felt at some level I did love Susan, could love Susan and could make the marriage work, maybe. When we were in the mountains I told Susan I loved her. She didn't say a thing. Just lay there. But even then I thought maybe when Witch Wendy came back, we could, as she always so charmingly put it, 'work through it'.

From then on, things went strictly downhill. First there was the school thing with Ben. Jesus! He obviously saw me with Melissa but totally exaggerated what he saw. Melissa and I had an enormous fight about it. She contended he couldn't exaggerate it because he wouldn't have known exactly what to exaggerate, which just goes to show how very little she knows about children. And Susan and I ended up on opposite sides of the fence and Ben jumped precisely into the neat little hole we'd dug together, which was exactly where he wanted to be.

Melissa became obsessed with Anna's baby. The day after the birth, her breasts swelled up as if she was making milk. I loved that about her, so instinctive, but I couldn't talk to her about it because the idea of a baby was such a minefield for us. She looked at the pictures of the baby endlessly, visited Anna constantly and probably drove her mad. I went along once to the hospital and we had the bad luck to run into Lisa. Even though I gave Lisa a perfectly plausible story, Melissa was convinced she 'knew'.

I was on edge, really on edge.

So we were back in counselling with Witch Wendy.

'Okay,' I said. 'We're into sex and love, which is my territory. My longings and desires, my needs not being met. All that, we finally get to look at.' I glanced at Susan but neither of us could hold it. It was too painful. 'Maybe we could even go to a sex therapist, God forbid!' I felt angry and sad, not thinking about what I was saying. I was trying, I thought. Did I want it or not? If it didn't work, could I leave with a clear conscience?

But Susan puts it on the table, straight up. There was no fooling around with love and affection at all. A straight deal. No feeling. She explicitly said there was no feeling.

'I'll have sex with you twice a week. I think that's fair.'

Even Wendy was a little taken aback but she was thinking about Susan, not about the metaphorical slap in the face Susan had just given me.

I felt as if I'd been hit by a lightning bolt but part of my brain kept working. The part connected to my smart mouth. Not that it mattered.

'So when does the week start?' I asked. 'Do we check in Monday or Sunday night, or perhaps even Friday night? And if I don't make it one week, can I use that one next week? Or could I even save it up and have an orgy for a whole week?'

'Stop bullying me, Martin,' said Miss Twice-a-Week. 'This is perfectly reasonable.'

'That's the thing about it,' I said. 'It's reasonable. It's fair. Trouble is, it's not passionate or caring or loving or any of those things. It's mechanical. It's got nothing to do with the relationship we're supposed to be having.'

'It's the relationship we've been having,' said the shop stewardess of love. 'It's exactly that.'

'Not the relationship I've been having,' I said, and immediately, guiltily, Melissa was there in my head.

'Really, Martin, we're just formalising what's been happening. How is this any different? And I'm trying. This is a starting point but I've got to be honest about where we're starting.'

'Isn't it the whole point?' I said. 'To make it different. For Chrissakes, we've been working through this list for a whole year, putting meaning and purpose into me mowing the lawn, finding our essential selves in paying the bills together in the cosy Thursday night ceremony. I'm the one who licks the stamps, aren't I? And now you reckon we should find transcendence and hope in our sex lives. Twice a week?'

'Perhaps we could defuse this,' said Wendy, but without much hope. Susan was in tears, I was in gorilla mode.

'I'm finished.' We said it together. The most synchronistic thing in our marriage. And I went home, packed my things and walked out of my house.

Melissa

I saw it was over with absolute and total clarity. I actually knew, in a confused sort of way, the moment he arrived with his bag. Don't ask me how I knew, but I did. And then, when he told me all with such passion and anger about Susan's betrayal, Susan's twice a week offer, Susan's insult, my position was crystal clear. I had been his insurance policy if it didn't work out with Susan. And maybe a bit on the side if it did.

It was finished for me.

Her twice a week sex offer. How enraged he was. How insulted he felt. How could she reduce their marriage to convenience? The way she saw relationships. Just a contract. No love. No sense of partnership.

So, I thought, this is what he's been after all along. A partnership with Susan. The real thing, and in the end she just wanted a marriage of convenience, which was what he claimed to have been having.

'We're free now,' he said.

'Free?'

'Free from her.'

'I always thought it was the kids.'

'It was.'

Then he saw my face.

'Don't worry, sweetie,' he said. 'I'm just mad at her. It was the last straw, that's all.'

'I thought it would be quite a good deal,' I said. 'Sex twice a week with an attractive woman you don't love. Or maybe you do love her and that's the trouble.'

'It's just the history, sweetie. And the coldness of it.'

'Don't call me sweetie.'

'You don't understand, Melissa. Let it go. This is the beginning of our new life together. This is where we start. We can do anything now.'

I shook my head. 'No, this is you cashing in your insurance. This is when you finally realise the marriage is kaput. This relationship has been all about you. You and me. You and Susan. You and your kids. You and your job. I've been a bit player, that's all. How could I have ever thought that Susan didn't matter? How could I have been so deluded? Susan was the main player and I was the bit player.'

'You know that's crap.'

'Then why leave now? Listen, Marty, if she'd said, "We'll try it your way. I love you. I'm sorry, sex is hard for me, but this is worth working on, because I feel something".' If she'd said that, you would have stayed.'

'No. I would have come here.'

'Crap, because if that was the case why weren't you here last year or two years ago? Why did it take Susan to say. "Let's get real. This is a marriage of convenience for the sake of our kids". Why did it take that?'

'She didn't say that. She wanted a contract with sex twice a week.'

'Marty, why *did* you want sex with a woman who didn't want you? Or love you? For all that time?'

'It's got nothing to do with us.'

'It's got everything to do with us, especially with me. Because this is what my mother, your sister Mary and Anna, and every woman of good sense has been telling me. And I haven't looked at it. I made my airy fairy choice for love and kisses and stolen moments.'

'I love you.' He said it with a superiority that infuriated me. I flung his bag at the front door. I pushed him towards the door.

'Go!' I said. 'This has been a toxic, destructive, horrible waste of time. If you stay I'll fucking kill you. You're totally deluded. This was bad, bad, bad.'

He went. I was devastated because I did love him. I howled and sobbed. And then I went to the people in my life who supported me. And I was ready to face this truth. But that old corny saying that the truth sets you free—is true. And I was angry enough to hang onto that.

He came back later, begging, explaining cajoling and bribing. Phone calls night and day. For a while I wanted him to understand the lies he had told me, himself and Susan. He didn't get it, any of it.

'It's finished. It's over.'

Martin

I was out of my mind when I left Melissa. I couldn't believe it was over. But I knew, I just knew from the way she was that this wasn't just a lover's tiff. This was it, the end. I wanted to forget, to blot it all out. So I took to drinking fairly heavily. There are worse ways to take your mind off things, but this time it didn't work. It just added in more fear, more rage, more upset, swirling around inside of me.

I was down at the local watering hole. Still the best pub around, even if it kept going up-market. Sometimes seems like the whole world is going upmarket. Funny though, there's always a place for the low life. And for the purveyor of tales about the low life. So it seemed natural to see my mate Cliff, who was now writing for one of the Sunday rags.

He'd described me a couple of weeks earlier as a 'society lawyer' which made me sound like a complete wanker. Anyway he was an old mate and I wasn't one to hold a grudge so I went over to have a drink with him.

Stupid bugger, he was pissed as a newt. Mind you, so was I.

'The famous society lawyer,' he said. 'Fancy house, fancy car, kids at that fancy school. Fancy wife, fancy girlfriend.' It was just the usual male bullshit, low level aggressive mateship banter, except he didn't have the latest info that there was now no wife and no girlfriend. And there was something offensively triumphant about his tone, as if he'd got the dirt on me.

'Fuck you,' I said and grabbed him by the shirt. Which sort of surprised me because I don't get into fights. I felt seriously out of control. And I'm twice as big as Cliff and twice as fit, which were all signs for him to cool it.

'Fuck *you*, you bloody peacock,' he said.

Then I was really out of control. I suppose, looking back on it, we were in the mode of giant apes who'd just been stung on the arse by a bee and we were both taking it very, very seriously, and very, very personally. I was ready to kill Cliff.

'Shut the fuck up,' I said.

Cliff had a lot of alcohol on his side.

'The lovely fucking girlfriend?' he went on, 'does she fuck better than the frigid wife?'

Well, the bar spun around and I spun Cliff around and gave him a personal relationship with the carpet. I was going to make sure some of his neurones took a permanent holiday. There was a crowd of punters pulling me off him. And suddenly, I realised, from the amount of blood that this was serious and I felt horribly and suddenly stone-cold sober.

And then I was kneeling down beside Cliff, saying 'Shit mate, fuck it, I didn't . . .' and I was staring at his tooth embedded in the carpet and the blood all down my shirt.

Some doctor who wasn't quite as pissed as the rest of us put his tooth back in and fixed him up. Thank God I had a few mates in that pub because this was assault in the eyes of the law and Cliff was a fucking journo.

Someone hustled me out of there and got me a cab. I couldn't cope with going back to the hotel where I was staying. For some reason I gave the cabbie the address of my old girlfriend Yvette. I mean I hadn't seen her since that wild night a few years back, but I just needed someone to talk to. I couldn't bear me and the mini bar together alone for yet another night. Plus I was pretty shaken up about Cliff and what I'd done.

I didn't even know if she still lived there, but I stumbled up to the door and rang the bell.

'Oh shit,' she said. But at least she didn't close the door.

'Could I sleep here?' I asked. 'Just for one night. I can't face a hotel. I'd neck myself, I think.'

'I'm the archetypal slut with a heart of gold,' she said. 'You can sleep here. One night, no sex. You look as if you've been in a brawl.'

'Big boys shouldn't get into fist fights,' I said, looking at my hand.

'It's a fairly unattractive quality,' she said. 'Your basic bad temper.'

'This bastard,' I explained. 'He's nasty when he's drunk.'

She gave me ice to put on my hand. 'Whereas you'd be a charmer.'

'Can't believe I laid into him like that,' I said. 'He lost a tooth. I mean he's a walking example of alcoholic decrepitude anyway. I'll pay his dental bill, but knowing Cliff he'll probably charge me to get his whole bloody head re-engineered.'

'So why aren't you at home with your lovely wife?' Yvette asked.

I began to cry. I sat there and cried. And cried. I've never cried like that before.

Later, I told her the whole bloody story. 'Jesus,' she said.

'I always told you marriage was a redundant institution.

Then we slept together but we didn't fuck. I was in no condition and she was in no mood. But she put her arms around me and slept close, the way I sometimes used to with my boys when they couldn't sleep.

Phil

I had ended up in 'bad company,' something I had always warned children in my care to avoid. They were two boys at the boarding school where I was a housemaster — lads of 15 and 16 — and much more experienced in the ways of the world than I was. I busted them creeping back into the boarding house late one night. And they persuaded me to smoke some dope. I was at a very low ebb. And then we went swimming naked in the school swimming pool but I forgot I was English and I can't swim very well. Especially when stoned. To cut a long story short, to prevent a scandal they sent me to a monastery and gave the boys a commendation for saving me from drowning. It was awful and irresponsible and I was glad to be in the monastery because I really needed to sort my head out.

People in Australia think there are only monasteries in Europe, and they exist solely to make exotic liqueurs, but there are quite a few in Australia. I'd always had a sort of longing for the cloistered life, and I certainly needed it at this juncture.

It was a Catholic monastery, a gorgeous place, picture-book pretty, surrounded by orchards, gardens and beehives, right out in the country. In fact, living there was a little uncomfortable. The rooms were musty, the apples from the orchard were small and sour and the cook couldn't make a decent loaf of bread despite twenty years of practice. Makes you wonder about the power of prayer, doesn't it? The place had all the hallmarks of a bunch of men living together, rather than a spiritual power-house. But perhaps all that made it the right place for me to put my life in perspective—my failed ministry, my failure as a teacher, my failure in love, that is, with Susan. I had poured an obsessional love into Susan, all the while knowing she was totally unavailable.

The brothers were very kind and certainly didn't intrude. But their calm and ease made me think I should ask for their help with my emotional life, which, left to itself, was swirling round and round in my head, taking strange flights of fancy and descending into black mires. So one day, out in the garden, I approached Brother John and told him all. He was kind to me, in a dry way, listening carefully and attentively.

'Sometimes,' he said, 'A cloistered life seems difficult but your path has been hard too.'

'I've made it hard,' I said, 'Not paying attention to reality.' And suddenly it hit me that my relationship with Susan had been about me, not about her. I had known about Melissa and I'd kept that knowledge from her because it seemed easier. As her friend, I should have told her.

That night was the long dark night of the soul. I saw my utter self-centredness, the utter falseness of my love for Susan, the utter pointlessness of my life. I'd thought I was unselfish not telling her because I was giving a chance for the marriage to survive. But it was cowardice, pure moral cowardice.

I went to Brother John the next day. 'I don't know what to do. I've behaved selfishly, egotistically.' I guess I looked crazy. I certainly felt crazy.

'Would you scrub out the kitchen cupboards today?' he said.

I worked all day, scrubbing out cupboards. Brother John came back at the end of the day.

He looked at my trembling hands. 'We have a three-day silent retreat,' he said, 'where you will find God's will for you.'

I didn't find God's will or I couldn't be sure if it was God's will or my own. But I was so agitated and upset about not telling the truth to Susan, that I set off to the nearest town, so I could make a phone call to her in private. Ring Susan, be honest. I rang that night.

'I love you,' I said. 'I've loved you for such a long time. You're my life, Susan. But that's not what I have to tell you.'

'Phil,' she said. 'You don't have to tell me anything. My life's all upside down too. Martin and I have separated. I'm trying to explain it to the boys. They're very upset. But it's all out in the open. It's over, and in a way I'm relieved.'

'So you know about Melissa?' I asked.

'Melissa?' Her voice was suddenly shrill. She didn't know about Melissa.

'Melissa is Martin's lover. I thought you should know.' There was a long silence. 'Susan?'

'How long has Melissa been Martin's lover?' she asked. She sounded too composed.

'I think it's been a while.' I said it too lightly. 'On and off.'

'On and off for how long?'

'Years,' I said. I could feel her pain.

'How many years?' And her bitterness.

'A lot.' I was tempted to lie, but the damage was already done. 'Going back to before that car crash Martin had.'

'1986,' she snapped. She had an absolutely phenomenal memory for recalling dates of even minor events. 'Five years at least.'

'Will I come back?' I asked. 'Help you with all this?'

'What? My very own Judas?' she said, and hung up.

Susan

Martin leaving had made sense. The boys were devastated, but even that was manageable. And I had a dawning sense of freedom. I was upset, but underneath I felt the right thing had happened. I told Dad that I'd take some leave. After a couple of months I'd come back and start up a branch office in Chatswood or out west, something with a bit of a challenge that would keep me busy.

'So you don't want him to lose the partnership,' Dad asked.

'I can live with this,' she said. 'And I'll need the maintenance.' He was a little surprised I was so calm. I must say, so was I, but I suppose it had been a long time coming.

That sense of calm lasted until Phil told me the sordid story about the other woman. Melissa was her name. It had been going on for years.

That was the day I threw his pottery kookaburra over the cliff. It was worth two thousand dollars. He'd tracked down the man who'd made it just a few months before. An artisan who made ugly things. It had made Martin very happy. He'd put it back on the table in the hallway. That made me feel even better chucking it over the cliff. Not my style at all, but there was a great satisfaction in that throw. I don't think I've ever been so pleased with a single physical action. Unfortunately I couldn't hear it smash on the rocks below. But I could imagine it.

The next day I put all the clothes he'd left in the house in a charity bin. I wanted all trace of him out of the house, out of my life. There was some vengeance in it too. It did cross my mind to burn his surfboards on the front lawn, luckily I couldn't find the garage key.

I sat down with the boys and told them what I had done and why, told them about the other woman, told them how angry I was. He had betrayed me and he had betrayed them. I told them we would be okay.

But that night it came out. Josh told me the boys had known. He sat there with tears in his eyes. Ben was there but then he went outside and jumped on the trampoline. Josh went upstairs, and I sat there in the dusk, listening to the thwang, thwang, thwang of the trampoline springs. Suddenly I ran upstairs, full of fury at Josh.

'You should have told me, Josh. Why didn't you? He betrayed me but you did too. I was the only one who didn't know. And Ben, you should have told me for Ben. How could you do that just to protect your father.'

'I didn't . . .' he started, but I walked out, bitter to my core. To have been betrayed by my own son.

It broke my trust with Josh. I was disappointed in him. Poor little Ben, he was the victim of this, of his father.

They were a little frightened. I was frightened too because I felt transported by my rage and hatred. I felt as if I was operating in another world entirely, that I was another person.

The sham of it. The pretence. Going to therapy had been an absolutely hollow exercise. That's when I knew he was sick. Well, not sick, because he had his own self-interest at heart. Keep his house, his wife, his children, his job. So for him the duplicity made perfect sense, I suppose. I could have understood if it had happened once. But this had been going on for years and years.

This whole experience was like being in the eye of the

storm. The world as I knew it ceased to exist. The people I knew didn't exist anymore. Their deceit, their trickery. People I had trusted and loved. My life support system failed. It was hideous.

When Phil had told me, he mentioned something about Mary, so I rang her. Mary had known since it began, pretending to be my friend. Keep the wife happy. I was encircled by the family, deceived by the family. She'd never see the children again either, not that they want to see her *or* their father.

Phil had known. All those years I trusted him as my truest and most loyal friend.

Lisa too. That's what I mean about the world as I knew it ceasing to exist. My own sister knew and thought I didn't want to hear it. Claimed she'd tried to tell me at one of our lunches. I have absolutely no memory of it. Something about an actress. Of course I would have wanted to know. It would have saved years of misery, years of deception, years of illusion.

I rang Dad. 'Did you know about this other woman?'

'What woman?' he asked.

'Swear to me you didn't know Martin had another woman?'

'Susan, of course, I didn't know. Who the hell is she? How long has it been going on? When did you find out?'

I gave him all the details and then I told him that I wanted Martin out of the company.

'Susan, you told me you wanted him here. He'll pay the maintenance.'

'No,' I said. 'I don't care about that. I want him out on his ear. I'm going to get every piece of property he has. I don't want him anywhere near us.'

'Susan . . .'

'Do you think it's right what he's done?' I asked. 'Should he be allowed to get away with it?'

'No, of course not.' There was a sort of resignation. And then, I thought afterwards, he's in the same boat with Marg and Mum. Except he's never been sprung. But he's lived that same lie. And for the first time in ages I felt just a tiny bit of sympathy for my mother.

Mary

Martin was devastated. He was just crazed with grief. Well, with grief and rage. He's got that Irish ancestry, so it's easy for grief to turn to rage.

It wasn't a pretty sight. Full of self-pity, resentment, anger, self-loathing, self-righteousness, pomposity, dishonesty and irritation. Under that he was also terrified and guilty. His life as he knew it had disappeared. Both lives in one go. And his work.

He couldn't understand how I could see Susan's point of view. He was even more bitter that I could see Melissa's. That was the ultimate betrayal. But he couldn't quite say it was a betrayal on Melissa's part because he still really loved her. He said she was too idealistic, she was too young, she had her head in the clouds. He couldn't see she was right.

The sad thing was that he had been lying to himself for so long that he didn't get it. Really and truly. That's when I stopped saying 'See', and just loved him again. He was my brother. So I was trying to see him through it, wanting him to find a life after this, to have a life, impossible though it seemed.

And yes, I could be superior and say I'd seen it all coming. I had, but I'd also denied it in some way. I'd denied the deep, bitter truth of it, the destructiveness of it. Not just the affair, the whole thing.

Mum and Dad chided him about the sin of divorce while secretly blaming Susan. His surfing friends knew all there was to know about waves, but not much else. And he didn't have legal friends any more.

When I was sure he wasn't suicidal, I sent him up to Byron Bay to live in one of my cottages and got him some local legal work. I went up regularly to check on him. He didn't surf and he did precious little legal work. But people recover from these things.

'I'm a doctor,' I told him. 'People die from cardiac failure but most of them recover from a broken heart.' I'm not the most sympathetic person but I wasn't sure he needed sympathy.

Susan was angry with everybody. I understood that.

'Not the boys,' I said. 'Don't take it out on the boys.'

She threatened me with a court order if I tried to contact the boys.

I still think my reasons for not telling her were okay.

I phoned Lisa to ask her to tell the boys I'd see them when things calmed down, but she'd been threatened with a court order too. Susan had found out she'd known about Melissa.

Same with Phil, who was in Queensland somewhere, saving his soul. We just had to wait.

CHAPTER 14

1992

Susan

I had refused to let the children see him for six months. The children didn't want to see him and I made sure they didn't have to. He went and lived somewhere up the coast so it was irrelevant anyway.

Rage consumed me absolutely and totally. I sold the house because he had loved it. I made sure Martin couldn't work in the firm. I would have done anything I could to ensure his unhappiness.

It was very hard. I couldn't decide not to be in a rage. I couldn't decide to act rationally. I had absolutely no motivation to do anything apart from be in a rage. I knew it wasn't the way I wanted to behave.

I apologised to my boys. I said that I understood them not telling me. It had been messy, uncertain, and they were unsure what to do. And, of course, Martin had denied it. But something in me still held it against Josh, and being Josh, he knew that. Maybe it was because he was becoming a man. He was tall and rangy like Martin, the same wild hair. I could not shake the feeling, the knowledge, that he had betrayed me. I hated that in myself.

I did some strange things. I told my mother about Marg— the affair with Dad, the flat, the double visits to the opera. I told her, not out of any sympathy for her, but because of her lack of sympathy for me.

'You should never have married Martin,' she said, 'but you didn't want my advice, as I remember.'

Her reaction to my revelation about Marg was probably predictable. 'Oh that little floozy,' she said, 'I've known about her for years.'

My father was furious. 'Stirring the pot when you've known for years,' he said. 'My private life is my private life. I've been a father to you, haven't I? How I conduct the rest of my life is none of your business.'

I felt all my ideals about life had been betrayed, that life itself was shameful and soiled. I saw no good in people at all. I stopped going to church for a while. Then I started going for June, Lisa's stepdaughter. It calmed me a little. I saw Wendy for a while. She offered me closure, letting go, all those fine sounding things. But the reality was, I wasn't ready. She did help me think more clearly about the boys, which was good. But the whole thing was like a kind of madness. No matter how I struggled, the rage took over.

It was the bitterness too, the deep, horrible bitterness, I could almost taste my own bile. It was with me night and day. It was the taste in my mouth, it was the pitying glances I got from other women, the curious glances from men. It was the hate, the absolute hate I felt for Martin. It was the wreckage of my life, complete and absolute.

When I sold the house, we moved to Woollahra. Finally I was away from the wretched ocean, the cheapness of the beachside. But it was no good. It made no difference to me. Fifteen years of waste. A shattered family. Two children with a father they couldn't have a relationship with. Betrayal for the sake of a little illicit pleasure.

Thomas Thomas

Bloody hell! Irene said she knew, but Susan told her a whole lot more than she wanted or needed to know. That's the thing, we'd had a way of living which encompassed this but it was never said. And now it was said, things got a bit of an edge up there in Pymble.

Things also developed a bit of an edge in Marg's flat in Elizabeth Bay. Thought I was long past women crying over betrayal. But no, it was all about which seats this one or that one had at the opera, who had which car. Anyway, I never had to go to the bloody opera again.

Irene had been pregnant when we got married. Could have been a terrible scandal, in those days you had to. I couldn't tell Susan. Now it's nothing but that wasn't the case then. Marg was the love of my life and she'd come back to me ten years later.

It had been complicated and tricky but it had worked, until Susan poked her nose in. Now we were all walking on eggshells.

Josh

I never heard my mother swear before this. I never heard her talk loud. I knew she cried, but she used to try never to cry in front of us. Now she just started crying any old time.

She said she wasn't angry with us, but she was. Dad was out of bounds. She had something called an AVO against him and then she was mad when that got into the papers. We weren't allowed to see Auntie Mary. We weren't allowed to talk to Phil. We weren't allowed to talk to Aunt Lisa and Uncle Jamie and our cousins, or even Grandpa and Grandma, and Nanny and Poppy were right off limits. We weren't allowed to go to the beach. She sold the house and bought another one without even asking us. She put all Dad's things in the garbage and she threw his kookaburra over the cliff.

Phil told me not to get angry back at her. He said she'd been through a lot. 'Forgive her,' he said, but that wasn't the point. Once, she even told my friends how bad Dad was when they came to the house. She was like a tape that just rewound and replayed again and again. She cried after and said she was sorry, but it didn't stop, all that stuff she said. My friends couldn't come to the house because I thought she might say things. She said the divorce had affected me badly. She wasn't the same mum she used to be.

She told me I should have told her about what Ben had seen. 'You were wrong not to,' she told me. 'Not as wrong as your father, but you protected him and left Ben and me exposed.' She didn't understand about Ben at all. She seemed to hate me, for a while anyway. I hated both Mum and Dad in a way. I still wanted to see Dad but she wouldn't let me. And I wanted to love Mum but she didn't want me to.

Ben was the angel now. Trouble was, he was a terrible angel. He slit open the seats in her car with a Stanley knife and told her Dad had done it. He did graffiti on the front wall of the new house but she knew he'd done that. She was super angry that day in a way I'd never seen before. Then she cried and said she was sorry and that it was Dad's fault.

I loved Mum, but I went out heaps to my mate's place. It was too hard being home. I couldn't even draw anymore. I felt guilty when I came home. I felt bad if I was happy. I tried things like making her breakfast in bed but she didn't eat hardly a thing.

I came home one day and she was curled up on her bed. She

looked tiny, like a kid. I wanted to tell her it would be all right, but I couldn't because she'd be angry or cry a lot. Nothing made it better. Nothing.

I sat on the bed and stroked her hair and she cried some more. Then she hugged me and said she was sorry for everything. I asked her what everything was, and she said 'just everything'. And we both started to laugh because we knew it was everything, and she didn't have to be sorry for that, but then she started to cry again. And it was a bit better because she was more like the mum she used to be, even though she'd never done anything like that before.

Ben was okay. He went back to school to please her, my school. He was good at drama. And fighting. He was in trouble a lot, but Ben didn't care about it and neither did Mum anymore. He went down the beach. He just didn't tell Mum the things he did. Neither did I.

I didn't have the dream anymore. I used to wake up, early in the morning, at four o'clock. I thought I could hear the sea and I thought Dad was in the house. Then I remembered.

Mary

You couldn't blame her but she was mad as hell. I owned a couple of cottages with her up the coast and she asked me to buy her out for some exorbitant price. When I wouldn't she forced a sale at auction. I was top bidder at a lower price than I'd offered her. She threatened to sue me. It was a nasty business. Really, she was a mad woman. I knew she'd come good, eventually. She looks tiny and soft but she's as tough as nails. That's not a put down. She's vulnerable but she's a survivor, too.

Mind you, I wasn't sure that our relationship would survive. But that's divorce. She was crazy that I hadn't told her about Melissa but I felt okay about what I hadn't done. I'm not sure that I'd do anything differently. After all, I had thought their marriage had had a chance. And I certainly didn't buy Martin's stuff about her offer of twice a week sex being the ultimate betrayal. It was pretty obvious from the start that Susan wasn't the sort of person who regarded sex as the heart and soul of the union. Twice a week seemed a fairly generous offer from her, although it was both sad and slightly comic. Same old human race.

I saw the boys, finally. She didn't want me to but I said to them we just had to be careful not to hurt her feelings by letting her find out. Ben could be a loose cannon but he was okay in the end. I told them why I hadn't told their mum about Melissa. I told them their father had behaved badly but he wasn't a bad man. I told them things go on in marriages that not even kids know about, and none of us knew the full story, and even if we did it wouldn't help us much.

They were hard to talk to, the combination of their ages and the circumstances. I used to take them to the movies and pizza afterwards, and it was then they told me things. They told me about Susan throwing his kookaburra over the cliff. I thought that was fantastic. I laughed and laughed and laughed. I think that helped them to understand that even though there was all this drama, some of it was ridiculous. And I thought it was great. Not like sensible, prissy Susan at all. An act of true passion. And she'd put his smart clothes in the charity bin. I was pretty impressed.

I saw Martin in the bolt hole I was renting to him up the coast and told him how the boys were going. Susan wouldn't let them see him, and in a way he couldn't face them, even though he was so self-righteous about Susan. For him, it was like a double divorce—Susan and Melissa. He was as crazy as she was.

'*I* made the decision to go,' he said. 'I left her. I understand she's angry. She's been full of repressed rage for years. That was the problem with our marriage, you know.'

'If she'd found out about Melissa she would have left you years ago,' I said. '*That* was a problem with the marriage too.'

'Maybe,' he said. He was gloomy, drinking too much and listening to too much Leonard Cohen. 'Melissa's the one I'll never understand.'

'And to think they said you had one of the finest legal brains in the country,' I said. Feeling sorry for Martin wasn't my forté.

'I might as well shoot myself,' he said.

'Yeah and really fuck up your kids' lives.'

'That's the only thing stopping me,' he said virtuously.

'Open the blinds, have a shave, get a job and get on with it,' I said.

Lisa

There's no doubt in my mind that I should have made her face the truth when I first saw the photo of him at Anna Giapoulos's wedding. Then the moment I saw him at the hospital, I should have told her straightaway. I'm her sister after all. So I'm sorry about that, really sorry.

She was furious with me, furious with everyone. Dad was banned for months, and Mum too. I didn't buy into that. She'd always been the one who was closer to them. In the end I ignored the ban. I just went there. I helped her move, even though she was as crazy as a mad thing. She threw all Martin's clothes into a charity bin. She'd already thrown the kookaburra over the cliff. That was the sad thing, that all that passion, all those fights they'd had over that piece of shit—I did agree with Susan on the aesthetics of that bloody bird—but it never really mattered. How can a badly made pottery kookaburra matter? But they had both thought it did. I guess it was just a symbol. Jamie and I tried to think if we had any symbolic things like that in our marriage—there was the awful carport he had built, but that was probably worth less than Martin's bird. I told Jamie he knew he was in trouble if he came home and found I'd burnt the carport to the ground.

I found the whole thing exhausting. I had a full-time job, June at home with her baby and Susan. Susan wanted to vent. Vent and vent and vent! It was too much but you can't say, 'Stop complaining about your ex-husband'. You just can't.

June's baby Oliver calmed Susan down. She was sort of losing it with her own boys. They were fantastic for adolescents, but let's face it, they were adolescents. And she was very hard on Josh for not telling her about what Ben saw.

'You've got to stop blaming Josh,' I said. 'Or you'll lose him. He's just a kid. He didn't know if it was Ben making up a story or Martin lying. Josh was protecting Ben. None of it's clear cut, Susan. All these other people who didn't tell you—who all knew—they didn't do it out of malice. They did it because they wanted to protect you.'

'I know.' She started crying. And I put my arms around her and she cried and cried. We made up but there was still a fair bit of rage left to go. I was glad because I could see the old softness in her. I knew she'd be okay but I hated she had to go through that.

As I said, the baby helped. I think it was his innocence.

Corny but true. In a way Susan has an innocent view of the world. She thinks she can get the people around her to behave according to her code. She doesn't take ordinary things such as bad temper or lust or adolescence into account. It was so hard for her to accept Josh growing up at that time. Of course he became a man! What else was ever going to happen to him? And there were sure to be parts of him that were like his father. She'd tried to eradicate that, poor Josh couldn't help being adolescent and himself.

June got religion which was a good thing because it stopped her sleeping around, or at least it stopped her sleeping around as often as she had been. A small mercy. She went to church with Susan. It helped them both.

June asked Susan to be godmother to Oliver. I must say I was a little peeved about that. Jamie said there was no sense in me being a godmother because I didn't believe in God. And sure, Susan bought the baby and June nice clothes and said nice things, but I was the one minding Oliver at six in the morning when June was too exhausted to get up. So I felt it would have been nice if she'd asked me. But no.

But I thought about it and, of course, Susan was the person she would choose. Even though her marriage was in ruins, Susan still gave an impression of being whole, being together. And maybe that together exterior made it harder for Susan to come to terms with that ruined marriage, that lost dream.

Phil

I was tossing up about converting to Catholicism and going back to live in the monastery with a view to becoming a brother. To tell you the truth I'm not sure the Brothers were all that keen on me joining them. They kept on saying how long it would take and how I'd have to study and develop more virtue. That's not exactly how they put it but that was the general drift.

I wanted a place, a home, a resting place where I'd just be told what to do and how to live my life.

'Perhaps,' said Brother John who was my spiritual advisor, a position I don't think he particularly coveted. 'But it's not what you need. Besides, you'd think life here could be improved. You're rather too worldly.'

That hit a nerve. He was right. I wanted the honey to be thicker, the apples sweeter and crunchier, the vestry tables polished with beeswax, fire Brother Mark who made their hideous bread.

'As a person of the world,' said Brother John, 'you need to make your peace with it.'

'I've tried the world.' I said. 'I'm not good in the world.'

'In any case, this place is still the world,' said Brother John. 'The world is the only place in this life, however we strive.'

I looked at him intently. I wanted an answer, not more talking in riddles. 'What is my problem?'

'You have no trust,' he said. 'Every time you hit a difficulty in life you don't turn to God, you turn away from him.'

There was some truth in that. I nodded. When I told Susan that I had known about Melissa and she had berated me, I had been angry with God. I didn't trust God to run my affairs. And as for the monastery and becoming a Catholic, that wasn't turning to God. That was a way of fooling God, pulling the wool over the divine eyes. Not possible with an all seeing, all knowing, all powerful God. And after all I'd been an Anglican all my life. Essentially it was the quality of my faith that was the difficulty, not the brand.

I told Brother John I'd go back into the world, that same old world and find my place.

'*And ye shall know the truth*,' he said, '*and the truth shall make you free.*'

The truth? I pondered it on the long bus ride back to Sydney. The bus was packed, and I was sitting next to a large angry man who ate onion sandwiches. I was tortured by lack of sleep and the smell of onions. I tried to think. I loved Susan but I loved her best from a distance. Maybe that was how I best loved most people, even God. That was the best I could do.

But I had talents and gifts. I had friends. I had a life.

I'd had visions of going to Susan, explaining myself. 'Have faith, have faith, have faith,' I told myself. 'Help me God, please help me.'

'Would you shut up?' said the bloke with the onion sandwiches. 'I need some shut-eye and you muttering your holy holy is giving me the willies.'

I was embarrassed. I don't usually mutter prayers in public places. I shut my eyes. I tried to make my mind free of words and images, for a prayer of trust to float through it, to make a wise choice. To be, for once, a wise man.

I got off the bus. Should I go to Susan's? To Mary's? To Lisa's?

I decided on going to Susan, but then I got into the taxi and gave the driver Lisa's address.

Sometimes prayers are answered.

Melissa

I was the one who had said the relationship was about love. I was the one who decided that love was my ideal. I believed in love, made love my Goddess.

It was not Martin's fault that he used that for his own convenience. Because that's what my love was for him—convenient. It allowed him not to make a choice. It allowed him to engage in this mammoth and pointless battle with Susan. It allowed him a regular sex life with two women. It allowed him to keep all the perks of his job and enjoy a family life. Okay, the family life wasn't perfect. In fact it was pretty damn nasty.

He wanted a woman who didn't want him. She wanted a husband she didn't love. She wanted her children and her social status. I was the patsy who made it all possible, made it run along nicely, made him sing and hum so he didn't pester her too much, gave him a safety valve when it all got too tense.

What Martin never understood was how much I loved him. I really loved him. And that's what made the year after so painful. The love. I still had it. He was in my head. He was imprinted on every part of my body.

I went into decline. I was sad. I had black circles under my eyes. My business withered. I played sadly with Anna's baby and felt a horrible envy of her for the first time in my life. I couldn't surf without crying. I was sad. Really sad.

Martin

I ceased to be Susan's husband. I ceased to be Melissa's lover. I ceased effectively to be a father to my boys. I ceased to be a partner in Thomas Thomas and Hargraves. I ceased to own a house on the cliff. Susan threw my kookaburra over the cliff, put my clothes in a charity bin. The person who was Martin Ryan ceased to exist.

Nor did I understand how that could have happened. I couldn't understand Melissa's reaction. She knew I was having sex with Susan. It wasn't as if the twice a week offer was a new thing.

That's what I couldn't get. How my whole life had gone down like a pack of cards. Puff, a wisp of smoke and it was gone. The whole thing. There wasn't a skerrick of it left. No routine, no kids, no job, no love, no house, nothing.

Mary was kind and unkind, but in general her unkindness did me no great harm and her kindness in keeping in touch with the boys and taking me up the coast did me a power of good. So I guess not everything was gone. There was still bloody Mary.

And surfing. But not for a while. Because surfing reminded me of Susan and the kids and Melissa and my house, and my life.

Melissa

I was over the romance of love. Thoroughly and completely over it. I'd been angry and bitter and I didn't believe in romance or love anymore. That made it harder to indulge in a romance to heal my broken heart which people started advising me to do. Because while I could see myself going through the motions, I didn't see myself feeling anything. And I'd always felt something, even if it was only a sense of connection and a bit of fun with a one night stand. But now there was this block of mistrust, of loss, standing in the way of my feeling.

I had so loved Martin that I exhibited the classic signs of grief. I pined. I lost interest in worldly things. My business suffered. I didn't care how I looked.

Anna and her little girl kept me going. Life was out there. I would get better. Life would improve.

My mother too. She kept telling me I'd done the right thing. At first I was bitter about the time I'd spent, the time I'd lost. Then I thought it didn't matter because I'd never have another relationship. Then, I thought I might. And I started to care about how I looked and I put a lot of work into my business and I wanted sex again and I had a brief fling which I knew meant nothing and wouldn't ever mean anything, but it gave me a sense that I was alive.

I began to come back to the idea of marriage and children, but in a conscious way. A family was an ideal, but one I was almost afraid to embrace. I had been an only child, then I'd lost my father, then my Greek family, so my mother and I didn't quite feel like a family. Martin seemed to confirm that pattern of loss.

I wasn't about to embrace another ideal, but I was optimistic enough to want it and to hope it would come my way. And, despite all the sadness, I was optimistic enough to remember I was a happy person who could enjoy life a lot. I think that's what Martin had always loved about me, that unlike Susan, I loved life.

I started going out with someone who I thought would make a good husband. He was called Angelo. At first I just liked the name, liked it that he was so different from Martin, liked he looked so different from Martin.

Mary came to see me now and then. I liked her but our relationship was all about Martin. One night she asked me to dinner. We were going somewhere flash so I made a real effort. I'd got out of the habit of doing that, but now I was getting back into life. It didn't feel real but I reminded myself that it was real. It was the stuff in my head that wasn't. Even though part of the stuff in my head was that Mary would tell Martin I looked great and he'd feel pain and regret. As if it mattered. But still.

'You look fantastic,' said Mary.

We chatted a bit, drank a bit, ate, and then walked out to get a cab for me. Now my business was back on track I could afford cabs again.

'Are you happy?' I asked her.

'Not happy enough,' she said. 'I'm good at friends. Occasional lovers and dramas are what I'm good at. I never thought I wanted more but maybe I did.'

She looked sad, which was unusual for Mary, so I squeezed her arm.

'It's okay,' she said. 'Not tragic. Just life. What do you want? You know, from life?'

For such a long time I had simply wanted Martin. And of course, I could have had him.

But we couldn't go back. We couldn't go from the ideal of love to ordinary love. We couldn't go back to a place where the lie hadn't been told or it had been smudged or fudged. He wanted to but we couldn't. We both carried that kernel of truth, the kernel of hurt. And that small thing made it impossible.

'I don't know,' I said to Mary. 'A normal life maybe.'

'Love?' she asked.

'Maybe.'

I didn't tell her about Angelo. Angelo who worked in foreign exchange in the bank and loved his middle-class well-paid job. His dad was Greek and his mother was Australian. I liked him and I'd told him about Martin.

But love? I wasn't sure.

Martin

What bothered me? Out in the surf in the early morning, my kids, that was all. I wanted them to be okay. I wanted them to know they had a father who loved them. Thank God I retrieved my board before Susan had thought to tip that over the cliff too. My lovely kooka. I was furious with her for selling the house too.

But then it came to court. For three years we'd been fighting like mad, letters going back and forth between me and Les Reese who was handling her side. I was barely working, just doing some criminal cases, fighting with old Thomas about proceeds from various cases, living in a shit unit back in Bondi Junction, close to where I'd started out. In fact it wasn't bad. I was near the surf and I never got into trouble with money because the flat was so cheap. After all the years of debt and striving, there was some freedom in the way I was living. When the boys came over they just bunked down on the floor.

The night before Susan and I were due in the family court I had a revelation. She could have it all. The lot. The Whiteley, the Cossington Smith, the shares, the cash deposits, the new house, the potplants, the jewellery, the cars, my underpants if she wanted them. She'd never let me have custody of the kids, but Josh was too old and I saw Ben plenty. So that was okay.

In the morning before proceedings started, I told her instructing solicitor. 'She can have the lot.'

Susan was disappointed. She wanted a fight. I told her she could have that too. Mud-wrestling, I suggested.

It was great: For once I had the moral superiority.

Out in the surf at Bondi, a few days after we signed off, I was thinking of the divorce and my life, as I was inclined to do. I didn't actually give away the whole kit. I'm not a saint. But out there, grey morning, flat sea, I thought of her, as she was, as we were. I got tears in my eyes. I think of the way Josh looks like her. Is like her. Of her trying so hard with Ben. And I was glad, in a good way, that I gave her the money.

Don't get me wrong. I didn't like her. I hadn't loved her for years. It was just the life we had.

That night, I wrote to her, told her I was sorry for my part in it, told her I had truly loved her, told her we should have never been together but we had been and we had two children and it mattered, even though it didn't work.

She never answered and I felt grim shame at my flash of moral superiority. That was a habit I didn't want to get into.

With the boys something had fractured. Mary said maybe it was just adolescence but they didn't trust me. Didn't trust life, a sadness in their eyes. Ben got drunk and he was only fourteen. Susan and I couldn't talk about it sensibly. Josh told me angrily he'd look after Ben. Shit! How did this happen? I know the answer to that.

I worked regularly. Made money and gave most of it to Susan for the boys. That was okay. I had enough and I bought a tiny flat at Bondi with a view over the beach so I could monitor the surf. Work was meaningless. It always was, but there used to be other things. I still missed Melissa, still didn't understand it. Mary told me Melissa was with someone else now. When I woke in the middle of the night, in the middle of my regrets, I could smell her, feel her, taste her. It was torture. There must have been someone else back then. We did fight a lot in those last months. Or maybe she thought I'd never come at a baby. I wrote to her, tried to explain, but in the end, it had gone. I knew that.

What was it? Love I suppose. Lust too. Sometimes it seemed a lot of trouble for nothing.

I may as well have cut and run the first day I met her. I did love her. I had loved Susan too. I thought maybe I hadn't learned some basic lessons in love, there was something I was missing.

Melissa is the one I can't work out. I still remember the shock of her rejection when it was all within reach. How did that happen? Melissa said it had all been an illusion, that it couldn't work, that it had been based on false pretences.

'You still don't get it, do you?' asked Mary.

No, I didn't.

I went to see Witch Wendy. It was part of my journey, as

people like Wendy liked to call it. Driving there I realised why I was going. I was looking for redemption. I just wanted a fifteen-minute chat, but she insisted on a paid consultation.

'I know what you used to call me,' she said. 'Witch Wendy.' But she had a smile on her face. I couldn't decide if she was well disposed to me or whether she was just being professional.

'The name's quite sexy, I think,' I said.

'It's quite insulting.' But she was looking at me as if I amused her.

'It was insulting,' I said, 'but then it became affectionate. I changed. Because you changed me. Despite myself. Despite the false pretences under which I came.'

'What false pretences?' She was being Witch Wendy again.

'Well, I was having an affair.' Of course she already knew that from Susan.

'But you were trying to repair your marriage as well?'

'Yes.' I smiled uneasily at her.

'It's a bit like drug addicts who come to counsellors and only want to talk about their childhood. It's a half story.'

'Maybe. I was sincere. In a way. I don't know.' I started to stutter, feel worse than I thought I would. I felt like the pebbled ceiling was sucking me dry. The tattered Desiderata was bringing back memories. Memories of hope, cynicism and despair, all mixed in together. What had I thought I was doing?

'The addicts are sincere too,' she said. 'But so deluded that it's hard to know where to start.'

'I don't see the parallel.'

'I didn't know where to start with you because I didn't know about this affair,' she said.

'I couldn't tell you because that would have ended my marriage.'

'Therapy is about change,' she said, 'and change is a very difficult thing. It's also about acceptance because most of us only ever change a tiny, tiny bit. But for even tiny changes or a tiny piece of acceptance, you have to be honest. So I'd be surprised if the therapy had changed anything.'

'I came to say I'm sorry,' I said.

'I'm not sure what you're sorry for.' She still had that smile. 'I got paid. You got what you deserved.'

Maybe that's when I started to see things differently.

Josh

I was waiting to leave school, leave home and leave the country. I was always worried about Mum, worried about Dad or worried about Ben. I was always defending Ben to Mum or Mum to Dad or Ben to someone.

'I'm going to Germany,' I said to Mum. I had a penfriend in Germany. She looked pretty sweet in her photos and I wanted to meet her. 'Then I'll go and live in China and learn Mandarin.'

'You're getting an education Josh,' she said. 'That's all there is to it.'

'I can't afford for you to go and live in China,' said Dad. He was always worried about money. 'You should go to uni first anyway. Your mother's right about that.'

It was always there. Your mother's right about that but not about this. Your father would have told you that. If you believe your father. You're like your father, like your mother.

'Go,' said Auntie Mary. 'I'll give you a round the world ticket when you turn eighteen.' But even she couldn't stop herself. 'I don't suppose either of your parents would like it, but I will.'

Lisa

Susan was into the travails of being a single parent. Bringing up two boys on her own. No money. No support.

'Yes Susan, no Susan, three bags full Susan.' You couldn't point out that she'd thrown a couple of thousand dollars over a cliff with that kookaburra, that she owned the house she lived in, that the boys' school fees were more than most families actually had to live on. But all that was just getting over the divorce, the end of the marriage. She was trying but it kept dragging her back. And it was hard because the people who wanted to support her were the same people who she felt had betrayed her, me included. But I could see her becoming herself again, I was waiting for her to become herself again, longing for it.

She got awfully religious for a while and prayed for me and my family. Mind you, some days we could do with a bit of grace thrown our way. And she started talking to Mum and Dad again. And to Phil. And the other people who had been banned. And she started studying law.

You hear how long it takes people to get over a marriage. Susan was walking, talking proof. She had been so unhappy with Martin it should have been possible for her to be happy. But a lot of the time she was still sad, less angry, but not really living her life. I guess it takes longer than you ever imagine.

Susan

About a year after Martin left, Lisa said I should go back into therapy. Told me in no uncertain terms that my 'rage was driving her crazy'. Well that made me angry, but I could also see her point. Except she, and so many other people, had lied to me over the years. Now they wanted to forget that. They want to forget there's unhappiness in the world. They want to gloss over all the problems.

Lisa was all about forgive and forget. All peace and harmony. But things get beyond that to a place that's raw and painful and you can't forgive and forget. Or they had with me. I didn't want to be there but I was.

I was happy to take June on for her. I was quite realistic about her, she was a sweet girl. It helped me to do something for someone who was outside the whole mess.

I loved my boys but there was sadness there too. They had been badly affected by the divorce. It cut the children loose too early. Josh thought he could make all his own decisions because he was finishing high school. So Ben thought he could too. There was no family to hold them.

I knew what Lisa meant by my rage, I really did. I didn't want to be like that, to feel like that. Sometimes I'd catch myself talking to strangers and I knew I sounded like a mad woman, pouring out the story of my marriage. It wasn't like me. Or not what I thought I was like. But I was like that. That was the painful part. Gradually seeing that, the rage lifted.

But when the rage lifted, a feeling of despair came down on me like a ton of bricks. Anger and resentment weren't healthy, they had poisoned parts of my life. But the thing was, it wasn't just a matter of deciding to give it up. It wasn't just a matter of making a decision. I needed to forgive Martin, but I couldn't do it. Even when he gave in about the property settlement, I was angry.

It was June who gave me the answer. We'd been at church

and we were driving home, she told me Martin had just sent her $200 to help her buy textbooks for the course she was doing. He's taken to this random charity—either to the boys, which I disapproved of very much, or to June, or I gathered, to all sorts of odd bods. Anyway she thought he was a nice man.

'How do you feel about him?' she asked.

'Angry,' I said. 'It's not very Christian I know, but I can't help feeling like that.'

'How do you want to feel?' she asked.

'I suppose I'd like to be charitable and forgive him,' I said.

'You don't have to forgive him,' she said.

'Why not?' I said.

'Because God will.'

Somehow, that changed everything for me.

Phil

I'm a dreamer. I had dreamed of Susan. I had dreamed of a ministry. I had dreamed of a career but I didn't know what to do in real life. I thought there'd be some point in life when I'd arrive as if life was a train journey, and at some point I'd step down onto the platform and people would greet me, welcome me home, and I'd feel terrific.

Trouble was, I'd never even got as far as buying a ticket for the journey, let alone finding out what platform the train went from.

I got a job back at the school teaching English and music. I'd never taught music before and I loved it. Taught Josh in his senior year. He was such a treasure that kid. He's got a light shining in him. Love him.

And somehow I was back coaching Ben's soccer team. Ben's one of those kids they say is a nuisance. I bet it's always on his report. But I reckon he's just a kid who's not suited to school. Once he's over that hurdle he'll be fine. Be able to do anything. Well, maybe not soccer.

I didn't teach religion anymore. Didn't use the title either. Just let it slide. It was a big relief, and somehow my spiritual life and my journey through life was greatly enhanced by it. I love the church but it's not my life anymore.

I saw Martin because of the boys and we started going to the footy again, sometimes with the boys, sometimes just the two of us. He was very unhappy for a long time but all that lawyer crap had dropped away. We were real friends again, in fact, more real than we ever had been. It was solid and important for us both. He talked to me about religion, and sometimes he even came to St James with me.

'Church is just for the music, you understand,' he said. But I knew it had memories for him. I knew it moved him. Once, I noticed, his eyes were wet after the service.

I saw Susan too. It was funny. Susan can just cut off parts of her life. Maybe she had to. All the anger over me not telling her about Melissa had gone, but by the time that went so had our former intimacy. She didn't want to discuss any of it.

But there was something there. A different friendship, an acknowledgment of the fact we had shared a lot over the years. I sort of fell out of being in love with her. I still loved her, and I was grateful for the way she handled the whole thing. She's got a natural grace, a sort of natural understanding of life that I just don't have at all.

Mary

What was it about?

Everyone got so caught up in taking sides, in making judgements of particular actions, in finding fault; they never knew what it was about.

I did a straw poll.

'Incompatibility,' said Phil. I saw Phil less now Susan wasn't giving lunches. I rather missed him.

'In what way were they incompatible?' I asked.

'Temperament,' he said. 'She liked things small and neat and he didn't notice. Couldn't notice. It wasn't in his nature.'

'It was illusion,' said Melissa.

'Illusion?'

'The illusion you can have a life that you're not having.'

'Sex,' said Lisa. 'He liked it, she didn't. That's why they were both so angry. He was prepared to have sex with someone who didn't want sex and she was prepared to have sex when she didn't want it. It completely fucks your head, that sort of behaviour.' She said it like a schoolteacher explaining a basic lesson.

'She didn't love me,' said Martin. 'And that was just too hard to bear.'

'Grow up, Marty.'

'It was the divorce,' said Josh. 'They were thinking about divorce all the time instead of thinking about being married.'

I searched for a neat explanation. There isn't one.

10 YEARS LATER

Mary

I'd got bored with real estate, although I still did a little of it, just as I did a little doctoring. I found a new passion writing detective stories and I was moderately successful, especially in Germany, which gave me a tax-free trip there every year.

I liked life but I felt a little lonely. I went on hormone replacement, hoping it was just the menopause, but that didn't really help. Most things are more profound than hormones and brainwaves, although we medicos always look for a magic bullet.

I saw Susan now and then with the boys. We actually had a civilised discussion at Josh's twenty-first birthday about me not telling her about Melissa. She could see my point of view. I thought what a civilised woman she was. More civilised than Martin. Martin kept his passions burning. Still, he and Susan had always done things differently.

When Susan's father, old Thomas, died she phoned me to get in touch with Phil who was staying at one of my holiday cottages up the coast for summer. Phil and I had almost lost touch, except he rented the cottage every year. Susan wanted him to do the funeral service for old Thomas. I said I'd come along anyway for the boys, who had adored their grandfather. Truth is I rather like funerals. They're very elemental and gloomy but you can't take them too seriously. People say such rubbish.

Old Hargraves was still alive, although barely and he rabbited on about what a good innings Thomas had had. Christ, life's not a bloody cricket match. It's more like swimming with the sharks if you ask me.

Then Phil did a eulogy. He surprised me. He did an excellent job talking up old Thomas. He paid due reverence to Irene as his wife, even though she's such a bloody witch of a woman. And he talked about how important Susan and Lisa and the grand-children were. Then, he surprised us all.

'And of course, there's Margaret,' he said, 'whom Thomas loved so very much and who was of such great comfort to him for so many years and particularly during his last illness. Who was his first and last love. To her, we offer our condolences for this heavy blow.'

Irene was spitting chips but I got the picture. Susan had told me that Irene had refused to visit Thomas in hospital and when he went home to die, he went to Margaret. It had been Susan who felt it was right to pay tribute to Margaret and she had organised Phil to do it. I heard she'd become quite close to Margaret. And it wasn't done out of spite towards her mother. She was quite dutiful towards her mother, but she'd given up trying to get close to her. She had thought it was the right thing to acknowledge Margaret. Very like Susan.

As a result, the wake was just fantastic! Everyone had an opinion.

So there was Phil back in my life, and in dog collar mode too, even if that was temporary. I wondered to myself why ever I'd stopped seeing Phil. He was just such a good man and such fun. Never cut out to be a minister, too curious and too much a seeker for that. But he so loved teaching and he'd got involved with a charity helping out street kids. And he had an excellent sense of humour.

We went home together after the funeral and we've been together ever since. He never wears his dog collar, even when we have sex. Sometimes I think it would be fun, but Phil points out that I have corrupted him and I must take him for what he has become.

We live like children, as only people without children are able to. We have ice-cream on our pancakes at breakfast. We go to the movies in the mornings and on long bushwalks at dusk and have strange people to stay the night. We don't care what people think.

Phil had been obsessed with Susan and that had got in the way of his life. But he was over that. Truth is, I'd always fancied him a lot more than I'd let on but there was no future in it when Susan was in his head all the time.

Naturally Phil and I talked about Susan and Martin a lot. It was an enormous part of his life and a big part of mine. It's more than ten years since Martin and Susan split. Here's what happened since.

Susan married a professor of law. She refers to it as a very 'civilised' marriage. Lisa thinks this means they only have sex once every six months. I don't think so. Phil and I sometimes go to Sunday lunch at her place in Woollahra and she has the light of happiness in her eye. She touches her husband all the time—on his arm, hand on his shoulder, a kiss on the top of his bald head. That says something, doesn't it?

Susan isn't bitter anymore. It's all gone and she looks lovelier than ever. She's very successful, only mildly religious, very organised. Once old Thomas died, she left the firm, even though she had qualified as a lawyer. She runs a gallery now, and what a gallery it is. Her eye is excellent and she's launched a number of young artists. She wants to launch Josh but he says that his art is purely personal.

Susan's children love her in the way the very best young men love their mothers, and she's an excellent godmother to June's child and a friend to June. All the people she fell out with are her friends again and she gives regular Sunday lunches. Very occasionally, she has dinner with Martin and the boys. Again, it's very civilised.

Martin has a funny, feisty girlfriend called Angela. They don't live together but they're warm and companionable and affectionate. He has a flat overlooking Bondi and he goes surfing almost every morning. The surfing is his freedom and he certainly isn't scarred by the trappings of domesticity. He has the same scruffy, cuddly look he had when he was in his twenties. He's lost the city solicitor demeanour. He's enormous fun and a totally outrageous drunk, but all that aggression he used to have is gone. Sometimes it feels as if it's been knocked out of him, and that feels a little sad, to me at least. But people like him although he's careful not to get too close to anyone, even Angela. He doesn't trust himself not to inflict damage.

'Don't trust myself with another relationship,' he says. 'Major ability to fuck up.'

He does a lot of work in the Children's Courts and is a major advocate for the rights of children. I was wrong about him being addicted to money and success. He liked those things when he had them, but in the end he didn't give a toss. He and Phil are both involved in the same kids' charity. He loves his own boys. Better than most men are able to, really. He goes to all Ben's plays and he visits Josh at least twice a year in Beijing.

Josh has been in Beijing for years. He's madly in love with a Chinese girl and wants to bring her to Australia eventually. He works for an export house that deals in art and furniture, and he studies ink brush painting under a Chinese master. Susan visits him regularly, but he puzzles her a little. She doesn't know what he wants. I think Josh is still looking out for other people, even Ben, although they live in different countries. Josh is a man who will never let anyone down. But maybe he lets himself down a little, is scared of wanting too much. He's warm-hearted and complicated, like Susan. He's got Martin's hair and you can see something of his expansiveness in Josh's art.

Ben is an actor. Or a waiter. Or a taxi driver. He's a boy who likes a good time with members of both sexes and a variety of chemicals. His parents worry themselves sick over him but he goes to great lengths to reassure them. He's a very fine actor.

Melissa is married to a man called Angelo. He adores her. They have tried every fertility treatment known to man and woman without success and now they're applying for an overseas adoption. Thailand, I think, because Melissa is a devotee of Buddhism. Melissa says that she and Angelo are very happy together. She loves being married but she is wary of saying she is in love.

Some things, she thinks, are better left unsaid.

Read all about it...

MORE ABOUT THIS BOOK

MORE ABOUT THE AUTHOR

WE RECOMMEND

Read all about it...

QUESTIONS FOR YOUR READING GROUP

1. How important is sexual compatibility in a marriage?

2. What are the most important ingredients in a successful relationship?

3. What was the impact of Ben's birth on Susan's feelings about her marriage to Martin and on her attitude to feminism?

4. Does divorce affect children more adversely than living with warring parents?

5. How important is sexual fidelity in a relationship?

6. How important are the other infidelities Phil talks about?

7. How can people successfully negotiate emotion-laden issues in a relationship?

8. Is marriage inevitably an institution that only imperfectly reconciles the different needs and desires of men, women and children?

9. Does the current divorce legislation make the end of a marriage more or less painful than in the past?

10. Do you agree with Melissa's choices in the book? Do you find them believable? Why or why not?

11. Do you think that the ends Susan was seeking justified the means of her choices and actions?

12. Do you think Susan and Martin were compatible despite their different backgrounds?

13. Martin kept secrets from Susan. Do you think real intimacy is possible in such circumstances?

Read all about it...

14. Did Phil's religious beliefs make it difficult for him to be happy?

15. How would it feel to be "the other woman"?

16. What effect do Mary and Lisa have on the marriage of their siblings?

17. Do you have a favourite character in the book? If so, can you identify why you liked the character?

18. How did Phil's character change/evolve throughout the story?

Read all about it...

Sydney and its environs feature heavily in *Love and Other Infidelities*. Here, Helen Townsend tells us more about the city she loves and how it impacted on the novel.

I came to live in Sydney when I was four, and my mother said, "Okay, you children don't need vests any more." And we were allowed to run around in bare feet. So I've always felt Sydney is a very, very free place. That's partly from climate, partly because it's such a cosmopolitan city.

I love the diversity of Sydney. Where we live has lots of people of Italian and Greek background, so at least once a week, I go out to morning coffee with friends, and have white beans for breakfast. I also love walking with dogs and friends round the bay where we live. I love the dominance of the harbour in Sydney, that flash of blue water down some grotty street, the pockets of bush. We often do walks along the Lane Cove River and when we go into town, we usually take a ferry.

"...Sydney is a very, very free place..."

I grew up on Sydney's north shore, which was then one of the posher areas of the city, lots of big houses, lovely gardens, but probably a bit more polite than the rest of Sydney. So I used that in *Love and Other Infidelities* as the setting where Susan grew up. People still talk about north-shore girls as being prim and proper. It's one of those stereotypes that has more than a grain of truth. But I did understand her nostalgia for the gum trees and those big backyards. And I understood how Martin hated it!

Martin, in the parlance of Sydney, is a westie. Being away from the ocean, the west has a very different character, more self-consciously working class, probably more tribal. When Martin went to university, particularly back in

the seventies, that was a break with his past. So
in a sense, both Martin and Susan, ending up
in a beachside suburb, are separated from their
roots.

I am a serious beachgoer. There's nothing
better on a hot weekday afternoon than to
go out to Bondi for a swim and Turkish pizza
afterwards. Sydney's beaches are just magic, and
I really understood Martin's devotion to that
beach life. There's something wonderful about
being with other people – all shapes, sizes and
ages, enjoying the simple pleasures of sand, the
ocean and an open sky.

Read all about it…

*"… There's
something
wonderful
about being
with other
people…
enjoying the
simple
pleasures of
sand, the ocean
and an open
sky…."*

AUTHOR BIOGRAPHY

Helen Townsend is the author of twenty books. This is her eighth novel and another example of her favoured theme of family relationships. She occasionally writes newspaper articles and has had one play and one radio documentary performed. She is married with three grown-up children and lives in Sydney – when she hasn't retreated to her creek-side home at Lake Macquarie.

AUTHOR INTERVIEW

What do you love most about being a writer?

I love being able to explore and imagine lives other than my own. I love the excitement of having characters change and develop in my head. And I love the process of writing.

"...I love the process of writing..."

How did you become a writer?

I'd always had thoughts about writing. When I married into a family of journalists, I had the chance to do some freelance writing. I enjoyed that experience a lot. And my first book grew from there.

Who or what has most influenced your writing?

I read constantly. I love Tolstoy, F Scott Fitzgerald and Alice Munro. I love to observe that process of creation, but my main influence is from people I meet. Often there's something interesting or eccentric about a person or something they say that's a starting point for whole new character and story.

Where do you go for inspiration?

Sometimes I overhear conversations on the bus, sometimes I find I'm grappling with things in my own life. I've written things that have been set off by an intriguing piece in the newspaper.

What one piece of advice would you give a writer wanting to start a career?

It's hard work so be prepared to work hard. Also, remember that this is a very solitary activity. I never had a mentor, but I think it would be a great help. And read, read, read.

What inspired you to write *Love and Other Infidelities*?

Strangely, my own very stable marriage. But I have seen many friends whose marriages ran far less smoothly. I wanted to look at why and how it happened in that case, but at the same time, not make judgements about the people involved.

***Love and Other Infidelities* shows us how the breakdown of a marriage not only affects the husband and wife, but also lovers, friends, parents and children. Was it difficult to write from all these different perspectives?**

I started making notes on all the different people involved, and I had all these scraps of paper and files. I began to see that in themselves, they had a particular power – to have these different voices and viewpoints, and it was a matter of fitting them together.

Which book do you wish you had written?

I think that to be able to write like Tolstoy would be the most fantastic gift. In *War and Peace* he was able to give so much insight into his characters and deal with the great themes of life.

When did you start writing? What was your first venture into writing fiction?

I wrote as a child and then I wrote as a journalist, a TV writer, a film researcher, radio writer and then moved into non-fiction. I always wanted to

"...I read constantly... I love to observe that process of creation..."

write fiction but I didn't have the confidence until I was in my late thirties.

Where do your characters come from, and do they ever surprise you?

My main characters start talking to me in my head. I worry if they *don't* surprise me. I think that's what inspiration is – a voice coming from some place you don't know about, but which is part of you.

Do you have a favourite character that you've created, and what is it you like about that character?

I tend to like all my characters, or at least have some sympathy with them. In *Love and Other Infidelities*, I loved Josh. In a way, he understood the situation with his parents, but he had a child's longing for things to be right in the world, as well as the power to imagine the darkest things.

What do you do when you're not writing?

Many things! Reading, walking, being with my family, swimming, enjoying art. I'm very domestic; I enjoy my house and my family.

"...I think that to be able to write like Tolstoy would be the most fantastic gift..."

A WRITER'S LIFE

Paper and pen or straight onto the computer?
I use notebooks, notebooks and more notebooks.
Then I have files on the computer and a total
sense of being out of control. Then it comes
into being.

PC or laptop?
PC. I have tried a laptop travelling, but I prefer
to use my notebooks.

Music or silence?
Silence please! I often relax with music and I love
to sing, but not when I'm working.

Morning or night?
Morning. I was trained by the school-hours
timetable. But as I get into a book, I burn the
midnight oil as well.

Coffee or tea?
Coffee. It's a serious addiction. I have tea as the
soft option.

Your guilty reading pleasure?
My hairdresser always asks me if I'd like serious
or serious trash. I never refuse the serious trash of
celebrity gossip which I read in the supermarket
queue too.

The first book you loved?
It's now very *not* politically correct. It was called
Little Black Sambo and it was about a melting
tarbaby.

The last book you read?
Riddley Walker by Russell Hoban. An amazing,
intriguing read.

Read all about it...

MY TOP TEN BOOKS

Some of these I keep returning to. *Voss*, I have only read once, but there are parts of it that feel like they are stuck to me. And some of these books I've also loved as films – *Mrs Dalloway* (& *The Others*), *Enduring Love* and *To Kill a Mockingbird*.

War and Peace – Leo Tolstoy
Persuasion – Jane Austen
Enduring Love – Ian McEwen
The Great Gatsby – F Scott Fitzgerald
Great Expectations – Charles Dickens
Mrs Dalloway – Virginia Woolf
The Makioka Sisters – Tanizaki
To Kill a Mockingbird – Harper Lee
Beloved – Toni Morrison
Voss – Patrick White

A DAY IN THE LIFE

I start off with coffee in bed brought to me by my husband, which is a very endearing habit of his. As I'm getting my teenage son to school and then taking the dog for a walk, my minds starts churning and I'm ready to start writing. I have lots of bits and pieces in my house which come from my family or from somewhere I've been, and they give me a sort of security. In my study I have my grandmother's china cabinet, a chaise longue and fabulous old framed illustrations from *Red Riding Hood* and *Alice in Wonderland*. I love to have those things around me. I also have my dog, who has a very sympathetic soul. I think it's essential to ignore e-mail until after lunch. You have to ignore things and people in order to get it done, and then you turn round and write about them. I've always got a notebook with me, and I take down phrases and thoughts and events. My family think it's a form of theft.

"... There's a certain ruthlessness in writing..."

In the morning, I do an awful lot of re-writing, going back, giving more life and colour to characters, or adding in things that I have discovered about them. At lunch, I usually have my head in a book while I'm eating. I try to phone a friend too, as writing is an extremely solitary occupation. I'm not someone who has to push myself to write. I have learnt sometimes it's better to stop writing and take a break for ruminating. I love to swim. I do twenty or thirty lengths and often that gives me good ideas. Sometimes, it's just getting away from the buzz in my head and getting a bit of clarity.

I write in the late afternoons, and sometimes go through till evening. I do more plot and character then, whereas the morning tends to be about the words on the page. I don't think you can write all day, but I like to write something almost every day. I read most nights – it's my greatest frustration that I can't read as much as I'd like. I find it hard to have a day off.

"...I'm not someone who has to push myself to write..."

If you enjoyed *Love and Other Infidelities*, we know you'll love…

Wednesdays at Four by Debbie Macomber

Every week a group of women meet, each has her own share of worries and troubles. Cancer survivor Lydia is anxious about her ageing mother. Alix's wedding plans have been hijacked by her meddling friends. Self-contained Colette's husband has only been dead a year but she's pregnant with another man's child. As friendships deepen these women start to confide in each other, but will listening and sharing be enough?

Everything Must Go by Elizabeth Flock

To those on the outside, the Powells are a happy family, but then a devastating accident destroys their fragile façade. When seven-year-old Henry is blamed for the tragedy, he tries desperately to make his parents happy again. As Henry grows up, he is full of potential but soon he questions if the guilt his parents have burdened him with has left him unable to escape his anguished family or their painful past…

The Mother and Daughter Diaries by Clare Shaw

Roberta and Cynthia are destined to be best friends forever. Unable to cope with her alcoholic mother, Roberta finds Cynthia's house the perfect carefree refuge. Cynthia's mother keeps beautiful butterflies and she's everything Roberta wishes her own mother could be. Years later, a stranger knocks on Roberta's door, forcing her to begin a journey back to childhood. But is she ready to know the truth about what happened on that tragic night ten years ago?